Through a Glass, Darkly

Through a Glass, Darkly

Bill Hussey

First published 2008.

Another Bloody Book.

www.bloodybooks.com

Bloody Books is an imprint of
Beautiful Books Limited
36–38 Glasshouse Street
London W1B 5DL

ISBN 9781905636280

9 8 7 6 5 4 3 2 1

Cover design by Head Design.
Typesetting by Ellipsis.

Printed and bound in the UK by CPI Mackays, Chatham ME5 8TD

Dedicated with much love to my family –
Mum & Dad, Carly, Georgia & Jon –
because they believed...

Acknowledgements

I owe a huge debt of gratitude to my grandfathers – Len Sanford & John 'Fats' Hussey – for inspiring me to write stories. My thanks go to Graeme Hills for his constructive criticism, mathematical contributions and, most importantly, his friendship. I have also been blessed with the support of Trevor & Keeley Lewis-Bettison, Dave & Lillian Bettison and Kasun Perera. Ben Mason is my dedicated agent and I thank him for all his hard work on my behalf. Professor Jane Rogers and several of the staff and students on Sheffield Hallam's MA in Writing have contributed to this book. Jane Mitchell and Dr Steve Baxter have both helped immensely with their knowledge of all things theological and medical. Finally, my heartfelt thanks go to Simon Petherick, Jonathan Wooding, Anthony Nott and all at Bloody Books for taking *Through A Glass, Darkly* out of the dreaming and making it real.

FRIDAY 25th OCTOBER 2002

If there arise among you a prophet,
or a dreamer of dreams, and giveth
thee a sign or a wonder . . .
                    Deuteronomy 13:1

One

Jack Trent stared into the bathroom mirror.

He could not fight it. *The dreaming* reached out and pulled him through the glass. Alone, always alone, he tried to scream but his cries were smothered beneath layers of darkness. On the other side of the looking-glass, the shadows around him began to define themselves into shapes, solid and tangible: tree-shaded meadow grass, dank earth, dripping hollows. Jack waited until the vision had settled. Then he stepped onto the path that cut through the dream-forest and strode out into the night.

Knowing that the environment through which he moved existed only in his mind did not slow the jackhammer beat of his heart. The fact that the thorns scratching his skin were not real, that his skin itself was a fabrication, was immaterial. With every step through *the dreaming* his fear quickened.

A chaos of birds taking flight broke the stillness. The beat of their wings passed overhead, and Jack felt a selfish desperation to move with them. Quickly, without guilt, out of the forest, abandoning the boy to his fate. But heroes do not leave children to die alone. He walked on, his torch illuminating the trembling leaves that overran the path.

At last, he reached the clearing. He tapped the torch against his palm to steady its light and began to search. Mist cordoned the glade, banking in a wall around its perimeter. There were no stars or moon overhead, no rustle of night-time predators, no forest scent. Jack soon became used to the sensory vacuum, so that when a whiff of smouldering charcoal stung his nostrils, the leaden coarseness of it was somehow shocking. He paced out the entire area. Empty. He had been certain the boy would be here. The screams had rung out, calling to him between the boughs of the denuded oaks. He peered into the darkness. There was no shade to it, just a wall of uniform black. About to draw himself out of *the dreaming*, Jack paused. A dusky red light had crept over the crenellation of treetops and, by its glare, he saw them.

They were just out of the reach of his torchlight. Two figures, as silent and rigid as waxworks. The first, tall and whip-thin, was standing upright. A smaller shape knelt by its side, frozen in an act of praying or repelling. A cold touch skittered at the base of Jack's spine. He took a step forward. As he did so, the figures retreated, their feet silent upon the carpet of dead leaves. Jack followed until he reached the opposing bank of trees. He glanced over his shoulder. Somehow, they had skirted around him. The moon burnt like a dying cigarette tip, throwing their long shadows at his feet.

About to retrace his steps, Jack stopped dead. A cry cut across the glade.

'Jack. Oh God, please, Jack. I've seen his eyes. He's shown me his *eyes* . . .'

There was something familiar about the voice. Jack started forward but, with the same horrible fluidity, the figures receded again into shadow. He stifled his fear and ran headlong after them, throwing the torch before him. Glass cracked and a yellow arc of light spilled across the ground. The torch rolled to a stop and flickered. It snatched the pair from obscurity in nervous stutters of light.

A man, or what appeared to be a man, stood huddled over the body of a young boy. Below the breast, the child's insides had been hollowed out into a gleaming crucible. The man's face rose up from inside the cavity, the taut white skin relieved here and there with smatters of red. Between his teeth hung bars of flesh, through which his tongue slavered, luxuriating in the taste of meat. He focused on Jack. Eyes, that were not eyes, pierced the distance between them. Then the stickman's lips hitched into a smile. Wiping his knuckles across his mouth,

4

the creature rose and, without a sound, slipped back into the forest. Jack watched the face shimmer between distant trees until, finally, it was lost.

The torch filament burned low and died. Encompassed by darkness, Jack waited and listened. Only his own thin breathing textured the silence. And then, a scraping, rustling, dragging sound reached his ears. Something was crawling towards him.

Jack put his fist through the mirror.

He gasped, as a newborn gasps its first unaided breath. A spray of blood flecked his face. The bathroom swam, and then everything became hard and rudely formed again. A hundred Jack Trents looked back at him from the shards of shattered mirror jewelling the washbasin.

Thank God . . . There were no dark tears on his cheeks.

He left the bathroom, padded to the kitchen and rinsed his hand. Four splinters, rusty with blood, provided some comfort. The pain they gave was real and immediate. Nothing more or less than exactly what it was: the tearing of flesh and nerve. He was grounded by it, but his thoughts soon snapped back to the vision. His first waking nightmare in twenty years. And so vivid, as if all the abstinence and training had itself been a dream and he was a child again, seeing shades of the future. A shadowland of possibility, his mother had called it. But it was not the *possible* he saw. It was the inevitable. *The dreaming* was back, and *the dreaming* was never wrong.

Jack touched the raw wound on each knuckle.

Her tan was fading fast. Dawn had hoped to come back golden and glamorous and, most of all, *over* him. Her friend, Samantha, had suggested a boozy holiday would help her come to terms with being dumped. A fortnight of watching Sammy down jug after jug of sangria, and flirt with boys to whom shaving was still a bi-weekly event, hadn't done the trick. On gritty Majorcan beaches Dawn could not forget. In cafes, where everything was served with chips, and her elbows rubbed raw on plastic tablecloths, she could not forget. And in clubs, with

5

their tacky floors and sticky teenagers, where she had felt her age, Jack Trent had been with her.

Now she was home. Face peeling, lips chapped and Jack fucking Trent still on her mind. She dabbed her nose with aftersun and started rehearsing the same old arguments. She didn't need a man. Her career required her full attention. It was tough enough for a woman to make her mark in CID without having to contend with distracting relationships. And he was a creep. A creepy, freaky creep. He wasn't even that attractive . . . was he? Okay, she had to admit that he was, in a peculiar sort of way. And he had been kind to her and to Jamie . . .

No. Remember how he ended it. Even if he wanted another chance, there was no way back now. If he had rejected her because of work complications, or another woman, or even because he didn't like her tits, she would have come to terms with it. It would have been sad, because she *had* felt something for him, but given time she could have shrugged it off. Maybe even forgiven him. But that particular rejection she could not forgive.

She finished moisturising and applied thick black eyeliner and lots of mascara. It made her eyes look mean. Through the thin bathroom wall her neighbour's stereo alarm sprang into life, belting out the first few bars of *Stand By Your Man*.

'Jesus Christ . . . Come on, Peter Parker,' she called, poking her head into Jamie's Spider-Man shrine of a bedroom.

He was just about dressed for school but still playing video games. With a little badgering of the carrot and stick variety, he was ready to leave.

The street was slick with frost, the sky as grainy as a poor TV transmission. As they walked, Jamie chattered about the fortnight spent at his grandad's. After thirteen years of parenting, Dawn had mastered the art of looking engrossed, and making interested noises, while her mind considered other matters. Usually bills, clothing budgets, work commitments, optimistic exercise schedules, but today Jack Trent dogged her thoughts. She remembered his voice on the phone, telling her why it

6

had to finish. He had sounded so frightened . . . Bastard.

Jamie gave her a self-conscious wave as he joined the swarm of kids siphoning through the school gates. Her mind elsewhere, she held up her hand in a stiff salute.

It was a short walk from the school to the station.

She wondered how many of her colleagues had guessed the real reason for her leave. On the request form the lie had been a cousin's sudden death (Dawn would not admit it but, like most well-balanced people, there was a corner of her brain given over to superstition. A cousin had been the target of the tragedy because she did not have a cousin that Fate might be tempted by). Everyone would have known that the excuse was so much BS, of course. Gossip in a police station was passed around quicker than a porn mag in a high school playground.

As she turned into the station forecourt, Jack was heaving a box from the back seat of his car. His washed-out blue eyes rested on her for a moment. She made a play of rummaging through her bag. When she looked up again, he was at the top of the concrete flight of stairs. She gave it a few minutes and followed. Entering the reception, she was irritated to see that he was only now sliding his security card through the automated lock. She glanced over the public notice boards, feigning interest in the latest posters for a drugs awareness drive spearheaded by DI 'Fat' Pat Mescher. The security door sighed into the jamb. She counted to a hundred, swiped her pass and entered the belly of the station.

He was waiting by the lifts. She thought about slipping back through to reception. Jesus, this was ridiculous.

'Jack? Can I ruin your day?'

Dave Fellowes, duty sergeant, cannoned into Dawn.

'Sorry, love. Jack, misper, here's the file.'

The lift doors grumbled open.

'Missing person? Surely that's a matter for uniform.'

'Sorry, buddy, I punch in the numbers and the wonders of technology strategically victimise. Maybe you abused an abacus in a former life. Here.'

Jack caught the file but dropped his box. Papers spilled

inside the lift.

'Christ, Dave! Are you the patron saint of arseholes?'

He wedged a foot in the door and attempted to retrieve his files. Without thinking, Dawn leaned into the compartment and pressed the door hold button. He looked up with whispered thanks.

'Dawn?' Fellowes smirked. 'You've been assigned to assist Jack on this one. No DCs available, and you should be all rested and raring to go.'

He flashed a toothy smile and left them to scrabble around.

'You don't have to,' Jack's voice slipped into her like a warm scalpel. 'I can sort somebody else . . .'

'No DCs available, if you can believe that,' she said. 'Anyway, it's been allocated.'

Dave Fellowes: the station's Grand High Stirrer of Shit. He must have known that Jack Trent had got himself some skirt at last, and would have guessed that her leave had signalled a break-up. Pairing them off on a case was just the sort of sick joke that smarmy bastard would enjoy.

'Can you help me?' Jack asked. 'I think this box has given up the ghost.'

Dawn kicked the remnants of the box into the foyer and elbowed a button on the panel. The lift gave an asthmatic wheeze and they were tugged upwards, cables and winches complaining all the way. On the sixth floor, eyes followed them down the corridor to Jack's office. Once inside, she relaxed a little.

'*Chronicle*'s already picked up the story. Brief article from today's rag,' she said, running her eye over the clipping stapled to the report sheet.

'Dawn, I meant what I said. It'll just take a call to get you re-assigned.'

Silence stood between them long enough for the muffled sounds of the station and the street outside to become distinct and jarring.

'Hurt your hand?' she asked.

8

'It's nothing,' he mumbled.

Nothing. Fine. She told herself she didn't care.

'Simon Malahyde,' she said, sifting the P61 misper form, 'seventeen. Lives in a village called Crow Haven. Reported missing by his mother on Tuesday. Didn't come home after a party. Uniform's been over, got the routine stuff done. The mother's insisting on seeing someone 'higher up', says she's got new information suggesting the kid's in danger. Must've been slow round here lately, why's CID getting mispers all of a sudden?'

'Lot of uniform's in training. 'Racism in the Force', that sort of thing,' Jack said.

'Very noble,' Dawn sighed, collapsing into an armchair. 'But a racist is the kind of arsehole that doesn't change its pimples, no matter how much training you throw at it.'

'Well, suppose we better get cracking. Can you call this Mrs Malahyde? Tell her we'll be over in an hour? See you in the car park in twenty?'

He left the room and she felt something inside ratchet loose and wind tight again.

Rain came in fitful bursts, roaring then pittering on the roof of Jack's car, rebounding off the pavement and throwing up a thin mist. Figures ran through it, zigzagging between the shelter of shop awnings. As they crossed the Black Friar Bridge, Dawn looked down the course of the swollen river, burgundy-black in the shadow of the cathedral.

'What does this lad do?' Jack asked, as they left the ring road.

Dawn flicked through the file. 'Student. Theology. First year. Pretty bright: he went to university a year early. Money-wise he's okay. Large annuity left to him by his father. Bank accounts haven't been touched for over a week, though.'

She felt a familiar anxiety as they left the city and Jack accelerated through the hairpin country lanes. She wondered why his dread of machinery in all its forms, from a hesitance to use even a battery-powered tin opener, to a firm belief

9

that he might one day hit the wrong button on his laptop and wipe the entire Police National Computer mainframe, did not extend to cars. Behind the wheel, he had a misplaced confidence. He was a terrible, and somewhat *terrifying*, driver. And today, due no doubt to the tightening coil between them, his driving was more erratic and fast-paced than ever. It was like being propelled about by a monosyllabic Warner Bros. cartoon character. She longed to break the tension with a careless question but pride held her tongue.

Twenty-seven miles out of the city, the car started to struggle up a steep rise. Hills are not a common feature of the fenland, so Dawn was surprised at both the height and the gradient of the ridge. Fringing the hill, and fanning out on either side, was a large forest. Dawn took out the AA Roadmap and traced the wood – Redgrave – with her finger. Flat and cramped on the page, huge and sprawling in her sights. As they crested the brow of the hill, they saw the village sitting in the hollow below. Cradled on one side by the rise, and on the other by the forest, the small community should have appeared comfortably snug. Instead, it looked cowed. They wound down into the village, past the school and war memorial, post office and pub.

'Is this it?' Jack indicated an opening in the bank of trees to their right.

'I think so. Mrs Malahyde said the house was just off the Conduit Road.'

Jack turned the car into a driveway, hemmed and tunnelled by rows of wych elm. The trees stretched away until their turning leaves blurred and fused together, giving the impression of a yawning yellow throat. The rain had stopped. Silence now, save for the rumble of the engine and the crack of gravel beneath the tyres. Dawn watched Jack's hands leave clammy traces on the steering wheel. A rill of blood seeped from beneath the bandage across his knuckles and trickled down his middle finger.

'Fuck it!' Jack shouted. 'Hold on.'

The seatbelt cut into her shoulder. As she jolted forward, she saw a huge metallic structure fill the windscreen. Stones

10

flew up from the drive and chinked against the wings of the car. The Ford Escort came to a halt a foot short of the gate.

'Dawn, I'm sorry. Christ, how didn't I see that thing . . . ?'

'Not your fault,' she groaned, massaging her neck. 'Looks like there should be a three-headed dog guarding it. You might've noticed it then.'

The gate was almost the width of the drive, and as tall as the topmost branches of the elms. It was a mesh of weathered metalwork with three praying figures at its apex. The eyes of these supplicants were smooth against their cheeks, their pupils long eroded.

'Cheery,' Jack murmured, getting out of the car. 'And padlocked. Can we call Mrs Malahyde?'

Dawn snapped open her mobile and shook her head: 'No signal.'

'Well, I reckon we could squeeze around the sides.'

He took a step back, judging the gap between foliage and frame. Pushing his back against the body of the gate, he began to ease himself through. He slipped on the moss-coated roots that ruptured the path, grasped the latticework and regained his balance. The figures atop the gate shuddered.

'Nothing to it. Come through.'

Dawn, being slimmer and more agile, made easier progress, but the roots were her only footing. She glanced down. The driveway sat on a raised bank of earth. On either side the ground fell away sharply. Her eyes swept along the almost vertical drop. Her head reeled. The forest bed, eight feet or more below, appeared to rush towards her. She stumbled. It came quickly: that sickening moment of a fall, when gravity sets about its work and you know that no amount of clutching at the air will save you. Resigned, yet afraid, she waited for the impact.

Jack's hands closed around her.

'You all right?'

As she righted herself, she saw his smile tighten. He snatched back his hands and folded them beneath his jacket.

'I'm fine. *You* all right?'

'Course,' he said.

They trudged up the path, away from the gate. Turning her back on those three figures, Dawn felt a childlike thrill, both exciting and dreadful. The kind she remembered from childhood, when her father had finished her bedtime story and was crossing the room to turn off the light.

They emerged from the drive and stood blinking in the sudden glare. A house of glass, beautiful and cold, threw the forest into their eyes.

Two

'Quiet Time' at St Augustine's Care Home for Retired Priests was never strictly observed. Today was no exception. There came the occasional fart from the unashamedly flatulent Father Janson; the careful hum of Fred Astaire numbers from the bibbed and drooling Father Mantou; insectile clicks from Father Connolly's throat. For Father Asher Brody there was only *the* voice, its words echoing to him down the years: *Do you feel it now, as your faith closes in about you?*

Filtered through the rain, October sunshine dappled the Day Room with spectrums of coloured light. Father Brody, sitting in the window, did not notice the display. In the place where the old priest's mind took him, there was neither colour nor beauty nor sunlight to warm his skin. Pretty lights had no place there.

Brody made up his mind. He reached for the telephone. There was a faint click before the hum of an expectant line. He hesitated, replaced the receiver and flattened out the newspaper on his knee.

Missing . . . last seen . . . Car abandoned . . . large build, dark hair, dark eyes . . .

The article sat above the lonely hearts, horoscope and WI pleas for jumble sale bric-a-brac. *Dark eyes.* Brody snatched up the phone and dialled. It rang once.

'Garret? You there?'

'Father Brody?' Christopher Garret's voice piped down the line. 'I didn't expect . . .'

'Forgotten our arrangement, Father? I was to be told of *anything* relating to the boy.'

13

'Really, Asher . . . You . . . you knew my views . . .'

'Our *arrangement*: if I left quietly, you would keep me informed about him. You took a fucking oath. I'll be in Crow Haven by nightfall.'

The receiver slammed into its cradle. Eyebrows rose upon the foreheads of nurses and volunteers, regarding the old priest as if he were a child that had stamped its foot in a tantrum. Brody glared back and heaved himself from the armchair.

As he left the Day Room, Asher Brody felt a twinge of uncharacteristic envy. Not of the stroke victims, who silently railed against the prison bars of their bodies, but of those whose minds had given up the hopes and terrors of the metaphysical. Once, in their days of useful service to the Church, they had probed and preached the questions of Immaculate Conception, Transubstantiation, Resurrection: the whole shebang. Now they cooed at rainbows and let saliva hang unchecked from their chins. A realisation slipped into Brody's consciousness: life without anticipation was what he craved.

Reaching his room, he made quick work of packing the few belongings he would need. Bones cracked as he hunkered down and selected three journals from the bottom of the wardrobe.

Crow Haven: 1976, Crow Haven: 1984 - '85 and *Crow Haven: 1995.*

The oldest diary, much like the seventy-six year old Brody, had a scored and weary appearance. When its first page had been filled, on 6th January 1976, he had already looked older than his fifty years: his hair, iron grey, his skin aged by half a century's exposure to an unrelenting sun. The Asher Brody who had made that first entry, however, had possessed boundless energy, equalled only by an industrious mind. And yet, a little under three months later, despair had nearly killed him.

He looked back at the forty or so other journals strewn inside the wardrobe. They had not been opened in years. He felt sickened by the perversity that only three periods of his existence meant anything to him: those recorded in these

Crow Haven diaries. The rest of his life seemed as if someone else had lived it. When he remembered the days of his youth in Darwin, he imagined them as he had once imagined the adventures of Huck Finn and Tom Sawyer. The boy who had camped beneath the stars of Kakadu, kayaked its canyons, discovered that its beauties and dangers were often the same thing, was no more real to him than the characters of Mark Twain's Mississippi.

The day his brother infected him with the adventure bug, even that seemed distant and unfamiliar. He had been six years old when his mother read aloud Charlie's first letter home. The world of violence and hazard, hinted at in that wartime correspondence, had excited him. He vowed that one day he would have his own adventure. His mettle would be tested. His courage would hold. But the fantasy of patriotic hand-to-hand combat was to go unfulfilled. Being academically gifted had been his downfall. His father determined that, while one son was a hero of the physical world, the other would be a champion of the spiritual. Arid land and cyclone devastation bred a hard, ferociously religious people in that part of the Northern Territory. His father had been one of the hardest. Asher had not dared cross the old man.

And so he was sent to the only seminary on the continent, the Ecclesiastical College of St Patrick, near Sydney. Under the tutelage of Father Samuel Willard, Asher Brody had found God despite himself. But faith did not dilute his zeal for adventure. During Vespers, meditation periods, visits to the Blessed Sacrament, he imagined himself the hero of some great battle. His war, shaped according to his studies, would not be manmade, like his brother's, but a crusade given by divine mandate. This holy quest, however, was denied him. After three decades of dutiful service, the passion in his heart for derring-do began to cool.

Then, arriving in the parish of Crow Haven, he had found an adventure at last. An adventure which had taught him that age-old lesson: be careful what you wish for.

Asher Brody looked back upon his past. For all the detail and colour, it seemed like a web of artificial memories. Only what had happened in Crow Haven in '76, '85 and '95 was real and vital to him. Now Crow Haven was calling to him again.

'Father? I'm sorry to interrupt. I knocked.'

Sister Agnes Hynter was not given to sweating, but beneath the brew of Vicks, talcum powder and camphor, Brody could detect a whiff of perspiration. He followed the look cast over his suitcase.

'I'm taking a trip,' he said. 'To visit my old parish.'

'You're feelin' worried, then? 'bout something in . . .'

'Crow Haven. You look ill at ease, Sister; it doesn't suit you. Unless Father Gregory's pinching your arse.'

'Father!'

The nun blushed and giggled. As Brody had planned, mock outrage defused the tension.

'What is it, Agnes? No secrets between us I hope.'

'Course not. It's jus' Father Garret . . . he phoned. Said you sounded upset.'

'He's more perceptive than I give him credit for. I'm *very* upset.'

'Well, Father Garret, he . . . He doesn't think you should go back. He didn't give no reason.'

Brody lifted his suitcase from the bed and patted the vacated spot. She sat, and he placed the Crow Haven journals in her hands.

'Three diaries, Agnes, covering nineteen years. But they concern one place. One secret. Tell me, how long have you been in God's service?'

'Forty something years.'

'And you feel His presence?'

'Every day.'

'And you've never questioned that presence? Never demanded proofs of His love?'

'Make demands of God, Father?'

'Why not? After all, the Church has done that very thing.

16

Many times, it has gone through jittery phases and cast around for tangible proof of the divine. Saintly relics, witnesses to miracles and crying Madonnas, stigmata. And then there are the devils.' Brody rapped the oldest diary with his knuckles. 'Possession and exorcism. The come-one, come-all, big-top hoopla of the Church; pure Las Vegas. I once thought of devils as the bogeymen of unenlightened priests. A stick with which to beat faith into the young and simple-minded. I know better now. One must be strong in the Lord to beat the devil down. When my time came, I was weak, and my weakness cost a young boy very dearly. Very dearly . . . It's all here. In these books. My testaments. I'll tell you a little of the story they contain, to make you understand why I *must* go back.'

Sister Agnes moved very little during Brody's long story, but the turning of the world never stops, even for the strangest tales. The afternoon sun retreated across the carpet. Gold turned ochre and, as Brody finished, twilight was deepening the shadows in the corners of the room.

'I thought this would be the last word on the matter,' Brody said, picking up the '76 diary. 'But, as I told you, more was to come. Now that Simon Malahyde has disappeared, I must go back. Something is about to happen. I can feel it.'

'Yes,' Sister Agnes said. 'Yes, I think I see now.'

Cawing came from the clump of copper beeches at the end of the garden. Brody went to the window and searched for the bird in the fingers of the trees.

'A crow, like tattered black cloth, flew into the clearing . . .' he whispered.

He did not need to consult his journals. The bird flew again inside his mind, plucking synapses as it went. His hand clutched at his chest.

There was a chink of keys. A *grind-click* as Sister Agnes locked him inside.

'Sister? What are you doing?' he rushed to the door. 'Sister!'

He pounded until his fists ached. Then he turned to the book that lay open beside his bed.

'Show me my path, O Lord,' he murmured. 'And sustain my faith in the dark days to come.'

Three

Anne Malahyde knew that she could watch the two detectives and remain unseen. It was one of the few redeeming features of this house. This glass tomb. The windows would reflect the forest and keep her hidden.

The woman was in her early thirties, thin beneath her winter coat. She stood with her back straight and her shoulders braced. There was challenge in that stance, but her gloved hands lay folded across her stomach, as if she were protecting something. Her face was impish but set hard. The man looked very young to be a senior officer. He seemed unable to keep still, forever straightening his clothes and ruffling his hair. Taken in isolation, his features shouldn't work: an overly-developed jaw, large eyes and an uneven tear of a mouth. Mismatched components that pulled together into a face that was striking, if not handsome.

In her youth, Anne would have pictured him undressing her. Imagined his fingers pulling at her knickers. She'd been insatiable then. Every man she met, every strapping young customer she had served in the tea rooms where she'd wait-ressed, had been cast in at least a brief fantasy. Of course, she had calmed down when she started seeing the wealthy Peter Malahyde. He had been older than her; so much *older* it had seemed. So less virile than the boyfriends of former days. That wasn't to say their sex life had been non-existent. Despite Peter's growing feelings of inadequacy, the sex had been okay. Right up until the time his face began to peel away.

Lust and craving: these emotions were remembered clini-cally now, for sex was part of living, and she hadn't lived in any real sense for such a long time.

They were here to ask about Simon. What did she know about Simon? Nothing. Weeks after Peter died, she had given birth to him without pain or passion. For years, he was just a little person who played in the garden, in the woods, and whom Anne made meals for when she remembered. Sometimes his resemblance to her late husband had shocked her into realising his presence but, by the time he was ten years old, his face had changed. At about that time he had gone to boarding school. She arranged for him to stay with minders at local hotels during the holidays. The only word she had of her son for seven years was end-of-term reports which always went unread. When he returned from an institution in Geneva last summer, they had exchanged a few inconsequential words. He had decided to stay at home while he studied at the university. Since then, he passed like a ghost through the house. Ghosts were things that Anne Malahyde refused to see.

Something had happened to Simon as a child. Just before he left for his first boarding school, that nosy priest had come to see her. The one who had been with Peter when he died. The priest had said some crazy things. Then, a day or two later, he had abducted the boy. Father . . . Father Bowman? Father Brodman? She could not recall. He was delusional, the younger priest – the man she now knew as Father Garret – had told her. He would be shut away somewhere. The police had asked if she wanted to press charges. It had seemed a lot of hassle. Now she wondered what that old priest had tried to tell her.

But what did she know about Simon? For seventeen years she hadn't given him much thought. Her life had been one long apology that could never be heard. Simon had played no part in it. No, she'd known nothing about her son until four nights ago, when he had woken her with a kiss. And now she knew everything. He had told her a truth that made all those years of grieving for her late husband a cruel sham. A truth that frightened her, because what she now knew about

Simon meant that death was not always the end: things could come back.

A house of glass. Shivering aspens reflected in the panes that ran the length of both storeys.

'I'd no idea there was anything like this in these parts,' said Jack.

'Art Deco,' Dawn murmured. 'Thirties design, though it doesn't look that old. Probably based on the Villa Savoye . . .'

She stopped. Jack was grinning at her.

'History Channel,' she said, starting towards the house.

It was so smooth. So dazzlingly white. Its skeleton of girders and skin of pre-cast concrete had been dressed with so much glass that she couldn't decide if it was beautiful or tawdry. As she faced it, she saw that the lower left wing of the house had no rooms, just a series of concrete pillars that supported an isolated second storey. Between the supports were trellis frames woven with the husk of a dead grapevine. Above, all the windows of that suspended level had been bricked up.

Dawn rang the bell. She had no time to withdraw her hand before the door opened. A woman, dressed in tones of black and grey, a headscarf tied under her chin, stood with disconcerting stillness upon the threshold. She made no move to greet them.

'Good morning,' said Dawn. 'I'm Sergeant Howard, this is Inspector Trent.'

Anne Malahyde did not respond, but stood aside. They entered a cylindrical hall with an iron staircase spidering around its walls.

'Beautiful house, Mrs Malahyde,' Jack said.

Dawn looked up to where the staircase met the first floor landing. Her eyes fixed on a door, very unlike its well-polished, dark wood sister across the hall. It was grey with dust and paint hung from it in thin, curling tongues. From a quick assessment of the layout, she guessed that it led to the bricked-up wing of the house.

'Dawn?'

At Jack's touch, she stirred herself. They followed Anne Malahyde through an archway and into a lounge full of dated '80s furniture. Dawn and Jack settled on a cream sofa while Anne lit a cigarette and stood smoking by the window.

'Now, before we move on to any new information, I want to go over a few areas,' Jack said. 'Your son disappeared Monday night. Bed not slept in. Says here you didn't hear him come home.'

'That's right.'

'We found his car abandoned at a quarry some way out of the city. Nothing inside to indicate his whereabouts. We have a witness who saw Simon that night. A Mr . . .'

'Father Garret,' Dawn said, passing him the statement. 'Was out walking and saw Simon pull into the drive at two a.m.'

'So he came home at two and drove off again some time before six, Tuesday morning. Which is when you noticed the car was gone. Now. What has Simon's behaviour been like recently?'

'Normal. Normal, I suppose.'

'He hasn't had any money worries? Asked to borrow anything over his annuity? No? Who were his friends?'

'I never met any friends.'

'Any relationship problems? You don't know. Did he have any stress from university work?'

'I've no idea.'

'This party he went to, where was it held?'

'I couldn't say.'

'It says here you were unable to give our constable a photograph for the Police National Computer entry,' Dawn said. 'We would take care of it, Mrs Malahyde. You'd get it back.'

'That's beside the point. I don't have one.'

'Are you saying you don't have a single photograph of Simon that we could take away with us?'

'I'm telling you I don't have *any* photographs of Simon.'

Anne responded to their stares with a simple shrug. The movement, sharp and sudden, almost startled Dawn. It was as if an alabaster statue had come to life.

22

'Seems you have quite a cool relationship,' Jack said.

'I don't like Simon,' she exhaled.

'Mrs Malahyde, you've asked for CID involvement in your son's case. We don't usually investigate such disappearances unless there are unusual features. Now, you've reported that there's some new information suggesting Simon might be in danger. We want to help but . . .'

'I don't have any new information. A friend suggested I tell you that, to get the case taken seriously. If Simon has been . . . hurt by somebody, I want that person caught. Punished . . . To do penance . . . I've told you what I know. Yes, I want to find Simon, but you're the detectives, so *detect*.' Anne stubbed out her cigarette against the window frame and threw the butt into the courtyard.

'All right . . .' Jack sighed. 'You told the constable that your son may have gone down to a workshop he has set up in the woods. That he often worked down there during the night? I'd like to take a look at it while Sergeant Howard goes over his room.'

'Fine. Follow the path to the right of the house and you'll come to it.'

Anne fished a key from her pocket and held it out.

'He likes happy families, doesn't he?' Anne said, as Jack left the room. She retied her headscarf and smoothed out the crinkles that sat around the crown. 'Must've had a happy childhood, I guess. All balloons and lollypops.'

Dawn said nothing. She thought Anne Malahyde's observation was probably well wide of the mark.

Jack strode down the path and into the wood. He was glad of the excuse to put some distance between himself and Anne Malahyde. Something about the woman unnerved him. Perhaps it was her cool façade and the sense of resentment that brewed just below the surface. Quickening his pace, he could not shake the sound of her voice echoing in his head.

I don't like Simon . . .

It began to slip into tones that he had not heard in over

23

twenty years. These, in turn, shaped words that came to him often in the long nights.

I'm afraid for my son . . . My son frightens me . . . What have you done, Jack? Stop them. Please God, make him stop them . . .

He refused to remember. Instead, he recalled the aftermath. Breathless hospital conversations. Corridors spilling over with family he had never seen before. Aunties and uncles crawling out of the woodwork, hearing the dinner bell of tragedy and coming to feed. And, in the waiting room, the unresponsive arm of his father as he tried to snuggle close. His father's eyes staring down. Eyes that tried to comfort, but could not help accusing. The doctor's voice:

'I'm sorry, Mr Trent, your wife was dead on arrival. Are you sure there were no signs?'

His father, a rational man, could not blame his son for doing something that was impossible, inconceivable. It was obvious, after all, what the 'signs' had been. If only she had listened and gone to a doctor sooner. Those superstitious ideas she had started having about their son. That Jack was dangerous. That he had been changed by his accident. That something unnatural was living inside him . . . Every now and then, however, young Jack Trent had caught a look of curiosity cast in his direction. After all, his father was only human, and even the most logical men sometimes lie awake at night and wonder if impossible things can be true.

Jack walked a little way into the forest and rested his back against an oak. Flashes of white came through the trees and dazzled him. Through shifting leaves, he saw the sun-baked whitewash of the house. Higher up, he caught glimpses of the grey breeze blocks that filled the windows of the suspended wing. The job had been sloppily done, he thought, and wondered at its purpose. He wiped needle heads of sweat from his brow and levered himself upright. As he did so, his palm brushed against the tree. He turned and looked at the trunk. With his forefinger, he traced a knotted valley in the bark. His heart skipped. He snapped his hand back.

These are the trees. No.

The trees from the vision. A coincidence.

The trees from the clearing. Can't be. Please, God . . .

The trees from the dreaming . . . .

He closed his fist into a tight ball. The teeth of the key cut into his palm. Pain brought him back. He stepped onto the path, his mind repeating the fading chant. Wind groaned through the forest, wagged the branches and bristled the sedge. Jack shook himself. It was his mind playing tricks. Had to be. He walked on.

The path ended at the door of the workshop. It was a sizeable tin-roofed shed with a stove chimney and a window curtained with coarse sacking. Jack scraped his shoes before he entered, leaving furrows of mud and the membranes of dead leaves on the step.

The key rasped in the lock. A smell of oil-based paint and sawdust mingled pleasantly in his nostrils. Dust billowed from the centre table. Catching the light, the motes danced in swirls and halos. A vice was clamped to the table but otherwise the surface was clear. Along the back wall, rows of tools hung off custom-made hooks: several types of saw, a file of hammers ascending in size, a pickaxe, a garden fork, a small scythe, a chainsaw. Each piece of equipment was well maintained and everything had its place. On the shelves, brushes without a flake of paint and pencils with sharpened points sat in jam jars. Bottles of white spirit, tins of emulsion and cans of weed killer were all neatly labelled and arranged.

Only a tangle of rope strewn beneath the window seemed out of place. The man who had built those tool racks and sat rubbing turpentine through those brushes was not the type to throw things into corners. Jack crossed the room and pulled back the sack curtain. He picked up the rope and fingered the frayed ends. A bright, sympathetic pain tore through him. The image of a child, its eyes wide, its mouth thick with blood, flashed into his mind. It was screaming, repeating a word over and over, but the scene unravelled in silence. A scene of pain, of dreadful torment.

A sound drew him back to the workshop: a yawn of wood

that came from the far end of the cabin. Sunlight from the window set filaments dancing before Jack's eyes. He caught a sudden movement beyond the glare. Breathing. Creaking footfalls. Eyes which drew the darkness. Knowing that what he now saw was not inside his head, Jack gripped the rope. The thing from his dreams, its face shining like sun-bleached bone, blocked the doorway.

Jack . . .

His name sighed across stunted teeth. Then the creature closed the door and stepped forward to meet him.

Four

Father Garret stared through veins of smoke. From an unhappy coincidence of lines in the patterned wallpaper, he began to draw out the likeness of a face. He pinched the tip of his cigarette between forefinger and thumb and knocked back a tumbler of scotch, his eyes never leaving the wall. The face was defining. Light and shade sharpened the rudimentary features. It stretched out from the paper. A perfect child's face, smiling and innocent . . . Garret's glass toppled and see-sawed on the desk as he recoiled from the trilling phone. His eyes snapped back to the wall. The face was gone.

Let it ring, he thought, *I'll just pretend I wasn't here . . . But* He *would know.*

Garret picked up the receiver. A warm, old-time radio voice crackled down the line. In his mind's eye, Garret saw the reptilian sway of the head. Saw the bloodless lips purring cruel words. He was asked if he understood and managed to draw enough saliva to answer, '*Uh-huh.*' The line went dead. Plans had changed, it seemed.

To wallow in the absurdity of it all, he phoned the operator and reported that he had just received a nuisance call.

'You must be mistaken, sir. No call has been made to this number since yesterday. Is there anything else I can help you with?'

'Not unless you're versed in stitching reality back together . . . ? I guess not. Good day.'

Asher Brody. There was still a chance to tell Brody everything. It wasn't too late: the boy was still alive. Mutilated, scarred both inside and out, but still alive. *Yes,* Brody would

27

help him. He fumbled with the receiver. It slipped through his grasp and pirouetted an inch above the floor, suspended by its wire. Shame and the urge to survive stopped him retrieving it. He looked up at the wall again and wondered what Man wouldn't do to survive.

There had been more blood last night. Groaning into consciousness, he had run his tongue through a big pool of it. He had picked reality from dreams and realised that the blood was real, soaking his head like some perverse baptism. He scuttled off the bed, took the red-flecked sheets with him. In the bathroom, he scrubbed his face until his skin cracked. Then the feverishness subsided and he had stared into the mirror.

'Who would have thought the old man to have so much blood in him?'

Hysterical laughter made his body ache until he reached the study, where he had calmed himself with scotch and cigarettes.

The phone rang again. Garret bolted upright, tipping his chair over as he went. He moved to the far end of the room. Pressed his back against the wall. The ringing stopped. His own voice frightened him.

'This is Christopher Garret. I'm either dead or otherwise engaged. Remember Coleridge's advice on epigram, and make yours a dwarfish whole, its body brevity and wit its soul.'

The beep cut in.

'This is Sergeant Dawn Howard, Father. I wonder if you're available for a short interview this afternoon. My colleague and I will be round at one, if that's convenient?'

There was a clatter and click. His thoughts turned to the cellar. Did he have enough morphine? *Time to think, time to think* . . .

He turned his face to the wall and traced the shape of the crucifix that used to hang there. The pressure in his head began to build . . . The face grew again from the wallpaper. It watched him. He was *always* being watched. Especially when he did bad things. The child in the wall whispered. Garrett

28

laid his ear close to the raised felt and heard:

As I lay me down to sleep
I pray the Lord my soul to keep
And if this priest kills me, well,
I pray the bastard burns in Hell.

A trickle warmed Garret's lips. He took out a brown-mottled handkerchief and wiped his nose. The face receded back into the paper.

These attacks were becoming more frequent. Sometime soon he was bound to have an episode in public. At the altar? Hearing confession? Holding mass? His tongue might then be freed and he would tell them his bitterest blasphemies, his darkest secret. Jesus, but the cancer was hungry: stalking inside him; using his body against him; making him piss and shit and bleed. But soon it would be over. Soon the promise would be honoured. Then he would be *whole* and could keep his soul safe from judgement.

He had to focus. The police were coming to question the last person to see Simon Malahyde. He went to the cabinet that reached across the back wall. He took out the Madonna figurine, stripped to a smooth nudity through years of handling, his good Bible and breviary, his rosary, vestments and soutane. Lastly, the crucifix complete with suffering martyr. After a moment's contemplation, he replaced the cross on the wall.

It was time to go to the cellar. To subdue the child. When the police had gone, Garret would have to go back downstairs and whittle away a little more of his soul. Afterwards, he would come back up into the house. Yet he sensed that a time was coming when he might never leave the cellar again.

Five

Dawn was forced to admit that, having pored over his belongings for nearly an hour, she still had little insight into who Simon Malahyde was. Toys that Jamie would love, a Scalextric set, action figures, the latest PS2 games, were set alongside CDs of seventies rock gods and a harlequinade of dolls housed in a miniature theatre. Then there were the books: the leather bound volume of Dr John Dee's *Liber Logaeth, or Book of Enoch*, 'offering the perfect truth of God through the language of angels'; the woodwork manuals and local history pamphlets; and the beautiful clockwork model of the solar system. Dawn gave Pluto a nudge, setting the orrery in motion, and wondered about the personality behind this varied collection of possessions.

'Dawn?'

'Look at this place,' she began, turning towards Jack. 'Jesus, what's wrong?'

His face was expressionless and livid, like a Pierrot mask.

'Nothing. I . . . I'm fine.' He glanced over the room. 'Kinda strange, all this.'

She stared at him for a moment. 'Yeah, well, 'kinda strange' is your speciality, not mine, so what do *you* make of it?'

A dumb look of hurt lengthened his face. Flustered, she said, 'Anyway, I can't figure it. I can just about believe that a seventeen-year-old boy might keep toys from his childhood stuffed at the back of a wardrobe, but some of this stuff's brand new. And these books: *De Lamiis Liber,* 'Book on Witches' by Johann Weyer, taken from the original 1577 text. Strange bedtime reading, don't you think? You know, you really don't look well. I've got an aspirin . . .'

'I said I'm fine.'

'Okay . . . Look, I've just phoned Christopher Garret. Told him we'd be coming over.'

The tip of a branch knocked against the bedroom window. Jack crossed the room and placed his palm against the glass, masking the tapping finger. His gaze fixed on the slowing solar system.

'So, are we going to turn this back to uniform?' Dawn asked. 'If she was lying about new information?'

'No, it's pretty quiet for us at the moment. It'll probably be a short job; we'll see it through . . . if you don't mind?'

'No. We can't avoid working together again, I suppose . . .'

'So, what did you think about mommie dearest's little outburst?' Jack asked.

'The whole wanting to see someone punished thing? Well, people never imagine that family members go missing of their own accord. If they did, it might mean looking close to home for the cause. It's easier on the conscience to think they've been taken. But that stuff about punishment or . . . What was the word she used?'

'Penance.'

'Sounds religious, don't you think? That was strange.'

'Have you found any notes? Letters? Does he have a computer?'

'No computer, no notes. I've been through all the drawers. No keepsakes, no photographs. Nothing with any scent of him on it, if you know what I mean.'

'Yes,' Jack said, 'there is no scent.'

He placed a finger in Pluto's path, causing the planets to come to an abrupt standstill. The kinetically powered sun pulsed a dull orange and died.

Anne Malahyde was left with assurances that the detectives would be in touch soon. They reached the gate and Jack opened the padlock with a key Anne had given them. The

31

rasp and clang of the batwing arms reverberated through the trees. The car doors slamming were like two gunshots in the stillness. Dawn knew that something was troubling him. She had not seen him this distracted and upset since their last night together.

'You sure you're feeling okay?'

'Where does Christopher Garret live?' he asked.

Mulch and fern fronds slid from the windscreen as he turned the car in the drive.

During the last days of her holiday, she had imagined this exact scenario. Thrown together on some case, her defences would falter. Despite her best efforts to hate him, she would find that she still cared. It was all panning out just as she had feared. Why the hell hadn't she refused point blank to partner him? Stupid question. You can't give the bastards an excuse to question your professionalism if you're a woman in this game. Sure, things were getting better, but prejudice in the force was like herpes. It took a bit of self-examination to find it, then it could be treated, but it was surprising how often the problem flared up again.

Yet that wasn't the only reason why she wanted in on this case. She liked things to make sense. Jack Trent, and the way she still felt about him, made no sense whatsoever. During the two months they had dated, she hadn't examined the Tortured Man of Mystery act with any real detachment. There was a chance, here and now, to strip away that act. She was certain to find that, as was the case with most single men, only loneliness and low-key desperation lived behind the façade. It would then be easy to dismiss him from her thoughts.

There was just one problem with all that. Deep down, she didn't believe that it was an act. She looked at him now and wondered how this clumsy man-child, in the space of nine short weeks, had managed to burrow his way under her skin. As a rule, she was always drawn to men who were like her: forthright, clear about what they wanted and how they would get it. She would never have believed that someone like Jack

Trent could hold any fascination for her.

Start at the beginning, her case analysis training told her. Sift cause and effect.

She'd transferred from Hounslow three months ago. It sounded corny, and if she'd read such a thing in a book she would never believe it, but Jack Trent had been the first person she met at the station. Fate, karma, kismet, it just went to show that God could do the Hollywood romantic set-up thing pretty well. Now, if only He could nail the endings. Entering the reception area, she had seen Jack trying to persuade the coffee machine to give him coffee. His negotiations weren't going well, and she had asked directions to DCI Jarski's office.

'Sorry? Oh. Let me . . . let me see. You don't have a fifty pence, do you? We used to have a woman come round with a trolley. She was difficult, too. I sometimes think she had an accident and they saved her brain and put it into this monstrosity. Like RoboCop. Except with coffee. To Serve and Percolate . . . Oh, fuck.'

She helped him pick up his change and managed, without difficulty, to order two coffees from the machine. With a half hour until her orientation with Jarski, they had gone outside and sipped their drinks on the wall behind the Magistrates Court. They exchanged opinions on the latest crime prevention policies and targets coming out of the Home Office, and found common ground in berating those bureaucrats who made a tough job even tougher. The usual cop-chat over, they soon ran into a conversational cul-de-sac. Then, taking her empty cup, he said something that had startled her.

'Don't worry about him. He'll do great things.'

Suddenly their conversation seemed a blur. Had she mentioned Jamie? His lacklustre grades were preying on her mind, but she never mentioned Jamie to strangers.

From that first meeting, Jack Trent began to intrigue her. What lit the touchpaper? His looks? No, although he possessed strong features he could not be described as handsome. Nor did she think it had been his intelligence or sense of humour, she'd had wiser and funnier. But there had been something. An immediate impression of sincerity. A quality very rare in the jaded world through which she moved. It was that brand of honesty common among children. The kind that doesn't stop a kid telling lies, but makes it difficult for them to disguise their natures. During their relationship, Jack most certainly *had* lied to her, but she had known (immediately? She couldn't honestly have said that) that he possessed a *good soul*. And, much as she wanted to hate him right now, she still knew it.

Her mother had used that kind of term. *Good soul, bad soul*, and the simplicity of those labels used to make the psychology graduate inside her cringe. 'Souls' in her mother's terminology, a complex patchwork of neural, psychological and chemical factors making up 'psyches' in her own, were neither good nor bad. Not even the clergy spoke about Good and Evil anymore. That sort of jargon was left to tabloid editors. When she met Jack Trent, however, she had been struck by the forcible impression that, beneath all his psychological ticks, there *was* a kind of purity. There was *goodness*.

After that first meeting, there followed a month of encounters so clumsily 'accidental' that she was certain he had orchestrated them. She found these awkward overtures charming. Still, she longed for him to get over his shyness and just ask her out. She had been about to take the initiative herself, when she heard that his father had died. She went to give her condolences and, before she managed a word, he had asked her to dinner.

They had been the only diners at the Basement Restaurant on Bates Street. Jack wondered if they might find Norman's decomposed mother waiting for them at their table. As she had not seen *Psycho*, the joke fell flat. The food had been bland. The conversation faltered at times but eventually found a steady course. He deflected questions about himself and she respected his privacy. Yet she had been curious about him. Perhaps for the first time since she'd met Richard, Jamie's long-gone father, she found herself really wanting to know the man who sat opposite her.

Looking back over the next two months of growing intimacy, it was odd that she had learned so little about him. Whenever she felt that he was about to open up, wariness would creep into his eyes and the conversation was turned around. At the end of the relationship, when he swatted her and Jamie away with *those words*, she had no real knowledge of Jack Trent beyond the few inconsequential facts he had let slip. Brought up in Cambridgeshire. His mother died when he was a boy. He'd had few serious relationships. He had loved his father deeply and he loved comic books. The scar between his eyes was a souvenir of childhood. He had sprayed a cousin's Barbie doll with an aerosol and set a match to it, only to have the plastic beauty blow up in his face. Two months and that was all she knew. She had only really ever known his *nature*: his lovingness, his tenderness, his *goodness*. And it seemed now that she'd even been wrong about that.

It was the third date she regretted. The night when she let her guard down and allowed him *in*. They had kissed on the first two dates (the second consisting of a pizza followed by a tension-free thriller movie). Both were funny, awkward little kisses, but she had found them exciting, like her first. Now she wanted to feel him inside her. She asked him to dinner at the flat.

She had not asked a man home in years, and had not made love in her own bed since Richard left over a decade ago. Since then, sex, both ho-hum and head-spinning, had taken place in either bachelor pads or motel rooms. After a while, these encounters merged into one big blur of limbs, genitals and Ikea furniture. Without knowing it, she had been ready for something more.

Jamie had gone for a sleepover at a friend's. She'd drunk a lot of wine while Jack stuck to orange juice. The conversation had been impersonal but entertaining. She noticed his hands inching across the table. Then Jamie burst through the door, his words tripping over each other.

'Hi,' he'd panted, 'Dan'sbeentakentohospital. Hismumthink

shisappendixhasexploded. Hisdaddroppedmeoff. Anyfoodleft? Hey, who are you?'

'J, don't be so . . .'

Jack interrupted: 'Nice Hulk T-shirt you got there, mate.'

'Come on, Jamie, adult time,' she said, trying to pull her son back by his rucksack.

'*Original Hulk?*' Jack read the motif. 'Can't be. Hulk wasn't green in the first issue.'

'Yeah, I know, he was grey. Cool. You know Marvel.'

'Well, mostly Stan Lee, Jack Kirby, Steve Ditko. Fantastic Four, Spider-Man, Daredevil. I'm not much into Blade and that stuff . . .'

'Crap . . . sorry, Mum. Blade's the bomb. Reed Richards is gay.'

Jack laughed and a debate ensued about the various merits of the Marvel pantheon. It was during these exchanges that she noticed a change in Jack. The child, caged behind those pained eyes, was let out to play. The surge of panic telegraphing, *Get Jamie Out . . . Get Jamie Out . . . Get Jamie Out . . .* faded in her mind. For once, there seemed no need to protect him.

They moved into the lounge. She told Jamie that he needn't drag Jack to his room; he could set out his action figures on the coffee table. J looked at her as if she had lost her mind, but didn't argue. He and Jack sat cross-legged on the carpet, shared their views and quarrelled like a pair of excitable academics. Occasionally, they dragged her into the fray, finding common ground as they joined together to tease her ignorance of superhero lore. It was past midnight when Jamie gathered up his toys and obeyed the command to go to bed.

Jack staggered upright, rubbing the circulation back into his legs.

'He's a bundle of energy, isn't he? Do you watch his E-numbers?'

'No. I mean. You see, he's not usually around when . . .'

They were in the hall. Jack brushed her hand with his forefinger. That deft touch imprinted itself in her memory as the first *real* token of intimacy between them. At that moment, the kisses seemed no more than polite formalities.

'He's going to be okay . . .' Jack said. 'Look, Dawn, if you don't want me to, I won't intrude on your home life. But I was thinking about a picnic. On Saturday. Maybe we could all go?'

The picnic. Three stark memories stayed with her from that day: the tingle-ache of her jaws caused by hours of laughter – Jamie whispering how much he liked Jack as they queued for lollies from a mobile ice cream truck – her and Jack under a weeping willow, its branches caressing the river while his fingertips caressed her arms.

Afterwards, Jamie had been bundled off to a friend's and they returned to the flat together. All the worries and fears she had about letting a man into her life now seemed silly and inconsequential. She still knew nothing about Jack, but that didn't matter.

She led him to the bedroom and undressed him, calming his trembling body with firm hands and light kisses. His touch, when it came, made her feel strangely fresh and unused. She slipped his hands beneath her clothes. For a moment, he looked very young. And then his face changed. His skin felt cold against hers. His fingernails scratched as he pulled away.

'I can't . . . I can't . . .' His voice tight. 'Too soon . . .'

'Jack? What's too soon? I don't understand . . .'

'It's inside. Still inside. I . . . My father.' He spoke the last words too quickly.

'You're still grieving?'

He sat unmoving on the edge of the bed.

'It's okay. Really, we don't have to rush things.'

She felt him flinch as she rested her hands on his shoulders. He stood up and pulled his pants over his semi-erect penis.

'We could cool things,' she continued. 'Have a break.'

'No. *Please*, no. Dawn, I need this . . . I need you.'

She comforted him that night, as she comforted Jamie when he had bad dreams, stroking his hair until he fell asleep.

A month passed. They spoke little about what had happened.

At first, Dawn believed that there might be some deeper, darker connection between Jack's behaviour and his father's death. She had known enough victims of child abuse to understand the length of those shadows. How often the trauma was never fully addressed until the death of the abuser. Was that the truth behind his pain? As the weeks passed, and he began to open up, the idea seemed less and less likely. It was true that victims of abuse often love their abusers but, from the softness that entered Jack's voice when he spoke about the dead man, Dawn could tell that his father had been undemonstrative but very loving. He had never so much as slapped Jack across the legs.

Time went on. In retrospect, it was strange, but only rarely did she think about what had happened after the picnic. Jack started spending a few nights a week at the flat. Often the three of them would have evenings out. Sometimes it would be a movie; usually an action film, during which Jack and Jamie would whisper *wows* at each other as CGI superheroes tussled on rooftops. She would roll her eyes when they suggested go-carting or a football match or bowling, but she loved every minute of it. Some evenings she and Jack would curl up on the sofa together and watch a *sick-chick-flick* (Jamie's terminology), and she would catch him watching her out of the corner of her eye. His expression made her feel warm and safe.

They took long walks together, wandering through the cathedral grounds until they reached the steps cut into the catacombs that led down to the canal. She remembered cool breezes blowing up from the estuary; an arrow of swans gliding downriver; the sun's last rays heliographing across the water. Only looking back did she realise how little they had talked. But on those walks she felt that she understood what mattered about him. She had been happy, and had loved his happiness, which seemed so bright and child-like. She asked him once, only out of politeness it seemed, if he wanted to talk things through.

'Soon,' he said, waves of wine-dark light from the moonlit canal reflecting on his face. 'I can feel it . . . I can feel it fading. In my mind . . .'

And, whatever it was, he had seemed to be tackling it. As time passed, his kisses became more prolonged and more passionate, his caresses more assured and more intimate. She had wanted him so much, but she respected his need to take things slowly. Happy as he seemed, however, there were still occasions when he would become withdrawn and melancholic. One such instance was when she asked him about his mother. His face blanched to the lips and he'd made some thin excuse to leave. As the weeks passed, those unexplained changes in mood became fewer.

Summer ended and Jamie's football practice started again. They'd gone to cheer him on at his first match and, as a commiseration treat (Jamie's team had lost 6-2), Jack had suggested a pizza.

'That'd be great . . .' Jamie murmured.

'But?'

'The guys are going to camp out at Liam's farm tonight. Can I go?'

'I don't know . . .' Dawn began.

'Ah, let him go,' Jack said. 'Here's thirty quid, J. Takeaway for the valiant losers is on me tonight.'

'Hey, we weren't that bad,' Jamie frowned, tucking the money into his pocket. 'If you wanna see a loser, how 'bout this?'

Ferreting in his bag, Jamie withdrew a neat little drawing of Reed Richards, aka Mr Fantastic, in full stretch mode with 'Wuss Man by JH' scrawled at the bottom. Jack held it at arm's length and grimaced. Dawn looked at him, and wondered whether his mock outrage was an effort to disguise the fact that the gift had truly moved him.

'Go on then,' she sighed.

Jamie high-tailed it out of there, calling over his shoulder, 'Thanks, Mum! See you later, Jack!'

'I had an ulterior motive in getting you all to myself,' Jack said, after they arrived back at the flat.

'Oh, yes? Are we going to play superheroes by ourselves tonight?'

'I was thinking maybe we could . . .'

He was blinking back tears. She knew then that the reason he had not made love to her ran much deeper than the death of his father.

Moments later they were naked, clambering onto the bed, kicking off the sheets as they went. Their kisses pressed, full and rough. She watched him move down her belly until his head met with her pubic hair. His tongue lapped in waves across her vagina and tickled her swelling clitoris. She squirmed, gripped by the little fires of pleasure igniting through her body. She placed her hands over his as they pawed at her nipples, causing a dull but pleasurable ache. Now he retraced the path he had taken, his hot breath never more than an inch from her flesh. They kissed and he left the taste of her sex on her palate. She turned him over and took his cock in her mouth. His body shuddered and she felt the muscles in his legs flexing and relaxing in time.

'Dawn . . . I want to . . .'

She lay beneath him, breathing shallow expectant breaths. Their eyes met and she saw written in his the enormity of what was happening. Why was this so important to him? It was just sex after all. Yet it was as if something crucial in his life hung upon this moment.

He was inside her, moving in slow, timorous pulses. She grazed her fingernails across his back: a gesture of reassurance. Tears fell onto her neck and breasts and ran in the light, oily sweat that covered her skin.

'Jack . . .' She drew breath. 'Jack, don't cry . . .'

Her vagina tightened. She put her hands to his face and wiped sweat and tears back into his hair. She barred his eyes with her fingers. The first flutter of orgasm made her mouth run salty. And then . . . she froze . . .

Jack had shivered to a stop inside her. It was not his climax. It felt like a death rattle. Between her fingers, she saw the colour drain from him.

'What is it?' she asked. 'What . . .'

'I can't . . . It's . . . God, *please*,' he whispered and withdrew

40

in the same moment.

He dressed without looking at her. Before she could bring herself to speak, he had left the room. The report of the front door made her cry out. She sat huddled on the bed for a long time. The telephone rang at last.

'This, it has to end. I'm . . . I'm sorry. If it was just you . . . It's Jamie . . . . What I mean is, I don't want to bring up somebody else's . . . I shouldn't have left like that . . . I'm sorry, but if we went through with things, you'd think I was serious . . . Maybe I would be if it wasn't for the . . . the boy . . .'

She hung up. *Those words* . . .

Now, sitting in the car and shooting sideways glances at him, she choked a little. It made no sense. Jamie had been his reason for ending it.

Six

'*Old Priory*,' Jack said, drawing Dawn out of her thoughts. 'Looks like a set from an old William Castle movie.'

He pulled the car into a gap in the line of dogwood shrubs that led up to the rectory, and they both got out. Dew dripped from the vines that crept across the Georgian façade and flew from the lion's head knocker. They waited for a moment beneath the portico, exhaling plumes of steam and wiping the mist from their faces. A short, stocky priest with a pinched face opened the door. Across from the house, the church bells tolled thick and heavy through the damp air.

'You're the police then,' Father Garret said. 'Come in. Filthy day.'

He stepped back into the vestibule and let Jack and Dawn shuffle past. Portraits lined the corridor. Beneath each was written the name and date of incumbency of the priest depicted. Daguerreotypes of heavy-whiskered Victorians filed away into obscurity. A colour photograph of a leathery-faced man named Brody headed the group.

'Good men all,' Garret said, opening a door to their right. 'With the possible exception of Father Brody there. He was somewhat . . .' He tapped the side of his head. 'Come in, dear.'

Dawn felt the accidental touch of a nicotine stained finger on her neck. She resisted the urge to flinch away. The study which they entered had all the cheer of a funeral home, with little in the way of decoration other than religious iconography. Father Garret sat behind his desk while Dawn and Jack squeezed onto a tattered sofa.

'Well, Father,' Jack started, 'we shan't take up much of your time. Now, in your statement you said you saw Simon Malahyde at roughly two a.m. Tuesday morning.'

'It was precisely two a.m. I heard the church clock toll.'

'How did he seem to you?'

'Hard to say. I caught only the briefest glimpse of him as he passed in his car.'

Jack fidgeted and got up. He walked around the room, ran his fingers over the surfaces and straightened the crucifix on the wall. He rested his hand on an old-fashioned radiator beneath the window sill, splaying his fingers between its ribs. To Dawn, it seemed that the priest kept a close eye on Jack's every move.

'Why were you out so late, Father?' she asked.

'Hmm? Oh, I was walking. Insomnia, you see?'

'What did you do after your walk?'

'I came home and read.'

'In here? This room faces the road. Did you see Simon pass again?'

'I was in bed.'

Jack didn't seem to be listening. He worked his palm up and down the undulations of the radiator.

'Did you know Simon well?' Dawn asked.

'Not at all. He wasn't a churchgoer; nor was his mother. In such a small place, you bump into people occasionally. I knew Peter Malahyde a little, his father, but that was a long time ago. I wasn't there when Peter died.'

'Odd turn of phrase,' Jack said, breaking out of his reverie.

'What I mean is, that was the last time a priest was ever at the house. Peter Malahyde was a Catholic. He died just before Simon was born.'

'Simon never knew his father?'

'No. And I *barely* knew him. It was Father Brody who administered the last rites . . .'

Dawn tapped the side of her head: 'That Father Brody?'

'*That* Father Brody,' Garret nodded.

'How did Peter Malahyde die?' Jack asked.

He took his hand from the radiator and Dawn saw that his palm was red and lathered in sweat. His knuckles had started bleeding again. He didn't seem to register any discomfort as he sat beside her.

'Well, I don't really know. A tissue disease, I think. They had oncologists, neurosurgeons. Even dermatologists, I believe. He . . . he fell apart.' Garret's skittish tone steadied. 'We're all betrayed by our bodies in the end.'

'Is there anything else you can tell us, Father?'

'I'm sorry,' Garret smiled. 'Mine eyes have seen the glory of the coming of the Lord, but not the going of Simon Malahyde, I'm afraid.'

As Dawn snapped the elastic band around her notebook, an abrupt clang came from the radiator pipes. Beside her, she felt Jack tremble. Garret's smile broadened.

'I don't think we have any further questions,' Dawn rose. 'If you think of anything else, perhaps you'll contact us?'

Jack grasped the priest's hand and shook it. The radiator rattled.

'I think you should get your heating checked,' he said.

The door closed behind them.

Garret rested his head against the banisters for a moment. Why the hell had he mentioned Peter Malahyde? It was becoming so hard to concentrate. He shuddered. Pray God the Doctor had not been there when the slip was made.

Garret opened the cellar door. Cold air coursed by, whistling as it cut a route through the house, slamming doors upstairs. He reached for the pull string and yanked. Electricity buzzed through the swinging bulb. Bent almost double, Garret ducked beneath the door frame and descended into the cellar. A welcome mat of light see-sawed at the foot of the stairs. It rocked across the face of the semi-conscious child slumped across the hot water pipes.

Not enough morphine, Garret thought. *Thank God I removed his tongue.*

He wrested a shovel loose from a tangle of gardening tools

in the corner. Its blade screamed across the cobbled floor. Resting it against the boiler, he straightened up, took a mahogany case from his pocket and levered open the lid. He removed a scalpel from its tissue paper. This knife once belonged to his father, Ethram Garret, a squeamish Edwardian doctor who had never had the stomach for surgery. Sometimes Garret thought he could still smell his father's cancer on the Gladstone bag and the gleaming instruments that he had inherited. The same cancer that bled through his own slowly dismantling body.

The moving light at the top of the stairs flashed across the blade.

'All done soon,' Garret whispered. 'Just tonight and then one more . . .'

He placed the knife on the stone flags in front of Oliver Godfrey. Sleepy eyes rolled from the scalpel to Garret's face. Drool slipped from the boy's swollen mouth. The stump of tongue clacked.

'Nawh . . . nawh . . . pleesth . . .'

Oliver shrank back to the wall. The chains around his wrists and ankles clanked against the pipes. His movements opened the wounds that had been nicked into his body to weaken him. Thin blood trickled over old scars.

'Nawh . . . Jethuth pleesth, nawh!'

Garret raised the shovel. His silhouette grew wide, focused and grew wide again in the pendulum swing of the light. During his time in the cellar, Oliver had screamed a good deal. The stump of his tongue choked his last cry.

Dawn laid the Malahyde file on a chair and removed her coat. Jack sat behind his desk and thumbed through her notebook.

'So,' he stirred, 'I suppose, Mother first. What do you think?'

'She makes a bit more sense after what Garret told us about her husband's death. I suppose grief can do that to some people. Make them selfish . . . I mean . . .'

Jack cut in: 'It's this alienation from Simon I don't understand.'

'Well, we don't know much about him. She said she didn't like him. Why? Drugs maybe . . . That room of his was a bit freakish.'

'But there's something more. If she's not bothered about him, why did she insist on seeing us? Why make up a story about new evidence?'

'There's a difference between not *liking* your son and not caring what happens to him,' Dawn said. 'It's too early to theorise over. We need to find out who his friends were, what might have been preoccupying him lately. Jesus, I need caffeine. You?'

'Please. Did you say there's been an article in the *Gazette*? I'll call them. See if they've heard from anyone who knows him.'

She was halfway out of the door when Jack said, 'Listen, if you ever go back to that house, and you need to go down to the work shed, take someone with you. It's just, when I went down there I . . . It's a bit treacherous. I nearly fell, and it's in the middle of nowhere so . . .'

'Sure,' she frowned.

What was the matter with him? He'd been distant and distracted ever since he got back from searching the cabin. On the return journey to the station, she had asked him if he'd found anything there. He hadn't answered, just slumped further into the passenger seat and gnawed his nails. And what was that idiotic warning about not going into the forest alone? A sort of hesitancy had entered his voice. The same kind of tone he had used during *that* phone call. He was lying, and lying didn't come easily to him.

She fed the drinks machine silver and punched in the order. Her mind ticked away as the machine whirred and ground. She took the coffees from the slide tray and was at the office door when she stopped.

Careful, she told herself. *Think it through: he's lying about something to do with Simon Malahyde's work shed.* Ignoring why

46

he would lie for a moment, she wondered about the other observation she had just made. *It was the same voice he had used when he told her he wanted to end it.* When he told her that he wasn't interested in a woman saddled with a kid. Had it been his intention to blind her with the ugliness of those words? To make her feel so repulsed she wouldn't question him about his decision? With a Styrofoam cup in each hand, she elbowed open the door.

'Why you take that sweetener stuff, I'll never know. Tastes like dried cat vomit and . . .'

The scene that confronted her withered the words in her throat. Jack was crouched on the floor, the contents of her bag strewn at his feet. Photographs from her holiday were in his hands. She tried again to speak, but her mouth was dry and cottony. The shock of this intrusion stunned her, and she felt bruised, disoriented.

Flares of colour darkened his cheeks. As he straightened up, her lipstick crumbled beneath his shoe, leaving a dusty cerise stain on the carpet. With eyes downcast, he stood like a wounded, indignant child, holding out the thirty or so prints. Splashes of coffee burned her hand as she slammed the cups on the desk. She snatched the photographs from him. The first shot showed her in a bar, her eyes glazed, standing between two men with Hawaiian shirts unbuttoned to their navels.

'What do you think you're doing . . . ?' she snapped.

'Your bag fell open,' he muttered. 'They dropped out. I was picking them up . . . Seems you had quite a time of it.'

'Fuck you. Fuck you, Jack.' The urge to lash out was hard to resist. 'You don't get to comment on my life. You're not part of my life.'

He took a short, trembling breath through his nose and the high-colour drained from him. Then, without a word, he moved to his desk and sat down. She started rearranging her bag. Someone thundered along the corridor outside. The shock-waves rattled the glass in the office door. The air conditioning clicked off. The intensity of her anger throbbed at her temples and made her movements hurried and clumsy.

'I'm sorry,' he murmured.

Collecting the crumbs of lipstick into her hand, she brushed them into the wastepaper basket. Her fingers, stained dark red, appeared hazy through a film of tears.

'You're right,' Jack said. 'I'm not . . . It's none of my business. Do you want me to . . . ?'

'No. God, how many times do I have to tell you?' she said, hoping that he wouldn't notice as she dried her eyes. 'Dave Fellowes will have told the whole station we're working on this. I don't want gossip.'

When she turned, she found him staring hard at the grain of the manila folder on his desk.

'Thank you,' he said. 'The Gazette . . . Someone's contacted them. A friend of Simon's. I thought we might see him tomorrow.'

Seven

It was dusk when the sun found its only toehold on the day. At the municipal playing fields, a burst of fire blinded the players and spectators. The display was fleeting. Twilight ran misty fingers over the city and floodlights lit the pitch. A whistle blew and the boys tramped to the sideline, steam billowing from chattering mouths and flared nostrils.

'How can you get so mucky on Astroturf, Jamie?'

'Don't know. Thirsty.'

Dawn reached into a plastic bag and handed him a Coke and a chocolate bar. Between chewing and gulping, Jamie picked at his legs. The sweet confection eased his anger.

'Can't believe we lost to those dickh . . . idiots . . . did you see Jim's goal? I set him up for that. Sort of. We should've had 'em. Should've been a piece of piss – erm, *pie*, easy as pie.'

'If you took a breath once in a while you might be able to avoid swearing altogether.'

'Hmm. Can I stay at Jim's tonight? Come on,' he nudged her shin, 'it's Friday. You could invite Jack round.'

She snatched the empty bottle from his hand and dropped it into the bag.

'Jim. I don't know Jim, do I?'

'New striker. He's got *Friday the Thirteenth* on DVD, and *Cannibal Holocaust* . . . Which we won't be watching, obviously . . .'

He smiled, his mind on the *Playboy* that Jim had swiped from his dad's collection.

'I'll stop picking this scab if you let me go.'

49

'I don't think so. I don't know Jim's parents . . .'

'Well, I think they've got a mutated son they keep in the attic, but otherwise they're pretty sound.'

'No, Jamie. Not tonight. Perhaps Jim can come over next weekend.'

'Oh, but, Jesus! Don't glare, you're not even religious. If you don't let me go, I'll start running drugs from my room. I'll get a girl in trouble . . .' he searched his mind for something that would really rankle. 'I'll join the Young Conservatives.'

'You sound overqualified for the Young Conservatives,' she said, deadpan.

'Fine,' Jamie muttered, tearing off a strip of scabs.

He wasn't that annoyed, but feigned an outraged stomp over to his kitbag anyway. Usually he would be pissed off with yet another of his mum's overprotective displays, but it was her first proper night home. Having said that, it would've been cool to have seen the *Playboy,* but at least Jim had promised to loan him the DVDs.

As he said his goodbyes to his teammates, he wondered if Jack *would* come over tonight. When his mum left to go on holiday – a holiday she insisted she'd booked months ago, though Jamie couldn't remember her mentioning it – she had given short answers to all his questions.

So, is Jack going with you?

No.

Why?

It was booked ages ago . . . I didn't know him then.

When you get back, can we go to Jack's house? He's got an alternative Marvel universe comic. Where Hulk kills Wolverine.

We'll see.

And one when the X-Men beat the crap out of the Fantastic Four . . .

Christ, Jamie, will you shut up a minute?

It hadn't been the play exasperation she usually used when he got excited. For some reason, she'd been really pissed.

One night, while his mum was abroad, he'd crept

downstairs and used his grandad's clunky old phone. As a little kid, he'd played with it for hours, loving the noise the Bakelite made as you put your finger in the holes and drew the spinning dialler around. That night the *click-click-click-click-whhuurr* seemed very loud in the quiet corridor below his grandad's bedroom. He'd copied Jack's number from his Mum's address book. The phone rang for ages before someone picked up.

'Yo, Jack?'

'Jamie? Is that you? Does your mum know you're . . .'

'She's on holiday, didn't you know? Have you had a row? She spazzed when I asked if I could call you.'

'Well, listen, J, I'm a bit busy right now. Could you . . . ?'

'Sure, I'll call later or something. Jack, maybe you could come over, we could . . .'

'I've got to go, Jamie. Sorry.'

He'd hung up. Every time Jamie stole a minute to call again over the next fortnight, Jack's answering machine cut in. Something *must* have happened between them. Jamie was determined to find out what.

'So, what we doin' tonight?' he asked, as his mother eased out into the Friday rush-hour.

'Well, I'm having a bath and going to bed. You can stay up 'til ten, and between now and then you can do what you like. Within reason.'

'*Ten*? Jeeze . . . So nobody's coming round then?'

'Nope. Listen, I have to go in tomorrow. I'll drop you at your grandad's for the morning, okay?'

'I could stay home, you know. I'm old enough.'

'Remind me to check the forecast later. If there's a possibility of patchy ice and snow flurries in hell, then you can stay at home by yourself.'

'Fine. Mum?'

'Hmm?'

'You said I could go over to Jack's when you got back . . .'

'I didn't say anything like that.'

51

'You did. I wanted to see his comic books. You said . . .'

'No . . . Look, pass me the aspirin from the glove compartment.'

'I'd just pop in and out. Anyway, you'd like to see him, wouldn't you? Have you seen him today? Do you think he'd . . . ?'

'Jamie, it feels like someone's doing the rumba in my head. Pass me the aspirin.'

'I will if you just listen,' Jamie said, leaning towards her. 'Have you and Jack argued? I'm sure it wasn't his fault. You can be a bit . . .'

'Sit back, I can't change gear with you there.'

'You've been horrible to him, haven't you?'

'Don't be so stupid. Move will you?'

'What have you said to him? No wonder we don't know anybody, normal people have friends come over. Nobody ever . . .'

'Jamie, I said *move* . . . Shit!'

Jamie's elbow knocked the car out of gear. The Range Rover leapt forward. Horns blared and tyres screeched. Headlights flashed in the rear-view mirror. Dawn fumbled for the brake and yanked the steering wheel right. She avoided the car in front by inches. The Range Rover bunny-hopped across the road and into a line of traffic cones which separated off the fast lane of the dual carriageway. The cones smacked against the front bumper and crumpled under the wheels. Jamie felt the slight jolt as they ploughed through the barrier and hit the partially resurfaced lane. A yellow sign advising of highway maintenance had its legs swept away and slammed onto the bonnet. The car stalled.

Dawn restarted the engine and, with apologetic waves to the trail of traffic behind, reversed out. The metal sign idled off the bonnet. She indicated left and brought the car to a stop on the hard shoulder. Jamie made himself as small as he could in the passenger seat.

'Jack doesn't want to see you anymore . . .' She stopped and shot a glance at her son. 'I mean he doesn't want to see

52

either of us, understand? You think I'm overprotective, don't you? Well, you know that nasty little feeling you've got in the pit of your stomach? The one that hurts because you've been rejected? That's what I protect you from. But you're a big boy now, aren't you? Maybe you don't need protecting.'

She hit the steering wheel with her palm. Jamie watched her, unsure of what to do.

The Ford tucked in so close to the kerb that its tyres flapped against the concrete lip. The driver wound down the passenger window and Terri approached with her usual caution. One time, she'd been caught unawares by some crazy who'd stuck her in the throat with a needle. A religious freak, the police had told her, 'down on whores'. She'd been wary ever since.

'Hi. I'm looking for Coral . . .' the man began, leaning over the passenger seat.

'She's away seeing her mother.'

Terri was savvy enough to know that men panicked if told their regular girl was ill.

'We . . . we . . . usually go to hers.'

'My flat's being fumigated. Look, sweetness, what do you want to do? If it's quick, I know a place.'

You might see the quiet guy tonight, Coral had told her, sniffing and rubbing Vicks across her chest. *He turns up when he feels the need. I reckon he's filth but he won't run you in. And it won't take long. He just . . .* The phone had interrupted her and Terri wasn't interested in the quirks of every one of Coral's clients.

The guy opened the passenger door. Terri ducked inside, ratcheted the seat back and adjusted her tights. She looked over and saw him watching the movement of her hands. He had a cute white scar between his eyes: a simple line of two shallow humps, like a kid's picture of a bird in flight. She told him to take a left at the Chinese and then a right onto the causeway. Perhaps he was just nervous, but his driving, jerky and too fast, made her feel a little sick. She turned the rear-view mirror to check her makeup. A clicking sound drew her attention. He was touching her bracelet beads with a fingertip.

'You like them?' she asked.

She reached down to take his hand but he snatched it away.

'They're very . . . very pretty,' he murmured.

'Next left,' she said.

The car rattled over the cobbles of a dead-end alley, crowded on either side by tall buildings. A dog appeared in the head-lights, picking over the contents of a split bin bag. To their left was the back of a theatre, its windows taped over, tired posters flapping from its walls. Opposite was the rear entrance of a trendy bar. Smoke and steam rolled from pavement level ventilation shafts. Neon lights flashed through frosted windows in time with a techno bass beat.

The engine died and the headlights dipped. He turned and looked at her. She suddenly felt exposed, as if her spirit, trou-bled at its edges, early in the stages of drowning, had been opened to him.

'Okay,' she said, 'what do I call you?'

'Jack . . . my name's Jack. Please . . . I can't touch you . . . I can't . . .'

'Hey, Jack. Jack, come on, don't get upset. It's cool, no problem. Look, I'll just . . .'

She pulled off her top, careful not to lose a sequin from the *Hot Bitch* motif. The bar's 'Rolling Rock' sign bathed her breasts in green light. Her nipples hardened in the dry air from the heater. She found herself relaxing quickly with him. He flipped open the glove compartment and removed a jar of white powder.

'Hey, no drugs,' she said, now less comfortable.

'No, it's just powder. Talcum powder. Here.'

He unscrewed the lid and she gave it a tentative sniff.

'Okay, I'm broad-minded,' she said. 'What's the score?'

He poured a little of the powder into his palm and dusted his hands with it.

'I can't touch you,' he said, the emotion tight in his throat. 'Not with my bare hands. I need - please, I need to *touch*. . .'

Terri put out a hand and rubbed his shoulders and back, not as she would usually massage her clients, but the way she sometimes reassured herself at night, when the edges of her life seemed too hard.

'Please,' he whispered, 'I need to touch . . .'

This was a new one on her, but as fetishes went, it seemed pretty harmless. His hands flinched as she enveloped them, but he did not snatch them back. The powder-rain falling between their fingers changed from white to red to yellow to green in the switching neon light. She placed his palms on her breasts. A white path marked the course of his hands along the slope of her neck. With the touch of a blind man making a mental picture, his fingertips explored the contours of her face. For five minutes, she felt his touch, smelled the lavender of the powder, heard the emotion through his intakes of breath. When she opened her eyes, she saw him rubbing tears from his cheeks, whispering his thanks.

He offered her a tissue to wipe away the powder traces. The lazy-eyed mongrel had taken its nose from the garbage and watched them like a mildly interested peeping tom. Now the show was over, it threw them a final frown and slunk away into the night. It was still early, and there was a city of garbage to pick through, but Terri felt exhausted.

'Take care, won't you, Jack? Hope I'll see you again. Don't . . . Well, just take care,' she said, getting out of the car. Her farewells were usually a clipped 'Bye.'

He might have smiled, she wasn't sure. The lower part of his face was in shadow.

She closed the passenger door and watched him reverse out of the alley and drive away.

Eight

Sister Agnes was wondering whether to call Dr Jamison again, when she saw the man on the monitor. As he approached the door, the trip lights fused, cloaking his face in darkness. The security cameras were working but, without light, only grainy images showed up onscreen. His short, bulky silhouette loomed against the glass panels of the door.

Agnes glanced down the empty corridor. Everyone was in bed. She was due to be relieved at 2:30 a.m. It was now only ten to midnight. Although she hated answering the door by herself this late in the evening, it hardly seemed fair to wake Sister Beatrice already. What with her rheumatism, the poor dear had little enough uninterrupted rest.

Beeeezzzz. The man pressed his finger to the buzzer. *Beeezzzz.* The image flickered. Agnes slapped the monitor. *Beeeezzzz.* The screen steadied and her eyes narrowed. Only one silhouette moved against the glass of the door. But on the monitor, another figure was displayed, waiting in the darkened vestibule. A ragged, gangly-looking fellow. He was shaking his head slowly, as if disagreeing with his fat companion.

Looks like Jack Sprat from the nursery rhyme, Agnes thought.

The screen went blank. She hit the box again. When the picture returned, the small man with the bag was alone once more. *Shadows playing tricks.* She went to the speakerphone.

'Hello?'

'Good evening, I'm Dr Ethram. I believe you called today asking for someone to take a look at a . . . Brody, Father Brody?'

'Oh. Jus' a moment. I'll let you in.'

'Thank you kindly.'

Sister Agnes pushed the door release button. The man who entered had a pinched, lean face that did not sit well with his plump body. He shook out his umbrella and came smiling to the desk. She didn't like his grin or his nasty yellow fingers. He sneezed and wiped his brow.

'Filthy day,' he said. 'Now, what's the matter with our patient?'

'I can't rightly say. He was his usual self, right up until this afternoon. Then we had a call from a Father Garret. I went up to see Father Brody and . . . well, the things he said . . .'

'Is he still in his room?'

'Yes,' she blushed. 'I locked him in. I'm not sure if I should have, but . . .'

'You did the right thing.'

'He showed me these books. I'm afraid, I'm *really* afraid, he's gone mad.'

'What room is his?'

'Twelve. Is Dr Jamison still on call? You see it wasn't an *actual* emergency, and Sister Beatrice wasn't on duty, so I didn't have anybody to discuss it with . . .'

'Give me the key.'

Rude little man. She turned to the back wall and the board where the keys were hung. A sense of betrayal, which she had harboured since locking Father Brody in his room, prodded her conscience. This is for Asher Brody's own good, she told herself.

As she raised her hand to the key, the lights behind her dimmed. She was about to make a throwaway comment about the state of the Home's wiring, when she saw *them*. Two shadows on the board. *Two people* standing behind her. The small doctor. And . . . *Jack Sprat, who ate no fat. Thin as a stickman from a child's drawing.*

Absurd. But there it was, standing shoulder to shoulder with the doctor. The shadow of its head inclined to one side, as if appraising her. Then the head rolled, passing across to the other shoulder, slipping in and out of the crevices of the

chipboard and over the key hooks. Lolling left to right . . .
left to right . . . left to right.

Sweat beaded Sister Agnes' forehead. Drops touched the
corners of her eyes and burned. A series of questions span
out in her head like a catechism: What is it? How did it come
here? What does it want? Is it really standing behind me? And
always the same answer: *Run, Agnes, run as fast as you can.*

'Sister. The key.'

The doctor's voice? No. Different. Older. So very, very *old*
. . .

She did not want to see, but an irresistible curiosity made
her turn.

*O, thank God. Stupid woman. No-one else there. No-one else
with the little doctor. No-one at all . . . But wait . . .*
There. Movement. Merciful Jesus, what is it . . . ?

Standing just behind the doctor, where the light barely
spread, where the dark held sway: something that should not
be. So still, except for its head, which swayed back and forth
like the tiring motions of a Jack-in-a-box. In the penumbra
of light in which the thing stood, Agnes could just make out
the shape of its emaciated body. Ribs poked through the torso.
The blades of its cheeks tented its face. A powerful resemblance
to Caravaggio's wasted figure of the crucified St Andrew
occurred to her. The association struck Agnes as blasphemous.
Good St Andrew had preached from his cross. This thing could
not preach. Could not speak. Could not think, even. Not with
its head so beaten in.

Set into the stranger's skull was a deep depression. It reached
so far into the face that there could be no left eye and precious
little nose. Straw-like hair moved in the rent, as if fingers
kneaded the crippled skull from beneath.

The figure moved away from its friend and towards Sister
Agnes. It slipped around the desk, its fingers raking the papers
arranged there. As if caught by a breeze, the pages fluttered
to her feet. She wanted to move, to obey the command and
run, but her legs felt as if they were cemented into place. It
was behind the desk now, its attention focused upon her. The

thing moved in close until she felt its fetid, dead breath on her skin. It spoke:

'Give me the key, Sister.'

She did not think. She held out the key. Something inside her head slipped and jarred, and she felt herself lost to the twin hollows before her. Hollows in which eyes had once been held . . .

'Thank you,' said the sightless man. 'And now for your reward. You believe in God, do you? Then you shall see God.'

In the pit of those hollows, Agnes saw her saviour. A wretched figure lost in a vast, incalculable darkness. She called out to him, beseeching the Lord to comfort her. Shuddering under the creature's gaze, the man–god turned his back and tended his wounds. It was then that Agnes felt the emptiness of the world close in around her. Like the lights outside, the bright parts of her mind tripped out, one by one, until all that remained was a single sliver of trapped consciousness. Focused through this, she saw the demon's face crack into a bitter smile.

'His light falls back before my shadow . . . Stay with me, Sister, and I'll show you things you wouldn't believe.'

SATURDAY 26th OCTOBER 2002

For now we see through a glass, darkly;
but then face to face: now I know in part;
but then shall I know even as also I am known.

I Corinthians 13:12

Nine

Jack closed the report he had requested on Simon Malahyde's abandoned car. The beautifully restored 1967 Triumph GT6 had been discovered parked on waste ground near a quarry. It had been unlocked but the ignition key was missing. No personal effects and no clue as to the whereabouts of its owner had been found. Below the quarry, a tributary of the Cam ran in a fast, sweeping arc. Divers would have to be sent down if Simon proved elusive.

Jack checked his wristwatch. 10:30 a.m. He thought they had agreed to meet at the station at ten. He was finding it difficult to recall yesterday's events with much accuracy. Memory lapses, like migraines and nosebleeds, were a side effect of *the dreaming*. One particular episode from yesterday seemed to have been almost entirely wiped from his mind. He remembered the interview with Anne Malahyde and her dismissive attitude to Simon's disappearance. He remembered talking to Father Garret, and the sensation he experienced as he touched the radiator: as if someone had called to him through the pipes. But there had been something between those interviews . . . The forest? No, think. *The work shed.* Something he had seen in the shadows. Something that had impelled him to warn Dawn not to go there alone. A figure? A face? It was no good. The memory would not come.

His eyes prickled through lack of sleep. As he rubbed them, traces of powder fell from his nails. Twelve hours later, and he could still feel the coolness of her skin against his finger-tips.

And the Nobel Prize for Dickhead Decisions goes to. . . Jack Trent.

He must have been insane to pick up a girl when the visions had only just started again. Yet after spending a day so close to Dawn, and remembering how she felt against his bare skin, he thought he would go mad if he didn't touch.

Don't make excuses, you fucking coward. It's unforgivable.

After he'd left the girl, he circled the city for a few hours, his mind disturbed by the possible consequences of such lapses. He'd parked the car and wandered through the municipal cemetery. The sky had been clear but the cuticle moon had given little light. He had gone straight to the Victorian burial ground. The ends of tombs, thrown up by subsidence, and collapsed obelisks had cast bold, angular shadows across a carpet of beer cans and condom wrappers. His mother's grave was at the new end of the cemetery. He had seen the modest cross only once: polished granite with a bed of stones the colour of sanitation tablets in public urinals. That smart headstone frightened him. He much preferred the company of those older, tumbledown monuments. It was a perfect example of the fact that, outside his head, he favoured a kind of romantic disorder to cold, unfeeling neatness. Inside the confines of his mind, however, he prized structure above all things.

After what had happened to his mother, he had trained his mind, sweeping away the chaos. It had been his last promise to her. To fight the darkness within him. He had achieved this by constructing a room in a part of his brain farthest away from his consciousness. Inside this room was a toy box. The contents had not been played with since the night of his mother's death. The room was kept locked and never visited. The box contained impossible things. His mother, influenced by the mythology of her faith, had called such things *Demons.* Even now, he didn't really know what they were, except that they seemed to be afraid of order. So, to drown their song, he disciplined his thoughts with mathematical problems.

He had recently immersed himself in a series of algebraic algorithms, using the Newton-Raphson method to approximate the value of certain functions. The exercise was pointless in that, working only analytically, the functions could never be solved. His purpose, however, was never to discover new proofs, he was too plodding a mathematician for that, but to order his thoughts as best he could. He was now working on an equally insoluble puzzle: a number series that aimed to ascertain a progressively more accurate value for pi. This particular exercise seemed to control the things in the box especially well. Jack wondered whether this was because, like them, pi itself was something sprawling that could be harnessed with logic. Perhaps that idea frightened them.

He allowed himself some diversions: comic books, old B-movies. Those were his flights of fancy and he rationed them. Films, art, books, they all fired his imagination, and he had learned from the very beginning that imagination was the thing that woke the *Demons*; the catalyst that altered their dark forms and gave them substance.

Twenty-five years of this routine had worked. His visions – *the dreaming* – the Demons' first gift to him, had weakened and disappeared. Yet part of the routine had left him sealed off from human contact. Their second gift was an ability to see the life, memories and dreams of another by the simple act of touching. Because this gift operated at some imaginative level, it gave them power. When they took such power – when he touched - they could bleed out of him. They could kill.

Bitter experience had now reconfirmed that he would never be able to control *them*. A month ago, hoping against hope to free himself from loneliness, he had reached out to Dawn Howard. And with that simple connection, they had reawakened, drawing renewed strength from his attempts at intimacy. He had pulled away, severed the connection, but it was too late. Now they were showing him the future again. Something terrible was about to happen in a clearing. In the woods. In Redgrave Forest?

The phone rang.

'Jack? Hi, sorry I'm late, I've had to drop Jamie . . . Look, I'll meet you at this lad's house. Where is it?'

He read out the address. He had *touched* her. Now the

darkness crept back in. His mother's killers were stirring in the hinterland of his mind.

The row with Jamie, and the guilt that followed, had exhausted her. She slept through her alarm and it was just after ten when she woke. She found Jamie, fully dressed and eating cereal in front of the TV. It was novel to have him up and ready to leave without any arguments, but she felt the sting in his dead-eyed glances and muted responses to her questions. Last night, he had made her feel angry and stupid, but that wasn't his fault. He just wanted . . .

A father? She didn't think so. It was obvious that he enjoyed Jack's company. They shared the same idiotic interests and the same stupid sense of humour, but they were friends. They spoke and listened to each other as equals. She'd seen no desire on Jamie's part to take on the subordinate role of son. But then what did he want? The answer came to her as she showered. He was anxious for *her* to have somebody. To be happy. And she had repaid his efforts as matchmaker by more or less telling him the hateful truth. That Jack didn't want *him*.

Jamie stood by the door, his hands tight around the straps of his rucksack. She pulled the Parka hood back from his face. He wouldn't look at her. In the car, he pumped up the bass and volume on the stereo. Two rappers, from some quarter of LA Dawn had never heard of, extolled the merits of their respective 'bee-atches'. For once she didn't tell him to turn 'that rubbish' off.

'Burger King tonight?' she asked, as she pulled up at her father's house.

'Sure,' he said, getting out of the car.

Watching her little boy wander up the path, she pictured herself delivering a swift knee to Jack Trent's groin.

She pulled onto the ring road. *Douglas Winters, 17 Berwick Ave.* It was little more than a ten-minute drive. Jack's disintegrating Escort was parked, with his customary disregard for the traffic laws, at a thirty-degree angle to the pavement and across a resident only space. He stood slumped against the driver's door, tie loose around his neck, a night's stubble girdling his chin. As she parked, he walked over and opened her door.

'Hi. You all right?'

'Yes. Couldn't get here any earlier. Shall we get on with this?'

Berwick Avenue was a street of terrace houses, each red brick, many bearing the hallmarks of student dwellings. Traffic cones and road signs, the spoils of many nights drunk, littered the pavement outside No 17. A desperate-looking potted plant baked in an upper window, and what appeared to be a piece of toast layered with jam was stuck to the outer side of a curtain. A sign done in gothic letters was attached to the post flap: *Jehovah's Witnesses selling weed and Avon ladies with big tits only please. All others are kindly asked to FUCK OFF.*

It took a good five minutes of Dawn hammering on the door before it was opened.

'Yep?'

'Doug Winters?'

'Upstairs . . . Hey, is Dougie okay?' the mass of hair and towelling dressing gown called after them.

'I don't know,' Jack said. 'Maybe we could talk to you later?'

'Sure . . . okay, sure.'

Nirvana's money-grabbing aquatic baby poster was tacked on a door at the top of the stairs. Above it sat a salivating cartoon dog with *Dougie does it Doggie* printed beneath in neat copperplate. Jack knocked.

'Who is it?'

'Jack Trent. We spoke yesterday.'

They heard a soft clap of slippers. A bolt whined free of its fitting and the door slackened in the frame. Jack pushed it open.

Doug Winters sat cross-legged on a futon. The walls around him were papered with posters of rock and Britpop icons, each positioned as though a spirit level had been used when hanging them. A collection of musical instruments: acoustic and electro-acoustic guitars, a banjo, a violin, and what Dawn believed was a jew's-harp had been mounted with care around the room. Books and colour-coded files were arranged on the shelves in order of size. The rest of the room was in total disarray. Crushed drink cans and furred pizza boxes lay strewn across the floor. A week's worth of washing, consisting of knotted shirts and cardboard-rigid socks, sat heaped in a corner. It was the stereotype of a student living in toxic untidiness, but the squalor did not ring true.

Doug appeared flushed. The skylight above his head was open and the sweet, earthy scent of cannabis was still in the room.

'Musician I see,' Jack said. 'Is that what you study?'

'Yeah, my dad wanted me to read economics; something 'useful',' Doug said, his voice uneven. 'Dear old Dad, he's like the contents of a whore's pants: a pussy, but he pays the rent.'

The boy gave a hollow laugh and plucked at the breast of his T-shirt. Despite the drowsy warmth of the room, and the amount of cannabis he had toked, Dawn could tell that he had not slept in days.

'Okay, Doug,' she began, brushing away strands of rolling tobacco that littered the desk and resting her notebook in the cleared space. 'What can you tell us about Simon Malahyde?'

'Whoa. Wait a minute. You're journalists, right? You said you were a journalist.'

'We're the police, Doug,' Jack said. 'On the phone I mentioned that you'd contacted the *Gazette*. You didn't ask who I was. As you know, Simon has disappeared. We need you to tell us about him.'

'I don't know anything. Listen, I just thought you were . . .'

Doug lapsed into silence. The stench of the room thrummed at Dawn's temples. Doug's eyes fixed on the door.

'Do you want me to lock it?' Jack asked.

The boy nodded, pressing his back against the wall. Jack flipped the bolt.

'Something bad happened.' Jack turned to face the kid. 'You couldn't tell your friends about it; too many questions. You couldn't tell the police; they'd want to follow it up. But you needed to make sense of it. You saw the notice in the *Gazette*. Thought you'd tell a journalist. Didn't matter if they believed you or not, you had to tell someone. You've been sitting in this room since the night of the party, ordering takeaway, afraid to go out, even to the launderette. Such a neat young man, living in this pit. Something must have really frightened you.'

'Can I smoke?' the boy said, his voice dirt-dry. 'A cigarette?'

'Sure.'

Doug took a roll-up from the pocket of his dressing gown and lit up. He drew on it, picking fallen flecks of tobacco from his shirtfront with shaking fingers.

'You won't believe me. I don't care if you don't. I couldn't tell Kate; I couldn't tell any of them . . .' he swallowed hard. 'The party hadn't really got going. By around one, people were either comatose or leaving. Joll - the cross between Marilyn Manson and Chewbacca who let you in - had just won the last drinking game. You threw food at the window, if it stuck, you had to drink. Toast on the curtain. That was mine. I was knackered, so I decided to crash . . .

'I found him here. Waiting for me.'

Doug flicked ash into the Diana memorial mug between his legs.

'He knew. Said he knew. Said he'd known from the first time he saw me. Said Kate was just a front. I told him he was talking bullshit, but I couldn't look at him. He has these *eyes* . . . He said we should take a walk . . .'

'What time was this?' Dawn asked.

'Like I said, 'bout one a.m.'

'Where did he take you?'

'The graveyard behind the cathedral. The Karlarney crypt.

You know the place?'

Yes, she knew it. She and Jack had passed it often on their walks. The granite mausoleum, erected in the seventeenth century by the Karlarney family, rose up in her mind. The monument, faced with colonnades, was not just a tribute to the dead, but a testament in stone to the huge wealth generated by the slave trade. Its grand archway entrance, now curtained with creeping plants, had been financially shouldered into place by those torn from their homeland and shipped to the New World by Tobias Karlarney. It was now a ruin, well known as a place of assignation for 'cottaging' homosexuals.

'It was dark,' the boy continued, his voice more even now, 'but the crypt has no roof and the moon was bright. I could see him plainly, you see? It's important you realise that. He was stepping over broken rock, broken gravestones. Stepping over the past. His voice was warm . . . cold . . . I don't know. "Survival is an urge," he said. "It has no time for niceties. It's the only instinct we have left that doesn't kowtow to conventions of polite behaviour. Our other drives have been stripped of their power. But the urge to survive is still merciless. It teaches us this: if we want something, we should take it". He came closer. "If you want something take it". His breath was hot against my eyes. "If you want something take it".'

Doug pressed his fingers to his lips.

'He has these eyes. The darkest eyes . . . But I couldn't . . . He.' Doug's voice died. It took him a moment to begin again. 'He took a wooden box from his coat. There was a blade inside, like a dissecting knife. I tried to push through the vines, but they were stronger now. Thicker, somehow. I had to stay and watch.'

The boy stared past Jack to the door. He held out his wrists and made slashing motions with his cigarette.

'He cut . . . right along. Right along his arms, elbow to wrist. The blood was thin. Like dyed water. Nothing living could have so little blood in it . . . "This is the power of unfettered urge", he said. "I wanted to show you, before I die, things you won't believe" . . .'

After a lengthy pause, Jack asked: 'Doug? Can you tell us what he . . . ?'

'He did things to me. Made me do things to him. Things I wanted. Things I didn't. Things that no-one would ever . . . He was *dry*. Hollow inside. His veins, withered grey. He showed me things. They came from the walls, from their graves. They told me I was dirty; told me I was damned. I still see them,' the boy cupped his forehead with his hand. 'In here. When I sleep . . . The moon was still bright when he left, and I was alone in the crypt. Alone with the dead. I waited 'til the sun came . . .'

'Doug, can you tell us what Simon was like?' Jack asked.

'No. No, I can't. I didn't know him. No-one did. The party was the first time any of us had seen him outside class. But I know one thing: he . . . he liked hurting people.'

'Did he physically hurt people?'

'No. It was emotional. Mind games. He's Janus-faced, you know what I mean?'

Doug shook his head, as if he disagreed with what he was saying.

'I think we'll wrap up there,' Dawn said. 'Listen, Doug, we need a photo of Simon. Do you have one?'

'I don't think so . . .' Doug reached into the drawer by his bed, his eyes still far away. 'Here. That's a video of a guest lecture I taped for my . . . for Kate. Some theology crap. He was there, asked some nuts question and made a bit of a scene.'

'We're going,' Jack said, taking the video. 'I'll send someone to talk to you, okay?'

'He had the darkest eyes,' the boy mumbled, 'the oldest eyes.'

'What did you think of that?' Jack asked.

They were standing by his car. Dawn scanned her notes and made little eye contact.

'At uni a whole group of us got stoned and convinced ourselves Bono was stripping on my bed,' she said.

'So why's he still scared out of his wits? Don't tell me he's still not come down.'

'Well, I'm not about to believe Simon Malahyde took him to a crypt just to do some sick magic trick. The kid's obviously going through some big life crisis. The only thing we can take from all this is that the big fur ball housemate confirmed Simon was here 'til one a.m. Monday night. *And* he said Simon left alone. That fits in with Father Garret's sighting of him at about two.'

'Okay. I'm gonna get the duty doctor to call on the kid,' Jack said. 'Shall we take tomorrow off? Come back to it fresh Monday morning.'

Dawn nodded and snapped her notebook shut. She was about to get into her car when he laid a hand on her shoulder.

'Dawn? I really am sorry about yesterday. The photos, honestly, I didn't . . .'

She shrugged off his hand.

'How's Jamie?'

She got into her car and slammed the door.

Ten

Jack completed the latest draft of the pi number series. It was becoming beautifully familiar. No matter how reassuring it was, however, it could not stop Doug Winters' words worrying his thoughts:

He had the darkest eyes . . . the oldest eyes.

The same eyes, perhaps, that had stared at Jack from *the dreaming*? Or could he put it down to coincidence again, just as he had with the familiar feel of the trees in Redgrave Forest? Maybe Dawn was right, maybe Doug's story was just a drug-addled delusion. The report from the doctor that Jack had sent round this afternoon suggested the kid was suffering from a mild persecution disorder, no doubt enhanced by his cannabis consumption. The doctor had asked Doug to spend a night in hospital, but the boy had refused and there were no grounds to section him. Diagnosis: any testimony from Mr Winters should be treated with a good deal of caution. And yet, to Jack something in that bizarre story rang true.

He went to the fridge and poured himself a glass of milk. Clearing a space between the piles of boxes heaped on the kitchen table, he sat down and surveyed the chaos. Two weeks and he still hadn't got round to unpacking. His striving for a tidy mind certainly didn't extend beyond the confines of his head. He pulled a box toward him and stared at the sterile contents.

When normal people move house, they have lorry-loads of memories, he thought. Whole attics full of trinkets and keepsakes from friends, family, relationships. Stuff they can't bear to throw away. Stuff that makes them laugh and cry. Even things that remind them to be angry or to grieve. Attics must be the soul of any house, but his attic had always been light on that kind of personal memory.

I have things, he reflected, *just* things. *Nothing with any depth. Someone will sort through it all when I die. Maybe they'll laugh. Or maybe they'll be sad, to find such emptiness.*

He had only one box of items that gave any context to his life. Inside were souvenirs from four special people. The first keepsake was a pair of horn-rimmed spectacles wrapped in tissue paper. The frames were heavy, the glass as thick as Coke bottle bottoms. As a boy, he would grab them off his father's nose, run to the bathroom and stare at his weirdly enlarged eyes in the mirror. He could still feel his father on the glasses. Two months ago, after the old man's funeral, Jack had given everything his father had owned to Oxfam. The smell of his clothes, the annotations in the books he read, even the funny cartoons he used to draw, had been too painful to keep around the house. His father had lived with Jack for six years and had never understood his son, but he had been the last person to love him unconditionally. Jack pulled his hair over his eyes, the way he used to when he'd been a kid, and remembered his dad's last words: *Live for me, son. Please try. Be happy, for me.*

The second item was a brooch. It was still necessary to put on gloves to handle it. The pain of his mother's death could still be tasted there, undiluted by the passing years. She had always worn the little cameo with the French lady's silhouette. It had been pinned to her nightdress when *they* . . . Jesus, he did not want to remember, but images snapped open in his mind: the black pool at his feet; the shrieks of vicious mouths; morphing limbs dragging across the floor. And the cameo. The last part of her still visible through the swarm.

She was to have been buried with it. The coffin had been kept in the parlour. He had listened through the wall until his father's muffled sobs segued into gentle snoring, and then crept downstairs. His eyes, round with fear, had been reflected in the shiny veneer of the elm casket. Careful not to smear the wood with his fingers, he opened the lid. His gaze inched up her body. Veins stood out in livid ridges along her neck. Her skin shone with horrible pallor against the black frock. He'd overheard his father saying that Mr Flannery, the under-taker, had not been able to get *that expression* off her face. Before he could look at her fully, he grabbed the brooch and covered it with the strip of sheet in which it now rested. His father never mentioned the disappearance.

The third and fourth items are new. A sketch of Reed Richards, aka Mr Fantastic, with 'Wuss Man by JH' printed beneath. And a photograph, somewhat out of focus. In it, she is smiling and motion trails lace out from her hair. He kept the snapshot in a plastic evidence sleeve.

They are my reminders, Jack thought, *of what I can never have*.

His skin tingled as he remembered those few exquisite moments when he had touched her. Felt her warmth, her hardness, her softness, the rough skin on her soles, the supple skin of her stomach. The coarse, damp hair of her vagina. The beauty of being joined with her.

He threw his glass against the wall. Milk splattered the fresh paintwork. Kicking the shards aside, he went to the window and opened it wide.

It was growing dark. Gusts of rain buffeted into the kitchen and cooled his skin. He had moved to the house a few weeks ago and the other properties on the new development had not yet been bought up. There were no garden fences erected and, whichever way he looked, he saw the black, empty windows of neighbouring houses.

There's something unnerving about an uncurtained window at night, he thought. *It draws the eye*.

A piece of tarpaulin, pinned beneath rubble, fluttered in the wind. Scaffolding groaned and settled. Jack saw himself reflected in the patio doors of the house opposite. The walls of his kitchen framed him in a yellow rectangle. His face was roughly defined: a pale oval with black dashes for eyes and a simple line for his mouth.

The reflection shifted, but he had not moved.

His body froze. His arms and legs locked. He tried to fight it, tried to move, but it was too late. He was out of his body, catapulted into his mirror-self. Huge black shapes grew up around him: the sentinel oaks of the clearing.

The dreaming had begun.

Jack was back in the glade. His torch smashed and . . . Yes, he could still hear it: something crawling towards him. The wind picked up, crackled through the trees and knifed across his face. Stumbling back, he met the forest edge. He felt along the web of bracken, but there was no breach in the barrier of branch and vine. No good running. No good screaming. *The dreaming* would not release him yet. Not until he had seen the face of whatever crawled from the darkness to meet him.

Everything was still. The dragging sounds had stopped. Perhaps the thing had vanished, like a will-o'-the-wisp, into the forest. Perhaps . . .

Hands dug into the earth a few inches from his feet. Nails were missing from some of the fingers, and the skin of a thumb was torn and peeled back over the bone. The hands ploughed deep. A head and torso emerged into the light. Lice, crawling through matted hair, bathed in patches of dark blood. Jack looked from the fingers that pawed at his legs to the turning face. It was ballooned and tinged throughout with streaks of yellow. Flaps of skin hung from it, mouldering like the pages of books kept in damp cellars. The whole body slithered into view.

A child. A dead child.

The boy pulled himself to his knees. Then he reached for Jack's shoulder and tugged himself upright. From stomach to sternum, the child's torso had been torn open and hollowed out. Rib-bones arched through the cavity and Jack felt them graze, like long hard fingers, against him. With every jerk upwards, blood and bile sloshed out of the child and splashed Jack's feet. The sound of each spill made him heave, but Jack managed to keep the vomit down. Through his shirt, he felt the stretch and flex of striated muscle, the heat of dripping flesh. At last, the child reached Jack's ear. His mouth lolled open.

'Jack, save me . . .' the voice gargled. 'Save me, Jack. Please . . . He's coming. He's so close.'

Jack knew the voice. He looked into a pair of striking jade irises and screamed. The only sounds he heard were the spongy movements of the dead kid's body and a faint ringing coming from far away.

'Don't let him take me. Jack, don't leave me here alone.'

The scene began to recede into the night. Before it vanished, Jack saw the child through the patio doors, as if he were standing in the empty house opposite. His face . . . rotting, dead, and so familiar . . .

Jack drew his fingers across his mouth. He staggered to the hall and picked up the phone.

'Jack? It's Dawn. Have you seen the news . . . ? Jack, are you there?'

'News?' he asked. 'News? No. No, I've . . . I've been asleep . . .'

'It's Father Brody. You remember, Garret mentioned him? Used to be the priest at Crow Haven when Simon Malahyde was a boy. Gave his father the last rites?'

'Dawn, is Jamie okay . . . ?'

'What? Of course he's okay. What are you . . . ?'

'Nothing. I had a nightmare. I'm sorry, go on.'

'Jack, you're worrying me.'

'It's nothing. I don't know what I'm saying. Still only half-awake, I suppose.'

He heard her take sharp breaths, as if she was about to challenge him further. Finally, she sighed and said:

'Last night, this Brody disappeared from the care home where he lived. A nun was knocked unconscious. It has to be connected with Malahyde's disappearance. I don't know how, but . . . Jack?'

'Yes . . .'

'What is it?'

'Dawn, there's something I have to . . .'

'I can't hear you. What did you say?'

He rallied himself.

'Nothing, sorry. I'm a bit light-headed. Can you come in tomorrow? I know I said . . .'

'Of course. Jack . . .'

'Goodnight.'

He replaced the receiver.

He had been about to tell her what *the dreaming* had shown him. That a child was going to be murdered. Tortured. Torn apart. Left to rot. And that the child in his dreams was no stranger. It was her son.

SUNDAY 27th OCTOBER 2002

As I was going up the stair
I met a man who wasn't there
He wasn't there again today
I wish, I *wish*, he'd stay away
Hughes Mearns, *Antigonish,* 1899

Let's talk of graves, of worms, and epitaphs.
Shakespeare, *Richard II,* c 1595

Eleven

Brody stood before the ladder that led to the derelict signal-man's box. He was back in the midst of Redgrave Forest, starting at the slightest sound. His body ached from the rigours of his clumsy escape. After Sister Agnes had locked him in his room, he turned to a game played often in childhood. A game practised by those seeking guidance as far back as the early Church: the *Sortes Biblicae*. He took up his bible, riffled the pages, and jammed his finger against a block of text. The passage so found was Matthew 2:14: the flight of the holy family to Egypt. The message was clear: Death had stalked the Nazarene. Death was coming for Asher Brody. Had Death, he wondered, in the shape of a Doctor, visited the Home the night before last?

Before he started to climb, he offered up prayers for those he had left behind.

Until the reforms of Dr Beeching, a branch line had run past the village of Crow Haven. This decaying watchtower was one of the few reminders of its presence. Redgrave had long reclaimed the ground that the railway had cut through it. After forty years, there was only the vague impression of a line beneath the cushions of lichen and wildflowers that strangled the tracks and fishplates.

Brody went gingerly up the steps. The rusted padlock gave way without much resistance when he put his shoulder to the door. Waving away clouds of dust, he peered into the gloom. Insect cocoons rotted in the corners of the filthy windows and webs hung between the levers stationed at the front of the signal box. On a small table stood a glass, as if full of milk, in which a spider had spun a thick grave.

Brody sat at the table and took a handful of pencils, a packet of foolscap and the three Crow Haven diaries from his bag. He had planned his course of action across the many weary miles of his journey to Redgrave. Now the time had come to put it into operation. The story he had to tell would be set out in three parts. The first would cover both the background history of Crow Haven and Brody's first encounter, in 1976, with the creature known as 'Mendicant'. The second would detail that period after Mendicant's 'vanishing' and the arrival in Crow Haven of Peter and Anne Malahyde in 1984. This second bundle would also cover Peter's horrific death and the birth of his son, Simon, in 1985. The last bundle would deal with Mendicant's return; with the 'soul-rape' of Simon in 1995 . . .

'With my final failure,' Brody murmured.

In order to write this story, he would refer to his old diaries for guidance. The diaries themselves, full as they were of other day-to-day matters and irrelevancies, could not serve. It must be a single tale, told fully. And he must write it with great haste: the man for whom these depositions were intended – the prophesied stranger – must soon take his part in this drama.

Brody began:

BUNDLE 1 –
CROW HAVEN: THE HISTORY

My name is Asher Brody. I have three diaries in front of me that tell of my own direct experiences in the village of Crow Haven. In each is a record of the crimes and depravities committed there by Dr Elijah Mendicant between the years 1976 and 1995. 'Mendicant' is not his real name, of course, and neither is it The Crowman, though he is known by both. I believe his true identity to be lost within the pages of his own dark history.

My aim here is to record these events in as full and frank

a manner as possible. I am convinced that somewhere in this story lies the key to the undoing of the creature that haunts my dreams and plagues my conscience. The nature of this key is a mystery to me, yet I feel certain that, if I give a complete record of my experiences, a wiser eye may pluck it from the text. I therefore beg for both your patience and your attention.

I ask these things of a stranger, for your identity is unknown to me. But it was foretold that you would make this last stand against him. I feel your time is drawing near.

Before I begin, I would like to give you a potted history of Crow Haven. This may be no more than stalling on my part (a cowardly act to postpone the moment when I must meet *him* again in the pages of my old diary) but I think you might understand things a little better when you realise it was no accident that the Doctor came here. By his own admission, he was attracted by the Darkness that dwells in this place. So let us follow Thomas Aquinas' instruction that, in order to first understand the particular, we must begin by understanding the general: in other words, you must know this village before you can understand how the Doctor was able to achieve his victory here.

Once upon a time, this entire area, including Crow Haven and Redgrave Forest, was part of a great marshland. Until the mid-sixteen hundreds, there was nothing in these parts but shifting bogs and sinking sands, layered with grey sea frets that knitted together land and sky. It was a dangerous place, and even the fen fishermen, who traversed it on stilts, were sometimes claimed by the marshes. Such places, with high incidents of accidental death, often acquire an evil, superstitious reputation. Suffice to say that there are many strange tales, and I have no time to set down all the stories of ghostly ferrymen or of rivers giving up their dead long before the time appointed in Revelation. But you must hear the story of Elspeth Stamp.

Thirty years before Crow Haven existed, Elspeth lived alone on an island in the heart of the marshes. It was a remote place, accessible only to those familiar with the topography of the swamp. Elspeth would leave it only to come to Darrow to sell corn dollies on market day. In the diary of Edward Stearne, Adjunct to the Witch Finder, she was described as a malicious, cunning old woman, well versed in the Dark Arts. The letters of Hector Fernival, Bishop of the See of Ely and defender of Elspeth at her trial, tell of a sour, misguided heathen, but clear her of any charge of witchcraft.

Elspeth was accused of murdering two children in 1623, of consuming their fat and of burning their swaddling clothes, so that she might take of their life essence and be made young again. There was precious little evidence, except the customary testimony of 'witnesses' (neighbours who bore a grudge, and fantasists) who had seen Elspeth 'converse with her familiars': a cat named Heggaty Tom and a great black crow called Lucky Wilt. Witches had been hanged on less. The defence of Elspeth by Hector Fernival (one of the few forward-looking clergy who did not take his cue from James I and see the Devil in everything) saved the woman. She was allowed to return to her island and there the matter may have ended.

In any other part of the country, it would have. But not here. The fen folk, who would later make up the residents of Crow Haven, waited until the bishop, the witch prickers and the justices left. Then they went to Elspeth's island. A well-read yeoman farmer, who had studied some European texts on demonology, led the group. They burned Elspeth alive, throwing her cat, Heggaty Tom, into the flames with her. Lucky Wilt was not found.

By the mid-seventeenth century, manorial lords and entrepreneurs were putting the fens to work. Using elaborate systems imported from the Nordic states, dykes and sluice gates were devised to drain the land. Two decades after Elspeth's death, the water receded and Crow Haven was raised. When completed, it was a fair size town, bisected south to northeast by the Conduit Road. It boasted a manor house built for Sir James Gratin, Earl of Walmshire (the man who had half-financed the drainage), a sizeable market square, a town hall, a brick-built schoolhouse and a tavern. The town was prosperous almost immediately, dealing mainly in livestock, wheat and barley and some textiles.

By the time of the Civil War, relations had soured between Sir James and the peasant farmers. The knight demanded more of the common land to be turned over to him, in recompense for his expenditure on the drainage scheme. Ill feeling festered for six years with petitions to an indifferent Parliament raised on both sides. In 1644, the militia was called in to calm rising tensions but the stretched unit was overrun. Sir James and his two young daughters were dragged from their beds and butchered in the town square. The girls were lashed, head-to-toe, between a pair of horses and pulled limb from limb. Sir James was made to watch and was then pilloried and stoned to death.

The captain of the militia reported to Oliver Cromwell (who was too involved with the Second Battle of Newbury, and his dispute with the Earl of Manchester, to much care) that, when the townsfolk had sated their bloodlust, what was left of Sir James was hardly recognisable. Just a mass of wet meat, of which the crows made short work. From a town of three hundred, five men were arrested and executed for the crimes.

As a side note, I must mention the crows. The town took its name from the flocks of these birds that plagued the newly divided fields. Superstition had it that the crows were descendants of Elspeth Stamp's lost familiar. They have, at any rate, guarded their lands jealously ever since. You will never hear the trill of a song thrush or see the fiery flight of a linnet between the boughs of Redgrave Forest. The crows suffer no interloper in their woods. But enough of them for now, they will take a larger role in this story later.

For three hundred years the rate of murder, rape, infanticide and other assorted violence in Crow Haven far exceeded that of its neighbouring towns. Although these crimes were sporadic, reference was made to their high incidence in history books. Few authors drew any conclusions. What conclusions could be drawn? That the town, which shrank to a village in 1840, was diseased? That it was a place of endemic evil?

The last incident on record before 1976 was the disappearance of a ten-year-old girl in October 1944. When Jessica Newhart didn't come home from school, her mother alerted the village constable. Door-to-door inquiries were conducted and, by early evening, the village had been roused and a search made of the Redgrave woods. Few people in Crow Haven ever went into the forest. Children were told stories of a witch, who had been burned years ago on an island when all the land hereabout was swamp. There was a raised area in the forest, so the story went, a clearing that she haunted.

Despite these stories, little Benjamin Bradstreet had seen Jessica wander into the wood. He had called to her, but she had not seemed to hear him. Throughout the night, Jessica's name rang through the trees, and did so for three consecutive nights thereafter until the search was abandoned. Jessica Newhart was never found and a fresh name entered the folklore of Crow Haven.

Thirty-two years passed almost peacefully. A bad place slept. Then, in 1976, the Doctor came to Crow Haven.

So many stories could be told here. A catalogue of horrors, but nothing compared to what was to come. Had Crow Haven been readying itself, I wonder? Preparing since Elspeth Stamp was burned on her island? And can I do anything but wonder about the innocence of that long-dead woman, knowing what I know?

Twelve

Earth rained between Jack's fingers, peppered his eyes, blinded him. He woke with a start, his body braced against the driver's seat, his hands clawing the dream-soil from his face. He had been inside his mother's coffin. Through the elm wood lid, he had heard his father's braying sobs somewhere above. His child hands (whenever he dreamed, he always saw himself as the twelve-year-old boy he had been the night of his mother's death) pushed at the velvet lining, as clumps of soil began to thud arrhythmically above. He had glanced down at his feet. His mother's cameo, shining in the gloom, was pinched between the fingers of something rippling and black. The creature, about the size of a large cat, began to skitter up Jack's body. Then the lid cracked open and dirt had covered his face.

Now he was awake and felt comforted by the biting cold. He dug sleep out of his eyes and checked the time. He'd nodded off for twenty minutes. He rubbed the steamed wind-screen and scanned the front of Dawn's building. Frost glinted on the pavement and on the windows of the cars parked outside the entrance to the flats. The street was empty.

This was ridiculous. He couldn't keep watch every hour until . . .

'Until he comes for Jamie.'

Vocalising it made it seem real. Otherwise it was just pictures in his head, and what he could read between the lines of *the dreaming*. In the first dream he had seen a man, or the semblance of a man, feeding off the corpse of a young boy. Last night's vision had shown that boy to be Jamie Howard.

Jack had thought long and hard during the hours of

watching. He still could not understand what *the dreaming* had shown him. When he had touched the Redgrave oaks, he had sensed that they belonged to the dream-forest. He had to believe that. Jamie's life might depend upon him accepting what he saw. So, a clearing, somewhere in that sprawling wood, was where Jamie would be taken. That surely meant that Jamie's murder would be connected in some way with Simon Malahyde: the geographical coincidence of Simon's home being surrounded by the trees from the vision told him that. Did this then suggest that Simon, the sadist of Doug Winters' story, would be responsible for Jamie's death? Possibly, but even if Simon's penchant for cruelty had developed into a more serious form of psychosis there were other puzzling factors to consider. Firstly, Simon – youthful and well-built – did not resemble the cadaverous killer from *the dreaming*. Secondly, where was Simon and why had he disappeared? Always, Jack came back to the same conclusion: the only point of connection in all of this was Redgrave Forest. And that was a connection so thin it was impossible to draw any inferences.

Jack got out of the car and wandered down the silent street. As the morning sun yawned across the city, night retreated, slipping under porches and stealing down narrow alleyways.

Last night, Jack had considered telling Dawn everything and then dismissed the idea. Tell the most grounded person he knew that he, Jack Trent, mild-mannered policeman by day, had superhuman gifts? That he could catch glimpses of her innermost thoughts just by touching her hand? That on their final night together, he had unintentionally probed deeper, and learned how she had loved and hated Jamie's father in equal measure. How she would rather die than ever let her son feel the sense of abandonment she had felt. And then he would have to tell her about the visions as well. He scooped some ice from the bonnet of a Lotus and held it to his face. Tell Dawn all those things? Impossible.

There was only one thing he could do. He checked the time. A little early, but he took out his mobile and dialled. A weary voice answered.

'Yeah? Peterson's Motherfucking Private Detectives. It's Sunday, for Christ's sake.'

'Bob? It's Jack Trent here.'

'What the motherfuck? Don't you sleep, Jack?'

'Not well. Listen, I need a couple of your boys to watch somebody. Day and night. I'll pay your usual rate plus expenses.'

'What? Aren't you boys capable of doing surveillance anymore? Got to outsource it like the motherfucking prison service?'

'My business. If you do this starting in . . . one hour, I'll forget to file the report about you keeping a loaded rifle in your office.'

'Hot fucking dog, Jack! You're a mean motherfucker when you want to be.'

'Cut the Yank bullshit, Bob. The nearest you've been to Dixieland is Country and Western night at the *Dog and Duck*.'

'That's where you're wrong, got my fourteenth trip to Graceland booked for Christmas. Let me get a pen. Susan! Pen! Okay, what's the name of the guy you want watched?'

Jack hesitated. A slender man in a long trench coat had stopped in front of the entrance to the flats. Jack took a few steps in his direction. The man took out an A–Z, checked the reference section and walked on.

'Jack? You there?'

'Jamie. The name is Jamie Howard.'

Thirteen

Dawn was still wondering about last night's telephone conversation. Jack's concern for Jamie puzzled her, but also confirmed some recent suspicions. She had been angry all Friday night and yesterday morning because she had lost her temper in the car and told Jamie the truth about Jack's reason for leaving – that he had no interest in the boy. As the anger cooled, she started to check the reality of Jack's behaviour against that reason. Now she saw, with breathtaking clarity, how transparent the lie had been.

They had to have this out.

Light flickered beneath his office door. She went straight in without knocking. The blinds were drawn. A TV and video unit sat on Jack's desk. His face was inches from the screen. His expression puzzled her: Guilty? Relieved? Unnerved? She couldn't decide. He punched the pause button.

'Hi. Morning.'

'Jesus, Jack, have you slept here? You look like shit.'

'Is Jamie with you? Have you dropped him off somewhere?'

Again, that strange, but genuine concern. Considering her reaction yesterday to his questions about Jamie, she was surprised he had the balls to ask again.

'Yes, at his grandad's.'

'The video Doug Winters gave us is no good. Too hazy.'

'Can I take a look?'

'No point. It's . . . defective. I'll see if Manny can work his magic with it.'

'Jack, I've been thinking things through and . . .'

As he ejected the tape, his mobile rang.

'Hello? Oh, yes, I . . . Hello? Damn these things! See if I can get a signal outside.'

Holding the phone out in front of him, as if he were checking a radiation leak with a Geiger counter, he moved away down the corridor.

Dawn slipped the tape back into the VCR, rewound two minutes of film and hit the play button. The scene was of the large lecture hall at the university: all dark wooden panelling and oil portraits of dead chancellors. The camera focused on an elderly man, dressed in black and purple robes and bent over a lectern.

' . . . so, the Transfiguration Story, whether mirroring the Resurrection or not, was seen as the objective deification of Christ. Man-God seen by mortal eyes. Questions?'

A hand shot up.

'Sir, Raphael's depiction of the Transfiguration poses some questions. Specifically, the unusual scene of the Apostles trying to exorcise a possessed child. Why do you think the artist added in this unscriptural image?'

'I'm not here to talk about artistic interpretations, Miss. Yes, you there.'

A whey-faced boy, barely out of puberty, squeaked, 'Professor, may I ask in what sense you see the Transfiguration as miraculous?'

'Well, I am inclined to agree with St John Chrysostom. It was a condescension to man. The miracle wasn't the sudden explosion of Light from Jesus. The real marvel was that he managed, throughout his life, to suppress his divinity and allow it to be shown only for a moment on the mountain. Yes?'

'Simon Malahyde, first year theology. If that's true, Professor, then may I advance a playful sociological argument? Let's turn the Transfiguration story on its head. Use it as a metaphor for man's own nature.'

There was a soothing quality in the modulations of the speaker's voice that was also somehow mocking. The camera stayed fixed on the aged academic.

'What do you mean?' he said, arranging his notes.

'I'm talking about man's transfiguration, the unveiling of *his* true self.' A few heads turned towards the unseen speaker. 'Just as Jesus suppressed his godliness when he walked the earth, I suggest that society is the lowlands where man suppresses what *he* is. But sometimes man will trek into the mountain and reveal his pure, primal urges.'

'I'm a theologian, not a sociologist,' the professor flustered. 'But there's certainly no suggestion, in the interpretation of the Fathers, that . . .'

'It's not a serious theological point. But we all have moments when lust, brutality, self-interest master us. When we feel freed from the constructs of artificial morality. It is these everyday anti-transfiguration stories that interest me.'

'To suggest petty human evil is in some form the antithesis, or dark equivalent, of Christ's revelation of his Goodness . . .'

'But cumulatively it *is* equivalent. The odd sheep will sometimes break off from the flock and become the wolf. The mild-mannered secretary who listens to her boss's complaints, day in day out, until, one morning, she snaps and thrusts a letter opener into his face. The schoolteacher who resists for decades until the day he finds himself alone in the storeroom with little Johnny. The learned academic who, five years ago, left a young cyclist to bleed to death after a hit and run . . .'

The professor grasped the lectern. Colour drained from his face, leaving it the sickly white of cottage cheese.

'We all have our dark transfiguration,' Simon continued. 'You know what I mean, Professor, when we see our morals die in the rear-view mirror.'

The old man, trying not to stare at the speaker, stuffed his notes into a folder.

The camera turned.

A tall, well-built man stood at the centre of an embarrassed group. Sunlight glanced through the lancet windows behind him and dazzled the camera. Then the lens re-focused. Simon Malahyde was dressed in black, his dark hair hanging down to his shoulders. His body remained very still while he spread out his hands before him, making a sweep of the entire room. There was something hypnotic in the gesture, and it was only when he turned to stare into the camera that Dawn focused upon his face . . .

A chill ran the length of her body. Her hand cupped her mouth.

Don't be stupid, she told herself, *there're a hundred explanations for what you're seeing. Of course he has a face . . .*

The figures in the background paintings could be made out, as could the expressions of the students sitting around Simon Malahyde. His body, the folds of his long coat and his powerful white hands were caught in every detail. It was only his face that remained indefinite. Whether she skipped ahead or paused the tape, the image was always indistinct: a blur of flesh-coloured pixels. There was the hint of features, but only in what appeared to be a flurry of motion trails. It was like a picture of a fast moving animal that the camera shutter had been too slow to capture.

'What on earth is it?' she asked, as Jack re-entered.

'Technical problem, like I said.'

He slipped past her and pressed the eject button.

'I don't know much about video footage, but I've never seen interference localised like that before.'

Jack seemed preoccupied as he moved around the room, drawing back the blind and sorting papers on his desk.

'Jack, we need to talk . . .'

'I've contacted the Brookemoor police; they're allowing us access to the Home.'

'So, do you think there's a connection between the disappearances?' she asked.

They were driving towards the Lincolnshire town of Brookemoor-upon-Fen. She was at the wheel, while he went through an early report into the disappearance of Father Asher

Brody. When he didn't answer, she said:

'On the face of it, there doesn't appear to be a connection. Brody left Crow Haven in '95, when Simon was ten years old. Father Garret told us Simon was never brought to church, and it's unlikely they had any contact after Brody retired. But doesn't it beggar belief that, the week Simon disappears, a priest who might've known him as a child vanishes as well? Maybe we should talk to Garret again.'

'Can you pull over?'

'Hmm?'

'Pull over.'

'*Jack*? What's the matter?'

The blood that gushed from his nose was striking against his chalky skin. She pulled the car to a stop on the hard shoulder. He jumped out. Blood sprayed over his shirt and across the passenger window and bonnet.

'Jack, what is it?'

'S'nothin',' he said, nasally. 'There's a toilet up there. I'll get cleaned up.'

He stalked off towards a concrete block of lavatories. She remembered how he had looked whilst at the Malahyde house the day before yesterday. Perhaps he was ill. She gripped the steering wheel: perhaps that was why he had finished with her.

It was cold outside, but the car felt stuffy. She opened the window and was refreshed by the slipstream of a passing lorry. A dull buzz droned from Jack's jacket on the back seat. She looked towards the toilets but there was no sign of him. As she lifted the jacket a piece of paper fell from its inside pocket. She retrieved it, and was about to answer his phone, when she noticed the initials in one corner of the paper: *JH*. It was the cartoon Jamie had given him.

She jumped as Jack opened the door. His face was clean but the blood was drying in brown blemishes on his collar. She unfolded the drawing and held it out to him.

'Do you know what a psychological fugue is?' she asked.

He slipped into his seat, passed a hand over his face and

took the cartoon from her.

'It's a sort of trance,' she continued. 'Something horrible happens to you, so your mind flees from it. My mind was in a fugue until recently. When you said . . . When you *lied* and told me that you didn't want to be a father to some other man's bastard . . . I was so disgusted I couldn't see beyond my anger. But I've been doing some thinking. You wanted me to hate you, didn't you?'

'I wasn't lying.'

It was a half-hearted attempt. She could hear the defeat in his voice.

'Don't bullshit me, Jack. That first night, when we played happy family, you could have let me send Jamie to bed. You didn't act like a man who sees kids as a burden. And if you hated him, why did you get so involved? In his hobbies? His football? Just to get in my knickers? Then why didn't you claim your prize? And then there's this concern for J. You're worried how the break-up affected him, aren't you? I can't believe I didn't see it all straight away. But the lie was too painful to examine. And it *was* a lie, don't deny it. That's why you had to tell me over the phone. That's why you can't look at me now. You're a pathetic liar.'

'Dawn. Listen . . .'

'I'm not even sure I want to know. The fact you used Jamie as an excuse . . . It sickens me. But these lies, they're damaging our work. So what do we do?'

Cars zipped past, rocking the body of the Range Rover. Tiny white silhouettes of wind turbines spun in the valley below, like toy windmills.

'I lied,' he said, staring at the drawing, 'because I didn't want to hurt anybody.'

'Worked like a fucking charm, five gold stars, you dickhead . . . For Christ's sake, just tell me why you really said those things.'

'I can't. I don't expect you to understand. But I can't tell you the truth.'

'Jack, I'm sorry for whatever pain you're going through,

but you need to face up to some things. You hurt me. You've hurt Jamie. That's something I never thought I'd be able to forgive. Maybe I still won't. But you have to tell me what's going on.'

'If I tell you everything, would you believe it? Sometimes even I don't believe it. And it's dangerous for you to know. Tomorrow morning, I'm putting in for a transfer. When it's over, when the case is finished, you won't have to see me again.'

She shivered, but maintained the defiance in her voice.

'What could be dangerous about us being together? Do you have a maniac ex-wife or something?'

'It's just dangerous. Take it on trust. A friendly warning then,' he said, responding to her derisive laugh. 'I care for you, and for Jamie. I wanted you safe, and the best way to make sure of that was for you to hate me. So that you'd stay away.'

Jack refolded the cartoon and gave it back to her.

'Makes no sense,' Dawn said.

'I hope it never makes sense. It's for your own good.'

'Don't be so fucking patronising. I can figure out what's best for me, but I can't make decisions like that based on nothing.'

'Fine. I'll make the decision for you. I will be bad for you. Bad for your son . . .'

'Bullshit, I don't get a say?'

'No.'

'This is something to do with your mother, isn't it? Just a guess,' she said, seeing his surprise. 'Intuition, maybe. When you spoke about her, there was something . . . What happened to her?'

'I'll be gone soon. No more questions. Please.'

'This is insane. *You're* insane. If you make this decision now, I can't ever have you back, you know that? I couldn't base anything on that kind of uncertainty. It wouldn't be fair on Jamie. Or on me.'

He said nothing. She started the car. They drove in silence.

Fourteen

Anne Malahyde kept her vigil by the door to the sealed room, as she had every day since Peter's death. There was no reason to now, but it was a habit of seventeen years and such things aren't easily given up. Beyond the door was the huge room in which he had died. She pictured the bed frame and drip-feed stand, laced with spider webs, illuminated by chinks of light straining through fissures in the bricked-up windows. Often, down the years, she had imagined his voice calling again from beyond the door:

Ahh-nnne. Plleeeasch. Aych need hurr.. Ahhnniiee. Pleeeasch . . .

Those pleas came night after night during the last months of his life. Cries that chipped away at the soft corners of her soul, leaving it sharp and brittle.

She prayed for the doctors to take Peter away, but his wealth had allowed him to indulge a selfish caprice. Instead of rotting in some state of the art hospital, he had decided to wither away at home. A private doctor and four nurses were hired. The latest equipment was borrowed at staggering cost and, through his connections, Peter obtained the newest experimental drugs, some of which had not been licensed. But not everything had gone his way. By the time that his nose had been eaten back to its skull snub, she'd had him moved from the main house and was refusing to share his agony.

She had been heavily pregnant with Simon during those long last months. Often she would have nightmares in which the shrieks of the dying man would pierce the amniotic sac. That the unfinished child would burst from her, slick with blood and mucus, and demand that they visit its father. The man without a face, whose screams echoed from inside the bricked-up room. But the child had moved very little inside her.

From the doctor's reports, she knew the full horror of Peter's death. Despite the precaution of the sealed windows, the light had stripped the skin from his body. His eyes had putrefied, shrinking in their sockets. His nose, lips and tongue, eaten away with deliberate industry. Unable to bear his ugliness, she had left him to face his miserable death alone.

Since Simon's revelation to her a week ago, she understood what the guilt of that abandonment had done. It had narrowed her world, focused it entirely on asking for forgiveness. That focus had been so unbending that she had been blind to what had happened to her son. She had not realised that, when he was just a child, Simon had been taken away. Had that been the priest's message to her all those years ago? That her child was a changeling? That, at ten years old, he had been impregnated by things that were dead?

Grief and shame had blinded her. And now grief and shame for Simon's fate drove her out of the house. Drove her to seek penance.

She had lived behind glass for half her life. When she had not been watching the door, she watched the forest. Remotely, she observed its cycles: the budding and falling leaves, the flourish and fade of the foxglove and bluebell, the span of the December moth from chrysalis to membrane and husk. With glass and brick between them, the wood had been a familiar friend, but now it seemed alien and threatening. Always whispering; always moving.

She reached the gate. The weeping figures looked down. They frightened her just as much now as the first time she had seen them. Peter had chided her – *'silly scaredy-cat'* – but the story he told, in the early days of his illness, of the gate, and of the man who built it, had only added to her unease.

'I don't see ghosts,' she said aloud, her voice terrifying her.

She walked out of the tree-tunnelled drive. Before reaching

the village, Anne took the headscarf from her coat pocket and put it on. That raw wound on her scalp, inflicted six days ago, might raise awkward questions if it was seen.

A line of pensioners, queuing out of the Post Office, watched her pass, regarding her as if she were a spirit that had no business appearing in the weak autumn daylight. Geraldine Pryce, headmistress of the primary school, called out a startled greeting, but Anne did not respond. Before she knew where she was, she found herself standing before the door of the Old Priory.

'I told you to stay at home. What are you doing here?'

'Why won't you answer your phone? I've been calling for two days.'

Father Garret poured a stingy measure of scotch and passed it to Anne Malahyde. When he had opened the door, she had been on the verge of hysteria, babbling about needing to get inside; that she felt the sky pressing down. To his knowledge, she had not left the house since Peter Malahyde's death. He supposed that quitting it suddenly had shaken her. She was as jittery as a dog full of fleas. Even if you discounted the fact that she'd been alone in that house all those years, he supposed that her madness was understandable. Six nights ago, her 'son' had flipped reality on its side and shown her its paper-thin edge.

'I've been . . . busy,' Garret answered.

Busy . . . Oh, yes. Very busy. On Friday, I murdered Oliver Godfrey. I was to have murdered Asher Brody too, but he eluded us. Tonight I must keep my appointment with young Mr Lloyd. But he will be the last. Then the promise will be kept. Must be kept.

'You said you'd help me,' Anne said.

'And I have helped you. I took care of everything. Nobody'll ever know what you did.'

'But I want them to know. I have to tell them everything. The police. Can't you understand? I need to do penance.'

'You *need* to keep calm, Mrs Malahyde. You must stay at home and behave exactly as we discussed . . .'

'No. I need punishment. For abandoning Simon, for not

99

seeing; for letting *them* take him. I should suffer.'

'You *have* suffered, my dear. Suffered dreadfully. I don't like to see suffering. As far as the murder is concerned, your conscience should not be troubled. Remember what I said on Monday night? You didn't kill Simon. You killed an abomination. Simon has been dead for seven long years.'

'I know all that. I know it wasn't Simon. But I did kill him, by neglect, all those years ago. I didn't see what happened to him. Didn't protect him. Please,' she snatched at Garret's arm. 'Please. How do I do penance for that?'

'Realise this, then,' Garret said. 'Telling the police would be easy. A quick fix. Not *real* punishment. You must live with it, alone, uncomforted, friendless. Live as you have lived. Put your little soul back into that empty house.'

'Yes . . .' she spoke slowly. 'Seventeen years for nothing. But it will be for Simon now. It will be real. Yes, thank you.'

Garret heard her footsteps, hesitant in the hall, and wasn't surprised when she spoke again.

'What did you do with the body?'

'Don't think about it,' he replied.

The front door whined and clicked shut. Garret wondered if he had done the right thing. Might she not phone Trent as soon as she got home and tell him everything? Even if she did, a sober-looking fellow like that would never believe her, would he? Still, it struck Garret as too dangerous a risk. She ought to be dealt with. But the Doctor had made it plain that she was not to be touched. Not yet.

The mantle clock chimed three. There was still time to visit the army surplus store before his appointment at the glass factory.

Just young Mr Lloyd, he told himself, *and then the Doctor must keep his promise.*

Fifteen

Jamie slammed the door. From inside the house, he heard the gruff, exasperated calls that told him to stop being a 'fool hothead'. The last bellowed admonishment – *Jees-us, Jamie, grow up* – sent him vaulting over the garden gate and sprinting across the farmland that backed onto his grandad's house. In the spring, golden light from this cornfield was thrown onto the ceiling of his grandad's sitting room. Jamie would lie dozing on the sofa and watch the rectangle of honeyed light sway above his head. Now the harvest was over and the field was desolate.

The wide-ploughed furrows made it hard going. *Like running in a dream*, he thought, *when you're being chased by a zombie, and you should outrun 'em easy, but your legs won't work and the air's thick as treacle.* He ran the width of three fields before collapsing beside a dyke. He laid on his back and felt the gutsy tattoo hammer inside his chest. A few gulps of air later, the beat steadied.

'Sonovabitch. Sonovafuckinbitch,' he garbled.

He wasn't sure who the insult was aimed at – Jack or his grandad – but he felt bad for saying it. But why should *he* feel bad? 'Jack doesn't want to see *you* anymore'. She'd corrected herself, to make it seem like he didn't want to see either of them, but the slip had been made. Jack hated him. That deserved a '*sonovabitch*' didn't it? And his grandad? Well, that old git had called his own daughter – Jamie's mother – a whore. A WHORE. Jamie punched the ground until his fists ached. *Sonovabitch . . . sonovafuckin . . .*

His temper ebbed and flowed. One minute he was furious,

the next the anger cooled and all that he felt was heartache at Jack's rejection. He watched bloated rain clouds inch across the sky. In the next field, a scarecrow nodded in the wind while a mangy crow stalked across its shoulders and pecked at its hat. Resentment continued to churn in the back of his mind. His grandad must have known that something was bothering him as soon as he brushed past the old man with a muttered 'Hi', and collapsed in front of the TV. Tom Howard had set out the Risk board on the dining table and asked Jamie if he wanted a game. A half hour in, and Jamie had just invaded Japan, when his grandad asked what was riling him.

'Come on, son, leave the yellas alone for the minute. Tell me the trouble.'

'That's racist,' Jamie muttered.

'Well, I'm always being told I'm something-ist. Racist, sexist. The only thing they'll let you be when you're old is defeatist. They positively encourage that. Come on boy, what is it?'

Jamie had burst into tears and blurted out everything. Then, after a few minutes' thought, his grandad called his mum a whore. Well, he hadn't *actually* said 'whore'. He said she'd had a lot of men – failed relationships (correcting himself quickly) – and that maybe Jack wasn't the only one to blame for the break up. Yesterday, Jamie would have had sympathy with this view. Hadn't he accused his mother of distancing Jack? Suddenly, he realised what was fuelling his rage. Shame: *Jack loves Mum,* he thought, *I know it. But he hates me. Hates me so much he broke up with her . . . But why does he hate me?*

Perhaps you're too pushy.

The thought jarred in Jamie's head, as if it hadn't been his thought at all. He tried to dismiss it, but it developed:

You're too involved, too desperate to see them together. Jack must have picked up on it and been frightened away. Maybe Jack wants kids of his own. Maybe you bug him with constant pestering about comic books and kiddy crap. Maybe . . .

Jamie sat up and listened. He had heard something outside that inner dialogue. Footsteps on wood. They seemed to come from the little bridge twenty yards or so downriver. But only that ragamuffin old crow strutted along the handrail, rearranging its plumage like a drunk adjusting his clothes after a brawl. He must have imagined it. Still, there had been an abruptness to the sound that didn't seem like the work of imagination.

'Trip-trap, trip-trap, trip-trap. Up jumped the troll. I'm going to eat you up,' Jamie whispered.

The Billy Goats Gruff had once been his favourite bedtime story. Whenever his mum adopted the grumbling voice of the troll, he had laughed and trembled, imagining that at any moment her lips would draw back to reveal wicked, needle-sharp teeth.

Rubbish, Jamie thought. *Baby stuff.*

Yet, glancing beneath the bridge, he half-expected to see yellow eyes staring back at him. A squat, grey-skinned body would be hunkered down low in the murky water.

Don't believe the storybook, Jamie, it would say, *I ate them all. I ate Little Billy Goat Gruff, I ate Medium-Sized Billy Goat Gruff, I ate Big Billy Goat Gruff. And I'll eat you, too.*

He scrambled to his feet, feeling stupid, but also a little frightened. He glanced down at his trainers. They were caked with mud. His mum was gonna have a fit. Shame-faced at his own baby-thoughts, he began to trudge back across the field.

Then he stopped dead. He had heard it again. Footfalls on wood. Cawing and a furious flap of wings sounded behind him. And footsteps, slow and creaking. This was ridiculous. He swung round. The chuckling stream and the laughing crow fell silent. The sun flashed across the fields. Across the scarecrow that stood upon the bridge. Watching him.

Although he couldn't make out the face beneath the shadow of its wide-brimmed hat, Jamie knew that it was staring directly at him. It remained so still that, for a moment, he wondered if somebody had propped it up against the handrail as an early Halloween prank. If he was stupid enough to approach, some fuckwit kid was bound to jump out of the hedgerow, screaming.

It was just a mangy old scarecrow after all. It wasn't as if it could . . .

It *moved*. The head tipped to one side, posing like Mr Fuckface Fosker when announcing particularly difficult homework projects. Then it raised its hand, its shirtsleeve hitching up over a fleshless wrist and forearm. It beckoned.

Jamie knew he shouldn't go near the bridge. That was the moral of the tale: trolls live under bridges. They grab and tear and rip. They eat you up. They grind your bones to make their bread. They take you to the dark places, far away from the watchful world. They take you to the woods. So he would stay put. He wouldn't go anywhere near the beckoning figure. Not a chance. However resolute this decision, it seemed not to communicate with his legs. He glanced down. In sudden, sharp jerks, like a poorly operated marionette, he was stumbling towards the bridge. The muscles in his legs flexed and braced as he tried to resist the force that dragged him on. It was no good. He could not stop himself. And then, all at once, the boy realised that the pressure *wasn't* external at all. There was an insane sliver of curiosity inside his own mind that impelled him to meet the figure.

I want to see its face, he thought. *Shit, NO! I don't want to see its face . . . I want to see its face . . .*

The wind blew the hood of his Parka across his head, but it did not obscure his view of the beckoner. The rags it wore remained unruffled by the breeze, but the brim of the floppy hat shivered. Below it, Jamie could see bloodless veins standing out in cords, as the head worked left to right, left to right, left to . . .

How had the scarecrow walked across the fields? How had it . . .

Jamie's stomach shrank. His bladder gave way. Gooseflesh puckered his skin and sent his testicles riding up into the cavity of his body. The scarecrow was still in the far field. It had not moved. The thing that waited upon the bridge was something other. An animated mannequin was frightening enough, but instinct told Jamie that whatever the scarecrow's doppelganger turned out to be, it was something much, much worse.

The tips of his trainers touched the bridge. He stopped. It wasn't a conscious effort. It was as if the decision had been made for him. He was close enough now to see the lower half of the thing's face. Thin, waxy lips drew back across a set of worn teeth. It smiled. The sandy skin of its jaw was broken in places, so that bone showed through like brilliant white pebbles on a dirty beach. Its mouth hitched open. Wider, wider, wider, until it resembled the wailing figure from that painting called The Scream. So wide now that Jamie thought, if it pitched forward, it could swallow his head whole. He saw himself consumed, torn apart inside that gangling frame.

But the figure did not move. The only part of it that stirred was the mouth, which grew ever larger. Saliva dripped between palate and tongue. Then, through that gaping hole, came the whisper of words. The lips did not form them; they echoed from the back of the creature's throat, like a voice projected from the depths of a cavern. Those words spoke of ancient, brutal things. And, as they rustled in his ear, like the leaves of old books, Jamie understood the terrors of a grown-up world.

Bob Peterson watched the boy being dropped off at the old guy's house. He noted the time – 09:51 – took out his thermos of coffee, and waited.

He wished he could do surveillance in his new De Tomaso Pantera instead of the shitty, but inconspicuous, Citroen Sedan. With its brutal Ford 351 4V Cleveland engine, the bright yellow Pantera was just like the one his idol, Elvis Presley, had bought in '71. While he rummaged through his tapes for 'Roger Miller's Greatest Hits', he contemplated firing a bullet into the dashboard. Then he'd be just like the King, who had shot at his own sleek motherfucker when it had refused to start one morning. He was in two minds, however. A shit-load of hours rooting through dustbins had gone into paying for the Pantera.

105

It was pure good fortune that Bob had chosen a spot giving a view of the back and front of the house. Bob Peterson relied on a lot of that kind of good fortune because he hardly planned anything. He was always in the right place at the right time. To take the spicy photo of the philandering hubby, to retrieve the incriminating credit card statement before the bin men collected. Well, if you will put KY Jelly and strap-ons on your MasterCard, you deserve to be caught out.

He was listening to Miller crooning '*The Last Word in Lonesome is Me*', when the skinny little runt banged out of the back door. Bob jumped out of the car and strolled along the public footpath, acting like he was out for a walk. The kid reached the dyke and lay down for a while. Then he got up and walked to the bridge, swaying like he was three sheets to the wind. Now the boy was talking to himself and stepping closer and closer to the dyke bank. Below, the water ran deep and fast. Bob made his dash.

'Hey? You hear me?' Bob said. He grabbed the boy's arm. 'You all right?!'

Christ, he hated breaking cover, but what else could he do?

'Huh?' There was something about the kid's eyes: was he stoned?

'Looked like you were gonna go ass over tit there,' Bob said. 'Who were you talking to?'

'Huh? What . . . ? I don't know what you . . .'

'Looked like you were talking to somebody.'

'I don't remember. Someone was here . . . I don't remember . . .'

With a troubled look from Bob to the bridge, the boy took off back across the field. Bob watched until he clambered over the gate and re-entered the house. Then the private detective stepped onto the bridge and rested his back against the handrail. Feeling the nicotine demon on his shoulder, he took out a strip of gum and chewed hard. That was when he saw the footprints on the slats. Wet footprints with maggots rolling at

106

their edges. They weren't the kid's. The kid hadn't come onto the bridge. Bob Peterson shuddered.

Once, an irate husband had cornered him in his office and shoved a shotgun between his teeth. Bob had noted with interest that here was a Benelli M1 pump action piece. The kind used by American cops up until a few years back, when the model had been succeeded by the Benelli M3. Not a bad toy, all things considered; Christ knows how that asshole had got hold of it. Then he'd grabbed the barrel, removed it from his mouth and told the stupid motherfucker to get out of his office. Bob Peterson was not easily scared. But, for some reason, those still-drying footprints would haunt his dreams for many nights to come.

Sixteen

Sister Agnes Hynter stared at the two detectives. Jack tried one last time:

'Agnes, if you can hear me, can you write down anything that might help us?'

The pencil faltered on the page. Then it was dropped again from the nun's balled fist.

'You can't expect miracles,' Dr Jamison whispered. 'The poor dear's lucky to have any motor functions at all.'

Soon after their arrival at the nursing home, Jack and Dawn had been introduced to this sad scene. A tiny room containing a tiny woman, aged suddenly beyond her sixty years; hunched over, child-like, trapped inside an ungovernable body. Sister Agnes had suffered her stroke on the night of Father Brody's disappearance, brought on, no doubt, by the blow that had knocked her unconscious.

'Did you know Father Brody, Doctor?' Dawn asked.

'I rarely saw him,' Jamison said, shining a pinpoint light into Agnes' eyes. 'He, like poor Agnes, had always been in robust health. A very powerful man, in fact, in mind and body. That's what's so strange.'

'What do you mean?'

'Why, Agnes' phone call that afternoon. She called my office, telling me Brody was behaving out of character. She was flustered, but it didn't sound serious. A lot of these old chaps go down hill without much warning. I said I'd pop in when I could. I was about to leave the surgery in the early evening, when I got a call from the Home saying Brody had recovered. I said I'd visit the following day.'

'Did you recognise the voice of the person who called?' Jack asked.

'No. But there are so many comings and goings here staff-wise.'

'Did Sister Agnes mention anything specific that Brody had said?'

'No. No, I . . . Wait a minute. There was a name. The name of a doctor, and of Brody's old parish. Some bird name . . .'

'Crow Haven?'

'Crow,' Sister Agnes murmured. 'Crow . . . man.'

She snatched up the pencil. Jamison made a move to placate her, but she swatted him away. Her eyes fixed on Jack. The pencil worked, scrawling two dark circles over and over until the paper had torn through.

'Crow. Doctor. Eyes,' the nun intoned, spitting over the page. 'Crow, Doctor, Eyes; Crow, Doctor, Eyes . . . Eyes – See – You – Eyes – See – Boy.'

Before Jack went up to Brody's room, he inquired if there had been any visitors on the night of the disappearance. The security camera footage had shown no-one arriving at the Home after six p.m. As it seemed that Brody had not been abducted, the working theory was that it had been he who dealt Sister Agnes the crippling blow. Dr Jamison had protested that, in her phone call to his office earlier in the day, Agnes stated she had locked the priest in his room, for his own safety. When the Brookemoor police arrived, however, Brody's door had been found open.

Jack did a circuit of the old priest's room. He checked under the bed and mattress and behind the headboard. He even pulled back the edges of the carpet where the tacks had come away. Finally, he came to the wardrobe. He rummaged beneath piles of clothes until he came across a collection of musty diaries. He carried each to the bed and laid them out in order. They spanned the years 1946–1994. As he arranged them, he saw that the journals had been written in a variety of locations: Sydney, Lima, La Paz, Cusco and, finally, Crow

Haven. All had been penned in a firm, bold hand. All except the Crow Haven diaries, these written in letters so shaky they were barely legible.

As Jack took a cursory glance through the journals written prior to the Crow Haven period, he noticed how detailed and full of colour they were. A trek that Brody had completed across the Andes to the forgotten Inca city of Machu Picchu was a prime example:

5/6/65- We reached the Sun Gate before dawn. The mountain terraces below were hidden in the boiling mist. I was left wondering how Hiram Bingham had felt - the first white man to see this sight in centuries - as he looked down into the valley and waited for the 'Old Peak' to unveil herself. As we watched, a condor broke through the blanket and heralded the dawn. In the same moment, the sun hit the top of the gate and the mist rolled back, revealing the ancient city. I was dumbstruck. Never before have I felt the utter inadequacy of language to express the stirring of the soul.

In fact, all the old diaries were full of these kinds of observations, stories and transcribed conversations. The priest had certainly seen the world, and had delighted in trying to recapture his experiences. It was only in the later Crow Haven diaries that an odd, staccato voice entered Brody's writing:

1ˢᵗ Jan 1977 — Bad dreams. Dead? We - the whole village - pretend to forget.

3ʳᵈ May — Keep thinking of books. Should we have burned them?

23ʳᵈ Aug — Mind easier now. Is he fading?

30ᵗʰ Oct — The children draw their pictures, sing their song. Call him The Crowman.

There were many years of these curt, sad little entries.

Dawn tapped the door. Her inquiries of the Home's staff and residents had yielded little more than the Brookemoor police had already ascertained. Nobody at the home believed the hypothesis that Father Brody had hurt Sister Agnes. Some lunatic had broken in and taken the old priest: Why had the security cameras not picked up the intruder? No idea, but Asher Brody is a good man.

'To be fair,' she said, 'Brody's involvement in the attack is based on circumstantial evidence. Any theories?'

'Well, Brody obviously told Agnes something extremely upsetting. Otherwise, why would she have locked him in here?'

'What are you talking about?' Dawn asked. 'The door was found open.'

'Then someone else opened it. Look at this.'

He waved her over to the window. It was made up of a large frame that held two sashes. Jack pulled the cord and lifted the lower sash. Cold, moist air crept into the room.

'Have you ever read the *Murders in the Rue Morgue*? Locked room mystery by Poe?'

'You don't think Brody was a giant orang-utan, do you?' Dawn frowned.

'You were the one who said 'kinda strange' was my speciality,' Jack grinned. 'But I think *that* theory's a bit out there, even for me. No, what I mean is this: when examining the room, DI Stephens and his boys have made the same kind of mistake that the police made in the Poe story. They found the door open but the window closed, so they just assumed Brody exited via the door. But feel the weight of this sash, if it's not clasped open from inside it'll fall back into place and lock. And look here, at the trellis frame outside the window, see how it's scuffed and pulled away from the wall? Jamison told us Brody was quite active for a man of his age. Suppose he heard the commotion downstairs as the nun was attacked. If the door was unlocked, he would have run down the corridor and taken the fire escape. Instead, he goes to the window, opens it and climbs down the trellis. The sash snaps back into place and locks. The intruder takes Brody's key but, finding the priest gone, he leaves the door open and replaces the key back on the hook downstairs.'

'That's assuming a lot,' Dawn said. 'I suppose your theory could be proved or disproved by taking prints from the outside sill, but it sounds far-fetched. Who was this intruder? Why would Brody fear him? And how did he avoid the cameras?'

'Okay, I get the point,' Jack said, snapping the sash back into place. 'But one thing I'm sure of: it wasn't just a knock on the head that turned that old woman's mind. She saw something she didn't like.'

Seventeen

It was after six when they arrived back at the station. Jack told Dawn that he needed to catch up on some paperwork and that he would see her in the morning. She brought him a sandwich from the canteen and left without a word. There was a single-mindedness about her that Jack admired deeply. She was able to set aside her personal feelings when working. Like this afternoon, when the average person would still have been smarting from his behaviour in the car, she had exuded professionalism.

It was past eleven when Jack cleared his desk. He took a couple of aspirin and tried to moderate his coffee intake. The nervous energy he was working on could tip over into a paranoid jitteriness if he wasn't careful. He stretched back in his chair and unwound the bandages from his knuckles. The cuts were still angry and weeping. His phone rang. In a few short sentences, Bob Peterson gave his first day's report. Jack replaced the receiver without commenting. He began to think about Jamie. Jamie spellbound before the bridge, staring at the wet footprints of a man who wasn't there. Jamie from *the dreaming*, dead and pleading:

'Jack, save me . . . He's coming. He's so close . . .'

Someone coming. Someone close. But who, or perhaps more precisely, 'what'? Simon Malahyde or that dark other from the vision? Jack brought his fists down hard upon the desk.

'The boy's sleeping. Now, a nice glass of merlot, I think. So, love, you gonna tell me what's the matter with our J?'

Tom Howard poured his daughter a glass of rich, sweet-smelling wine. Dawn rested her back against the trembling refrigerator and felt some of her exhaustion melt away. Her father told her how Jamie had spilled the beans about this Jack character. They'd had a little chat, and the boy got the wrong end of the stick and took off. He'd been distracted and tired when he came back, so Tom had sent him up to bed. There hadn't been a peep out of him since.

'Something's going on with him,' said Dawn. 'And with Jack. I just don't know.'

'Boy's obviously fond of the fella. You too, I reckon. Don't turn your head, love.'

Dawn burst into tears. She felt her father's arms around her. He lifted her head and brushed her face with gentle fingers. For the first time in her adult life, Dawn found herself confiding in him. His quiet questions made her wonder why she had not sought his comfort and counsel in all these years. In her youth, he had been her first port of call in a storm but, since Richard left, she had been too ashamed to go to him. She asked herself why this was and could think of no satisfactory answer.

Bringing her story up to date, she said, 'I don't know what's wrong with him. He crumbled today. He admitted he'd lied and then pushed me away again. I felt this morning like I was pushing against a false wall and now the wall's broken down. But there's nothing behind it. And that's worse, in a way.'

'He said he would be bad for you and J. Do you believe him?'

She shook her head. 'It makes no sense.'

'And this asking after Jamie,' her father continued. 'Why's he doing that?'

She finished the merlot in three long gulps, appreciating it only as an aftertaste at the back of her throat.

'He's concerned. I think he wanted to make sure J was handling the split okay.'

'Right, so what're you basing your *real* worries on? Let's say he just wanted out. Men don't always have their reasons.

What else worries you?'

'I don't know.' Hot tears began to slide down her cheeks again, but there was something functional about them, they did not burn her eyes this time. 'He's putting in for a transfer. It frightens me, Dad. I don't know why. I've never relied on anyone really; to feel safe. But him going away. It makes me feel . . . vulnerable.'

Dawn poured herself another drink and stared into the ruby red of the merlot.

'Why?'

'Because . . . don't laugh, Dad, I swear . . . because he's *good*.'

'Sound like your mother.'

'I know. It isn't like me to say things like that. That's why I think it must be true. He *is* good, and he's terribly worried about something, and I think it must be to do with Jamie. That's why I can't let it go.'

Jack Trent stood on the towpath overlooking the canal. A bitter wind cut up from the estuary and whistled over the lip of the catacombs that towered above him. Prisms of ice floated downriver, glinting like stars and cracking wide as the frost took hold. There were days in his memory, only a few weeks old, when smartly painted barges and narrow boats passed along the waterway. Children played into the late evening along the hedgerows on the far bank. Games that the modern world could not touch. Often, Dawn brought stale bread and they fed the grebes and mallards. Now the birds and the children and the boats were gone. Now she was gone, and it was cold and dark.

The great solstice clock of the cathedral tolled twelve. Jack roused himself and decided to go back to the office. There was no point in heading home only to be haunted by questions. Work would calm him. He started up the stairway.

As he ascended, his gaze passed over the catacombs. These ancient subterranean burial recesses, banked one on top of the other, reached up a good forty-five feet from the canal path to

115

the cathedral grounds. Their hiding place had been discovered when work on the cathedral foundations was begun in the eleventh century. Overnight, so the story went, the tombs had been stripped bare, the spoils of long dead heathens divided between the bricklayers of the new temple. Eight centuries later, the Victorians restored the crypts and, in their peculiar desire to emulate the ancient world, sanctified the ground and packed the recesses with their own dead. A stairway had also been installed for mourners to parade up and down. Steps were laid against the graves and iron girders driven deep into the pits.

Now many of the nineteenth century sealing plaques had crumbled away. In several places across the wall, dark mouths yawned, their lips dusted with pebbled stone.

Jack was halfway up the stairs, the catacombs at their ninth layer, when he heard the voice.

'Help me. Please, is someone there?'

He looked over the handrail. The towpath was empty. There were no hedgerows on this bank, no places to hide. From where had the voice come?

'I can see you.'

Jack stumbled back against the handrail. The voice – closer, louder – had echoed out of the recess just level with his head. The plaque – inscribed, 'Mr Edward Peakes, Born 1810 Died 1892. '*The Lamb Walketh At My* ' – was half torn away. The hole was quite large enough for a child to crawl through. It had been a child's voice that called out to Jack. He approached the aperture.

'Hello? Are you trapped? Can you hear me?' His voice boomed in the cavity. 'Listen, I can't see you. I have a torch in my car. Just wait and . . .'

'Don't leave me. I'm afraid.'

Jack put his face to the opening. The moon threw a tongue of light into the tomb, just enough to see an accumulation of sweet wrappers, takeaway boxes and crushed drink cans. Beyond that, there was no telling how far back the hollow reached.

'Are you there?' Jack called.

'Yes. In the dark.'

'Can you move?'

'I can't get out of the dark.'

'Let me . . .'

'I'll never, ever get out of the dark.'

'Look, I'm going to get my torch. Don't be frightened . . .'

'I'm falling!'

Jack thrust his hand into the grave. At that moment, clouds veiled the moon and the light was lost. Jack's fingers, his hand, his arm, disappeared into impenetrable blackness. He felt around, meeting only stone chippings and sweating rock. There was nothing in there. No child. No-one at all. He started to withdraw his hand when something tickled the tips of his fingers. Something cold. A cry caught in Jack's throat. At first, he imagined the impossibly preserved skeleton of Edward Peakes, sprung out of its casket and leering like a hideous jack-in-the-box.

'Is that you?' Jack asked.

The left side of his face flat against the catacomb wall, veins roped his neck and arms as he strained further into the hole. Fingers clutching, he met something that felt like a hand. He snatched at it, and the extremity responded, holding him fast. But there was something wrong. The contours and pressure of the hand were not those of a child. Jack tried to pull himself free, but the grip transferred to his wrist and tightened. His cheek ground against the stone as cold fingers interlaced his own. The voice spoke again, deeper this time:

'*Non Omnis Moriar.*'

This was not *the dreaming*. This was not the *Demons*. This was something else. Something equally frightening and perhaps even more real. Jack had never seen a ghost. He had seen visions of the dead and dying. He had seen those creatures that nestled inside his mind, but although they were monsters, they were at least living things. He knew, with an instinctive certainty, that whatever was inside the recess, gripping his hand, was dead. And now it was moving. He could feel the cool touch of it reach along his arm.

Jack strained with every muscle. He managed to drag his shoulder free but his forearm remained locked in that vice-like grip. Moonlight broke through the clouds and now he could see once more into the recess. A body, no larger than that of a fair-size dog, clambered through the cavity and approached the little envelope of moonlight. Its skin, caked in filth and streaked with clotted blood, gave it a coat like brindled fur. Bright, baleful eyes added to the animalistic nature of the thing.

Jack put his foot against the wall. He kicked at the plaque and felt his hand slide out of the grasp. He cracked his tailbone as he fell into a sitting position. Sickened, dazed, he held up his hand to the moonlight. It was sticky and red, but the blood was not his. As he looked up, fingers, with nails bitten down to the quick, arched over the plaque.

'Non omnis moriar.'

The voice still echoed, but was close now to the opening.

Jack scrabbled to his feet and turned, as if to retreat back down to the canal. He caught sight of what lay below and stopped dead. A dense mist had banked along the towpath and was now swirling at the foot of the stairway. If he went that way he would have to go slow. There were no railings fencing the canal. An image of himself tumbling into the waters filled his mind. He saw his struggle to break the surface. Saw the hands that reached out for him from the polluted depths. Hands like those that now caressed the lips of the tomb.

He made up his mind. He would have to climb the stairs to the cathedral. That would mean passing within three feet of the recess. He put his back to the railing and edged up the steps.

'He's coming for Jamie. You cannot save him.'

Jack inched along the rail. Felt his bladder tighten. Tried not to look, but could not help staring into the catacomb. Coils of frayed rope lashed the child's wrists. Beneath them,

118

old weals started to weep. He paused. A memory stirred: frayed rope on the cabin floor. Someone watching from the shadows of the workshop door . . .

'Remember, Jack,' the boy in the catacomb whispered. 'Remember well. Remember *him*.'

The child crept into the light.

Jack screamed. His muscles bunched and weakened. He dropped to his knees. He could do nothing now but sit and watch.

Agony, defined in terms of flesh, emerged to meet him.

The child's head, swollen to twice its natural size, sat slant-wise upon a broken neck. The force of the skull trauma had crushed and tugged his features into grotesque positions. Whatever facial characteristics remained as perceptibly human were only recognisable as such in the way a fractured nose, or elongated eye, might be picked out of a funhouse mirror. The mouth, toothless, was dragged down to the chest by a shattered jaw. The left eye had been punched back into the cranium. The nose, torn from the face, had left behind a pair of tear-shaped slits. Overall, the effect was as if someone had peeled away a young face and moulded it to fit an ulcerated skull.

Jack stared. The horror of what he saw made the world fall away and even the darkness retreated. Everything narrowed and focused on the impossible thing climbing down out of the hole.

'Jesus Christ . . .' Jack whispered.

The boy was naked. His chest was caved in and ribs poked like white spears through his skin. He shambled forward in awkward, jerky movements. It appeared that his legs were intact, and Jack wondered if he had been dead so long that he had simply forgotten how to walk. The boy staggered as far as the rail and collapsed. He laid his head in Jack's lap and began to cry. The weight of the skull told Jack that this was not a product of his imagination. There was a child sitting here beside him, dead, but still suffering from the blows that had killed him. Jack laid his hand against the boy's crown and felt the pulse of fluid trapped there.

'Who did this to you?'

The stump-tongue clacked out the words:

'He is coming, Jack. Not long now, not long at all. He is coming and you must be ready. The Doctor will see you soon . . .'

The boy's breathing became more even. His misshapen head lay still in Jack's lap. In the darkness of the catacombs, and upon the cathedral steps, the dead were sleeping.

MONDAY 28th OCTOBER 2002

Knowledge is of two kinds. We know a subject ourselves, or we know where we can find information upon it.

Samuel Johnson, quoted in *Life of Johnson* by James Boswell, 1791

A library is but the soul's burial-ground. It is the land of shadows.

Henry Ward Beecher, 1813-1887

Eighteen

It was still night. That was all Stephen Lloyd knew when he came round. Before he realised how much his head ached and how painfully the chains cut into his wrists and ankles, he saw that he had been stripped. Fear sat like a hot brick in his chest. The gag in his mouth made him want to barf, but he held it back. Where was he?

Try to think.

He had planned to meet his dad at nine-thirty p.m. on the Renton playing fields, hoping that the conditions would be fair enough to observe the 51 Pegasi star of the great Square of Pegasus. His dad told him that it would be quite faint but, with a clear night sky, they should be able to see the distant sun. Stephen had gathered together his binoculars and a down-loaded sky-map and set out. Before leaving the house, he stuffed his dead brother's baptism dress into his rucksack.

The priest. Fuck, yes: the Priest.

The priest who had met him as he walked home from choir practice at St Brigid's just a week ago. The priest who'd said how sorry he was to hear that Stephen's little brother had died at only a month old. And who, after buying him a McFlurry and blah-blah-fucking-blahing for ages, offered Stephen forty quid for the dead baby's baptism stuff.

'You want Kyle's clothes?' Stephen had asked.

It had seemed odd, but experience told Stephen that priests always had weird ideas. Bread into flesh, water into wine, that kind of bullshit. His mum said he had to respect them, but his dad, who blamed his mum's church-shit for their break-up, said that priests were the weirdest headcases going.

'*Most of 'em are little boy-type queers, Stevie. So you kick 'em in the orbs if you have to.*'

'His baptism dress, yes,' the priest said. 'We have lots of funny ceremonies in the church. You know that, being a good altar boy. Now, one of those ceremonies involves the baptism dress of your dead brother. No need for you to worry about the whys and wherefores, but you must bring it to me. Traditionally the Church makes reparation, which means I give you money, for the loss.'

'Why don't you ask Mum?'

'The Bible tells us that a sibling must give the clothes freely. You remember that passage?'

'Course,' Stephen lied.

'And anyway, why share the booty? I need these clothes so that your brother's soul may ascend to heaven. You want him to be at peace?'

I don't give a monkey's, Stephen thought.

Ever since Kyle stopped being Kyle and had become 'Dead Baby', things had gone bad. His mum was always at church, lighting her stupid candles. His dad had pissed off long ago. Stephen didn't blame his old man, but resented the bastard's hypocrisy. It was all right for *him* to leave the twenty-four-seven wail-a-thon, but '*You stay and be strong for your Mam, Stevie*'. But if things were going to the shits then there was only one person to blame: Dead Baby.

Without fully realising it, Stephen had started capitalising that moniker the day his dad left. The kid had been cute when they'd brought it home. All pink and a bit yellowy, and smelling clean, like a deep, sterilised cut. Stephen had liked him when he'd been Kyle. But Dead Baby - purple-lipped, frozen-faced, little fists clenched at the sides of his head - he had ruined everything. So, sure, the priest could have his clothes. Stephen would be quids in and it was one less thing for his mum to blub over.

They'd arranged to meet at nine-fifteen, but not at St Brigid's and not at the Lloyd house. Stephen had asked why and had been given the kind of look that could curdle milk at fifty paces. Hadn't he read his Bible? Didn't he know that this very special rite – this offering of baptismal garments - could take place neither on hallowed ground nor at the place where the child had died? It must happen somewhere secret, somewhere that was special to Stephen. There followed a long pause. Stephen was unsure. Ah well, the priest had shrugged, if he couldn't think of a suitable venue then the money – a good sum of money - could always be put to other uses . . . The paper factory on Steers Mill Road, Stephen suggested. Perfect. And afterwards the priest had offered him a lift to the Renton playing fields.

That'll really piss Dad off, Stephen had thought, *seeing me pull up in a priest's motor. Can't wait to see his face.*

The factory forecourt would be the meeting place but Stephen had arrived early. He decided to take a look inside the old building. Getting into the abandoned factory was easy. The local council or whoever kept boarding up the back window and Garry Skeet – head nutter of the gang Stephen sometimes hung around with - kept prising it open with his crowbar. The only difficulty was hitching your bike up and lowering it in.

Grit peppered Stephen's face as he freewheeled his BMX through the old shop floor. The bike had been a guilty present from his dad, and Stephen took every opportunity to plough it through stone chippings and broken glass, relishing the dumb look of disappointment when he'd turn up for their weekly stargazing with scuffed tyres and scratched alloy rims. He spun a few tailwhips, nearly skewering himself on a broken water pipe, and tossed the bike into a corner. Then he climbed a heap of pallets to the high windows and watched the switch-on of the dump floodlights. Most people thought he was tapped, but he loved the way the stink rose from the garbage hills and turned the light hazy shades of orange and purple. Those swirls of colour made him think of gas clouds raging across the planet Jupiter.

Stephen's eyes snapped away from the dump. A juddering

thunk-thunk-thunk-thunk-reeech sounded from the front of the building. The factory's rolling steel doors had ratcheted halfway up and jammed. Headlights shone bright blades through the holes in the grille and silhouetted the lower body of a man standing outside. The priest ducked beneath the unresponsive roller door. He had a sheet of tarpaulin rolled under his right arm, and a pair of bolt cutters, which he dropped with a clang on the concrete floor. He stared at Stephen without saying a word.

'I've . . . I've got it here,' Stephen said, pulling the robe from his rucksack.

'Come here. Into the light.'

This was fucked up. The priest was different. Not the funny, soft-touch old bastard he'd been a few days ago. He was dead-eyed, his movements sort of mechanical.

Most of 'em are little boy-type queers, Stevie . . .

He eyed the BMX. It'd take too long to shoulder it up through the window and the priest's car was blocking the front. The best way out was to dodge past the old fucker and duck under the grille. He dropped down from the pallets.

Have to make it look natural at first, though, he thought. *Then make a sudden break.*

As he walked towards the priest, he looked up, casual like, into the rafters. The ticking over of the car engine rumbled between the struts and beams. He wondered why the birds that nested in the roof hadn't scattered at the sound of the snapping locks. It seemed that they had abandoned the factory. Maybe they had all migrated. All save one. A single black bird or crow. High up, hopping around as he passed under its rafter, cocking its head and watching Stephen's progress.

Inch by inch, as he approached, the shadows withdrew from the priest's face and the glare of the headlights seemed less like a halo about his head.

'Well done, boy,' the priest said, taking the baptism dress.

'Yeah. The. The, erm, money?'

'All in good time . . . Tell me, do you feel a twinge in your soul as you sell your dead brother's clothes?'

'S'just Dead Baby things,' Stephen replied, wishing that Garry or one of the gang would just please turn up. *Make the break. Any minute.*

'Pragmatic child . . . I wonder, can you see him? No? Some can, some cannot. Strange, as he's standing right behind you.'

Stephen turned – *Fucking Dumb Ass.* Pain licked across the back of his skull. His brain bellowed. Then there was nothing. No. Wait. There had been a split second when he'd woken up inside a kind of box, like a coffin. He'd heard the car engine. Everything was dark. He must have passed out again.

And now, here he was. Chained like one of those dancing bears he'd seen in a wildlife appeal on TV. He half-giggled, half-sobbed, as he thought:

Dad's gonna be really pissed when I don't show . . . ha-ha-ha . . .

His stomach clenched and felt small. He realised that, as frightened as he was, he was also very hungry. Just then, as if to taunt him, he imagined that he could smell the scent of roasted meat. It grew stronger. It wasn't imagination. There really was a salty, rich aroma wafting from behind him. It sharpened his senses. His eyes focused. He made out more of the cellar.

Orange light danced on the sweating walls. A shovel, encrusted with brown smears, stood against the boiler. Slats of wood were nailed across the window above his head. A blade of moonlight sliced between the boards and cut across the neck of a dead boy sitting opposite. Stephen's cries died in his throat. It was as if he knew that a scream would be a poor response to such a sight.

The kid's head looked all out of shape, like a roughly plumped pillow. Beetles skittered in the matted hair and some-thing shiny and black suckled in his torn, hanging mouth. At last, Stephen found his voice and started to cry. He kicked out with his trussed legs, trying to get upright. Instead, he slid lower down until his feet pounded against the torso of his dead cellmate. The smell wafted through again. Cooking. Cooking meat. Sunday roast.

There came a squeak of metal and a wall of heat hit Stephen's back. Something flashed in front of his eyes. A thin knife held in the priest's yellow fingers. If he hadn't been sick with fear, Stephen might have laughed at the stupid rubber suit the old boy was wearing.

'Hello. Awake, are we? Not to worry, you'll sleep again soon,' the priest promised. 'Oh, I see you two have met. This is Oliver. Oliver, this is Stephen. There's no time for you to become friends, I'm afraid. Now, Oliver, let's get to work, shall we?'

The priest tugged Oliver's legs and the body toppled to the ground. Then, sitting astride the boy's thighs, the man plunged his knife into the stomach. There was a little blood, not much. Throughout what followed, Stephen Lloyd's reason dripped away under the white heat of his terror. He alternated between screaming and pleading, but the old man's work went on uninterrupted. Finally, Stephen realised that it was no good appealing to the priest (*I won't tell, I promise. Even if you take another kid. You do what you like to them. Just please let* me *go.*) and he turned to God. His whispered prayers, mocked by the unimpeded passage of the blade, went unanswered. And so he gave up on God, too, and waited quietly for his turn to come.

If he had been rescued from that cellar, Stephen's mind would never have recovered from what he witnessed there. During long nights in psychiatric wards, he would have recalled the glint of dead eyes, and a broken jaw stretched into a rakish grin. It was a blessing then, in some ways, that Stephen Lloyd was not rescued.

His time came. He saw the feet planted before him and waited. Seconds stretched beyond their allotted span. Maybe the priest had changed his mind. Maybe. The shovel fell and he felt the rolling shock of fractures snake across his skull. His head on the stones, he experienced the second blow as something distant. Chunks of his brain were closing down and he could no longer understand the sensory signals telegraphing pain. It was with only mild curiosity that he felt the tug of the spade nestling inside his head. The metal was cool against the heat of his mind, against his thoughts. He almost resented the fact the priest worried the shovel free. At last, it was torn out, and his brow, fringed with a patch of hair, went with it. His vision darkened. All that was left to him was the whistle of the spade, the crack of bone and the suck of pummelled meat.

In the dim reaches, he felt a tiny hand steal into his own.

'I'm sorry, Dead Baby,' he said. Kyle giggled.

He lifted the baby and kissed its forehead. Then, with his brother clasped to his chest, Stephen Lloyd crossed the space between worlds.

Nineteen

It was 00:12 by Jamie's *Friendly Neighborhood Spider-Man* alarm. Sleep would not come. However many times he went over what had happened by the bridge, all he could remember was his anger. Then nothing, until the fat bloke with the Elvis quiff had asked him if he was okay. Whenever he concentrated on what had happened in between his mind started shutting lots of doors. The only thing he recalled was a feeling. A realisation that he'd been too hard on Jack; that he should forgive him. That if he didn't, something terrible was going to happen.

The child vanished like a drawing on steamed glass. Jack held out his hands, as if to recapture the image. He longed to comfort the dead boy, to ease his wounds and banish his nightmares. At first, he thought he still heard crying, but the sound defined itself as the sough of the wind. Fingers outstretched, Jack dropped his keys into the gutter. Somehow, he was no longer sitting before the catacomb. Instead, he stood on the kerb just outside the cathedral gates. Snatching his car keys from the foamy drain water, he wasted no time in getting into his car and driving to the station.

His nerves were shot and he yearned for the stability of solid police work. He went straight to the basement and sandwiched himself between the stacks and a row of computer terminals. His eyes burned in the green glow of the microfiche.

Doctor: both Sister Agnes and the dead child from the catacombs had mentioned a 'doctor'. He ploughed through records and case notes, but was unable to find mention of a physician who had lived in Crow Haven in the last fifty years. He moved on. At two a.m., having cross-referenced several names through both paper and electronic files (Malahyde, Simon; Malahyde, Anne; Malahyde, Peter; Brody, Father Asher) he found an original one-sheet report, dated 5/6/95, that detailed the brief abduction of Simon Malahyde, ten-year-old male, by Father Asher Brody. Jack found that he was not surprised by what he read.

Geraldine Pryce, headmistress of the Crow Haven primary school, had reported Simon missing at 1:34 p.m., after the child did not appear for afternoon registration. A search was begun, conducted by PC Clive Grainger. It was Grainger who found the boy at five-ten p.m., wandering out of Redgrave Forest and towards the school. Simon was unharmed, except for bruising to his wrists and ankles, where he had been bound. He told Grainger that Father Brody had taken him to a clearing in the forest and held him there for four hours. Remarkably, the child seemed unperturbed by his ordeal.

Brody, who was later found dishevelled and exhausted, had minor lacerations to his face and hands and a slight cut beneath his ribs. He was unresponsive to questioning, and would not say why he had taken the boy, or how he had sustained his injuries. He would only speak to his friend, Father Garret. As the child was unharmed, and his mother had shown no interest in pressing charges, the CPS decided not to prosecute. The condition insisted upon, however, was that Brody be retired into the care of a secure home.

PC Grainger initiated an extensive search of the forest, in order to ascertain the location of the clearing for evidence gathering purposes. However, his team was unable to locate the glade. When Simon Malahyde was later questioned by a child psychologist, he would only say that he and Father Brody had been 'playing a little game'.

The July 2nd edition of the *Gazette* for '95 reported that Father Brody had been sent to St Augustine's Care Home for Retired Priests in Brookemoor-upon-Fen. The abduction was not mentioned. The article cited exhaustion as the cause of retirement.

Discounting the possibility that Brody was crazy, what did this suggest? Perhaps that he had known something was wrong with Simon. Known it and had taken the boy in order to . . . To do what? Once again, Jack found that he had no answers.

Grey hints of morning strained through the pavement level windows above his workstation. He switched to his other night's researches. His plan had been to begin from October and work back through the missing child reports on the Police National Computer. There were only three unresolved P61 missing child forms filed from the area for this year.

Turning over the details of a runaway found living rough in Nottingham, he was confronted with the school portrait of Oliver Godfrey. He had expected to find a photo of the boy in the records but the living, unmolested face, frozen in the photograph, shocked him nonetheless. Those were the gimlet eyes that had stared from the darkness of the catacombs. Those were the hands, with the bitten down nails, that had clawed out of the tomb. This was the boy whose arms had been bound by the frayed rope from Simon Malahyde's cabin. Oliver's disappearance was dated 21st June 2002. Had Simon abducted and murdered him, or had the mysterious thin man from *the dreaming* been responsible? And did Oliver's fate now await Jamie?

'What are you doing down here?'

Jack folded the report into his jacket pocket. Dawn moved between the stacks, took a seat at the cramped desk and glanced through the Brody notes. She looked tired.

'Had a hunch about the priest,' Jack said.

'Interesting . . . You know, this gives me an idea,' she said. 'When I was at uni, I did a module on Stockholm Syndrome. In some kidnap cases, victims begin to identify with their abductors and with the ideas which motivate them. It's common where someone has been taken, threatened with death, but shown tokens of kindness. Hostages have even joined the same terrorist groups as their abductors rather than be set free. It says here that Simon showed no antipathy towards Brody after the kidnap. Say the relationship endured. Maybe they wrote to each other secretively. When he's old enough, Simon breaks Brody out of his confinement . . .'

'He was ten years old when he was taken, Dawn.'

'An impressionable age.'

'No. I've read about these cases. Simon was abducted for only a few hours. I don't think that's enough time to bond with a kidnapper. In any case, Simon, unlike Brody, has never abducted a . . .'

'I think it's possible that he has. That's why I came to find you. The body of a little boy was found this morning in a lay-by on the Saxby Road. The kid hasn't been officially iden-tified, but I've checked the PNC upstairs and reckon I've got a possible ID: Oliver Godfrey, disappeared June this year. This was found at the scene. Might've dropped out of Simon's pocket when he dumped the body.'

She held out a plastic evidence sleeve. Inside was a car key and fob that sported the Triumph motor company badge. Jack was certain, even before he saw the inscription on the back of the fob, that this was the missing key from Simon's aban-doned car. He turned over the evidence sleeve and the word 'MALAHYDE' glinted before his eyes.

Oliver Godfrey's corpse was a dirty brown colour, shot through with licks of green that reminded Jack of a patina of oxidation on copper. His hairless body was bloated; oddly flabby looking. There was severe trauma to his head. Cut into the boy's stomach were deep, diamond-shaped incisions.

Jack approached the slab. There was no doubt. This was the mutilated face he had seen a few hours before. Only then, it had been ghostly. The sounds of the mortuary seemed distant: the ticking refrigeration unit, the squeal of the gurney being pushed down the corridor, the *plink-plink-plink* of water drip-ping from swan-neck taps into stainless steel sinks.

'Inspector Trent? Jon James, I'm one of the technicians here.

We're still waiting on Professor Jackson, the forensic pathologist, and either coroner or parental consent for the post mortem but that, of course, is a formality.'

Later, Jack would find it hard to remember the face of the technician, Jonathan James. He had listened attentively enough, but his vision was turned inward. The slits in the corners of Oliver's mouth made it look as though the dead boy was grinning. Oliver Godfrey, the child from the recess, now the child on the slab, was confirmation of the reality of what he had seen in the broken catacomb. Confirmation also of Oliver's warning: *He's coming for Jamie.*

He: for once, Jack forgot about the skeletal figure from *the dreaming*. The key was concrete evidence and it gave him a real figure upon whom to pin his fears: Simon Malahyde.

'Now, I've seen a photo of Oliver,' James said. 'This is him. Same facial spacing, same skull shape. We'll confirm ID in a few hours. He was beaten with a flat, wide object. Probably a spade. The killer stood in front and above him. If you look here, you'll see that the back portion of the parietal bone has been crushed with downward thrusts. I'd say he's been dead for over twenty-four hours. PM lividity,' James pointed to the deep purplish-red of Oliver's feet, 'is complete and rigor is well advanced.'

'From our information, Oliver was abducted on 21st June,' Dawn said.

'He's certainly not been dead that long. There's nothing much in the way of decomposition. I should say he's been dead no longer than two to three days. Prior to death, he's been kept chained. You see the bruises on the wrists? The grit and mould under his fingernails are too ingrained to have worked in there after death. So my guess is that, for the last few months, he was kept in a damp, stone building. A cellar or outhouse. His tendons have also been cut, probably to stop him running away. From the uniformity of these smaller cuts, I'd say he was kept naked for some time. The nicks at the corners of his mouth have been made to open it wider, so that the tongue could be removed. Maybe to stop him screaming.

It's my opinion that these wounds were made long before death; you can see the healing on the stump. And then there are these . . .'

James pressed against the diamond-shaped wounds.

'They are about three inches deep. Clean cuts, as a surgical knife would make. See, there's no untidiness as you would get with a serrated blade.'

'Taken as trophies?' Dawn suggested.

'You're the detectives,' James said. 'But this is interesting, help me turn him over.'

Despite James' comments about rigor mortis, Jack expected the body to feel rigid. Instead it was cool and pliant, as if the will to be cohesive had left it. Cut into Oliver's buttocks were narrower, but deeper, incisions.

'The cuts were taken from high-fat content areas of the body,' James said. 'Now, if one looks at similar cases reported from the States, these are precisely the type of wounds one would expect to find. This boy wasn't cut for trophies. My opinion: I think whoever did this wanted to taste the fruits of his labour. This boy was cannibalised.'

Twenty

Dawn had a hard time keeping up with Jack. He took the mortuary steps three at a time and stalked off down the corridor. She called after him, insisting that they return to the station and appraise DCI Jarski of the new development. He would not listen. Her stomach, already cramped after what they had just seen, lurched as Jack drove them, with more than his usual recklessness, to the house in Redgrave Forest.

From the moment she opened the front door, Jack was brusque, to the point of aggressiveness, with Anne Malahyde.

'We found a child's body this morning,' he said, after Anne had shown them into the ivory-white lounge. 'A little boy. Beaten. Tortured. Cut up. And, right next to the corpse, we found this.'

He threw the plastic bag containing Simon Malahyde's key fob onto the coffee table.

'Many people who live with predatory murderers are ignorant of the fact,' he said. 'Either that or they build up walls in their minds. Explain away odd behaviour. They avoid looking in garages, lock-ups, tool sheds, because they can't handle confirmation of those niggling doubts and suspicions. But, looking back, you'll find there were always signs. What signs did *you* miss?'

'I've no idea what you're talking about.'

Dawn kept a close eye on Anne Malahyde. To a casual observer, the frosty indifference with which she had greeted them appeared to remain fixed. But the woman drew too often on her cigarette. Moistened her lips too frequently. The listless detachment was segueing into well-masked apprehension.

'Look at these photos,' Jack continued. 'Your boy's handiwork.'

He spread out a series of Polaroids before her. Snapshots that he had taken of Oliver Godfrey's corpse before they left the mortuary. Anne blinked, but did not turn away.

'Oliver Godfrey was eleven years old. He was abducted from a church picnic in June. Since then he has been kept, barely alive. His tongue was ripped out to keep him silent. His body was mutilated. His head was smashed in. Look at the photographs.'

'Jack, can you give me a minute?' Dawn said.

'This boy's name was Oliver Godfrey. The oldest child of Jim and Eileen Godfrey. He played hockey for his school. He liked fishing on Sundays with his old man. When he was taken, he was wearing a Hull Stingrays T-shirt. He loved ice hockey. Was going to see the team play the week after he was taken by your fucking son.'

'Jack. A word. Now.'

Dawn steered him down the hall and into a large conservatory.

'What the hell do you think you're doing?' she asked.

'I'm not putting on kid gloves to deal with that bitch,' Jack spat. 'She knows something, Dawn. You see that, don't you?'

'What I see is you throwing this case away. If there even *is* a case: you know as well as I do that the key makes only the flimsiest of connections between Malahyde and the dead boy. You also *know* you can't conduct interviews like that, not unless you're going to bring her in and question her formally. Anything you get from her on these terms would be inadmissible. Now, tell me, what the hell's getting to you?'

'The kid,' Jack said, scraping his shoes against a stone imp. 'Seeing him, I just . . .'

'Bullshit, Jack. You've handled child murders before and stuck to the book . . . Christ. You know, I think all this has something to do with us. I'll be honest: I'm worried you're losing it. We need to talk this out properly.'

Jack shrugged and turned away.

'Then I'll go to Jarski, tell him I'm concerned about your objectivity.'

'Dawn, I'm leaving. I told you, after this case, I'm gone. If you're worried I'm cracking up, fine, just please let me finish this before you strap on the straitjacket, all right?'

He barged back into the glazed corridor. Dawn kicked the green mottled imp. What the fuck was she going to do? Her gaze travelled over the rows of untended flowerbeds, each colonised by straggling weeds. A small balcony, jutting out of the back of the second storey, caught her attention. Through its rusted rail wound a rotten grapevine and a stringy weed with white trumpet flowers. The balcony door must lead into the isolated wing of the house, Dawn guessed. Into the room with the bricked-up windows . . .

When Dawn returned to the lounge, she found Jack replacing the Polaroids in his pocket.

'I'm sorry, Mrs Malahyde,' he said, 'for being . . . over-zealous.'

Anne made no sign of accepting his apology.

'Mrs Malahyde, do you have any idea why your son's car keys should be found next to this little boy's body?' Dawn asked.

'I can tell you this,' Anne Malahyde said. 'Simon is not a killer. He's an innocent. A victim of . . .'

'That remains to be seen,' Jack said, a touch of the former acidity entering his voice. 'I should warn you, we will have a warrant sorted before lunchtime. I want this house searched. Top to bottom. If Simon *is* innocent . . .'

'Sorry, sir. The front door was ajar.'

A uniformed officer poked his head into the room.

'DCI Jarski wants you back at the station. Right away, he said.'

'I'm not taking the case away from you, Jack; I'm just taking over line manager duties. You'll have responsibility for the day-to-day running of things.'

DCI Jarski spread out his hands, in what he hoped looked like a conciliatory gesture.

'We don't need a team, sir,' Jack replied. 'The investigation will lose its focus.'

'Not your decision, Jack.'

Fuck him, Jarski thought, *I've a good mind to hand it over to that fuckwit Mescher . . . Oh, good judgement, Jarski. Cut off your nose to spite your face.*

'Look, this isn't a common or garden missing person case anymore. It's a fucking child murder. You've got a good task force, a great Scene of Crime Officer, fresh out of forensics training. A fully kitted out incident room downstairs. You'll use these facilities, Jack. Understand?'

'But, Sir, listen: this case doesn't need man-power and gizmos thrown at it.'

'You know your trouble, Jack? Not a team player. You're what, thirty-six? You could be the youngest DCI this station, fuck the station, this *force*, has ever seen. You're a good detective. No unresolved files, no Code D4s. Since you came over to CID, every case you've worked on has been successfully prosecuted. You know how rare that is? You know they call you Sixth-sense Trent, both uniform and our lot? But you won't get early promotion. Know why? Because you're a loner, a misfit. Won't share the ball. Example: you should've come straight back here after seeing the Godfrey boy this morning. Should've done exactly what I did when I heard about it: set up the team, organised the media. Well, you'll share in *my* playground, sonny, or you're off the case, got it?'

'Sir.'

'And call me Roger. You're my only DI who calls me 'Sir'. Makes me feel like a fucking headmaster. Now, I think a search of the house and woods where this Malahyde lived. I know, as it stands, we've only got the car key to link him, but what with his suspicious-as-fuck vanishing act I don't anticipate any problems with warrants. Okay, you've been downstairs to the incident room, yes? What name did that gingery git DC give the case?'

'Paulownia.'

'What? What the fuck does that mean?'

'Apparently it's a Japanese tree with heart-shaped leaves.'

'Next one in the dictionary, hey? Don't like it. Call it operation . . . Hansel, that'll do.'

'How very inappropriate, *Roger*,' Jack said, halfway out of the door.

'Make a note, boyo: press conference at six-thirty. Mescher will be there.'

'Mescher? Why?'

'He was officer in charge of the Godfrey boy's disappearance.'

'Fuck-*ing* great,' Jack sighed.

'Don't twist your panties. As usual, Mescher fucked it up. He won't be in the team, but he knows the Godfrey parents. Best for him to be there, show a familiar face. By the by, a dicky bird told me you'd been over to Brookemoor, asking about a missing priest or some such. What's that about?'

'Father Brody. He knew Malahyde when he was a boy.'

'Good lad. Hunches like that solved you the Greylampton case, I remember. Anyway, stick it in your report. I expect a full summary of all this bullshit tomorrow. Oh, and, Jack? Have a fucking shave. You'll be on TV for fuck's sake.'

'Mescher?' Dawn said, after Jack had related his interview with Jarski.

'OIC on Greylampton before I took over. Hates my guts. It was before your time . . .'

'Five girls, all under fifteen, all blond. It *was* national news, Jack.'

It was now late afternoon. Jarski's task force had swung into action with breathtaking speed. Dawn had even managed to coax grudging admiration for the DCI's organisational skills from Jack, with the caveat that it would achieve nothing.

As they stood talking in the courtyard, a buzz of activity droned from the house behind them. The Scene of Crime

Officer had arrived with a colour-coded plan and organised three forensic teams into 'hot areas'. A DC had been sent into the local community and managed to muster a small search team that had already begun to scour the forest. Curiously, the volunteers all came from the outlying villages, none from Crow Haven.

All this activity made Jack strangely petulant. He kicked at the gravel, scuffing his shoes like a moody child. Dawn supposed the news that Mescher had any involvement in the case had not improved his humour. If canteen gossip was to be believed, the Greylampton case was unusual, not only because no-one had ever really figured out how Jack had solved it so quickly, but because of the intense animosity between the two senior officers involved.

Due to the grisly nature of the murders, the case had been big news. It stayed big news because of Mescher's inability to find the killer. Five girls had been taken in 2000, all from the Ely area. Mescher's team had worked for a year, turning up neither credible leads nor suspects. The Chief Constable had insisted that a new task force be brought in. DCI Roger Jarski headed the Major Crime Unit, with Jack Trent as his immediate subordinate.

Within three days, due to Jack's efforts, a bank manager named Greylampton was arrested. Trophies taken from the girls were found at his home, pickled in gherkin jars. When Dawn transferred three months ago, people had still been speculating as to how 'Freaky Jack Trent' had fingered the nonce bank manager. There were clues alright; small details which often get missed in the chaos of large-scale investigations. Even so, Mescher had overlooked too many. Within twenty-four hours, Jack had drawn them all together and wrapped up the case. He just seemed to *know*. And now it was common knowledge that Mescher was aching for revenge.

'So where's Mrs Malahyde?' Jack asked. 'Kicked up a fuss about all this, I expect?'

'No, she's been quiet as a mouse. You probably scared the

shit out of her with those pictures. I'm gonna question her again before I leave. *Responsibly.*'

'Good luck. By the way, did you notice that the morgue guy said Oliver's body had been dissected using a surgical blade? Remember the knife Doug Winters described to us?' Jack glanced at his watch. 'Oh crap, I have to get going. I'll be finished at seven, if you're still around?'

'Sure. But Jack, I meant what I said earlier. We have to talk, okay?'

She expected another fight. Instead, he looked at her intently and she saw the weariness in his eyes.

'Yes, we have to talk. There are things you should know . . . Jesus, Dawn, I don't know what to do.'

He turned and walked away down the tree-tunnelled drive.

The crime scene coordinator had not yet designated a team to investigate the bricked-up room but, at Dawn's request, he had examined its door. He reported that, due to dust deposits and the corrosion of the lock, it was certain that the room had not been entered for many years. Clearly, it had nothing to do with the case. Nevertheless, something about it captured Dawn's interest. She stood staring at the warped and peeling paintwork, wondering what Jack had to tell her.

'Do you have children?'

Dawn drew a sharp breath. She had not heard Anne Malahyde approach. Turning, she found that the gaunt face, framed by the ever-present headscarf, was not fixed in its usual distant expression. Anne's eyes were wide and trembling. Her lips, usually tightly pursed, as if she were concerned that her supply of words was finite and had to be rationed, moved freely.

'You look like you do,' she said. 'Mothers know. But don't you think that's a name to be earned? Mother? You're not a *mother* just because you store a child for nine months. You're an incubator. To be a mother you have to nurture. Protect. I'm not a mother. I was an incubator once, that's all.'

'Mrs Malahyde, *if* Simon did this, you can't blame yourself.

142

As Inspector Trent said, many people who live with . . . disturbed individuals, just aren't aware of the fact.'

'He was just a little boy,' Anne continued, oblivious to Dawn's words. 'And I didn't see. There's a kind of cruelty, you know, that's passive. It's worse, in a way, than active cruelty, because people who wouldn't consider themselves cruel can indulge it. I *let* it happen. Here. In this room.'

Anne took a key from her pocket and fitted it into the lock. Dawn looked around at the sister door across the hall. She was anxious that no-one should come from the main house to interrupt this moment. With some effort the key turned. The barrel ground and there was a snap as the tumbler restrained the bolt.

'My husband died in this room,' Anne said. 'They cut him up afterwards, but they never found out what killed him. He screamed my name every night for months. I overheard the nurses, in the last days, say that he was quieter. But isn't it eerie, they said, how he chatters away. He really thinks there is somebody that visits him in the night. In the dark.'

Anne's grip tightened on the handle. Her voice grew hard.

'I mourned for him for seventeen long years. Now I know, *things can come back.*'

A tide of dust flew into their faces. Fingers of light intersected through cracks in the bricked windows. *Like a cage of light*, Dawn thought. Empty bookshelves stretched along the walls and towered over the bed and drip feed stand at the far end of the room.

They must have seen it in the same split second, for as Anne whimpered, Dawn gave an involuntary shudder. Imprinted in the dust, passing through the bars of the light cage and approaching the bed, ran a trail of tiny footprints.

'They took him,' Anne said. 'And kept him.'

Questions tripped over each other in Dawn's mind as she advanced into the room. What could Anne Malahyde mean? Who was the child that had managed to get into this isolated room? Was this the place that Oliver Godfrey had been kept?

Impossible. There was only one set of footprints leading into the room: none accompanying them, none coming back.

Pinpricks of lights scanned her until she reached the bed. From this distance, Anne looked very small in the doorway. The footprints ended here. There were no hiding places. Dawn knelt down and traced the outline of a shoe with her finger. The print was so small it made her heart ache. Then, through the mesh of bed springs, a square of yellow paper caught her eye. She looked back. Anne was gone.

A breeze whistled through the cracks in the bricks. The concrete, comforting outside world grew thinner. The door was swinging to. Dawn snatched at the yellow paper, leapt to her feet and started running. She sped through the needle-point beams, her feet slipping on the thick dust. Inches from the door, her fingers brushed the panels. A final effort and . . . it slammed shut. She groped for the handle but found none. Digging her nails into the gap along the jamb, she tried to prise the door open. It would not budge. The lock must have jammed. Desperation to get out of that dreadful room mounted. She called and hammered. There was no reply.

To concentrate her thoughts on something other than claustrophobia, she examined the child's drawing in the beaded half-light. It was a picture of a clown. Nothing out of the ordinary. The kind of effort proudly displayed on fridge doors up and down the country. As her sweat spotted the paper, she saw the dedication:

For Daddy and his friend - Mr Funnyface. Love Simon xxx.

Dawn felt herself go cold. The sense of entrapment heightened. Standing there, a prisoner in the spaces between light and darkness, Father Garret's words came back to her:

' . . . *Peter Malahyde . . . He died just before Simon was born . . .*'

Twenty-one

As incompetent as Pat Mescher was, Jack had to admire his people skills. Here he stood, four months after the abduction of Oliver Godfrey, as clueless now as he had been at the outset, and the parents of the dead boy were thanking him for his efforts. It was sick. When he caught sight of Jack, Mescher smiled and the burst vessels in his cheeks stood out angry and red.

'Jim, Eileen, may I introduce Jack Trent.' Mescher steered the bereaved couple across the room. 'From today, he will be taking over the case.'

'You *will* still be involved, won't you, Pat?' Mr Godfrey asked.

'No, no. I'll give Jack any help he may require, but DCI Jarski thought it best to put together a new team. Rest assured, though, Jack here is a fine detective. He solved the Greylampton case single-handedly. So the story goes.'

Mrs Godfrey looked at Jack as though he might strike her at any moment.

'I will not forget Oliver,' Mescher said, enveloping Mrs Godfrey's small hands in his flabby grasp.

'Gentlemen, ladies!' Jarski had mounted the platform. 'Are we ready?'

The press room was packed. A few nationals had got wind of a new kiddy killer and sent their crime correspondents. The local hacks watched the London pros like a cluster of schoolgirls viewing the pretty new addition to the class, with a mix of suspicion and grudging admiration.

Mescher enfolded Mr and Mrs Godfrey in a bear hug before they ascended to the platform. Just as Jack was about to follow, Mescher touched his elbow.

'Watch yourself, Trent,' he spat in Jack's ear. 'I might not be in Jarski's team, but I'm watching. If you slip, it'll be you giving talks to pre-pubescent pot heads.'

'Listen to me,' Jack's quiet voice shook. 'Your incompetence allowed that bastard Greylampton to gut those little girls, one after the other. I won't let you jeopardize a life pursuing some vendetta against me. You understand?'

Mescher's jowl trembled. Bellicosity and colour drained from him.

'Settle down, please.' A fragile kind of hush followed Jarski's instruction. They were all seated now at a long table: the DCI, Jack, the Godfreys and a police press officer. 'Now, as you're all aware, the body of Oliver Godfrey was found early this morning at a lay-by on the Saxby Road. In a moment I will hand over to Officer in Charge, DI Jack Trent.' Murmurs from the crowd. Jack thought he heard the name 'Greylampton' muttered somewhere in the hall. 'He will fill you in on the person we are looking for. We have a physical piece of evidence to connect this man, Mr Simon Malahyde, to the crime *but*, and I must stress this, Mr Malahyde is *not* an official suspect at this stage. Indeed, we are very concerned for Mr Malahyde's own wellbeing. If anyone out there has seen this gentleman, or has knowledge of him, we would appeal for you to contact us. Now, I'll pass over to DI Trent.'

Autumn sunshine glanced through the dirty windows of the signal box. Brody rubbed sleep-starved eyes. He put down his pen. Long hours of writing had cramped his hand but at last the tale was told. Now he prayed that he was right. That somewhere in these pages lay that vital undetected clue to the Doctor's destruction. The clue that the prophesied stranger *must* now find. Yet, as a familiar pain teased at his heart, Brody knew that he could be sure of nothing. All he could do was follow the same old Crow Haven pattern: grope around in the dark and hope for the best.

He reached into his bag for the ball of string and the packet of brown paper he had bought en route to Regrave Forest. Then he began wrapping the depositions into their three bundles: one for each phase of his life in Crow Haven.

As he packed up the last of his manuscript, the horror of his story and of what was to come began to overwhelm him. The old priest tore his collar loose and went to the door of the signal box. Outside, the forest crowded him. The trees chattered in the wind. Their ceaseless conversation chilled Brody to the core. He had to leave this place. Had to be among people before this forest drove him mad.

Forever glancing this way and that, he left the signal box. Forty minutes later, he was sitting in the nearest pub outside Crow Haven, sipping a pint of yeasty ale and cradling the bundles in his lap. His sense of unease had just begun to subside when he noticed the television above the bar. A ticker passed across the screen: POLICE PRESS CONFERENCE: CHILD MURDER LATEST. Brody asked the landlord to turn up the volume. The picture focused on a man identified by an onscreen caption as 'Det Insp Jack Trent'.

' . . . you may have unusual information,' said Inspector Trent. 'You may be reluctant to come forward, thinking you would not be believed. *I* would believe you. Please, Father Asher Brody, contact me. I need to speak with you. You can call me on . . .'

Brody heard no more. He stared at Jack Trent and knew that this was the man he had waited twenty-six years to meet. The scar - a crooked white bridge that spanned the gap between the stranger's eyes – told him all he needed to know. Brody offered up a prayer of thanks. He had found *him*.

After Jarski and Mescher had put the Godfreys in a taxi home, both behaving as if they were placing fine crystal in packing cases, the DCI asked Jack to join him for a tête-à-tête (Read: '*bollocking*', Jack thought). Jarski adopted the old good cop bad cop shtick, swinging between the two with schizophrenic ease.

'I know your methods are a little . . . different,' he said. 'I

147

didn't interfere with you during the Greylampton case, and I appreciate the results. But you can't handle a press conference that way. PR. Police work is ninety percent PR these days.'

Jack, propped up against the wall, gave way to a full-body yawn. On reflection, he supposed, that wasn't the best way to receive Jarski's discourse on modern policing.

'This is exactly what I fucking mean,' the DCI exploded. 'People fucking skills, Jack. You just stand there yawning at me like a mardy tart. When I handed over to you in there, I expected details of this Malahyde bloke: height, weight, appearance, last seen. I wanted you to impress upon those arsehole scribblers that, as we'd found a piece of evidence to link Malahyde with the killing, we needed people to come forward with sightings. You barely mentioned him. Just went on about this fucking priest who, it seems to me, has hardly anything to do with anything.'

'Fine, Roger. Now, I do have a case to deal with.'

'Fuck off,' Jarski said. 'And remember, I want a full progress report tomorrow.'

It was now nearing quarter to eight. There was little chance that Dawn and the forensics team would still be at the house. The search of the woods, as it was only an evidence gathering exercise, would have been abandoned long ago.

The time had come to tell her everything. The whole Biography Channel, Sixty-Minute Story of My Life deal. In glorious technicolour lunacy. Even if she didn't believe him, he had a moral duty to give it to her straight. Before the discovery of Oliver Godfrey's body, there had been a thin strand of logic, twisting in his mind, which had told him: *steady, wait and watch, it might all be coincidence.* But, as the case progressed, and increasingly stranger things came to light, that rubbery strand of logic had wound tighter and tighter. When the corpse of the boy he had seen in the catacombs had been found this morning, logic came to the end of its elasticity and snapped. This was all real. Jamie was going to die. She must know.

Jack opened the door to his office. Under the aching glare

of the halogen lamp, missing person reports were spread across his desk. Dawn sat by the window, framed by a nightscape of smog-blurry stars.

'Something weird happened at the house,' she said. 'Weird is your department.'

She passed him a scrap of torn, nicotine-yellow paper. In the centre of the page stood a clown, dressed in a gaudy suit, balloons or lollipops spinning around him. Two stick figures had been drawn standing behind the clown. The dedication below read: *For Daddy and his friend - Mr Funnyface. Love Simon xxx.*

'I've checked: Peter Malahyde died three weeks before Simon was born,' Dawn said.

'Well, children do write letters and draw pictures for dead parents,' Jack said.

'Do you know where I found this? In the bricked-up room. The room, according to Mrs Malahyde, that has not been opened since Peter's death.'

'What are you suggesting?'

'I don't know.' Dawn cupped her forehead with one hand. 'Nothing. I just scared myself, I suppose. I got stuck in that room and freaked out. One of the forensic guys had to get me out . . . Maybe Simon did manage to get in there when he was a boy. Left the present for his dead father. He was probably craving affection, I'm sure he got none from his mother . . . It's probably nothing.'

'I think it's something, Dawn. It's another piece.'

'So,' she sighed, 'you ready to tell me what's going on?'

'Not really. It's a question of where to begin.'

'Well, like the King of Hearts said, begin at the beginning and go on 'til you come to the end: then stop.'

'Okay. But can you do two things for me first?'

'Stalling again? What is it?'

'First, I want to know how Jamie is. Has he been acting strangely lately? Has he . . . ?'

'Yesterday. He had an argument with my dad. About us, actually. He hasn't spoken much since.'

'Has he mentioned seeing any strangers hanging around?'

'No. I can't stand this, Jack. What're you afraid of?'

'It's going to be fine, Dawn. Trust me. Now, the second thing: you've been going through these reports. I reckon we're thinking along similar lines. You've noticed that odd little detail in the Godfrey file, haven't you?'

'I think I know what you mean. It was just a footnote, really. Oliver's sister died a year before he disappeared. Cot death. A week after the kid's abduction, Mrs Godfrey found that the baby's baptism dress was gone. Seemed strange, maybe part of a fetish killer's MO. I've been going through some unresolved mispers.'

'We should phone the parents in any missing child case still active,' Jack said. 'Ask if any baptism clothes disappeared at about the same time. It's not the sort of thing they would necessarily report.'

'And then you'll tell me what's going on?'

'Promise.'

They divided a bundle of reports between them. Dawn manned the landline while Jack used his mobile. The hours ground away and, with every phone call, Jack felt the hope and despair that began and ended each conversation press heavily upon him. There was an unintended cruelty in calling these people, who had lost such precious things. Some had seen the press conference and, when he told them who he was, he could hear the conflict in their voices. It had to be bad news. Their child was dead, murdered like little Oliver. There was horror and grief in that, but there was also a kind of relief. Months of waiting, their lives suspended in an emotional amber, was over. Now they would at least *know*. And here was the cruelty: Jack was not there to free them, to give them permission to grieve at last. He was there only to ask more questions.

'I'm sorry, Mr Lewis, we are still looking. Good night.'

That was the last name in Jack's bundle. He reordered the papers, and was about to start on last years' batch, when Dawn caught his eye.

' . . . so, you reported Stephen missing at eleven o'clock

150

last night, Mrs Lloyd? Yes, I understand . . . Do you have any other children? I'm sorry to hear that. My sympathies. Was Kyle baptised at all? At St Brigid's . . . ? Now, this may seem an odd question, but has Kyle's baptism dress gone missing? Yes, I'll wait . . .' Dawn hit the mute button. 'Stephen Lloyd, supposed to meet his dad last night at the playing fields down Renton way. Didn't show. I almost overlooked it 'cause it was only put on the PNC this afternoon.' Dawn punched the button again. 'Yes, Mrs Lloyd, I'm here . . . It's gone? Could Stephen have taken it? No, this is just routine follow-up. Maybe a colleague and I could pop over to see you tonight . . . ? Fine, we'll see you then.'

Dawn replaced the handset.

'She couldn't say whether Stephen took it, but it was definitely at home yesterday afternoon. We better go. You can tell me what I need to know in the car.'

As Jack grabbed his coat, his phone rang. He answered. A voice cut in before he could speak:

'This is Asher Brody, Mr Trent. Can you speak freely?'

'Just a moment,' Jack turned to Dawn. 'Bad reception again. I won't be a minute.'

He walked to the lavatory and fastened the door behind him.

'Father Brody, I must talk to you . . .'

'It's not the time to talk. At a quarter to midnight, you must be at the door of the Yeager Library. Are you familiar with Jericho College?'

'Yes, I was a student at . . .'

'Forget what you think you know. At the Porter's Lodge ask for 'Willard'. When you are let through, take a right at the Primary Quad. Follow the Cloister, keeping your shoulder always to the back wall. Just before the tower of the Watching Window, there is an archway. You will pass through it and enter an older part of the college. A quad . . .'

'Do you mean the Cardinal Quad? But . . .'

'It will be dark. You'll have to feel your way. When you come out of the arch, you may see lights from rooms away

151

in the darkness. Do *not* stray from the wall. You'll reach the Yeager Library soon enough. Ring and wait for the librarian. Ask to see *The Transmigration of Souls*. Read it quickly. You must leave the premises at the stipulated time. The librarian is quite particular. Tomorrow, I want you to visit Geraldine Pryce, the headmistress of Crow Haven School. After that you will be prepared for the story I have to tell. Ready to know what Simon Malahyde really is.'

'I'll do as you say, but I must . . .'

'Good. And, Mr Trent, be on your guard. If I have identified you as the one who might bring an end to this, rest assured *he* has too. He will attempt to tease out your weaknesses and set your fears against you. I wouldn't be surprised if he has tried already. Goodnight.'

Jack left the lavatory. The light was still on in his office. Dawn's silhouette grew large against the glass. He crossed the hall, eased open the fire exit door and started down the stairs.

Twenty-two

A hoarse croak descended from the heights of the Damascus Gate, Jericho's looming tower entrance. Jack found it difficult to pick out the bird from the array of mythological beasts set on plinths around the walls. Then something shifted, and he saw a crow perched on the scorpion tail of a manticore. As he passed under it, the bird cried out again and circled down to the cobbled street. It paced to-and-fro, keeping a tiny eye fixed on him. Stepping through the gate, he heard a final bad-tempered squawk and the clapping of wings.

Jericho accepted few lodgers, but the place was unnaturally quiet nonetheless. Beyond the gate-tower, the crew-cut Primary Quad was illuminated by electric lights set in antique lanterns. The Lodge was in darkness. Jack rapped on the visitor's window. From nowhere, the porter appeared and drew up the sash. Even in these ancient surroundings, the sallow-faced man looked comically antiquated in his Edwardian-style clothes. He leant across the sill and thumbed the brim of his bowler hat.

'I'm here to see Willard,' Jack said.

'What? What name did you say?'

'Willard?' Jack repeated.

The porter pulled down the sash. Through the single plate window, he tapped his pocket watch and mouthed: 'Go through.'

The light in the Lodge went out. Jack entered the open court and stepped into the cloister that ran along the northern edge of the Primary Quadrangle. On the opposite side of the court was the Master's Lodge, the Combination Room and the Lower Library. Lights and laughter came from some of the dorms. A low hum of conversation and the chink of glasses echoed out of the Combination Room.

Keeping his shoulder to the wall, Jack moved along the cloister. A cold wind whistled through the arch at the end of the covered walkway. The lanterns, slung from the cloister roof, rattled nosily. Jack reached the base of the tower abutting the archway and looked up to where the Watching Window was situated. The panes were as black as the lead that held them. He saw no face pressed against the glass.

He remembered the tale of Jericho's ghost from his student days: a story he had thought of as mere superstition. Professor Rowland Mewes, fellow of the college in 1850-something, had been engaged, for his own amusement, in an archaeological project. He had been trying to trace the location of the lost Cardinal Quad. Before the University acquired the land, a sect of Thomist monks had built a library on this fabled quad in the late fourteenth century. A group of fellows at the University had been desperate to acquire the land of these learned brothers. Neither promises of advancement nor threats would part the monks from their library. And so a whispering campaign against the brethren was begun, citing their use of arcane lore and even witchcraft. There are no records of how things escalated but, on Christmas Eve 1392, the entire order was herded into its library by a cadre of masked men. The doors were barred and the place burned to the ground. The Cardinal Quad was destroyed and the new college was built on the land.

Five centuries later, Professor Mewes began his researches. He was convinced that the brothers had been aware of the danger threatening their lives. And so, desperate to protect the knowledge they had accumulated, the monks secreted their most valuable books in a vault beneath the library. Fired by the desire to unearth some of the treasures lost in the Dark Ages, Mewes spent three years scouring the land that surrounded the college. At last, he came to the conclusion that the site of the hidden chamber was beneath Jericho's stable yard. He applied for permission to excavate the area. A convocation of the Master and senior fellows turned down his request, due to lack of proper evidence.

Mewes, bitterly disappointed, retired to his room overlooking the stables. He sat in the window, night after night, staring at the scrap of land, wondering what ancient learning lay beneath it. One night, the porter saw Professor Mewes burst out of his rooms and run down the cloister shouting:

'It's there! Jesus in his heaven, it's there! Impossible but . . .'

Mewes disappeared beneath the archway that led to the yard. The porter followed moments later. He found the enclosure empty. The horses dozed in their boxes. The watch-dog, chained to a spike at the mouth of the arch, started barking only when the porter appeared. There were no footprints on the dusty ground. Mewes had vanished. He was never seen again.

The casement, from where the Professor willed the lost Cardinal Quad to give up its secret, was afterwards known as the Watching Window. Over the next hundred and fifty years, students, professors, masters and porters have reported seeing a figure standing in the window, his livid face pressed against the glass.

And now, Jack thought, *I'm following in your footsteps, Professor.*

The stables had been torn down in the thirties and the yard tarred over. Jack knew that only the lecturers' car park lay beyond the archway. But the tunnel was very dark and he could not see the tarmac space beyond.

Jack stepped beneath the arch and out of time.

Twenty-three

Beyond the fact that their son was now potentially the second victim of a child killer, Harry and Fran Lloyd knew nothing. Stephen may have taken his dead brother's baptism dress, Mrs Lloyd wasn't sure. Had he been acting strangely in recent weeks? She didn't think so. Had he mentioned meeting any strangers? No. Dawn noted the responses and wondered, for the hundredth time, where the hell Jack had got to.

'She don't notice nothing,' Harry Lloyd said, cracking open a beer and licking the foam from the rim. 'I'm surprised Stevie was able to swipe the kid's stuff. It's hard to find a minute when she's not bawling over it. Just *look* at this place.'

A row of little porcelain dogs rattled as he ran his finger along the mantelpiece. He held out two grey digits in front of his wife's face.

'He was supposed to be with you,' Fran screamed. She turned to Dawn. 'He's trying to blame me. He blamed me for Kyle. I put him on his back, I didn't smoke around him, I made sure the room wasn't too hot. Everything they told me. He was blue. His little eyes were big. He was supposed to be with *you.*'

'Can't you understand, Fran, I'm *not* blaming you? If you'd just let it go . . .'

'Forget, you mean.'

' . . . I'd still be here. Stevie'd never have to go out to meet me then, would he?'

'You were supposed to meet Stephen last night, Mr Lloyd . . .' Dawn began.

'Bloody Church is her problem. Even got my boy involved.

156

Choir boy. You can imagine the stick I get at work about *that*.'

'You're Catholic, Mrs Lloyd?'

'Too right she is. That's what's screwed her up. Love to wallow in misery, the bastard Catholics.'

'And Stephen, he was confirmed? Involved in the Church?'

'Course he was,' said Harry, crushing his empty beer can and throwing it into the grate. 'They love to get their claws in early. Bastard Catholics.'

Harry Lloyd seized one of the china dogs and dashed it against the stone flags of the fireplace. He stood looking at the broken pieces for a moment, then squatted down and brushed them into his palm.

'I don't know what to do,' he murmured. 'Frannie, I don't know what to do.'

Fran Lloyd slipped from her armchair and knelt beside her husband.

'We haven't lost him, Harry. He's our own. Jesus will keep him safe.'

'Please,' Harry rocked forward in her arms, his forehead resting on the flags. 'Please, Jesus, keep him safe. Bring him home to us.'

As his father begged for his safe return, Stephen Lloyd was being methodically dissected. Although he had not been as committed a Christian as Oliver Godfrey, he had intoned the name of God before he died. His prayers were brief, however, and Father Garret believed that, in the end, the boy had accepted his fate.

When Garret murdered Oliver Godfrey, he had not anticipated what a messy business it would be. Stupidly, he had worn his everyday clothes. He had learned his lesson, however. Over the weekend he had purchased a rubber decontamination suit with matching gloves from the army surplus store. Now, the suit squeaking with his every move, Garret sliced diamond-shaped cuts from Stephen's buttocks. Stephen, of course, had been kept in the cellar for only a day, and so his blood was full and rich. How different poor Oliver's had been, after weeks of draining and being chained in the dark.

Garret turned the boy over and started working at his stomach. A strip of moonlight flashed a bright mask across the devastated face. Pressure built in Garret's head. He looked down at the hunks of meat in his hands and felt the blood becoming sticky between his fingers. As the light flickered across them, those features of Stephen's face that remained intact raced towards Garret, receded, and then thrust forward again. The lustrous eyes snapped open. Lips moved.

'You have disappointed me, my boy,' the voice - not a child's - croaked. 'Where is your backbone? I bore it, so should you.'

Stephen Lloyd was gone. Dr Ethram Garret, shining with the cancer that had killed him, lay at his son's feet. He was exactly as Garret remembered him: very tall, very softly spoken, every fibre of his body racked with pain. He was so yellow that he seemed to glow with a light of his own.

'This is what my son has become. Pathetic,' the dead man sneered. 'A murderer of children. Tell me why, Christopher.'

'Because I watched you die, Father.'

Christopher Garret could not bear to look into the uncomprehending eyes that stared up at him.

'I - I saw your pain . . .' he stammered. 'I could have killed myself, I suppose, but . . . but I was offered another way. *He* came to me. He showed me that I might be damned in such a way that I would never see Hell.'

'Foolish boy. You *will* see Hell. You don't have the stomach to cheat Judgement.'

Garret blinked away his tears. When he looked back, his father was gone. Stephen Lloyd lay upon the stone floor, still and dead.

'You're wrong,' Garret whispered, feeling the pressure in his head ebb. 'I shall never be judged. I will be forever.'

The specially adapted metal tray in the furnace clanked as it expanded. Garret opened the grille door and threw the cuts into the hot pan. They sizzled and spat and smelt good.

This is the end, Garret thought, as he watched the meat turn white. *The end, thank God.*

A trail of viscid fluid drained away from the cooking flesh. It flowed down a channel indented in the base of the pan and out through a perforation in the side. A glass jar collected the fat. Garret burned his fingers in the dribble as he peeled off the Robinson's Marmalade sticker. He screwed the lid back onto the jar, sealing it airtight. Then he placed it in an alcove in the cellar wall. It nestled there, amongst the containers of Oliver Godfrey's fat and the baptism dresses of Kyle Lloyd and Jessica Godfrey.

Fran and Harry Lloyd were arguing again. For a moment, as they comforted each other beside the fire, Dawn had seen a vestige of the love that grief had wrung out of them. It was fleeting, however. She left them with as many reassurances as she could but she knew the similarities between this disappearance and Oliver Godfrey's were too striking to be a coincidence.

She went back to the station. For the next hour, she sat in Jack's office trying his home number at five-minute intervals. No joy. She called at his house on the way back to her father's. No-one answered her knocks. Pulling into her father's street, she tried Jack's mobile again – *Sorry, you cannot be connected . . .*

To divert her mind, she switched back to thinking about the case. The Church seemed to be the key. Oliver had been a devote Catholic and a committed Christian Youth Group member. He had been abducted from a church day out. Stephen was also a regular churchgoer, though in his case it seemed this was due to parental pressure rather than any real faith. Both siblings of these abducted boys had died of cot death. Both siblings had had their baptism dresses stolen. She asked herself why Simon Malahyde would feel the need to seek out two boys with such specific histories. She thought over the little she knew about him, but there seemed no clue that answered the question.

And then something struck her: she was beginning to assume, without question, that Simon Malahyde *was* the killer of these boys. She knew only too well that, in police work, such assumptions were dangerous. Of course, there was the linking evidence of the key fob but, as she had pointed out to Jack, it was a circumstantial link. Not real, stand-up-in-court evidence. What's to say the murderer hadn't also abducted and murdered Simon, and that he had planted the fob as a blind? Okay, it would be unusual for a kiddy-killer to go from targeting pre-teens to a seventeen-year-old, but it wasn't unheard of. It was also feasible that Malahyde could have dropped the key in the lay-by several days ago, and that the cases were unconnected. As Jarski had pointed out at the press conference, Simon was not an official suspect. Not yet.

Dawn realised that it was Jack's own firm conviction of Simon's guilt that had subconsciously swayed her. That and perhaps the sense that something wasn't quite right about young Mr Malahyde. She remembered the feeling she had got while examining Simon's various possessions. That sense of a fractured, inconsistent personality.

As she dragged her bag and briefcase from the car, she noticed the Citroen Sedan parked across the street. There was nobody at the wheel. She could have sworn the same car had been parked outside her apartment block this morning.

Has he mentioned seeing any strangers hanging around?

She went over to the car and peered through the windows. Cassette tapes littered the floor, a brown leather coat sat on the back seat and a bag of Haribos on the dash. The gear stick acted as a bookmark for a copy of Hustler magazine.

She tried Jack again. *Sorry, you cannot . . .*

'Jesus Christ, where are you?' she said. 'Jack, I'm frightened.'

160

Twenty-four

The air was cold and molasses-thick. Jack pushed against the darkness that surrounded him. He remembered this as a short passageway yet he had taken maybe fifty steps and was still not through it. His feet ceased to clack against the cobbles. The ground shifted beneath him like sinking sand. And the worst of it was, he could feel *them* awakening. Squeals and shrieks rang down the corridors of his mind and echoed in the chambers of his soul.

He brought the door of their prison to the forefront of his consciousness and peered through. The toy box lid was open a crack. Clustered eyes, spider-like, stared out, while black fluid seeped from the gap.

Pi over four equals one minus a third plus a fifth minus . . .

The flow of their mercurial bodies froze.

. . . plus thirteen over fifteen minus seventy-six over one hundred and five plus . . .

The dark matter shivered – hissed - ebbed back towards the box.

. . . two thousand five hundred and seventy-eight over three thousand, four hundred . . .

The lid snapped shut. Jack pushed the room back into the farthest recess of his mind. His senses returned.

He was out of the tunnel and standing before a large wooden door. The legend, *'Yeager Library'*, was burned into the central panel. Turning back, he saw the archway and his own uncertain footprints on the clay path. Across the court to his left, candlelight passed a series of mullioned windows. For some reason, he took great comfort from those lights. He wanted to get away from the intimidating hulk of the Library and visit each cheery-looking room. He remembered Father Brody's advice, however, and turned back to the bell-pull set into the cornerstone.

The Yeager Library was a structure of stone and wood. The door was wide and arched at the top, mirroring the six lancet windows on either side of it. No lights illuminated the stained glass, but away to his right Jack saw a few glimmers shining through tiny octagonal holes set into the wall. These reached, like a string of sparkling beads, far into the distance. He put his ear to the thick timber. The echo of the bell rang through distant rooms.

The door swung open.

'Your business, Mr Trent?'

The face of the figure in the doorway was masked by the glare of his lamp. Jack saw only that the man was perhaps five foot ten and dressed in black robes.

'I've been sent by someone who . . .'

'Why are *you* here?'

'I was told to ask for a book . . .'

'A book is only a tool. What do you want?'

'Truth, I suppose.'

'This library has collected books down the ages. It houses knowledge that spans millennia. But there is no truth here. Only a signpost or two perhaps.'

'A signpost is good enough.'

The monk stepped back and allowed Jack to enter a large, circular hall. The stone flags of the floor, worn to a shiny finish, were dusted with straw. Four fluted pillars rose to support an elaborately ribbed and traceried ceiling. Between these pillars stood three doors marked *Archives, Reading Rooms* and *Library* respectively.

'So, Jack Trent, do you wonder how I know you?'

The face that turned to Jack was full of strong features: a jutting jawline, a prominent forehead, pronounced cheeks raised above small, sunken eyes. It was as if an excess of bones had been squeezed into too small a space.

'I might wonder, if that was the strangest thing that had ever happened to me.'

'Indeed,' the monk's eyes narrowed. 'I see them, you know.'

'Them?'

'Inside you. The ancient Romans may have called them 'numina', spirits that preside over a certain thing or place. In this case, your gifts. They drive your abilities, but they are also enslaved to you. Like the engines that came after my time, you need them to power your visions, but they also rely on your emotions for sustenance, for fuel. You know that already. There are books here that could tell you what they are, how they came to live inside you. Books that could tell you how to control them, so that you might reap the benefit of those powers without the curse of isolation. Books that could tell you how to rid yourself of them, if that was what you wanted.'

Jack almost staggered under the weight of the librarian's words.

'Is that possible?'

'Of course. But you have a choice. There is no fee for the first visit to this library, but there is a limitation. You may read only one volume, unless, of course, you decide to stay. Your choice: read the book you were sent to read or the book that will set you free.'

His years stretched out behind Jack in one long, lonely sweep. If the librarian was to be believed, he might walk back to the world and have a chance of becoming part of it. He could have friends. He could have a family. He could have her . . . But could he? With Jamie dead, and knowing that he had this opportunity to discover how the boy might be saved, could he rest easy as he held her through the long nights?

'*The Transmigration of Souls*.'

'Noble, Jack,' said the librarian. 'And in the long run it may be the wisest course.'

The monk's touch was gentle. He led Jack to the door with '*Reading Rooms*' inscribed upon it.

'Do you live here alone?' Jack asked, trying to turn his mind away from the recent choice.

'My brothers, those who were sealed within the night the fellows burned us alive, still abide here. Presently they are at prayer.'

The librarian took a stone key from his robes. Numerals and arcane designs decorated the shaft and teeth, but Jack had no time to make them out before the key was fitted in the lock. The door opened, and Jack, expecting another large ante-chamber, was surprised by the low, long corridor. Red doors with brass nameplates stretched away in a crimson blur.

'The reading rooms. All our visitors are assigned one for the period of their stay. Although that, of course, can never be accurately guessed.'

The librarian shut and barred the way behind them. He ushered Jack down the passage, the light of his lamp burnishing the nameplates they passed. They had gone some way down the corridor, straw muffling their footsteps, when Jack stopped before one of the doors. On its brass plate was written:

Kit Marlowe 1593 -

'What is it, Jack?'

'Kit Marlowe? Christopher Marlowe? He was here?'

'He *is* here.'

The librarian pointed to the gap beneath the door. In the strip of light, Jack saw a shadow pass and re-pass.

'Many have come to seek knowledge. Some famous, some forgotten. Mr Marlowe is one of our more venerable guests. He came to us after a little trouble in Deptford, a ruse on his part to avoid a charge of treason, so he told me. He wanted to lie low for the night and be on his way in the morning. He became rather too absorbed in his studies, however . . . You may also have heard of Mr Marlowe's near neighbour here.'

The librarian held up his lamp to the nameplate on the opposite door.

'Professor Rowland Mewes, Eighteen Fifty-Three,' Jack read.

'I hear Professor Mewes is quite the celebrity these days. He also keeps late hours.'

Through the door, Jack heard the scratch of pen on parchment.

'This may be an opportune time to give the customary warning . . . Ah, here we are.'

Two doors along from the playwright's room was a plate marked: 'Jack Trent'.

'The dates of your incumbency shall be added later,' the librarian said, opening the room.

Again, Jack expected something very grand, but was confronted by a simple sandstone chamber with only a desk and a chair for furniture. The ceiling was high and, at the rear, there was one of the octagonal windows he had seen from outside. On the desk sat an oil lamp, an hourglass, a pile of yellow parchment and a notebook.

'The warning, then,' said the librarian. 'Each visitor is given the amount of reading time I deem necessary for his needs. This hourglass represents your allotted time. If you are still in this room when the last grain of sand is spent, then here you will stay. You shall never leave, but endure through the ages, confined within these walls. Like the good doctor, you shall simply disappear from the world. You shall, of course, have all the books you want. Even Mr Marlowe, however, has found that the pursuit of knowledge for knowledge's sake grows rather irksome after a few centuries. Are you ready?'

Jack took his seat. He brushed the parchment with his fingers, fearful that it would crumble at his touch. The paper was strong, however, and merely crackled. The text was written in Italian, but scrawled in a hurried hand on the notebook beside it was a translation.

The librarian turned over the hourglass.

'Then begin.'

Twenty-five

THE TRANSMIGRATION OF SOULS.
1600 Anno Domini. Anon.
Translation from the original Italian by
Father Asher Brody - 1976.

Know then that many of the beliefs of our pagan forefathers were based upon blasphemous precepts, but not all their erudition was at fault. There were kernels of knowledge that the philosophers of antiquity plucked from a greater body of Truth than they could know. We blessed generations, who have come after the Advent of the Lord, should not discard the old learning, but instead focus it through the perspective glass of the True Faith. Then might we not see the Glory of Creation in subtler tones, and better recognise the snares of the Devil before they draw tight about us? I say all this to defend myself from a charge of heresy, for my story touches on the accuracy of a particular ancient, though heretical, belief.

To begin: I propose to tell you nothing about myself or my history. To do so would make me easily marked. The most you will know is that, for five years before the dread events of which I write, I had been travelling through Wallachia and Transylvania, collecting stories of the most fantastic kind, with a view to compiling a volume of Folk Myth and Rhyme. Many of these tales came from the town of Bistritz, on the trail of the Borgo Pass, which was at that time plagued by a pack of lycanthropes and other night creatures.

Leaving Transylvania in the summer of 1593, I made my way through Hungary, into Austria and then north into

Bohemia, where I settled for a while. I had not planned to stay long. I was keen to reach Saxony before the New Year, where I had heard that a magician was to be brought before the Leipzig Supreme Court accused of reanimating his dead wife. I was tired, however, from many months on the road, and so I decided to rest for a week in a small town that nestled on the River Oder, overlooking the Prussian diocese of Breslau.

I will not give a name to the town. Suffice to say it was a pretty backwater, with meadows of corn poppies, bluebells and sweet red campions. I took a room at the inn and, indolence not being among my vices, I made my name known by purchasing drinks for the house. I soon found myself sat among grateful companions, who regaled me with the myths of the locality. When I retired to my room, I had a thirst from the yeasty ale and a catalogue of trite tales, variations of which I had heard many times before. Here was the story of the little orphan children lured to the crone's sugared cottage. And there, the tale of the wicked nobleman who murdered all his wives and stored their bodies in a bloody chamber (the origin of this last I had long ago traced to the monstrous alchemist, Gilles de Rais). Perhaps resting for a week in this place had been a mistake.

By the third day, I had packed my trunk and purchased a trap to take me as far as Prague. It was late when I finished arranging my portmanteau, and I was about to take my rest, when a note was slipped under my door. The letter, unsigned, was written on weighty paper, folded thrice and sealed with wax.

Mr Dear Sir (it ran)
   Word has reached me of your fascinating employment. If it would suit you to pay me a visit this evening, I believe I could furnish you with a most singular experience to add to your collection. My carriage awaits downstairs at your convenience.

I was full of curiosity and, pausing only to collect my cloak,

I descended to the public bar. To my surprise, the place was in darkness. I left my host a note, saying I would return late and asking him not to bar the door.

Outside, a fine closed carriage awaited me, drawn by a pair of palomino beauties worthy of the chiefs of Saladin. The driver was a jovial fellow, always laughing when he spoke. He threw me a bearskin and said that I should get some rest, as we had a fair distance to cover. The air was cold, which I thought would sharpen my senses, but ensconced in the carriage I fell into a deep sleep. I could not guess the duration of our journey, for when I woke there was no moon to gauge the night's progress.

'Here we are, Sir,' the driver called. 'You look fair rested.'

'Is your master's house in this great glen?' I asked, stepping from the carriage.

'Follow the path leading into the valley and you will see what you shall see.'

'What? See here, I shall not gallivant up hill and down dale . . .'

'I should do as you are told,' the driver laughed.

He pulled up his doublet, exposing the dagger slung from his belt. I had met with dangers before on my travels, and had never seen the merit of risking one's life for the sake of arrogant notions of bravery. Pulling my cloak close about me, I began to move down the treacherous incline.

The forest was dense and, halfway down the vale, I cursed myself for not having demanded the brute give me his lantern. The darkness began to work at my imagination. I recalled in an instant all the tales I had been told, from Sicily to the Baltic, from Seville to the Black Sea. Faces grew from the shadows around me: incubi, succubi, vampyr, and the fading gods of the old religions, their aspects changed into mischievous imps and fairies. Like Dante's pilgrim, set about by malevolent forces, I descended into the unknown.

I came out suddenly into a glade. At its centre burned a fire, stoked by a young woman who possessed a hard kind of prettiness. She sang a coarse tavern ditty as she worked. Like a midwife attending her patient, she would sometimes press her hand against the big round belly of the stewing pot which hung over the fire. Then she would shake her head and feed twigs into the flames, the lights of which danced gaily against the sleeping trees.

The woman paid me no heed, and I was about to creep away when I felt a hand on my shoulder.

It is easy to say that, from the moment he touched me, I had a presentiment of Evil, but perhaps hindsight darkens my memory. He was a man of average height, slow and graceful in movement and voice. That is all I can tell you, for he wore a hood pulled low over his face. I gave my name and bowed.

'You have seen much,' he said, raising my face to the light, 'but you wear your learning as a fop wears the latest fashions; proud of how it looks to others, but having little comprehension of the subtlety of its stitching. You have a chance tonight, my fine chronicler, to understand something momentous, something exquisite.'

In other circumstances, I might have been insulted by his words, but dread had overwhelmed me. I had heard of these covens many times, and they were always most secret affairs. Orgies of depravity in which Lucifer was summoned and often appeared. There was little chance, I thought, that having witnessed this blasphemy I would be allowed to live. But he had called me 'chronicler'. What did that suggest?

'Time is short,' he said, taking my elbow and guiding me towards the fire. 'You must tell me quickly, what do you know of Metempsychosis?'

'I confess, I have not heard of it,' I replied.

'You surprise me,' he said, sarcastically. 'Well then, Metempsychosis is a rather ill-defined belief, with many variations the world over, but at its heart is the idea that a soul may be transferred between organisms at the point of death. Herodotus tells us that the Egyptians were the first to recognise it. Pythagoras instituted societies for the spreading of the belief. It was even accepted as a passage of new life by a few

Gnostic sects of the early Church. For years, I searched for a fabled book, often spoken of in the poetic accounts of the old philosophers, which contained a ritual of rebirth. A manual, if you will, describing a form of metempsychosis in which a man might, by design, transfer his soul into a new vessel. Two years ago, I found a copy of the volume in the private collection of an old Castilian cleric who had retired to Granada. He gave it up rather . . . unwillingly.'

His hood did not cover the lower half of his face, and I saw a smile play across his lips. It was as he reached into his robes, taking out a small book covered in what appeared to be dried pig's skin, that I noticed his fingernails. Long and sharp, those talons were, pitted and grooved, like well-worn bone.

'It is the *Ritual of the Transmigration of Souls*. To my knowledge, the rite has not been attempted in a millennia. It is your task to record it in a new gospel.'

'This is an affront to God,' I said.

'You are free to leave if you wish,' he replied.

Terrified as I was, my love of learning and spectacle would not allow me to flee the grove. Was it possible? Could a man truly eclipse one soul with another?

'Observe and learn, hypocrite,' my host laughed. 'You shall see that God has withered on the vine of mythology, like Pan and Odin before him. This world, which Man has tried to order, was thrown together in that firmament,' he pointed to the heavens, 'and there is nothing there but cold, dark chaos. No love, no compassion, just indifferent eternity. The universe does not care what we do here. It has a single lesson for us: Exist. At all costs, Exist.

Bring out the children.'

I had been so spellbound by this eulogy to the cosmos that his injunction shocked me out of a kind of trance. I had once seen a conjuror from the East mesmerise a serpent by playing a sweet harmony on his flute, and I wondered then whether my host's mellifluous tones had had a similar effect upon my own senses.

The young woman brought forth three ragged children

from the forest. They were bound together by the wrists, blindfolded, gagged and without clothes. I guessed the oldest to be perhaps thirteen; the youngest no more than ten. They were clearly peasant children. I noticed that they did not struggle as they entered the clearing. It was as if the will had been drained out of them and replaced with the unquestioning compliance of a dumb animal. At my host's instruction their blindfolds were removed.

The two younger boys were brutish-looking things, but the older was quite beautiful. As golden-haired and fair-faced as Paris. He seemed insensible, staring at us without expression as he was tethered to a tree. His two companions were lashed to stakes beside the fire. They were obviously very weak, and it was only when the pretty woman unsheathed her knife that they began to scream. Strident yelps, as a pig makes when its throat is to be slit.

'What do you mean to do?' I asked. 'For pity's sake, these are but children.'

'They are keys. Only keys,' my host said.

Circling behind the boys, the woman took her time with the initial selection. She examined her knife in the firelight, running her thumb along the belly of the blade. Satisfied with its sharpness, she approached one of the boys, hooked his ankles with her foot, grabbed a handful of hair, and thrust his head forward. She then grazed the tip of the knife along the length of his spine. Watching her, I was reminded of diviners using their rods to seek out underground springs. Whatever forces guided her, she made her choice. Slowly, by fractions of inches, she slipped the blade into the bucking child. Screams roared out of the clearing as the knife worried a route through sinew and puckered the awning of skin. The cries did not move her. She worked diligently, cutting three intersecting lines. Blood dripped from the hilt of her dagger and stained her snow-white hands. Weakened, the fight had left the boy, and he did no more than shudder and writhe like a fish expiring upon the deck. A grimace, worked by exhausted muscles, bunched his features, as the lady pushed her fingers into the cuts across his back and prised a hunk of meat loose. The boy saw his flesh passed before his eyes and fell in a dead faint against the post that held him.

The worst of it was the cold indifference with which the beautiful creature accomplished her work. If she was mad she might have enjoyed it; if she had a soul, she would have run in horror from it. As it was, her glacial eyes said: I do not care; these children are so much meat to me. As if to prove this point, she threw the flesh into the cauldron and watched as it roasted over the flames.

The other child had come to his senses. He pulled away from the stake so hard that his bonds cut into his wrists. When the woman approached, he kicked out at her and somehow managed to break free. In a flash, he was halfway to the woods. My heart raced with him, my spirit willing him to escape. Just as he reached the trees, however, the laughing coachman stepped across his path.

'What's your hurry, boy?' he said. 'Come warm yourself by the fire.'

With that, he struck the child hard in the temple. The boy staggered back, clutching his head. Picking up the little body as if it weighed no more than a feather pillow, the driver strode towards us. He threw the pitiful creature on the ground and the witch went to her work. Soon she was drenched in the blood of two innocents. She eased the last cut from the unconscious boy and threw it into the pot.

I began to weep. I looked down at my shoes and saw them red in the firelight. Blood was still pouring from the boy who had been delivered by the coachman, but the first child was now utterly drained. With his lips drawn back across his teeth, his eyes, pain-crinkled at their edges, it looked as if he were trying to imitate an aged man.

My host left me in the care of the driver, and approached the fire. The woman ladled the juices from the cooked child-flesh into an earthenware container. This she passed to her master.

'This is the viscous fluid of the sacrificed,' he said. 'I drink it, to take of their essence. To power the change.'

He tipped the jug to his mouth. I heard the fat sizzle against his lips.

'Bring the swaddling clothes,' he gargled.

The woman took a bundle of tattered cloth from the ground beside her and held it before him, as if she were paying homage.

'These are the clothes of the baptised dead,' he said. 'The dresses worn by the infant siblings of the sacrificed. They are burned to show my passage.'

He threw the dresses into the flames. Immediately, a strange black smoke rose from them. As if it had some conscious purpose, it curled around his form and did not dissipate into the night. It wound itself tight and then threaded out, snaking across the fire in a dense coil. It approached the fair child, who had remained so calm and glassy-eyed during the murder of his friends. With black fingers, the smoke probed his handsome face. At last the vapour touched his lips and flowed into his mouth. For the first time, a spark of intelligence showed in his eyes.

'Please,' he said. 'What's happening? Fingers touch inside me. They dirty me.'

His eyes surveyed the carnage before him: the unmoving corpse of the first, the still twitching form of the second. His mouth opened and closed, but no sound came forth. Without a word, my host went to the boy. He pulled back his hood and the child found his voice. From my viewpoint, I could not see the face that was revealed. I thanked God for that at least.

This man, this thing, then squatted down and, to my horror, began to tear at the child's breast. The attack was one of concentrated frenzy. Skin hung in tapering strips from those husk-like nails. The outer layer was soon breached. I could hear the rending of stronger tissue. Strands of dripping matter garlanded the monster's wrists and forearms. He cleaved ever deeper, ploughed into the secret flesh of the poor child, the hot blood he spilt steaming the air. He thrust the meat between

173

ravenous jaws, palming as much as he could into his swollen mouth. The boy, his lungs now unable to give vent to his cries, shivered violently. Something about the way he quaked spoke of a terrible finality. Even on the far side of fibres grove, I could make out the scrape of fingernails upon exposed bone. The inner frame of the child had been reached. Surely the madness must now draw to an end.

The sounds of slaughter aside, there was only the crackle of fire to be heard. The coachman had long since ceased his laughing. Only that black-souled woman continued to look on unaffectedly.

'Do it now.' The command was choked from a gorged mouth.

She did not hesitate. She crossed the glade, pulled back her master's head and swept the blade across his throat. My eyes were lowered, but I heard thick, guttural noises, like sucking mud on boots.

When I looked up the child was dead. His mouth gaped. A hole, rived from his chest, glistened darkly. Within it, I fancied I could see the white of rib-bone and the ruddy, unmoving sacs that were his lungs.

What devilry now, I thought. I was soon answered. In a single impossible collapse the body of my host crumbled to the ground. Nothing remained, except an exposed skull and skeleton and strips of grey skin that fluttered away in motes on the night air. At first I did not see the dull red light that burned low in the folds of his cloak. It rose, growing brighter as it ascended. I felt my soul shrink from it and my skin crawl as it bathed me. The little orb made straight for the dead child. It plunged into his mouth and I saw the back of his throat lit scarlet. There was stillness for a time. The fire cracked. The wind whispered. We waited.

The boy's eyes snapped open.

I had seen murder that night. I had seen cannibalism. I had seen depravity of the most wicked kind. But nothing chilled me so much as those beautiful eyes focusing again on the world. As I watched, the child's lungs inflated. Fibres laced

174

across the wound that had been rent out of his chest. He was whole. He was living.

The woman went to the boy, cut him loose and kissed him. The dead face smiled and he looked in my direction. He passed over his former body, kicking through the desiccation so that it powdered his feet. He stood before me. I almost cried, for I saw something infernal, impious, perverse and beautiful.

'Soon you shall return to the world and tell of this true resurrection.'

I had, of course, guessed the nature of this Godless creation, but still the rich tones of that voice harrowed up my blood. I fell to my knees, half in horror, half in worship.

TRANSLATOR'S NOTE: The anonymous author then goes on to describe how he was taken to a large chateau that rested in the saddle between two mountains, so that he could pen his 'testament'. The main features of the rite that I have drawn out are as follows:

1. Only the body of a child-spirit, on the cusp of adulthood, may be taken.

2. The order of the rite is not set in stone, but the following acts are essential: (i). the fat of two children must be consumed to power the possession. (ii). the baptism clothes must be burned to show the path into the child (the vessel). (iii). the spirit desirous of new life (the possessor) must partake of the vessel's flesh. (iv). the possessor's exhausted life must be ended.

3. After his death, the possessor has the grace of ten days in which to enter the vessel. After that time, his psychic substance will deteriorate to such an extent that possession is impossible, except in one unusual circumstance [see the ADDENDUM to this manuscript.]

4. To take advantage of any special gifts of the vessel, the possessor must first ensure those gifts have been fully realised by the vessel at the point of possession.

5. When possession is complete, the possessor cannot end

his new life by self-destruction. The life must either be taken by another or by natural decay. That said decay will be a living decomposition. A terrible rending of form and spirit.

'Dear me, Mr Trent.'

Through bleary eyes, Jack looked up from the text. The librarian was holding the hourglass.

'It appears that you have run out of time.'

'No, a little longer.' Jack's hand shot out towards the librarian in a pleading gesture. Papers flew off the table. 'There's more to read. An addendum . . .'

The monk tapped the hourglass' empty chamber.

'Terms and conditions, Mr Trent.'

'No. I can't stay here. I have to go. Please, I have to save the boy.'

'As I read the situation, Jack, you have things somewhat upside down. Much better for you to remain within these walls. Out of reach. Out of Time . . .'

TUESDAY 29th OCTOBER 2002

Behold, I shew you a mystery;
We shall not all sleep, but we shall all be changed.
I Corinthians 15:51

The Doctor will see you now.
Oliver Godfrey, *Post Mortem*

Twenty-six

Jamie had been awake for two nights straight. His eyes ached for sleep, but whenever he closed them he saw terrible things: a chalk-white face in the half-light of a forest; an axe head cleaving through skin and bone; a little boy called Simon drawing a picture for his dead father. And blood, washing down centuries.

He wanted to tell his mum and grandad. But tell them what? That he was scared shitless to close his eyes? That he had seen something on that little bridge that had made him piss his pants, but he couldn't remember what it was? They'd think he was cracked. Before you could say 'I'd like pink polka dot pyjamas, please, and a warm milk for my invisible friend', two Lurch-like attendants would be locking the padded cell.

He was dozing. Had to stay awake. He switched on the TV.

Jack had taken him to a retrospective of fifties sci-fi movies at the old ABC in the summer. In one sitting, they'd watched spooky kids with pudding-basin haircuts in *Village of the Damned*, giant atomic ants devastating LA in *Them!* and the ET robot from *The Day the Earth Stood Still*, who could only be stopped by the command 'Klaatu barada nikto'. The old black and white, just starting on the TV, had been his favourite: one man's fight against listless pod-people in *Invasion of the Body Snatchers*.

The film's hero, Dr Miles Bennel, slammed on the brakes to avoid the kid who'd run out into the road. As Bennel and the boy's grandmother talked on the dusty track to Santa Mira,

Jamie's mind wandered to the third row of the ABC. He longed to be back in that musty theatre now, with its hard seats, sticky floors and the soft, flickering light beam overhead. And Jack, sitting next to him, nudging him at the good bits. It was a safe, warm memory.

He was so sleepy . . . The Sandman sprinkled his dust . . .

And then Jamie was wide awake again.

Something had jarred in that last sliver of consciousness before sleep took hold. Something in the room? At the window? His eyes darted and focused at last on the TV. Dr Bennel had got back into his car and roared away but the picture had not switched to the next scene: Bennel's surgery. The empty highway, with the regiment of telephone poles stretching into the distance, was frozen on screen. *Must be a technical fault*, Jamie thought. But the soundtrack still played, looping the rustle of the wind through the trees and the scuttle of grit on the road. Jamie blinked. Surely it was just an imperfection in the film. No, it was moving. A tiny dot coming down the road. A man, his head swaying rhythmically. As it approached, the shape of the figure became clearer: a bone-thin body wrapped in tattered clothes.

Jamie snatched for the remote. It slipped through his fingers and fell under the bed. He wanted to dive after it, but found he could not move. The shadows of the celluloid trees glanced over its withered form as the scarecrow-figure came fully into view. It stopped inches from the screen and blocked out the road behind. Beneath its hat, Jamie could see a scarred mouth tense into a smile. The scarecrow's voice crackled through the speakers:

'Don't worry, Jamie. Later you won't remember. Later you'll think: it was just a movie.'

A maggot crawled between the cracks in the monochrome face. Then it pushed out into three dimensions and writhed on the surface of the screen.

'Just a movie.'

The maggot plopped onto the floor and rolled there, fat

and white. Identical gyrating bodies grew from the television until the screen was filled. Squeezing between the maggots came other creatures: beetles, spiders, centipedes, bluebottles, locusts. Below the TV, a carpet of exoskeleton and carapace formed and crawled out towards the bed. The mass buzzed and hissed, mating and devouring, as it moved like a dark battalion across the floor. An advance guard of mosquitoes landed on the counterpane. Jamie tried to swat them away. He managed, with a huge effort, to flick the fingers of his right hand. The mosquitoes took off, only to circle and come back, fixing him with tiny red eyes. Now the swarm was creeping across the bed. It tickled along his arms, up his chest, and rolled over his chin. Still Jamie could not move.

'Just a movie.'

The hum of the fricative choir grew louder. Then the sound became at once intimate and muted as tiny forms skittered into his ears. Soft and hard, smooth and barbed, they fanned out across his body. They crawled between his toes, slipped between his buttocks, chattered in the forest of his hair. He felt their wetness, like miniature tongues, slip into the folds of his skin. Legs scampered through his pubic hair and mouths bedded deep into his penis. He whimpered, but could not brush them away. His hands were dead weights at his sides. A spider strained across his face, hefting a sac of eggs behind it. This webbed womb raked over the jelly of Jamie's eye.

'Just a movie.'

A sea of black flooded into his nose and mouth. He swallowed, and felt a large insect curl up and drown in his throat. Pinpricks of pain fired across his body. Wings, massed with tiny veins, cloaked his eyes. Something must have traversed the chambers of his ear and reached his brain. It was the final horror, that alien presence probing the tissue of his mind.

'Just a . . .'

He could no longer hear, no longer feel. His senses gone, all he could do was lie there, encased in an undulating cocoon. These things would soon devour him; strip his flesh to the bone. But before that, he would become a nest. A place to feed and breed, in which to eat and, in turn, to be eaten.

Jamie thought of his mum and his grandad. He thought of Jack Trent, who might have saved him. And then there was nothing left to think. He gave himself up to the inevitable.

'Wake up, Sir. You say you found him like this?'

'You came round the corner just as I laid eyes on him, Constable.'

'Hmm. Doesn't look like a tramp. Do you get many of those?'

'In the gateway some nights,' the porter said, thumbing the brim of his bowler and scratching his temple. 'Not laid over the Master's parking space.'

The man, sprawled across the tarmac of Jericho's private car park, was lying on his stomach, his hair jewelled with frost. His hands were covered in what looked like brick dust. In fact, there was a layer of dust all over his head and clothes, as if he had stumbled through a building site. Beside his lips stood a puddle of oil-like fluid. The man stirred.

'The sands ran out,' he said, pushing against the tarmac to raise himself.

'I'll get 'im a blanket from the lodge,' said the porter.

The man's coat, half-frozen, cracked as he eased himself onto all-fours. Dust rained across the reserved car port which had been his bed for the night. Dawling helped him to his feet.

'Now, Sir, had a bit of an adventure, did you? Want to tell me . . . Jesus Christ.'

The stranger, who Dawling now realised was no stranger at all, blinked in the light that had just touched the spire of the Watching Tower.

'I was out of time. I thought I'd . . . How did I get out?'

'I don't know, Sir. I think it's best if you come with me. We'll get you some breakfast.'

'No. I have to see somebody.'

Dawling put a restraining arm on the man's shoulder, but

he twisted loose. The constable stumbled backwards and tripped over the little porter. He heard the clatter of the gate.

'What were you doing, creeping around behind me?'

'I'm sorry,' the porter said, meekly. 'I see our friend has escaped. Ah, well, only a vagabond. Didn't outstay his welcome here at least.'

Dawling grunted, opened his notebook and scribbled: *Insp Trent - found sleeping rough - J College - 0700 hrs.*

Jamie ate his cereal in front of the TV. He seemed engrossed by the discussion of Chelsea's chances of overthrowing the Manchester/Arsenal domination of the Premier League. He looked very pale and Dawn asked if he felt unwell. 'M'fine,' he muttered.

'I don't think he's up to school,' Tom Howard said, as she packed Jamie's lunch.

'For God's sake, Dad, it's probably just his hormones.'

As she watched her father grow smaller in the wing mirror, Dawn began to 'tidy her mind'. First off then, Jamie had nothing to do with this case. Common sense insisted that, whatever was concerning Jack about her son, it was a separate business to the murder of Oliver Godfrey and disappearance of Simon Malahyde. Secondly, the picture she found yesterday was exactly what Jack had said it was: a present for the father Simon never knew. Thirdly, nothing was wrong with Jamie. It *was* hormones.

She turned to check the oncoming traffic. Jamie was staring at the 'End is Nigh' evangelist preaching on the opposite side of the street. *Staring, but not seeing*, Dawn thought. The horn of the coach behind wailed.

'Okay to go, Mum,' Jamie said. His eyes were sharp, his voice normal.

They arrived at the school. He was getting out of the car when Dawn touched his arm.

'You're all right, aren't you, J?'

His head lowered. All she could see was the hood of his Parka. The school bell sounded. A huge-breasted teacher clucked around the playground, gathering up the children. Jamie looked up.

'Please, Mum, I want to see Jack. I need to.'

'But J, I . . .'

'Jamie! Hey spacka, you weirdin' out again today? Oh, hello, Mrs Howard.'

A ginger-haired boy, who Dawn remembered from football practice, dragged her son away. To her surprise, Jamie fell into animated conversation and did not look back.

He's fine, she told herself. *Everything's fine.*

'Where the fuck is he, Dawn?'

DCI Jarski was at Jack's desk, rifling through papers.

'I don't know. What on earth are you doing?'

'Let me tell you something that may have slipped your notice, Sergeant: This is a murder investigation. Two kiddies dead *and* the press sticking to me like chewing gum to the cat. I told Jack I wanted a full report this morning, including this crackpot priest idea of his. I've got nada, so I'm looking for his notes. You know what? There are none.'

'Two? What do you mean two?'

'Am I running this case solo now? Have you even checked in with the Incident Room downstairs? Found, this morning, on the playing grounds near Renton.'

Jarski tossed her two black and white enlargements. Taken from different angles, they both depicted the severed head of a young boy. In the first picture, the left side of the kid's face was resting in the churned earth between two goalposts, so that only the right eye could be seen, staring low across the ground. In the second, the head had been rolled over. Dawn found it difficult to pick out the cherubic features of Stephen Lloyd from the pulped mass that filled the close-up.

'Before we found him, I had a call from his folks,' Jarski said. 'I was ready to give you a bollocking about needlessly upsetting the public, but it seems you and Trent were on to something there. That alone, Dawn, is your saving grace. You and weirdo boy are fucking good. But don't push it.'

'Don't push it?' Dawn snapped. 'This is getting beyond a joke. I think I'd rather you give the case to Mescher; then at least I wouldn't have to hear your constant whining.'

'Talking of Mescher,' Jarski looked up from the paperwork and pointed to the chair opposite. 'He brought PC Dawling to see me this morning. Now, *I'm* going to tell you what Dawling found lying around like a fucking hobo in the grounds of Jericho College at seven a.m. Then *you're* going to tell me what's going on with Jack.'

Crow Haven Primary School. Opened 5th September 1850.
In Memory of those teachers and children who lost their lives in the fire of 1848.
'Sleep after toil, port after stormy seas
Ease after war, death after life, does greatly please'.

A streak of bird shit had crusted over the stone plaque. Jack spat on his handkerchief and rubbed hard until only a faint outline remained. From inside the building came the hesitant chant of children reciting their times tables. It sounded almost religious, like a group of novices intoning mass for the first time. He was trying again to remember how he had escaped from the Yeager Library last night, when a voice interrupted his thoughts.

'The fire was started deliberately, but the culprit was never found.'

A figure pushed through the glass entrance doors. In its wake, Jack caught that smell of damp coats, boiled vegetables and cheap disinfectant so redolent of school. The woman, probably in her fifties, had shoulder-length grey hair and a confident brusqueness of manner.

'I would love to have seen the old schoolhouse,' she continued. 'It was built here with the town, you know? Sixteen hundred and forty-two.'

'It was completely destroyed?' Jack asked.

'You can still find the odd brick in the forest, I believe. Strange how that happens, isn't it? How the corpse of a building can spread out, as if the fabric of the place was returning somewhere. Still, the old school, like the town, didn't have the happiest of histories. Perhaps whoever burned it down thought that he was purging the place. I'm not sure the children had to die, though . . . So, Mr Trent,' she said. 'I believe it's time I introduced you to Simon Malahyde.'

Twenty-seven

'Father Brody wants you to hear my story, though I don't care to relive it.'

The wall behind Geraldine Pryce's desk was a riot of colour. Plastered across every available inch, the children's pictures lit up the room. They struck a discordant note with the austere Victorian furniture and pocked, industrial grey paintwork. On her desk sat a mug with *World's Best Teacher - Florida* printed in faded gold letters. *It should look hokey*, Jack thought. But, because it was hers, it didn't.

'He's contacted you?' Jack asked.

'Last night.'

'And you didn't think to report it?'

'Mr Trent, I believe, from what Asher Brody told me, that you understand this business. You know Asher is a good man.'

'I don't know anything of the kind. I just want to know what he has to tell me. And quickly.'

'I think he's preparing you. Perhaps it's like viewing the Bayeux Tapestry without knowing what it depicts. You can guess at what might be happening in it, but if you don't know the history, the people, then you'll be asking yourself, 'Why're they fighting?' and 'Who's the chap with the arrow in his eye?' It's possible that you already see the tapestry of this story, but the why escapes you.'

'All right, Miss Pryce,' Jack sighed. 'Paint me a picture.'

The playtime bell rang through the corridors. A wall of noise raced past the headmistress' door: feet stomping, excited chatter, calls of 'Quietly!' 'Slow down!' and once an exhausted

'Jesus, I need a fag'. Then everything was still. Geraldine Pryce began.

Her words washed over him. He was so tired. The story Geraldine told played out like a film in his head . . .

Crow Haven: September 1984 – January 1985

Over the long summer holiday, Arabella Nugent, seventy-three-year-old headmistress of the Crow Haven Primary School, received notice terminating her employment. She seemed to take it very well, chatting about ideas for her newfound leisure time: planning an herbaceous border; re-reading *Middlemarch* and other big fat classics; brewing her own cherry brandy.

She was found, a week later, dead in her bathtub. She had clipped her wrists with a pair of secateurs.

The note she left was short and to the point. She saw no reason to go on without her work and her children. '*The little ones occupied my thoughts. Kept me from thinking about that which we never mention. I had hoped to be treated better, bearing in mind the things I know. But rest easy, Crow Haven. Arabella knows her duty. She shall take it all to the grave*'. There were no questions raised at the inquest about the meaning of the letter, and a verdict of suicide while the balance of her mind was unsettled was recorded.

In the last week of the holidays, Geraldine Pryce arrived in the village. Because it had been a last minute appointment, there was a great deal to organise. She did not have an opportunity to meet the villagers until the beginning of the school year. As it turned out, she was surprised to discover that there were only twenty children from Crow Haven who attended the school. The eighty or so other pupils came from neighbouring villages. From the first school day, Geraldine was struck by a marked difference between those pupils native to Crow Haven and the outsiders. The two groups mixed only when instructed to do so, and seemed to be always suspicious of each other. It was not unusual, in her experience, to find that kids new to school preferred the company of children from their own area. Once a child feels secure, however, he or she will usually spread their circle wider. Not so here. The reason may have been that some of the Crow Haven children possessed a strange kind of deformity.

Geraldine could not put her finger on any specific malformation. Nevertheless, there was an impression of abnormality in some of their faces that she found quite disturbing. Sometimes it seemed that she was looking at those little Crow Havenites as if in an old mirror, its surface mottled and warped. And then the spell would be broken. She would see that they were just children after all. Somewhat pale perhaps, but not monstrous. No, not monstrous.

At the end of the first week, Geraldine fell into conversation with a mother from New Gransham.

'If there was any other school local, I'd send my Jules there,' the mother sniffed. 'The kids are weird in Crow Haven. Everyone knows it.'

When Geraldine tried to remonstrate, the mother gave her a pitying look:

'You'll know soon enough, Miss Pryce. Look at 'em over there.'

The Crow Haven children were gathered together in a solemn huddle in a corner of the playground.

'Things happen here. Even them bairns know, but there ain't one of 'em that'll tell.'

For the next month, due to the organised chaos left by Miss Nugent (more chaos than organisation, actually), she barely had a chance to explore her new home. She had rented a house on the outskirts of the village, her nearest neighbour being the *Old Priory*, and had only ventured into 'civilisation' for little shopping trips. Completing her lesson plans one uncomfortably warm evening, she decided to take a walk in the woods.

As she crossed the Conduit Road, a car came skidding around the corner and sent her reeling into the undergrowth. There was a screech of tyres and the opening and slamming of car doors.

'I'm so sorry. Are you hurt? Don't move. Anne, get a

189

blanket from the boot.'

'I'm all right. But, dear God. If a child had been . . .'

'Gerry? Bloody hell, it is you.'

It didn't take long to place the voice. She had not seen Peter Malahyde in years. Not since university in fact. They had both studied law at Bristol from '62 - '65. She had thought of him a few times since then. More than he had thought of her, she guessed. In their first year they'd 'had something', but things had not ended well. She'd had one too many drinks and slept with his best friend. He had not been angry, that wasn't his style, but afterwards he treated her as unworthy of his attention. After graduation, she had sent him a few postcards, but they went unanswered. He seemed much more cordial now.

'Gerry Pryce, who'd've thunk it? Oh, I'm sorry. This is Annie, my wife.'

A beautiful, pale young girl walked towards them, a tartan blanket folded over her arms. Peter must have caught the slight frown that furrowed Geraldine's brow.

'I know, young enough to be my daughter. Dirty old man and all that. Look, sorry about this, we're in a bit of a rush. Meant to be having the local clergy round for a drink. Why don't you come with us?'

'You live around here?'

'Just moved in last week. Come on, it'll be good to catch up.'

As Geraldine followed Peter and his young wife to the car, she noticed the bump straining against the girl's low-cut shirt. Again, Peter must have followed her gaze.

'My first born,' he said, cupping his wife's stomach. 'You better be a boy.'

Anne gave a thin smile and, without a word, ducked into the back seat.

'No, Anne, sit up front with Peter, you shouldn't ride in the back,' Geraldine said.

'She's fine, Gerry. Hop in.'

By the time they reached the gate in the woods, Geraldine

had been brought more or less up to date with Peter's life. After university, he had tried his hand at a few occupations: solicitor, timeshare operator, copywriter. Then his father had died. The hated patriarch had not carried out his repeated promises to cut his son out of his will ('He used to call me a grey sheep. Said I didn't have the balls to be black.'). There was just short of a million tied up in numerous portfolios, yielding comfortable annual dividends, shares in a cup-winning race horse, and a beautiful house, which his father had thrown in as an afterthought it seemed.

'You always were a lucky bastard, Peter,' Geraldine said as they pulled up before the gate. 'Good Lord, are those to guard your stores of treasure?'

'Annie doesn't like them, do you Annie?'

Peter jumped out of the car and swung back the gate. He looked up at the three praying figures sitting on the apex of the frame.

'They're coming to get you, Annie.'

He stalked back to the car. Reaching Anne's window, he grimaced and gurned, pressing his face to the glass. Geraldine laughed, until she saw that Anne was paying no attention. The girl's eyes were fixed on the lime-green effigies. Now that Geraldine looked at them, they *were* rather sinister. Their bodies contorted as if in great pain. Their mouths, open a fraction too wide, appeared to scream rather than intone prayers. For a moment, she had the absurd impression that there were tears running down their faces, but surely it was only dew against those metallic cheeks.

'Is that the house?' Geraldine asked as they cleared the trees. 'Peter, it's beautiful.'

Beautiful, yes, but not happily situated. It did not seem to Geraldine that the sleek art deco structure, so calculated and synthetic, sat well in its surroundings. Those long windows should be reflecting a snow-capped serration of the Alps, or a flat glassy lake in Switzerland. It would be at home with those clean, sure lines of Nature as it was not here, amongst these trees that seemed to bend and twist into shapes that the eye could not follow.

'Do you know much about this area, Gerry?'

Geraldine helped Anne from the car as Peter strode up to the house.

'No, I really haven't had time, my predecessor left things rather . . .'

'It's my new hobby. Local history. I need a pastime, now I'm a man of leisure.'

This did not surprise Geraldine. Whenever she thought of Peter, she had the image of a magpie in mind. His interests were always varied and short-lived: Australasian politics, rock bands, vintage cars, the history of the Commedia dell'arte. But he would only light on the shiny surface of these subjects. Once the 'pop' veneer was scratched away, he would become bored and move on to a new obsession.

'I've researched the surrounding area, but can't find much on Crow Haven. I know it was once marshland but not much else. The odd thing is,' he opened the door and ushered them in, 'I tried to find out about the guy who built this place - yes, through to the lounge - drew a complete blank. He bought the land in '75, had the house built, and that charming gate Annie loves so much, and moved in early '76. Lived here alone until the spring when, hey presto, he up and vanished.'

Geraldine blinked in the glare of the brilliant-white room. She sat down on one of the three white leather sofas, amid storeys of packing cases.

'Please, Peter,' Anne murmured. 'I don't want to talk about that.'

Geraldine had thought Anne was in her early twenties, but her voice sounded younger. *She may be no more than seventeen* . . . Geraldine glanced from that pretty, sullen face to Peter's. He looked his forty years, and the little sneer that played around his lips did not improve his appearance. Geraldine wondered whether Anne was anything more than another 'project', which he would tire of soon enough.

'My father bought the house from a charity,' Peter

continued. 'The missing guy's heirs must have given it away, can you believe that? Are you making tea, darling? She's a peach. I met her at a shitty little fundraiser for leukaemia research. She was a waitress. Didn't have a penny. Ignorant as a newborn . . .'

'Peter, don't say things like that . . .'

'It's alright, I'm broadening her mind. Books and plays and things.'

'So, what's this about the local clergy popping round?' Geraldine said, irritated.

'Father Brody. Called a few weeks back.'

'What an honour. I haven't had sight nor sound of him, and he's my nearest neighbour.'

'Well, you're a heathen interloper, aren't you, Gerry. I did mention to him that I was thinking about reaffirming my faith.'

'Project number three,' Geraldine whispered.

'What? Oh, wait a bit, I didn't tell you about the *room*, did I? Well, dear old Dad never bothered coming here. Said it was just an investment. So no-one's actually occupied the house since our Mystery Man disappeared. I gave it the once over when I got here. There's this door on the second floor. On the plans it's one big room. I've tried all the keys, the door won't open. I'm gonna take a sledgehammer to it tomorrow . . .'

'May I suggest a little caution, Mr Malahyde?'

A large bear of a man stood in the doorway. He had a tired, grizzled appearance, but his grey eyes were alert and focused on Peter. Beneath his short beard sat a roman collar.

'Father Brody?' Peter asked, getting up and greeting his guest.

'I apologise for my lateness,' Father Brody said. 'Mr Malahyde, I wonder if you would like me to bless the house? It would involve short prayers at the doors to all the rooms. It would take no time at all.'

'Well . . . That's to say, yes, I suppose, if . . . Is this quite usual?' Peter asked.

'Every house has bad memories. It is a habit of mine to do this service for my new parishioners. Starts a young family off with a clean slate, you understand?'

The priest was lying; Geraldine was sure of it. Not about wanting to bless the house, his abrupt question had shown a strange anxiety in that regard. It was his reasons that rang hollow, though she could not say why.

'Well . . . That sounds grand, Father. By the way, do you know Geraldine Pryce?'

'Miss Nugent's replacement? We're neighbours, I believe?'

'And this is Annie, my wife.'

Geraldine wondered how long Anne had been waitressing before she met Peter. The tea things clattered about on the tray as she handed out cups and saucers.

'You'll have to baptise our kid when the little chap comes along, Father,' Peter said.

Geraldine noticed Brody's lips twitch at their edges as he raised his cup.

'We were discussing the history of Crow Haven,' she said. 'How long have you been here, Father?'

'Eight years.'

'That's about the time this place was built, wasn't it? Did you know the owner?'

'I knew him, yes.'

'Well, don't keep us in suspense,' Peter said. 'There must be lots of local theories. What happened to him? Aliens, I reckon, or tax fraud. What was it?'

'He is gone, Mr Malahyde. Just gone,' Brody said, and would not be drawn further.

It was nearing sunset when Brody offered to walk Geraldine back to her cottage. During the afternoon, he had proved to be a dour, monosyllabic guest, speaking little about himself and his parish. Now, however, as they walked beneath the trees towards the gate, he seemed to want to talk.

'You know Mr Malahyde well?' he asked.

'Not well, no. We were at university together. I've not seen him in years.'

'I'm not sure it was wise for him to have brought his wife here. She's very young. I'm sure she'll find it quite tiresome to be cooped up in the middle of nowhere.'

'She will do as Peter tells her, I expect.'

'And a baby on the way,' Brody continued, as if he hadn't heard her bitterness.

They moved closer together as they passed through the gate. Geraldine felt the priest shudder and noticed that he kept his eyes on the path. Overhead, the sun glanced through the treetops, gilding the leaves so that it appeared they burned with dying embers.

'So who was the mysterious builder of the house?' she asked.

'Names,' Brody said, quickening his pace. 'I was told once to mistrust them.'

Jack leaned forward in his chair, his tiredness banished by Geraldine Pryce's tale.

'So, my new, rather eccentric friend saw me to my door,' Miss Pryce said, topping up Jack's coffee, 'and I didn't think much more about him. I was very busy with the new school term, and didn't have a chance to visit Peter and Anne for a few weeks. By the time I saw Peter again, he had opened the door and was already dying.'

Twenty-eight

Dawn left Jack's office. Inside her mind, questions clamoured for answers. Some of them were her own, some echoes from DCI Jarski's heated inquisition. Where was Jack? Was he on drugs? Did he drink? Why would he sleep rough in a college car park? Was he in some kind of trouble? What was wrong with him? What was the nature of their relationship? And to each, especially the last, she had to answer: I don't know.

She decided to drive out to Crow Haven. For the moment, she could make no sense of Jack's behaviour and, for the sake of her own sanity, she felt the need for a diversion. In any case, it was time she spoke to Father Garret again.

She pulled up outside the Old Priory, and was halfway along the drive before she saw the figure crumpled against the door. He was conscious when she reached him, but his breathing came in irregular gasps.

'I'm fine, I'm fine,' Garret kept repeating. 'Just help me to the house.'

Dawn got her arm under him and heaved. Yellow fingers clutched at her shoulder.

'The key. My trousers.'

With some difficulty, she managed to slip two fingers into his pocket. During her time in uniform, she had been flashed at, vomited over and urinated on countless times. It had been necessary to develop an unemotional response to these incidents. The bulge of Garret's testicle against her forefinger, however, was the first unwanted physical contact in years that made her feel sick.

She opened the door and guided him to the study. He fell into a chair and pointed at the scotch decanter.

'Let me get you an ambulance,' she said, passing him his drink.

She picked up the phone but he laid a clammy hand over hers.

'There's nothing they can do. I have brain cancer. A virulent strain, so my doctor tells me. I am . . . what's the saying? Ah, yes, up the proverbial creek without the proverbial paddle. I don't even think I have a canoe,' Garret laughed. 'I'm drowning in it.'

Dawn could detect no hint of self-pity. A scathing inner voice sneered: *How brave he is, to face death alone. Who are you to be repulsed by him?*

'Nothing can be done,' he continued. 'I've had all the tests. I won't have chemo. Not because I'm a man of God and hate science, or because I don't want to lose my hair; I'm too oddly shaped to be vain. I want to be clear-headed at the end. And I have an insurance policy, you see?'

'Your faith.'

'Yes. Faith in the endurance of the soul, as reward for services rendered.'

'Are you sure I shouldn't take you to hospital?'

'Quite sure. 'Hell hath no limits' but science does, I'm afraid. Now, what can I do for you, Sergeant?'

'You heard Inspector Trent's appeal on the television last night?'

'I don't watch television. I was reading. Macbeth:

Light thickens; and the crow makes wing to the rooky wood.
Good things of day begin to droop and drowse;
While night's black agents to their preys do rouse.'

'Yes. Well, we believe that there is a connection between the disappearance of Simon Malahyde and the murder of two young boys.'

'How dreadful. Upon what is this connection based?'

'A personal item of Simon's was found beside the body of a boy named Oliver Godfrey. It appeared to have been dropped there.'

'I see.'

'As far as we can establish, the boys didn't know each other. No shared interests, they attended different schools, one lived in the city, the other in the countryside. But there are points of connection. They both had siblings who died in infancy; they must both have arranged to meet their killer, because they took their dead siblings' baptism dresses with them. And they both had a connection with the Church. What I want to know is, does anything strike you about how the killer might have targeted them?'

'Well, as far as the deaths of the siblings are concerned, there are church records of course.'

'Do the public have access to them?'

'Officially, no, though I have to confess that I leave my own lying about the church.'

'Can you imagine any reason why two Catholic boys would be singled out?'

'That's surely something in the line of abnormal psychology,' Garret said, pouring himself another drink. 'A grudge against the Church? I don't know.'

'Or maybe it was for reasons of convenience,' Dawn said. 'Assuming the murderer doesn't have a fixation on Catholic boys, what are we left with? Someone who kills Catholic boys because they are easy targets for him. He has a way of knowing who they are, what they are like, what families they come from. That suggests someone who is part of the local Catholic community. Is there a diocese magazine that would include articles about young people in the Church?'

'*The Good News Gazette.*'

'And that would be sent to Catholic hospices, retirement homes . . . ?'

'Free of charge.'

'That leads me to my second question. I think you may

198

have omitted to tell us something about Father Asher Brody.'

Jamie skived both first and second periods. He had been sitting in a cubicle for the best part of two hours, staring at patterns of ghostly graffiti. Each morning Mr McGregor, the caretaker, would scrub away at the doors, but traces always remained. Jamie now took a strange comfort from this everyday cycle of filthy scrawls and harsh bleach. It was predictable. It was *real*. He rested his head against the cold plywood partition and asked:

What the fuck's wrong with me?

Sophie Antmar would say it was a tumour. That was her explanation whenever someone acted out of character. It was probably because her mum had died from a tumour when she was little. Maybe it was a tumour pressing down on his brain, fucking up that area where memory was stored. After all, he couldn't for the life of him remember what had happened on Sunday behind his grandad's house, or what had happened last night in his bedroom. There were only two impressions growing in his mind, though he could make little sense of them. The first was visual: the Scarecrow, the Batman villain who terrorized all Gothamites with his toxic nerve gas. The other was emotional: a senseless desperation. It had begun as a niggle, no more powerful than the guilt of putting off homework. Now he found it hard to hear his own thoughts above the cries in his head:

You must see Jack. He will save you . . . Save me? From what? From what you saw. From what waits for you on the bridge . . .

The door at the far end of the lavatory block sighed open. It was probably Mr McGregor doing a skiver inspection. He waited for the high Glaswegian voice to shriek: 'Ah ken spy y'ah tootsies, boy.' Instead there came a quick burst of teacher's-out-of-the-room-chatter from a nearby classroom. Then, with a pneumatic hiss, the door clicked shut.

Pipes clanked and urinal sprays spluttered and whooshed. No sounds came from the newcomer. Jamie swallowed hard.

The hum of the tube lighting overhead stammered. In a series of *plinks*, the lights switched off, one by one. Splodges of bleach-layered graffiti shone in the sudden gloom.

Darkness and silence. And then a scraping sound, as of someone dragging their nails across a blackboard, screeched along the cubicle doors. It was not Mr McGregor. Jamie glanced up at the frosted windows above the partition. A black shape fluttered against the glass and perched on the sill. From the playing fields came the pip of Mr Grayes' whistle and cries of 'Foul! Cheating bastard!' Through the wall behind him, Jamie could hear Fuckface Fosker's monotone drone. For the first time in his life, he wished he was taking notes on the causes of coastal erosion.

He is here. *Who . . . ?* He *who whispers to you.*

Jamie tucked up his legs and held his knees to his chest. He shuffled along the seat until his back rested against the cistern. The urinal sprays fizzled out and the water glugged away. Below the door, a lean shadow glided across the floor. Jamie knew that your shoes could be as clean as the Queen's arse, but you always left a mark on those piss-gleaming tiles. There were no marks, however, because *He* did not walk.

Those scraping nails reached Jamie's cubicle and tapped upon the door. *Tick-Tick-Tick.* And at their insistence the boy felt a tickle at the back of his throat. He gagged and coughed up something wriggling and black. The beetle rolled onto its back, legs kicking, mandibles pinching at the sputum that coated its body. Suddenly, Jamie saw himself lying on his bed, woven inside a living husk. He remembered the chatter in his ears, against the lobes of his brain. He remembered the taste of pupa, the crunch of carapace, the sting of probosces and pulse of larvae. And he remembered the certainty of death that had overtaken him.

A voice rasped, 'Let's play a gamey, Jamie.'

His mum used to say that. *Let's play a gamey, Jamie . . .*

'Please . . . please go away.'

Tick-Tick-Tick

'Open up. It's your old uncle Funnyface come to call.'

'No. Fuck off . . . Please, just . . .'

'Now, now. There's only one person who can make me go away, and he's not here. It's time we had a little face to face, Jamie. You remember my face, don't you? Once seen never forgotten, eh?'

Jamie's bladder gave way. Piss soaked through his trousers and dribbled over the toilet seat. The flow stung his hands, but he did not – *could not* – move. There was a click as the lock snapped up of its own accord.

'Oh, yes, I'll let you see me one more time. Just once more before the end. When next we meet I'll be picking your flesh from between my teeth.'

Fingers, as twisted and brittle as twigs, arched around the door. A rotting stink began to overpower the brew of shit and piss and bleach.

The door opened. A foot fell upon the beetle, cracked it apart and smeared its soft insides across the tiles.

'Time for a little screaming, I think.'

Twenty-nine

' . . . so, as I said, I hardly looked up from my desk for a month,' Geraldine Pryce continued. 'But as busy as I was, I was growing more aware of the uniqueness, for want of a better word, of Crow Haven. It seemed to exist in a kind of vacuum. Outside events did not register in the consciousness of its inhabitants. I was in the post office the day the IRA bombed the Tory conference and happened to mention it. Blank faces all round. During the years I've lived here, I have never heard a villager speak of news from the outside. Tianaman Square, Diana, September 11th: these things don't penetrate Crow Haven. It has enough of its own tragedy, I suppose. Anyway, it was the day after the conference bombing, actually. I was feeling unwell . . .'

Crow Haven: October 1984 – January 1985

Two days before, Geraldine had found a small, hard lump beneath her left breast. Tests would later show that it was benign. Within weeks it had been removed. On that October morning, however, she had been sick with fear. By the time she reached the surgery, she was finding it hard to keep the terror out of her voice.

'Miss Pryce, to see Dr Hathaway.'

'Take a seat, Miss Pryce.'

The receptionist beamed. Geraldine recognised that wide, faintly patronising smile as one that she might use herself fifty times during an average school day. *I don't want to be humoured and I don't want to wait,* she screamed inwardly. *Will they take my breast? I'm very plain, not womanly at all, but don't take my breast.*

She told herself to stop being silly. But already her femininity felt like it was slipping away. She looked across at the paragon of womanhood sitting opposite. Golden hair, sensuously bowed lips, full breasts. The girl seemed to notice eyes on her body. Flustered, Geraldine recognised the young woman.

'Anne. I'm sorry, I didn't see you there. Funny how that happens at the doctor's. So wrapped up in our little ailments, we look right through people.'

Anne Malahyde drew her cardigan around her and slouched in the seat. Geraldine was anxious to explain why she had been ogling the girl, but could not frame the excuse. They sat in silence. In the moments that followed, Geraldine's embarrassment gave way to a prickly irritation. Surely the child wasn't so stupid as to believe . . . She must ask Anne a question, or she might say something regrettable.

'Are you here for a prenatal check-up? You're over the morning sickness, I hope?'

'Peter's ill.'

'Really? What's the matter . . .'

'Nappy rash, I'm afraid,' Peter broke in. 'Hello, Gerry. Better not kiss me.'

The other patients in the waiting room each found something to become engrossed in as Peter came out. Geraldine couldn't blame them. His face glowed bright with ointment but beneath the balm, his skin was peeling badly. Boils and sores rimmed his hairline and the corners of his eyes.

'Good Lord, Peter, what's happened to you?'

'They think it's a rather nasty form of psoriasis. We've just got back from the Seychelles, but three weeks laying about didn't seem to help. We're seeing a specialist tomorrow. I only came to this quack for something to relieve the itching. How are you, Gerry? Not seen you since I ran you down.'

'School's been murder. I promise I'll visit soon.'

'Good girl. By the way, did you hear about poor old Brody? Had a heart attack. Only a warning, thank God . . .'

Despite her promise, Geraldine did not see Peter for another three weeks. Ten days after her appointment, she received the all-clear, but she could not set her mind at ease until the growth had been removed. Dozens of times a day, leading up to the operation, she would feel the small, hard pebble in her breast and convince herself that it had grown. Doctors, after all, were always making mistakes.

In fact, during this time, she didn't give Peter a second thought. But a few days after the operation, when the world fell back into place, she decided to honour her promise. It was now early November, and the school day began and ended in darkness. At five o'clock on a Friday afternoon, she hurried through the last of her tasks. She finished writing a letter to a disgruntled governor, explaining why his son hadn't been picked for the intramural spelling competition, and left the caretaker to lock up the school.

No-one, save herself, moved through the streets of Crow Haven. A blustery wind chattered around the village like a delinquent child, upturning dustbins and throwing their contents into the road. Geraldine strode along the Conduit Road until she came to the opening in the trees. Reaching the gate, she glanced up at the three praying figures. It looked to her as if they were trying to reach through the branches above them, like prisoners grasping at the free world through a barred window.

She cleared the avenue. There were lights coming through the slit windows of the sealed room. She rang the bell.

'Peter's too ill to see you,' Anne said, before she had fully opened the door.

'I'm sorry to hear that. May I . . . ?'

'Annie? Who is it?' The voice sounded anguished. A word she would never have thought of associating with Peter Malahyde.

There was movement at the top of the spiral staircase.

'Mrs Malahyde, I believe it would do Peter good to see Miss Pryce.'

Brushing past Anne, Geraldine mounted the stairs and joined Father Brody on the first floor landing. He stood before a dark, heavy-looking door that was part-way open. The old priest looked greyer and frailer than she remembered.

'How are you?' she asked. 'I heard you've been unwell.'

'It was nothing,' Brody whispered. 'Miss Pryce, you must prepare yourself for a shock.'

'Is he that ill?'

'He's dying.'

'Dear God . . . I thought it was just psoriasis . . .'

'It's a degenerative tissue disease, that's all they know. It's not infectious, but he is wasting, Miss Pryce. He is quite . . . changed.'

The staircase rattled as Anne Malahyde ascended.

'Mrs Malahyde, please join us,' Brody said. 'Your husband needs . . .'

A strange mix of fear and hatred twisted Anne Malahyde's features. She disappeared into the main house without a word.

'She won't see him?' Geraldine asked.

'Nobody can convince her.'

'But if he's dying . . .'

'You may sympathise with her a little more in a moment. She *is* only a child.'

Brody opened the door.

'Peter . . . *Oh*, sweet Jesus . . .'

It took several seconds for the horror to subside. After the initial shock, waves of revulsion rolled through Geraldine Pryce, remoulding her insides into sickening shapes. At last, she mastered herself and walked to the bedside. She sat down and talked as soothingly as she could. A nurse circled the room, checking the expensive-looking machinery and, at intervals, applying lubricant to the corners of Peter's eyes and lips.

His skin, where it was not cracked, looked almost translucent. In those places where it had split apart, sores festered in patches of yolk-yellow. The rest of his face was a network of veins; broken blue lines which would burst if the slightest pressure was applied. Starved of blood, his lips had drawn back over his teeth, giving him a wolfish appearance. Geraldine took in his wasted form. She remembered, all those years ago, his body moving against hers. A virgin, she had panicked that his penis would tear her. Now she wondered whether it, too, had withered along with the stick-thin frame beneath the sheets.

'Annie won't come,' he rasped. 'But it's a nice room, isn't it?'

The hurriedly prepared bedroom had that feeling of emptiness, while not actually being empty, that newly used rooms often possess. The adjustable bed, the drip-feed, the monitors and other equipment were all brand new. Ranged along the walls stood long, empty bookcases that looked like the only original features.

'She'll come,' Geraldine said, touching his bandaged hand. 'Give her time.'

'She won't. She's probably got someone with her now. Some young buck between her thighs. A hot, juicy cock in her cunt . . . I have lots of visitors, though,' his mouth bled as he smiled, but he seemed not to notice. 'You and my doctors and Father Brody. And, just as I fall asleep, another visitor comes. He says he's a doctor. He's a great comfort . . . Father, you won't believe this, but we used to be sweethearts, didn't we, Gerry? Christ, she was a charity case, though. I used to have her climbing the fucking walls . . .'

Brody suggested that they let Peter get some rest. When they reached the landing, he said: 'You mustn't take that to heart. He's on a lot of different drugs . . .'

'No, of course, I understand . . . Tell me, is it safe for him to be here?'

'He is probably shortening his life by not being in hospital, but that's his decision, and he's lucid enough, most of the time.'

'And what about her?'

'She has no friends in the area,' Brody said. 'Perhaps on your next visit you might talk to her. Don't pressurise her into seeing him, just listen to her fears.'

'Do you think he'll live to see his child?' Geraldine asked.

'Perhaps it would be better if he did not.'

Geraldine tried to call often in the following weeks, but Peter had been away to London, and once to Denmark, for tests. The nurse, left behind at the house in case of a sudden return, had been given instructions that Anne did not wish to receive visitors. The young wife had not accompanied her husband, it seemed.

On her eighth attempted visit, Geraldine thought that she must have missed Peter again. There appeared to be no lights on in the sickroom. It was only when she was within a few feet of the front door that she saw the windows had been bricked over. The house looked very odd now, one wing of it always watchful, while the other had had its eyes put out.

She was let in by the nurse and taken straight upstairs. Anne was nowhere to be seen and Father Brody was also absent. The room was lit by a table lamp positioned a good distance from the bed.

'I know Mrs Malahyde wouldn't want you here,' the nurse whispered, 'but he needs some company.'

'What happened to the windows?' Geraldine asked.

'He can't bear any light on his skin. He wouldn't have curtains. He insisted on the windows being bricked over. All on account of his imaginary friend. Oh, yes,' the nurse said, noting Geraldine's frown, '*he's* always here apparently. Telling Mr Malahyde stories. His friend doesn't mind the ugliness, Mr Malahyde tells us, being so ugly himself. But he prefers the dark. He doesn't like to visit if there's a risk of light. Mr Malahyde'll do anything for this new friend, and so . . .'

The nurse swept her hand over the huge grey breeze blocks filling the windows. There was a kind a playful mockery in the young woman's words that Geraldine didn't care for. She decided to change the subject.

'How did his tests go?'

'Not well. They're none the wiser. Closest they can guess is a strain of leprosy. It's a complete cellular breakdown. Dr Stoker lives in the house now. He said that Mr Malahyde's bones, organs, skin, they're all losing cohesion, falling in on themselves.'

'How is that possible?'

The nurse shrugged.

'And Mrs Malahyde?'

'They tried to get her to sign something so they could remove him. You'd think she'd jump at the chance. I think she was too frightened. She knows she's wrong not to visit him. Doesn't want to add to her guilt by going against his wishes.'

'Gurr–hee?'

The voice croaked from the far end of the room.

'Yes, it's Miss Pryce come to see you.' The nurse steered Geraldine by the elbow halfway down the sickroom. 'Go ahead, I have to take a pee.'

At first, Geraldine could not discern his features from the crisp, white bed sheets. A hand twitched on the counterpane. It was bandaged, but Peter's fingers were exposed. The white sheen of bone shone through the skin. His face was heavily swathed and there were blotches of red throughout. On his head, only a few patches of hair remained. The colour seemed to have been bleached from these thin tufts, leaving them a weak straw-yellow.

'Schee wchont caurrmm,' he choked. 'Maicchh hurr caurrmm.'

'I can't . . .'

'Aychh'll taychh schaa bay-bee. Chell hurr, aychh'll taychh hurr bay-bee.'

His black tongue, no larger than her little finger, flickered out as he spoke. In fact, his entire body appeared strangely reptilian. But it was his eyes, seen between the slits in the bandages, which really frightened her. When he blinked, his irises showed through the skin, as if his lids were as thin as tracing paper.

'Miss Pryce? Mrs Malahyde wishes to see you.'

'I'll be back in a moment, Peter.'

As she followed the nurse out of the room, she heard Peter

sobbing quietly to himself.

She followed the nurse through the main house and into Anne Malahyde's bedroom. Anne was sitting at a dressing table, her hand resting on her stomach.

'I don't want you coming here anymore. I don't want you seeing Peter.'

'Look, Peter needs company. He needs . . .'

'Then I should be the one who gives it to him. Not you. He didn't even like you, he told me. He just felt sorry for you. I should be the one . . .'

'But you're not. You can't stop me coming here just because it makes you feel guilty. That's worse than not going to him yourself.'

'I saw the way you looked at me,' Anne said. 'Filthy pervert in my house.'

Oh, let her believe what she wants, Geraldine thought. Peter seemed so far gone that perhaps it was pointless to continue visiting anyway. She had to acknowledge that, in truth, she was thankful for this excuse not to return. How much longer would he last, and would she be able to look at him in the final days?

'I'll leave,' she said. 'But, Anne, if you don't go to him now, you'll have to live with the knowledge you abandoned him for the rest of your life. Can you do that?'

'*That*, in there, is not Peter. I won't sit by the bed of a corpse and watch it rot.'

'I didn't see Peter again. He died a few days after the New Year.'

'How did you feel?' Jack asked.

'I didn't like Peter very much,' she said, after a moment's thought. 'I would never have wished on him a fraction of what he suffered, but I found it difficult to cry for him. When Brody gave me the news, all I could think of was my last memory of Anne Malahyde. When I left the house, I saw her standing at an upper window, looking out onto the forest. I think I knew then that I was seeing her future. She reminded

209

me of Tennyson's Lady of Shalott. You know the poem? The lady doomed to stay forever in her tower, only able to see the world through a magic mirror. That's Anne: locked in that house. Inside her guilt. In her island in the forest.

> *Four grey walls and four grey towers,*
> *Overlook a space of flowers*
> *And the silent isle imbowers,*
> *The Lady of Shalott.'*

'How did Peter die?' Jack murmured. 'Did they ever find out?'

'He opened the room. But that's Brody's story. All I have left to tell is what I know about young Simon.'

Geraldine opened her desk drawer, removed two pieces of card from a plastic sleeve and handed one to Jack. It was a school portrait, composed of the customary lines of pupils bookended by teachers.

'That's from 1994. Simon was nine years old. He's third from right in the first row.'

A small boy, with lank black hair and startling blue eyes, smiled from the photograph.

'What was he like?'

'He was remarkable only in that he seemed to be a happy child. Quite an achievement growing up in that environment. Otherwise, he was very average academically, enjoyed sports, could play up occasionally. No different from any boy his age. A year after that photograph was taken, he changed. Suddenly. Terribly. This was taken in the summer of 1995.'

Geraldine passed him the second photograph. It was almost identical to the first, except that the children were a little taller. Some of the teachers, a little wearier. And Simon Malahyde did not have a face. Jack recalled the lecture theatre scene from Doug Winters' video.

'The photographer developed several rolls of film; each was the same. He could not explain to me why Simon's face appeared to have been rubbed out of existence.'

'What happened to him?'

'Well, that's the question. I remember he had been speaking about his father around that time, asking me questions. Mr Trent, all I can tell you is that one day I knew Simon Malahyde as a lively, cheeky little boy, and the next he was something very different. He seemed . . . *Old*. Old beyond reckoning . . . A week after this photo was taken, Asher Brody abducted Simon and took him to the clearing in the forest. That is all I know. That is all I want to know.'

'But you must have some idea why Brody took him.'

'Let me tell you about Asher Brody. I have got to know him well since Peter's death. I have no faith, no belief in God or Providence, but Brody believes in those things, and it comforts me that he does. He took Simon to save him, Mr Trent, and I believe nobody else could have. He failed, that I know, but he tried.'

There was finality in her voice. Jack got up to leave.

'Mr Trent, you remember I spoke of the Crow Haven children being different? On your way out, you will find our Halloween gallery. The pictures drawn by the Crow Haven children are all on one board, I'm sure you'll find them most… unusual.'

Jack made his way down the corridor. Eventually, he came to the gallery which was bordered on each side by rows of little coats. On the main board, beneath bright orange letters spelling out OUR HALLOWEEN DRAWINGS, was the usual collection of pumpkins, witches, vampires and Frankenstein monsters. To the side was a smaller board with only twelve drawings. Whereas the other pictures were brightly coloured, these were done in pencil or charcoal. Each depicted the same scene: a cleared area amongst a grove of trees. Twelve identical stick-thin men stared out at Jack. Their arms were held out at their sides, their clothes, ragged and worn. Patchy hair was drawn standing on end.

Jack felt suddenly cold. In each of the drawings the figure had been given dark holes for eyes.

Thirty

Father Garret was worried. This woman wasn't a fool. He wondered how much she knew about what had happened in the clearing between Brody and the young 'Simon Malahyde'. She could have easily found out about the abduction, he supposed, and it would appear suspicious if he did not tell her what he knew.

'Why didn't you tell us that Father Brody had kidnapped Simon?' she asked.

'Well, it was *years* ago. And I wasn't aware that Father Brody had anything to do with your investigation. If you want to know, what happened was that one day Brody just took it into his head that the boy was possessed. I believe he had prior experience as an exorcist, possibly in his ministries abroad. Exorcism is a little outdated in my book. It has been known to affect the minds of priests.'

'But why do you think Brody centred his attention on Simon?'

'I don't know . . . Asher had known his father, and Peter Malahyde had died rather dreadfully. Perhaps that was the key. I must say, I lived with Asher and *did* notice a few signs. Forgetfulness, growing paranoia.'

'In our reports, it says Simon was unharmed but Father Brody was injured.'

'Self-inflicted, stigmata-type wounds. Confirmation of his mania, I suppose.'

'Have you kept in touch with him?'

'Christmas cards. He has quite lost his mind, you know.'

'Do you think it's possible that Simon might have developed

a relationship with Brody? A kind of emotional dependency sometimes flourishes in these cases.'

'No, I must say, I think your case in Brookemoor and Simon's disappearance are quite unrelated. As for these poor murdered boys, well, I really can't say.'

'All right. Thank you for your time.'

As she got up, Garret noticed that her eyes swept the room. Her gaze fixed on the wall opposite his desk.

'Have you lost your crucifix, Father?'

'I've had a clear out. Felt I needed some new things.'

He did not care for the tight smile she gave him. He followed her into the corridor.

She knows. Get her out before she . . .

'Wonderful.' She stopped beside the stairs. 'I thought this house must have a cellar.'

Didn't close the door . . . Holy Jesus, I forgot to close the door.

'I love the cellars in these old places,' she said. 'All the horrible changes people make to these beautiful old houses; knocking through rooms, plasticky Swedish furniture . . . but they hardly ever touch the cellar. May I?'

She was at the top of the basement steps. Beads of sweat sprang out at Garret's temples and lathered his hair, making his scalp itch. A simple push. Then the scalpel . . .

'No,' Garret smiled as naturally as he could. 'I'm afraid it's not safe down there. Now, please, I have a sermon to prepare.'

Once outside, Dawn reconsidered her ideas. She had no reason to suspect Garret of anything, but she could not shake that gut feeling about him. And then, seeing the cellar door, she had wondered 'What if?' The mortician's words came back to her – *My guess is that, for the last few months, he was kept in a damp, stone building. A cellar or outhouse.*

She tried to think of any reasonable argument that would convince a magistrate to issue a search warrant. There was none. The dead boys had no connection with Crow Haven and Father Garret had no connection with Simon Malahyde.

213

She could not very well request a warrant just because Garret's house had a cellar. In any case, it was imperative that she stuck to procedure. Jarski was on her back. It was becoming difficult enough to shield Jack's eccentricities from the DCI, without her throwing the rule book out the window too. If she wasn't careful both their careers could be up the Swanee.

Still troubled, she looked back at the rectory. A crow, perched atop the portico, returned her steady gaze.

Every muscle in Jack's body screamed. He was unsure how long he had spent sleeping on the cold tarmac of the Master of Jericho's parking bay, but the shooting pains in his back told of a few hours at least.

Since he had been found by the uniform and the porter, it felt as if he had wandered in a daze. Coming to the school, hearing Geraldine Pryce's tale, had been dreamlike, as if he were out of phase with reality. Just like the Yeager Library. Perhaps he was readjusting to the world after his escape from the reading room. And that was another thing: he still couldn't remember just *how* he had escaped. There was no time to consider that now. He had sleepwalked through the morning, and it was only as he left the school that the stories of Yeager and Pryce sparked against each other.

Jamie was not going to be murdered. Not in any conventional sense. His fate was actually far worse. Jack snapped open his mobile and called Bob Peterson.

'Bob, it's me. Do you have a hand gun?'

'Don't think I heard you right there, Jack.'

'It's a simple question. Do – you – have – a – hand – gun?'

'Look, Jack, what do you want me to follow this kid for anyway?'

'My business, Bob, as I told you. Now, for the love of Christ and all the fucking saints in heaven, do you have a *hand gun*?'

'No.'

'I'll have a warrant issued, and if I find one in that flea pit

214

you call an office . . .'

'All right! Christ Mother! I've got a Walther P99 semi-auto. Takes the point 40 Smith and Wesson rimless cartridges . . .'

'I didn't ask for the specs. I want you to carry it with you when you tail Jamie. Whoever takes over your shift should have a weapon too.'

'I can't do that. I'll lose . . .'

'I don't want to make trouble for you, Bob. Carry the gun. Use it if you have to.'

'Je-*sus* . . . Is this kid Witness Protection or somethin'? Someone coming for him?'

'Yes. Someone bad.'

'Whoa, whoa, just a minute. Does the mother know?'

'No. And you don't tell her *anything*, got that? Now, where's the boy?'

'Hold the line, I'll call through . . .'

Jack heard Peterson swearing under his breath while dialling another phone.

'Hi, yeah, it's me. The boy? What? Why the hell haven't you reported that? Tell you what, next assignment for you two butt-munchers: picking the sweetcorn out of my turds, reckon you could manage that? Jack? You there? The boy's skipped school. Done a runner. It's all right, though, my monkeys have found him. He's at that new housing development near Ridgeby, you know it? Look, I'm sorry about . . .'

Jack threw his mobile onto the passenger seat, started the car and drove fast out of Crow Haven. He adjusted the rear-view mirror and looked at himself for the first time that morning. His face was smeared with dirt and scratched in several places. He ruffled his hair and a shower of dust and a few stone chips fell into his lap. It was odd, he thought, that Geraldine Pryce had not commented on his appearance. Perhaps living in Crow Haven had inured her to the odd.

He threw the car around the country lanes, reaching seventy on the straights.

Thirty-one

'How y'doing, buddy?'

'Not great . . . Jeeze, Jack, you don't smell too good.'

Jack joined the boy sitting on the doorstep. He followed Jamie's gaze to the dark blue Fiat Punto. The driver spoke into his phone and, a moment later, pulled away.

'He's been following me,' Jamie said. 'Is he a private detective?'

Jack nodded and blew into his hands.

'He's crap, don't you think . . . ? Jack?'

'Yep?'

'I'm scared.'

'Me too, buddy. Me too.'

The boy bowed over and put his head between his legs. His shoulders trembled as he sobbed. Tentatively, Jack put a hand on his shoulder. He felt the ferocity of the fear working through the kid. For Jack, this demonstration of dependency was something entirely new. He felt proud, somehow, but it was pride tinged with uncertainty. Could he really save Jamie? Hadn't he just been groping around in the dark, hoping to find answers and defences?

'Come on, let's get you inside.'

He led the way to the kitchen and cleared a space at the table. Jamie was still trembling, so he turned up the central heating and Irished their coffees.

'How did you know where I lived, J?'

'I just knew. I keep seeing things . . . Bridges, doors, corridors. Every time I try to think about it, my mind kinda shuts off. Something happened last night . . . today. I can't remember.

216

All I had was this feeling that I had to see you. I needed to tell you that something was coming . . .'

Bridges, doors, corridors. Hadn't someone described Simon Malahyde as 'Janus-faced'? Jack remembered his father, years ago, reading to him from a book of Roman myth: Janus, God of bridges, passages and doorways.

'I saw this horror film once, where this guy thinks his wife's a witch,' Jamie said. 'He becomes kinda manic and gets the whole town to hunt her down. They catch her and lay her on the ground and put a door on top of her. Then they start piling rocks on the door. It creeped me out . . . I feel like I'm being crushed, Jack. Like someone's piling rocks on me. Pushing me out bit by bit . . .'

Jack's mobile rang. Jamie spilt his coffee across the table.

'No-one's gonna hurt you, J. I promise. Look, there's a stack of old Green Lantern comics in the corner. I'll be back in a minute.'

Jack stepped into the corridor and flipped open his phone.

'Yeah, Jack Trent.'

'Mr Trent? Asher Brody, how are you progressing?'

Jack kept the kitchen door open a crack. He watched Jamie pick through a box of old DC issues.

'The picture's becoming clearer, yes.'

'Good. I know you've seen Miss Pryce. It's almost time for answers. But first . . .'

'It's time for answers *now*. I won't run around on some paper chase of clues. I know you think you have to introduce me gently; though I'd hardly call sending me to a library that might have imprisoned me for the rest of time the 'softly-softly approach'. I know weird, Father. Believe me. I really don't think you're gonna shock me.'

'I wonder. What do you think you know?'

'Peter Malahyde couldn't face the death that awaited him. He found out about the metempsychosis ritual. Before he died, he murdered two boys, performed the rite and possessed the body of his unborn child. Simon Malahyde was a vessel for his father. My guess is that the possession is finite, seventeen years or so and dad has to vacate the premises. He organises a second ritual, kills Oliver Godfrey and another boy and sets his sight on a new vessel. How'm I doing?'

'Metempsychosis cannot be worked in the way you're suggesting. An unborn baby cannot be used as a vessel. It must be a child on the cusp of adulthood. But before we consider who or *what* Simon Malahyde was, we must see how things stand now. I've seen the latest news report; a second child has been found dead.'

'Stephen Lloyd?' Jack asked, remembering the name of the boy whose parents he and Dawn had arranged to meet last night.

'That was the name,' Brody confirmed. 'The fat of both boys must already have been harvested. If we surmise Simon died last Monday, on the day he supposedly 'disappeared', then the spirit that possessed him has only two days left to effect a new metempsychosis. By Thursday, the ritual must be complete or the spirit will be too weak to invade a new body. We must locate the intended vessel and . . .'

'He's reading comic books in the next room.'

'What?'

'Trust me, I know the boy he wants. What I don't know, is how to protect him.'

'I'll take care of that. I'll be in touch.'

The phone went dead. Jack stood at the door for a moment and watched the boy. He had studied the changes that fear had wrought on his own face over the years. Subtle alterations around the eyes and mouth that only the truly fearful can recognise but, if asked, could never describe. He saw how fear was now beginning to eat away at Jamie Howard.

'J, I think you should phone your mum, tell her where you are.'

'OK . . . Mum won't believe this, Jack. She's not the sorta person who sees things.'

'She'll have to believe. Call her. Tell her I have to talk to her.'

Jack waited at the kitchen table, flipping through the comic Jamie had been reading.

'She's not answering. My grandad's not about either. She's supposed to be picking me up from footy practice at half-six.'

'Good lad. We'll wait for her there.'

'Jack, you know you've got about thirty messages on your phone?'

When Dawn returned to the station, she found that Jarski's temper had not improved. Jack had still not shown up and there was another press conference scheduled for later that afternoon. As much as it was obvious that the DCI was not averse to hogging the limelight, and despite Jack's recent TV performance, it was clear that Jarski felt that the star of the Greylampton case would be beneficial in a PR sense.

'And where the hell have you been?' Jarski bellowed, as she entered the Incident Room.

'Interviewing a witness.'

'Well, can you inform me before you swan off? *Christ*, I've got enough on my plate with Jack going AWOL.'

'I keep telling you, Roger, Trent's a loose cannon.'

Pat Mescher had been hanging around the Incident Room since yesterday, attempting to make himself look inconspicuous. A task nigh on impossible, Dawn thought, when you take up half the room and possess a face that glows in the dark like a jack-o'-lantern. He stood beside Jarski now, spraying the DCI's arm with pasty crumbs as he spoke.

'I thought you were supposed to be babysitting school kids,' she said.

'This Trent's bit, is it?' Mescher smirked. 'How unprofessional can you get?'

'Pat, fuck off,' Jarski exploded. 'And stop spitting crap all over me. Waddle back to your office and do some fucking work. Dawn, come with me.'

Jarski led the way, barking orders and pushing harassed-looking DCs out of his path. Dawn followed him into an unoccupied interview room. She perched on the edge of the table and ran her fingers over the dints and cigarette burns.

'Look, Dawn, I don't want to discipline Jack. And I sure as hell don't want to reassign the case to that useless tub of lard, but put yourself in my position. Jack's OIC and, on the first proper day of operations, he's found sleeping rough in one of our more prestigious colleges. If he *does* have a drink problem . . .'

'Jack doesn't drink. He's never touched a drop.'

'OK, so what's the score? Why's he suddenly away with the fairies?'

'Has it occurred to you he's following up a lead? Or . . .'

'Then where's the fucking prelim report? Let's say he fingers the bastard who killed these boys. Any decent defence brief'll go into the case operation notes and tear us to pieces. Now, look, I know you're close. Drop what you're following up at the moment and find him.'

'No. No way. I *am* worried about Jack, but I do have my own career, you know. Jack Trent isn't the be all and end all, saviour of CID. Two kids are dead and I have a job to do.'

Dawn barged out of the interview room. She pushed through a throng of journalists, all chomping away on sweating pre-packaged sandwiches. She would be lucky if there was anything left in the canteen. After an eternity of queuing behind the representatives of the Fourth Estate and listening to their numbskull questions – '*So . . . I take this ticket and you bring me my food? Do you bring cutlery? In that tray? Do you bring ketchup? In that tray? Napkins? In the tray. The trays?* – she found a secluded spot behind a plastic trellis frame interwoven with plastic ivy. She ate off a plastic plate with plastic cutlery and wondered if it was possible that her pasta was, likewise, plastic.

'Dawn? Have you seen Jack?'

'Oh, *please*,' Dawn muttered into her lunch. 'No. I have not seen Jack, and when I do . . . Manny? Are you all right?'

Manny Steiner, the audio/visual bod for CID, looked nervous as hell. Dawn was used to seeing him in his tiny office next to Archives in the basement, basking in the glow of half a dozen monitors. The Prince of the Pixel, the Audio Oracle, were a few of his self-styled monikers. Within his kingdom of loops and filters, he was supremely self-confident. Dawn sometimes imagined the cool, collected Manny in the outside world and found it difficult to picture him other than downloading pornography while his mother called him for dinner. Now that home-life version of Manny stood before her, twisting his fingers around a video cassette.

'Is that the lecture hall video Jack gave you?' she asked. 'The one with the glitch?'

'There's no glitch. I cleared up the image late last night.' He said the next sentence slowly, giving weight to each word. 'Dawn–it–scared–the–shit–outta–me. I've run it through every filter program available, even used the Video Image Stabilization software developed by NASA for the Feds. It's not been tampered with; no cheapo special effects, this is real. It is what it is. Look, I've heard the stories about Jack, who hasn't? I never believed them though.'

'Manny, what are you talking about?'

'He's a magnet for this stuff, isn't he? The Greylampton thing? I heard he spoke to those dead girls with, like, mind powers. But this. I've cleared up the image, printed out stills and enlargements, but that's it. Finito. I don't wanna see this shit again.'

Manny tossed a package onto the table and headed for the lifts, no doubt returning to the comfort of his subterranean lair. Dawn gave up on her pasta and opened the envelope. She took out three A4 stills. Each was a shot of Simon Malahyde, standing in the audience of the theology lecture. A time code was printed in the bottom left corner of the frame, recording the moment from which the image had been taken. Fractions of a second separated the shots.

She flipped through them several times. Her mind raced, searching for explanations but knowing, deep down, there were none. It seemed that her initial impression on seeing

Doug Winters' video had been partially correct. Simon Malahyde did not have *a* face, after all.

He possessed several.

She spent the rest of the afternoon reading through transcripts of interviews from the usual collection of cranks and attention seekers that come forward after a TV appeal. Five murder confessions, none mentioning the extraction of fat. One haunted mind had claimed that the voice of Johnny Morris, speaking through his Yorkshire terrier, had told him to kill the child. A DC, who obviously hadn't thought her transcript would be read at any senior level, had scrawled- 'Copy To: Jack Trent – Plausible, don'tcha think?'

Dawn always double-checked these 'freak' confessions. The OIC on her first major case had told her: '*Remember, you ain't lookin' for one crazy in the midst of a bunch of sane people. Out there, they're all crazy.*'

For every ten minutes taken up reading the masturbatory fantasies of would-be killers, she would spend twenty examining the stills. She supposed she had to believe Manny when he told her the video had not been digitally altered. An elaborate prank then? The lecture was a set-up. The faces were masks. She could hardly see the university allowing its most hallowed lecture hall to be used like that. And then there would have to have been a conspiracy between the students in the audience, which surely would have come to light. But if it wasn't a joke perpetrated on the day, and the film had not been tampered with, what then? She threw the stills into her bag. It was time to pick up Jamie from practice.

By the time she reached the playing fields, she had tried Jack's phone a half dozen times. Always the same message greeted her – *you cannot be connected.* Rain drilled the windscreen. She grabbed her umbrella, stepped out of the car and slammed the door. She would drop Jamie at her dad's, drive straight to Jack's and wait outside until he returned. All bloody night if she had to.

The pitch was deserted. It was only six-fifteen by her watch.

A group of boys traipsed across the field, their heads low against the driving rain.

'Hey!' she called. 'What's happened with practice tonight?'

A kid she recognised as one of Jamie's team mates came running over.

'Mrs Howard? No, called off. Coach thought it was too wet. Look, is J with you?'

'He's not with you? Where is he?'

'He bummed off school. Look, he owes me a . . .'

'I don't care what he owes you. Don't stand there like a bloody halfwit . . .'

'Hey, chill. I don't know where he is, okay? I gotta go.'

The boy rejoined his gang. He said something and they all looked in her direction and laughed. She pulled out her mobile and grunted. The battery was dead. Where the hell was her little boy?

'Dawn, he's with me.'

Jack. She felt a strong urge to kiss him. To put her lips to his face. To bless the bridging scar between his eyes. Jamie was with him. That meant her son was safe.

'Where is he?'

'I told him to wait in your car. Don't you ever lock that thing?'

For some reason, his question seemed very funny. She burst out laughing.

'What's going on, Jack?' she asked, breathing hard. 'Why's he with you? Where were you today? What happened last night?'

'I'll answer your questions, Dawn. All of them. But you have to believe what I'm going to tell you. For the sake of . . .'

'I saw his face.' Jamie, standing behind her.

Dawn was about to throw her arms around him, in one of those public displays he hated so much, when she saw what he was holding. One of the stills of Simon Malahyde. The most disturbing, most impossible of the three. The first of the

223

faces, taken at 06:06:01, was weird enough: the little dark-haired boy. The second, timed at 06:06:02, showed a pallid, middle-aged man, his cheeks wet with tears. The child and man resembled each other strongly and the same expression was imprinted on both faces. Horror, agony, revulsion. The third face – 06:06:03 – the one Jamie held out to Jack, was quite different. The features, if features was the right word, withered and decayed, the expression, malevolent.

'This is him,' Jamie said, his voice small.

'I know.' Jack took the picture. 'We've met. In my dreams.'

'Jack? What the hell's going on . . . ?'

'Dawn, it's time you heard the truth. About Simon Malahyde. About Jamie. About who I really am.'

Thirty-two

Jack's Story

Jack Trent pulled his mother and father close, as if they were a pair of recalcitrant bookends. They walked on, a snug little huddle. All along the pavement of Oxford Street the snow was a well-packed, slippery carpet. Occasionally a bus would trundle by, careful of kamikaze Christmas shoppers who dashed between the stores. Jack was wearying of the bustle. He'd not been to London before and, exciting as it was, it seemed as if everyone and everything had something to prove. In his village, things were happy with what they were. Small church, small houses, small noises. Even the people seemed smaller, though perhaps that was because Londoners collected themselves into big, bad-tempered herds and crashed about the place.

'So, boy, your mum's off to get a few surprises for the Big Day. What'll we do?'

'Why don't you take him to the Father Christmas Grotto in Hamley's?'

'Mum, I'm twelve, I'm not a baby.'

'Hear that, Claire? He's not a baby. Better scratch the playpen off the list. Tell you what, there's one of those new American hamburger restaurants not far from here. Fancy that?'

'Here, you can't go into a restaurant with a dirty face,' his mother said, spitting into her handkerchief. 'What'll the waiters think?'

'Urgh, Mum, get off. That's disgusting.'

'It's how cats wash, and they're the most hygienic creatures going.'

'What? Like next door's cat?' Jack laughed. 'It sits around

licking its bum all day. And it does this thing where it . . .'

James Trent caught his wife's eye and tried to stifle his laughter.

'That's enough of that, toilet gob,' he said. 'Come on. We'll meet up in an hour outside Woolworths.'

Claire Trent waited for a kiss from both her boys, and then they went their separate ways. Hand in hand, father and son jostled along the pavement, Jack trying to keep his footing on the ice. He looked back once, scanned the crowd for his mother and saw her swallowed up by the press.

'Look lively, son.' The fatherly grip tightened and the boy felt reassured. 'Keep up.'

They passed a Salvation Army band on the corner of New Bond Street, and James sang along boisterously to *Good King Wenceslas* while his son cringed.

An hour later, they stepped out of the fast food joint on Regent Street. Jack licked tomato sauce from his lips and belched, savouring the flavour.

'Glad we got you washed up for that unique culinary delight,' James Trent said.

'You're such a miserable old fart. Better hurry up, we'll be late for mum.'

Jack held on tight to his father. He looked up at the grainy pink strip between the tall shops. He had never seen the sky that colour before. It was just like the rest of the city; jostling for space and making itself horribly different in order to stand out. He was tired now and, as much as he had liked the taste, his dad was right about the food. The burger felt like it had reassembled itself in his gut and had taken a wander back up his windpipe. Any minute now it was bound to make a reappearance. Jack swallowed hard.

As he walked, it seemed that he had to push, not only against the people, but against the glare of light and white noise. He hardly noticed the sky open up as they crossed Oxford Circus. Shoulders shoved against him and he felt the phantom burger move further up his throat. His hands ran wet in his gloves. If he was home now, he'd be curled up in front of their twenty-six inch Keracolor TV set, devouring egg on toast and watching a Batman re-run. A mental image of Eartha Kitt in her tight Catwoman outfit diverted his mind from the crush and swell, but he still felt nauseous.

'You all right, boy? Not far now.'

The real faces advancing on him looked cruel and hard, while the plastic ones that flashed by in window displays were jovial but frozen. He felt bruised and dirty by the time he saw his mother. She was standing on the opposite pavement, trying to wave at them while labouring under a dozen fit-to-burst bags. A motorised tableau of the nativity whirred away in the window behind her, complete with holy family, shepherds, barnyard menagerie and the Three Kings, robotically offering and withdrawing their gifts.

Jack waved, certain now that he was going to puke. Then a string of tinkling Christmas lights overhead caught his attention and he forgot his upset stomach. His eyes followed the wire to a lamp post on the other side of the street. Nearby, at the same level as the lights, a group of men stood in the cradle of a cherry picker. Clipboards in hand, they appeared to be making a bird's-eye inspection of the thoroughfare.

'Come on, son. Quick as The Flash,' his dad said, pulling him between the traffic.

They were halfway across the street when it happened.

Jack saw the cherry picker's lorry jolt forward. Above, the men in the cradle called out in alarm. Newspaper reports would later blame a faulty brake for the accident. At that moment, however, it seemed to Jack that the crane had come to life. Like some mechanised brontosaurus, it rumbled towards the lamp post from which the Christmas lights were strung, its great neck swaying this way and that. The cherry picker crashed into the post and its cradle juddered and dropped three feet. The men screamed as the vehicle's hydraulic arm cut through the wire that held the lights. There was a vicious metallic twang. Sparks flashed. The lights flickered. Jack screwed his eyes tight shut.

Against the blackness, he imagined the sounds around him

– cries, shouts of warning, the whoosh of the wire – in comic-book style captions. Then a glare, fierce as lightning, flared against his closed lids. In the same split second, he felt the explosion against his face, so strong it launched him off his feet. He seemed to be airborne for ages before falling against the hard, wet ground. The scent of burning skin filled his nostrils.

Jesus, I'm on fire . . .

Then there was PAIN. Pain so huge that he was able to sidestep it and marvel at its enormity. Confused shouts and screams, and a thunder of feet roared around him. He felt his arm plucked from the ground and a finger press into his wrist.

'He's gone.'

'Bring him back. Please, you have to bring my boy back.' His father's voice, rolling like a slowed down record.

'What are you talking about?' Jack asked. 'I'm all right. I'm . . .'

'Please, Jesus, take my child. Let him pass quickly through Purgatory.' His mother. 'God, our Father, Your power brings us birth, Your providence guides our lives . . .'

'He's not dead, Claire. Stop praying. He's not dead.'

I am. You're wrong, Dad. I am dead. My eyes won't move and my breath isn't steaming no more.

He could feel nothing. Not even the touch of snow against his face. He was speaking to them, but they couldn't hear him. All that he could see of his parents were their shoes: brown brogues, black boots, slurry-stained. A circle of shoes had gathered around him and, oddly enough, he could read fear and agitation in the way they shifted and pawed at the ground. Between a pair of high heels and rubber galoshes, snaked a trail of multicoloured broken eggshells. At first he didn't recognise them as the Christmas lights.

A few feet from his head, two red stains sat upon the snow. Blood. His blood. Scary, *big* pools of *his* blood. So big, he doubted there could be much more left inside him. A cable lay across the puddles and fizzed blue at its frayed end. As his mind began to drift, and his parents' pleadings and the cries of the crowd became muffled, he watched the blood spread and sink. The world was slipping away from him. It was okay, really it was. He found he didn't mind the growing dark. He was about to surrender to it, when he heard the sound.

Ripping. As if a thick piece of fabric was being torn along a seam. It was unnatural, jarring: the report of something that shouldn't be happening. He saw the tear. It started as a paper-thin slit, running from the base of the nativity tableau. There was a gasp, and the rent widened and lengthened. Mary and the baby Christ were torn apart, their faces flapping on either side of the aperture, as if they were no longer solid forms but painted on canvas. The tear opened wider still and Jack saw all that was beyond it.

Whirling beyond the fissure: at once a world, a universe, a single entity, a mass of beings, a macrocosm, a microcosm. Later, he would not remember his comprehension, but now he saw and understood in a moment a new dimension in its generality and specifics. A dimension of impossible suffering. Of chaos.

The wheeling kaleidoscope began to settle. At first, Jack thought that everything beyond the breach had lapsed into darkness. It looked like the coldest night. Perhaps the last, when the universe was spent, or the first, when the stars had not yet been strung out.

Then something stirred.

One slick body moved against another. *Things* were gathering at the opening. As they moved forward, jostling for space like the Christmas shoppers, the light from the window display shimmered off their oily limbs. The rent had stopped at five or so feet, but hands reached now from inside, grasped the frayed edges of this world and stretched the oval wide. As their heads reached through, the shrieks began. Not from the crowds still gathered around Jack, they did not seem to see the creatures, but from the mouths of the monsters themselves. From the opening, six came screaming into the world, dragging their soft, spongy bodies behind them. Tendrils lashed back into the void, as if part of them wanted to remain in that chaotic womb. As the last of the six stepped out, the tear began to heal itself, closing off thousands of other beings. The figures of Mary and Jesus were stitched back together. The nativity returned to its three dimensions. And now another group, not told of in the Bible story, had gathered beside the manger.

Contorted, disfigured, they had no uniform features or shape. As their eyes fixed on him, some clustered, some seemingly blind, Jack had another intuitive flash. In the first few hours of their lives, they had possessed the same form. Some cruel art had mangled their bodies, reconfigured their limbs and grafted additional features into already crowded faces. They were, in fact, living experiments that had escaped some vast laboratory. As with his earlier understanding, this insight was later lost in a memory characterised only by confusion and dread.

They crept, scuttled, dragged themselves to the window. As one, they passed through the glass as if it were water, and advanced towards Jack. Their feet made no impression on the snow. Colour drained from Jack's vision. The broken bulbs became grey, the snow turned whiter and the faces of the unseeing people blanched. Everything was the silvery mono-chrome of a black and white film. Everything except his blood, which remained shockingly red in the washed out world.

Tentacles writhed through the snow and touched the sinking pools. In the midst of terror, words read by his father years ago, entered Jack's mind:

Her skin was white as snow, her lips as red as blood, her hair as black as ebony . . .

They closed around him, chittered and shrieked, until their voices rang in his mind.

'He's dead.' His mother. 'Dead without the blessing. His soul isn't clean . . .'

They had come to take him. Hell was beyond the breach. Hell that he had glimpsed; hell that waited now.

I'm good. I am, please. Please, don't let them take me. Dad, please . . .

Their faces began to melt. Heads caved into torsos, rippling bodies collapsed. Pouring into each other, becoming a single uniform slime, they pooled over the bloodstains. Errant eyes, ears, claws and tongues rose to the surface of the ooze. Having gathered itself, the mass banked a hair's breadth before Jack's eyes. He saw his own dead face reflected in their surface. Splinters of coloured glass were embedded in his cheeks and forehead. The skin between his eyes was bubbling, burned and black.

A needle-point span out. Jack screamed, but in the reflection he saw that his mouth did not move. *They* punctured his pupil. Their mass grew smaller. Jack felt *Them* slipping coldly into his mind, dripping through his brain, creeping into his thoughts. In a moment, the pool was gone and only his blood remained upon the snow.

Thirty-three

Jack's Story

There was no sulphur, no brimstone, no Devil with his black book. But Jack knew that this was Hell nonetheless. He had never imagined that there could be anything more frightening than the damnation of his nightmares. Strangely, the demons that populated those dreamscapes would now be welcome faces in this emptiness. There was neither light nor colour here, neither shadow nor shade, no smell, no sound, nothing to stimulate his senses. He was alone in a forgotten corner of reality. Alone for all time . . .

And then he felt a sliver of visceral sensation. That meant he had a body. How many times had he heard Father Soames preach that only the Spirit, divorced from the Flesh, may pass over? Something was now moving inside his *flesh*. This was not Hell.

This 'something' was embedded deep inside his mind. *Mind* wasn't the right word, because he could feel the substance lying against the tissue of his brain. Lodged there like a kernel of corn stuck between teeth.

Them.

The creatures from the rift. Their gentle movement sounded like a thickly silted sea lapping against the shore. Maybe they were feeding from him, parasites sucking away his bones and organs from the inside. No. No, he *knew* they were sleeping. He could sense their exhaustion. And he knew, without knowing how he knew, that as dangerous as they were, they would not harm him. He was their home now. Their sanctuary. He took strange comfort from *them*. For, if they were sleeping inside him, then he could not be dead.

★

Shadows moved across the gauze of bandages. He tried to sit up, but the sheets were tucked tight, pinning him like a butterfly to a card. A trundling sound passed by. He pictured a trolley, pushed by the big fat matron who had straitjacketed him to the bed. The trundling stopped.

'Good morning, sleepyhead.'

No big fat matron had any right to have a voice that sweet.

'M-morning . . . where am I?'

'You're on the Aikman Memorial Ward. Shall I get your parents . . . ?'

'Why are my eyes bandaged up?'

'You've got a few burns and bruises. I'll get Dr Shelley to take a look at you.'

'Please stay.'

Not long ago – at least he didn't think it had been long ago – he had thought that he would never again hear another human voice. Now he was awake, surrounded by smells and sounds and shadows. He had never realised before how beautifully crowded the world was. Tears smarted against the cuts and burns around his eyes. His body didn't seem able to contain the great heaving sobs that worked through him. An arm was placed around his shoulders and drew him close.

'It's all over now, Jack. You're safe. There's nothing to be frightened of.'

'Now, Jack, you remember what we talked about? You might be a little shocked by the scarring, but remember, you were very lucky. Coming back after being clinically dead for four minutes is no mean feat.'

Jack wriggled free of his mother's hug. He felt that he should face this alone. He squinted as the bandages were unfurled. The air was cold against his parched eyes. There were three people gathered around him, and it was from their words, rather than from their shapes, that he recognised them.

'How is it, boy?' his dad asked. 'Do you see us?'

'Blurry . . .'

'I need to take a look in your eyes now, Jack. Try not to move them.'

The doctor's torch burned into his pupils. Red-etched veins floated before the light. The muscles of his optic cords felt so tight he was sure they would snap.

'Okay, that looks fine. It's going to take a few days for your vision to settle. You've had over a week for your eye muscles to become lazy, but I don't foresee any problems with recovering your sight fully. Right, let's show you the scarring.'

'It's not bad, Jacky.'

'Mum, don't call me that.'

'Any chance of giving him a new nose, doc?' his dad said. 'He got that one from my mother-in-law.'

'James, for God's sake.'

It was the first time Jack had laughed, and the first time his dad had made a joke since the accident. It was nice to have the old fart reading to him every day, putting on comical pirate voices for *Treasure Island* or scary voices for *The Jabberwocky*. But it was in those periods between reading, when his old man just sat by the bed, holding his hand and whispering – *'Glad you made it back, son. You're gonna be all right. No question'* – that he missed the jokes. They were much more comforting than those whispered reassurances.

Dr Shelley brought a small, vanity-style mirror close up to Jack's face.

'Now, I confess I don't understand you, young Jack. We wondered whether you'd have to have stitches, but the lacerations healed almost in hours. That's what's known in the medical world as a miracle. (I might write to the Pope and demand canonisation!) So, no scarring on that count. The burn, however . . .'

Since he had been told what had happened: that a live wire had swung into him, peppering his face with glass and burning 240 volts between his eyes, Jack had imagined himself hideously deformed. In his dreams he pictured the bandages being removed and his mother and father standing back, horrified and repulsed.

'I wondered if that would be your reaction,' Dr Shelley would say, 'so I took the liberty to procure this . . .'

He would bring out a heavy iron mask. Like the one worn by the disfigured mastermind, Doctor Doom, arch nemesis of The Fantastic Four, or the illegitimate king in the Dumas novel. His father would strap the mask securely in place.

'Oh, no,' his mother would complain. 'I can't bear seeing that over the breakfast table each morning. Hideous. Can't . . . can't we send him back, Doctor? To the dark place? He could live there forever, and the things that crawl inside could keep him company . . .'

He stared hard into the mirror. His face appeared to be the same shape it had always been. A little swollen perhaps, and there were a dozen or so angry scratches where the glass had been removed. There was only one startling blemish: a white scar, bridging his nose and wiring his eyes together. Jack gripped his mother's hand, but it was a reaction of relief. It wasn't so bad. In the right light, it might actually look pretty cool. He could live with . . .

Something shifted. Something cold, surging away from his mind. He snatched his hand back.

'You still with us? As I said, Jack, you were very lucky,' Dr Shelley said. 'You've just got that white blaze as a souvenir.'

And Them, Jack thought, *I have Them, too.*

A few days later, his vision sharpened. Within a certain proximity he could make out faces quite distinctly. He was squinting at the *Sub-Mariner* comic his dad had brought him when the honey-voiced nurse ('Nurse Alice', so she had told him, with a wink) drew back the curtain around his bed.

'Morning, sweet cheeks,' she said. 'You're leaving me today, I hear.'

'Yeah . . . sorry . . .'

'I should think so. You're the most handsome patient on the ward. Don't tell Mr Sheridan that; I always tell him he's

235

the best looking.'

Jack felt his face grow hot. He couldn't believe how he'd embarrassed himself in front of her the other day, bawling like a little kid. Being able to see her now didn't make things any easier. She was so beautiful that he found it difficult to think about what he was going to say, so everything came out wrong. She leaned over him, checking the few remaining dressings on his burns. Her heavy breasts rubbed against his chest.

Holy Shit. Not now! Jack panicked.

His penis stiffened against her arm. She must have felt it, but she stood up and smiled, as if it was nothing unusual.

'S-sorry,' he stammered. 'You know. About the other day. Being a baby and . . .'

'You're a sweetie. Gonna break some hearts someday.'

She straightened up and smoothed the creases out of her uniform. As she checked her lapel watch, Jack leant forward and took hold of her hand.

'I want to tell you something. I haven't told Dr Shelley or my parents. It'll sound stupid, you won't believe me, but I still feel them . . . I need to tell someone . . .'

'All right, Jack, calm down. Let me close the curtain, okay? Then we can talk.'

She drew the plastic screen around the bed and sat down beside him. His mouth felt dry. Should he tell her? He hadn't told Dr Shelley. The day he'd woken up, the doc had asked him if he had experienced anything during the time he had been 'clinically dead'. Something in Shelley's attitude had told Jack to keep shtum. Shelley had gone on to say that, if he *had* seen anything, there was no need to be scared. It was all just chemical reactions in the brain. It wasn't real.

Her hand was cool in his.

'The night I had my accident. I saw . . .'

His shoulder grew warm. How to say it. How to even come close to describing what had happened.

'In the shop window. Not the window. This thing, opening up and . . .'

A painful tingling reached down his arm . . .

' . . . They came out of a tear . . .'

'Go on.'

'A tear in the world. I saw . . .'

'It's okay.'

'Oh, Jesus.'

. . . reached like a strip of fire and stretched into his fingers.

'Jack? What's the matter?'

He looked down at his hand, expecting to see it engulfed in flames, burning the pretty white fingers that interlaced his own. He tried to pull away, but the invisible heat seemed to fuse them together. Without knowing how, he turned his vision inward and saw the little black sac that nestled in a nook of his brain. It was empty.

His consciousness shifted again. No longer cognisant of the pain, he became aware of *them*. They were all around him, smothering him, dripping from his mind and coursing through him, like cold blood. Alice's face, the enclave of his curtained off bed, the exterior noises of the hospital, all vanished. He was conscious only of the deafening rush. Of being borne through his own body, encased in *their* dark mass. *They* screamed through his arm. Split him between his fingers. Drew him out of his body. Into her. He saw . . .

Don't you ever tell Mummy, Alice.

. . . himself, through her eyes. He was speaking slowly, his face blank, his eyes rolled white in their sockets.

Mummy won't love you anymore, if you tell her what we do. Now touch it, baby, touch it like I showed you.

He saw Alice's father. And the playroom. And the red-spotted knickers that she had spent all night trying to clean with soap and scalding water. He saw her hands, not white and pretty, but swollen and raw.

They shrieked as she pulled her hand away. Over *their* screams, he heard the rush again, this time running backwards. He moved with *them*, through the widening space between fingers, back into his body, which felt as cold and unwelcoming as an abandoned house. As his senses slotted into place, he felt

237

them coalesce into the sac.

Alice the nurse, Alice the little girl, backed away from the bed.

'No-one has ever been inside me since him.'

'I didn't know. I'm sorry', Jack said, his vision returning. 'You saw them, didn't you? Please, I'm scared; I want to know what they are . . .'

'You were *inside* me.'

'I know. I'm sorry. Please, help me. What are they? I don't want them inside . . .'

'Inside me. Like *him*. Not like him. He was never in here,' she brushed her temple with shaking fingers. 'What are you? Something bad, something very, very bad . . . Stay away. Don't ever come near me. Don't you ever, ever come near me.'

Thirty-four

Jack's Story

'There's something very wrong with him, James.'

Jack crept downstairs and sat shivering on the bottom step. Through the gap in the sitting room door, he saw his dad by the sideboard pour brandy into two glasses.

'He's not been the same since the accident.' His mother – out of sight – 'And now Miss Simpson says he's daydreaming in school; that he's alienated his friends. All he does is sit in his room, reading comic books and playing that racket.'

'He's almost a teenager, for crying out loud, Claire. And he's just getting over a pretty nasty experience. Here, stop bloody pacing about. Drink up.'

'It's not just that,' his mother sighed. Her thin arm came into view and took the drink. 'He doesn't want to be near me. He doesn't even kiss me goodnight.'

'Well, show me a twelve-year-old lad that likes kissing his mother.'

'Why won't you believe me? There is something different about him. Did you notice how that nurse looked at him when we came to take him home? She'd been so fond of Jack and then, when he said goodbye, she looked . . . I don't know, she looked frightened.'

Jack tiptoed back upstairs. He closed his bedroom door gently behind him, switched off the light and crawled into bed. Stretching his hand into the darkness, he skipped the needle of the record player back an inch and turned down the volume.

How could she think he didn't want to be near her? He was desperate for her to comfort him, to tell him that everything would be all right. That they were still in Kansas, Toto. And how could his dad think that his behaviour was normal? As if those parasites sleeping inside his skull were as welcome a change as the downy hair growing around his dick.

He should tell them.

God, no. Then even his dad would consider calling in a nut-doctor. Or worse, he might laugh and insist that 'the creatures' demonstrate what they could do. Jack shivered. What if his old man told him to stop being a weirdo and give his mother a goodnight kiss? With his lips touching her cheek, what secrets would he discover? He was old enough to know that his parents had lived different lives before he came along. Lives that he had taken no interest in before, and that had only been hinted at. If the creatures laid out his parents' sins and tragedies before him, would he ever be able to look at them in the same way?

He must take care not to touch anyone until he figured out what these things were. What they wanted. But it was so hard, and he felt so alone.

He had not dreamed since the accident. At least, when he woke, he couldn't remember dreaming. There had been this boffin on TV once who'd said that dreaming was the mind's safety valve. It was the 'catharsis' of the soul. Jack had looked the word up (it'd taken some time because he'd heard it as 'cats-fart-sis'). It meant getting something out of your system, like punching a smaller kid if your folks were going on at you. If we didn't dream, the TV egghead said, we'd be a mass of 'new-row-sis'. Jack hadn't looked that up, but he now felt he understood what it meant. It meant going nuts, having a case of the heebie-jeebies, being (no joke) one bulb short of a full set of Christmas lights.

By early February, they had started showing him things, not from a person's past, which he only saw when he touched, but things about to happen. The future, laid out in mirrors and windows. Always dreadful things that he could make no

240

sense of until it was too late. Accidents like the one that crippled his grandmother, which he had seen as brief flashes of stairs, flailing limbs and compound fractures. This, coupled with the inability to touch, was almost too much to bear.

One day, as he strolled along the river, skimming stones across its icy surface, he had come across Dan Foster and Jane Rye. They were too busy to notice him. He watched them, not caring if he was seen. What he witnessed made him feel as though he were frozen. Something was happening between Dan and Jane that he would never experience. It would happen to all his friends at some point, and he would be left behind.

His friends. They had been great at first. The girls cooed over him and the boys had hailed him, as if he were a mythical hero returned from the Underworld. From the start, however, he was sullen and distant. They had all been patient, but after a while their sympathy ran dry.

It was a Saturday, mid-way through the month, when he heard voices in the forest. He recognised them at once and crept within earshot. From behind the base of an alder tree, Jack watched the boys at work in the hollow. There was Dan Foster, Carl Walters and four or five of his old buddies, busy with saws, hammers and scraps of ply. In the old days, they would have asked Jack to help build their fort. He was good at that sort of stuff; always coming up with inventive but practical designs.

'I saw this flick at the Regal,' Danny said, through a mouth full of nails. 'This scientist is trying to bring his wife back from the dead. He has this whole lab set-up. He puts these electrodes on her and turns on the juice. She comes back, but she's got the soul of this ancient Egyptian Queen or something . . .'

'Are you saying Jack's an ancient queen?' Carl Walters laughed.

The other boys giggled too until a look from Danny dried up their laughter.

'I'm just saying you don't know what happened to him.

241

Maybe Jack ain't Jack no more.'

Jack took off. He ran as fast as he could, back through the woods towards home. Trees passed in a yellow blur. His feet cracked on the hard earth, juddering his bones. His heart raced against his chest and his spit was thick and coppery. Just over the next ridge was Doyle's Rise. Some kids called it the Shiiiiit Skids, but to Jack and Dan and the old gang, it had always been the Death Bank. It was so steep nobody dared climb it. If you slipped, you'd never stop yourself. You'd plough head-long, forty feet down and count your lucky stars if you managed to peel yourself off the road alive. No need to put on the brakes just yet though. There was plenty of time.

He was moving fast when he tripped. His legs wheeled beneath him and he pitched forward into a copse. A tree stump speared his stomach. Air wheezed out of his lungs as he tumbled, tucking and rolling. Leaves slipped through his fingers and he found no purchase on the frosted ground. Caught between screams and laughter, he tipped over the Death Bank.

He saw the descent in snatches: feet framed against the sky; cushions of bright green moss speeding his descent; woodpigeons, frightened by his screams, exploding from the trees overhanging the precipice. The road growing larger . . . larger, larger. LARGER.

Roots slashed his skin. There was a dull snap and he felt his right arm trail behind him. Gravel spat into his face like shrapnel. The pain and fear was blinding, and it wasn't until he felt the chill of *their* hands grasping along his optic nerve that he realised *they* were moving. There wasn't time to worry about it. Soon nothing would matter. Soon his skull would be cracked open on the road and *they*, together with his brains, would splash across the tarmac. One last inward burst of crazed laughter: *Goodbye, cruel world!* And a final, sober plea: *Please, God, make it quick.*

He tried to close his eyes. They wouldn't shut. Everything went dark anyway. Cold, wet tar filled his nostrils.

The impact did not come.

When his vision returned, he found himself squatting on all-fours in the middle of the road. The arm, which he had guessed must be broken, supported him steadily. Looking sideways, he saw his path cut through forty feet of broken thicket. He should be dead. At the very least, he should be rolling around in agony. The only pain he felt was a slight sting between his eyes. Blood dripped from his nose onto the back of his hand. He wiped his sleeve across his face and was about to see if he could stand, when he looked again at the black surface of the road.

It was moving; flowing under his hands and feet. Something thick and gummy dripped from his eyes into the pool. The puddle shifted. *They* span towards his face and re-entered him as coldly as they had left. Resuming their position inside his skull, they lapsed back into sleep.

Jack fell into a sitting position and tried to think. *They* had saved his life. Did this mean he owed them one? The thought made him tremble. He coughed a mouthful of vomit onto the road and waited for his breathing to steady.

'Please, Jack, tell me what's the matter.'

Jack shivered. He was wrapped in a blanket, huddled over the electric fire. The TV was on, but he had the volume turned right down.

'Can't,' he said, his voice hollow.

'Jack, I won't have that sort of nonsense. I'm your mother and . . .'

'You won't understand.'

He drew the blanket around him and stared at the bright filaments of the fire. Why had they saved him? He had thought they were evil because they looked monstrous. Perhaps he'd been wrong.

'Come on, love,' his mother said. 'You can tell me anything. There's no need to be frightened. Jesus is with you always.'

'Is he?' Jack murmured. 'Where was he when I died? Where was he when *they* came into me?'

'Jack, what are you talking about?'

243

He bowed his head. The fireguard gave a violent prang. He drew himself further into the blanket and watched a silent Orinoco scamper around the Womble Burrow.

'Jack, tell me this instant.'

Orinoco fell off a ladder.

'All right,' he whispered. 'You asked for it. I'll tell you. In fact, I think *they* want you to know.'

Thirty-five

Jack's Story

'I wanted to figure it out on my own,' Jack said, bringing his story up to date. 'I thought if I told someone, I'd be laughed at. But I keep seeing things, in mirrors, in my head . . . I can't handle it anymore.'

'Jack, I'm so sorry,' his mother said. 'I didn't know you felt so alone.'

'What are they, Mum? What do they want?'

'Listen, you're very upset. I know things have been tough at school. Let's go and see Dr Shelley, maybe he can recommend someone who . . .'

'I don't need a psychiatrist!' Jack shouted. 'I need someone to *believe* me. I need someone to take them out of me. I need . . . Jesus, don't touch me!'

She drew a sharp intake of breath as his foot connected with her stomach. Fear and self-loathing rocked his senses. His mother, doubled over, stared at him through bars of hair. The pained, confused look she gave almost made him wish he *was* lying crushed on the road beneath the Death Bank: a cold buffet for birds and foxes.

'I didn't mean . . . you can't touch me. I told you.'

'Jack . . . it's the . . . accident. You're . . . not . . . fully . . . You're imagining . . .'

'How? How am I imagining things? I *saw* what that nurse's father did to her.'

'Tell me truthfully,' she said, her breathing coming more steadily. 'What's wrong?'

Jack tore strands of hair over his eyes.

'Jesus Christ! *They're inside me.* Please, Mum, *please* believe me.'

'But, love, don't you see it's impossible?'

'And manna falling from heaven *is* possible? Trumpets blowing down walls and talking bushes and dead people getting up and walking around, and all the rest of that *bollocks* you make me sit through every week; all that *is* possible?'

'But what you're saying, God wouldn't allow it.'

'Oh, wouldn't He? Well He *did*. And I've prayed, Mum. I've prayed and prayed and He doesn't hear.'

'That's enough.'

'You know what I think? I think He's dead. Or maybe He's scared of them. Yeah, that's it,' Jack laughed. 'God's scared shitless of the things living inside my head . . .'

'I know you're upset, Jack, but I won't have blasphemy in this house.'

'Too late,' he muttered.

The heat from the fire made his eyes water. He looked at his mother through stinging tears.

'You won't ever believe me will you?'

'I . . .'

'You have to. Mum, I'm sorry.'

Jack threw off the blanket. Shivering, dressed only in his pyjama bottoms, he reached out to touch her.

'Jack? What're you doing?'

His fingertips quivered an inch from her hand. His chest, still shaped like a child's but beginning to stretch and broaden, heaved as his breath shortened. Suddenly conscious of his exposed torso, he placed his right hand over his breast. His heart sang against his palm. He gripped her wrist.

Fire exploded down his right arm, licked into his fingers. It was quicker this time. There was no chance for second thoughts, for turning back. They pulled him inside her and he saw her fully, as no-one else ever had.

At the forefront of her mind was discipline, authority, morality, control, stamped through with the strictures of the Church. But behind that breakwater lay an ocean, beautiful and fathomless. *They* saw it too, and Jack sensed their excitement. Before he could think of stopping them, they plunged into the tumult, dragging him behind. Secrets unravelled as he drowned in her hopes and fears and fantasies. He saw her, and was proud and sickened.

Without knowing how, he drew *them* together and felt his way back. In a moment, he was in his own body again and was aware that he was speaking.

' . . . and you want to believe it. That if you're good, it'll all be all right. But you know it's not true. No-one is ever saved . . .'

He pulled his hand away.

'Mum? Are you all right? I had to, you see? I had to show you. I had to . . .'

'It's *dreaming*. Shadowland of possibility . . . *dreaming* . . . I saw them, Jack,' she said, stepping away from her son. 'I saw them . . .'

Things changed in the last week of his mother's life. To the outside world, he was sure that there was no noticeable difference in their relationship. When they met her friends in the street, or when they attended Mass, she behaved as she always had. Fussing over his appearance and manners. But at home things were different. She treated him with a mixture of over-attentiveness and suspicion. As she tiptoed around him, being all bright and cheerful, Jack thought he could feel her fear and hatred.

On a few occasions he tried to bring up the subject of what had happened. She would never be drawn. The only comfort he took from her newfound horror of him was the certainty that she would not tell his father about *Them*. James Trent loved to joke and fool around, but he was a very serious-minded man. He didn't believe in monsters.

It was two days later when Jack found out just how wrong he could be.

Dan Foster had picked a fight with him at break time. The head had told them to shake hands. Jack refused and had been told to go home and think about his behaviour. His dad had been away on business and was not expected back until the weekend. As Jack eased the front door to and tiptoed down the hall, hoping to sneak up to his room unnoticed, he was surprised to hear his father's voice from the kitchen.

'Right. Let me get this crystal fucking clear. What you're telling me is – I can't actually believe I'm going to say this – Jack, our son, is *possessed*? You *are* joking. You have to be joking?'

'I don't expect you to believe it,' his mother said. 'If it's not backed up by reports and graphs it doesn't exist, does it? Well, the Devil doesn't come with a Kitemark.'

'I'm away for three days and come back to the Salem Witch Hunt . . . Look, if Jack's been a bit off since the accident, who could blame him? And these mood swings? He's growing up, changes in personality are normal. Come on, Claire, not even the Church believes in the Devil anymore.'

'There is a darkness deep inside him.'

'Mother of God! You know what I think? I think *you* should see a doctor.'

'I'm going to talk to Father Soames tomorrow.'

'About what? You're not seriously going to tell him our son is . . .'

'I saw them, James. They came from him. They bore him into me. Demons.'

'Claire, this is a difficult time, what with Jack's accident,' James Trent said, sounding conciliatory. 'Of course you've taken solace from your faith but this... what you're saying is practically medieval.'

'They're real, James. I've seen them.'

'Christ. You know what? I think you should talk to Joe Soames. Maybe when he tells you you're a fucking lunatic, you'll believe it.'

'You think you know so much. James Trent, Renaissance Man. You're just an ignorant child. There is a Devil. Evil exists. There are Demons living inside our son.'

'Claire, I don't care if our marriage suffers. I don't care if you hate me for the rest of my life, but listen very carefully: my son will not be subjected to your lunatic beliefs.'

'I won't stand by and let them take him, James. I won't be frightened of my own child. I'll talk to Father Soames and we will drive them out.'

The kitchen door flew open. Jack raced upstairs. He leaned over the banister and watched his father's long shadow stop at the front door.

'Over my dead body, Claire. You hear me? Over my dead body.'

★

The Chordettes version of *Mister Sandman* blared out from downstairs. There was only one reason why his dad, who disliked all forms of music, had the record player cranked up so loud. He was really pissed off and he didn't want to talk to anybody. The barbershop harmonising of the Chordettes melted through the floorboards. The sound set Jack's heart jangling. He flopped onto his bed and opened the latest issue of *The Uncanny X-Men*. His gaze swept over the grids and speech bubbles, taking in none of the story, registering only flashes of colour. What will she say to Father Soames?

He ran his fingers into his hair and pulled the long locks tight. Just two months ago he had been happy. He'd had good friends, he'd had a family. He had never felt alone in his entire life. Now, since the accident, since *they* had forced their way into his mind, he was a leper. His friends stayed away, or wanted to pick fights with him. His mother crept around the house, trying to keep their encounters to a minimum. He didn't feel like he was her son anymore. It was as if he was an unexploded bomb that could only be defused with a mixture of quiet prayer and hysterical argument. He had caused that change in her. He had driven her into the extremes of her religion. And he was responsible for his dad's growing hatred of her.

Recently, Jack had begun to think of what it was to be human. It was like clinging to a cliff face. Your safety line was family, the niches for your hands and feet were your friends. As you climb higher, as you grow, you can look down and see more of the cliff. Understand more of where you have been and where you might be going. But what if the safety line snaps? What if you lose your footing? If you're lucky, you might find a ledge and spend the rest of your life there, going no higher, becoming no wiser, remaining a child. Jack sensed that he had found a ledge and was grateful for that at least. But the rock face around him was smooth and sheer and a dense cloud had wrapped itself around the heights of the cliff.

It was *they* that had cut his line. *They* that had chipped away the niches. *They* that clouded his route to the summit.

The time had come for a little chat.

Thirty-six

Jack's Story

Drawing them out without having to touch was easier than he had expected. He imagined a hand reaching into his mind, the fingers growing ever smaller. He began to probe the membranous tissue of his brain, seeking out their resting place. It didn't take long to find. The sac they occupied pulsed in a channel at the interface between the right and left hemispheres, overlooking the cord of his brainstem.

They were sleeping. Strand by filmy strand, he teased the little sac away. It was as the last fibre detached that the screams and shrieks started. Quickly as he could, he plucked them out of his mind and along his optic nerve. Up ahead, he could see light passing through the gelatine composite of his eye. As the light grew brighter, *they* lengthened and sharpened into the needle with which they had first pierced him. The needle-point slipped into the back of his eye and he was fired into the surface of his body.

Nothing could prepare him for the pain of re-entering his senses. It was a hundred times brighter than the fire that licked into his fingers when he touched. He was sure his brains were melting and that, any moment, his head would crack apart. Black tears ran down his face and dripped at his feet. They pooled into a living puddle. Jack began to make out crude shapes forming from the mass.

'What . . . are . . . you,' he choked. 'What do . . . you want?'

A soft gurgle answered him. As the last of the fluid slipped down his cheeks and joined the pool, another voice came from outside the room.

'Jack? Are you still awake?'

'No. Mum, don't come in.'

'I have to talk to you.'

'I said NO. Leave me alone.'

'Look, I know I've been . . .'

'Doesn't matter.'

'It does,' she whispered. 'We have to talk. About *them*.'

'For God's sake, just leave me the fuck alone!'

'I won't. You have to listen . . .'

His mother opened the door.

'Jesus in heaven.'

She stood in the doorway, her mouth open, her hand resting, almost casually, on the jamb. What was she thinking, Jack wondered. Was there a scrap of comfort she might take from the horror unfolding before her eyes? Something inside that said: if these *are* demons flowing forth from your child, then it follows that there *must* be a God.

'Go. Get out,' Jack screamed.

Gripping the edge of the bed, he spat up a mouthful of blood. It sat foaming on the surface of the pool. He watched his mother enter the room. Her voice trembled when she spoke:

'Is this . . . ?'

He nodded and wiped red streaked saliva from his mouth. He saw the terror working the muscles of her face. She began to mouth silent prayers.

'Mum. Please, you have to go.'

'No.'

She did not look at her son. Her concentration was focused entirely on the emerging shapes at his feet. She gave a sudden start as a spine lashed out from the ooze. The nodules of bones prattled across the floorboards. Other bodily components joined it, thrashing about in the mass, fighting to take form. It took only a few seconds for the assembly to be complete. The grind of bones, the snap of vertebrae, the screams of rebirth. The six, which he had not seen fully formed since the night they had entered him, staggered and slithered into being.

'God, Holy Father, keep and protect us,' she murmured. 'Strike down your righteous anger on this abomination.'

The little huddle looked from Jack to his mother. A harsh chirrup interrupted her prayers. She saw them in their entirety and faltered.

'In His name . . . Oh, *God* . . .'

She half-turned, her fingers reaching for the handle, when the door slammed shut.

For a moment, no-one moved. Not Jack nor his mother nor *them*. The hornbeam tree in the garden tapped the window with a bony finger. The floorboards groaned and settled. *Mister Sandman* hummed from downstairs. Jack thought of his father, asleep in the armchair, his fingers loose around the neck of a drained bottle. What dreams had the Sandman brought him? No nightmare to equal this.

'Leave her alone . . .'

There was a smart *click-click-click-click* as insectile legs skittered around and six faces peered at him.

'Mum, please go . . .'

'I can't.'

'Go! They won't hurt me . . .'

Hopelessly, she said: 'The door. The door won't open.'

Jack could have sworn that all six mouths smiled. Then, with moonlight on their backs, they scuttled towards her.

He watched his mother's faith drain away. Her back pressed to the door, she stumbled over prayers and passages. All his life, she had told him that every day she felt the love and comfort of God. How cruel it was that, in these last moments, she should look so abandoned. She *was* abandoned. And not just by God. Jack wanted to move. To go to her. To save her. But he was afraid.

His mother's crucifix fell from between her fingers. Paying the talisman no heed, they stepped over it and surrounded her. Claws caught at her dress and grazed her legs. An excited squeal rose from one of them.

'What have you done, Jack?' she murmured.

Her eyes never left his as the creatures slipped their hands

253

beneath her nightdress.

'Stop them.'

She pleaded. Pleaded for intervention, heavenly or human. None came.

'Please, God, make him stop them.'

Jack tore at the bed sheets. There were fractions of seconds during which he thought he had the courage to move. Then fear would roll through him again, scraping bile from his stomach and washing it into his mouth.

One of the creatures gave a contended purr. Claire Trent's head bucked forward. She began to shudder as she felt the first licks of pain between her legs. She stared wild-eyed at her son. Darkness deepened in that far corner of the room. It was as if the creatures were drawing shadows to them, cloaking the horror of their actions from uncomprehending eyes. Jack could no longer make out his mother. He could only hear her fevered breathing. Yet when she spoke, her voice came in a strange, sing-song tone.

'Inside me . . . Oh, Jack. They're inside me. Moving further and further inside . . .'

He heard it. The intimate sound of fingers reaching too deep. Soft and velvety, it prompted Jack to empty his stomach onto the floor. Over the dry heaving that followed, he heard his mother take a shocked intake of breath. Then came the report of something snapping, as of a high-tension wire being plucked in two. She did not scream. Not even when the tearing began. It became a frenzy, and Jack could only imagine the violence of it. Something broke, like a wishbone cracking between fingers. A wet, heavy splatter hit the floorboards. In the same moment, Jack wished the darkness away and prayed fervently that it would remain. Further sounds assailed him, each speaking of damage that could never be repaired.

'No! Fucking get off her! Fucking get off her! You fucking...' he screamed.

Below, he heard shattering glass and his father's frightened voice. The record skipped back across the *Mister Sandman* lyrics.

'Mum,' he whispered.

From beyond the door came a clatter of feet up the stairs.

'Jack? Open up! Jack! What's going on? Is your mother in there?'

His dad hammered on the door.

Jack got to his feet. His legs shook as he moved through the room.

'Mum?'

There was blood on the bare boards. Trails of it, as if she had tried to escape but had been dragged back into that dark corner. A broken fingernail, skin adhering, stuck out of a splinter of wood.

'Mum?'

Silence. He stepped forward, into the shadows

His mother, her face laced with blood, was lying on the floor. She was not moving. Unidentifiable trophies sat in the crook of her legs. Beneath her skirt flowed a thin evacuation of clear fluid.

They were back in their composite form. The matter touched her feet and started moving up her body. She flinched; that was all. Jack watched and was thankful for the silence. The quiet working of the thing made it seem almost natural. Her legs and abdomen were soon filmed. The mass trickled in a single finger up her front, between her breasts and along her neck. When it touched her lips, she shivered. It fanned out behind her, capping her head like a bonnet.

'Mum?'

'Jack? Is that you?' his father shouted. 'Open the door! Has she hurt you, son?'

They wrapped themselves tight around her. A living winding sheet.

Jack knelt down beside her. There was nothing left. Only the vaguest of impressions beneath the casing. Nothing, except the brooch. The white cameo of the French lady she always wore at her breast. His frustration, his shame, his anger exploded.

He would tear them off. He would rip them from her. He would save her. The moment he touched it, the fluid withdrew. It drained away from her face, unmasking dead eyes. Before his brain registered the ripple moving up his arm, one thought drowned all others: *I let them kill her.* He did not react as they flowed, triumphantly, back into his mind. He reached out and touched her face.

The door splintered open.

'Jack? Jesus. Jack, stay here. Stay with your mother. I'm going to get help.'

Footfalls raced downstairs. He heard his father giving their address. Describing how he had found his wife.

'No, she's just . . . She looks dead . . . No, there're no injuries I can see.'

Jack started. The blood had vanished from her face. The scarlet trails on the floorboards were gone.

'Jack... you must fight them...'

Her lips moved, but her eyes remained fixed.

'For the rest of your life... fight them. Find a way. Keep them from the world. Do you promise me?'

They were sleeping now. He felt them wound tight in their nook. As she continued to stare up at him, her cold, dead hand slipped into his.

'Promise me. In His name.'

He nodded. He had no tears. Her hand went limp.

Thirty-seven

'The thing with Trent is, not only is he a prissy little know-it-all, but you can bet he's never had it tough. I guarantee mummy and daddy powdered his arsehole 'til he was thirty.'

Dave Fellowes looked up from his log book and smiled.

'He's really got you riled, ain't he, Pat? This all still 'cos of Greylampton?'

Mescher banged his pint mug on the desk, spraying the log book with tea.

'Hey, steady, Big Man,' Fellowes complained.

'Y'eard about what happened this morning, didn't ya?' Mescher spat. 'Trent was found sleeping rough in a fucking college car park. I found out, took it straight up to Jarski. You know what that self-important dickhead said? He said he didn't have to explain his personnel decisions to me.'

'You're breaking my heart here, Pat. You know what? You and Jack should go on *Jerry Springer* or somethin'. Get some relationship counselling.'

'It's fucked up, that's all I'm saying. Trent's not shown his face today and he's still OIC. What?!'

A WPC had addressed Mescher as she descended into the holding area.

'PC Dawling, Sir. Says he wants to see you.'

'Can't get any lower,' Mescher grumbled. 'I'm taking orders from uniform now.'

He trudged upstairs, his face level with the WPC's buttocks. For the first time in weeks, Mescher felt his dick harden a little. Before they reached the security door, he groped inside his trousers and gave himself a quick squeeze.

Dawling waited in interview room six. There was a woman sitting on one of the plastic bucket seats, her head between her legs, vomit dried into her hair. Her clothes were cheap flash. Just a nigger tart, Mescher thought.

'Fuck me,' he muttered. 'Can't you uniform boys handle a prossie round-up no more?'

'I don't want *him*,' the woman said, pointing at Mescher. 'I told you who I want.'

'She says she's been drugged by a client, Sir,' Dawling said.

'And? What's it got to do with me?'

'Terri?' Dawling said soothingly. 'Can you tell DI Mescher who you asked for when we brought you in?'

'How many times? I *want* pretty eyes. Dumb dick here won't listen, I'll tell *you*.'

She got to her feet. Swaying as she walked, she made for Mescher. Her multicoloured beads clacked as she prodded him in the chest.

'I want scar eyes. Get scar eyes. He'll stop them hurting me. They doped me up. They raped me. Nobody here gives a shit. Get my pretty eyes . . .'

Mescher guessed who she meant, of course. Excitement sang through him. *This is it,* he thought, *I've got you, you piece of shit.* The prostitute nodded and smiled at him. He gripped her arm and shook her. The WPC made a move as if to stop him, but the look he gave her stopped the bitch dead in her tracks.

'Tell *me* who you want,' he said.

The whore laughed. Mescher took a quick look at Dawling and WPC Tits. They were pussies. He could handle them. He hit the girl hard across the face.

'Now,' he grunted. 'You gonna tell me?'

'Sca-scar eyes,' she gasped. 'I saw him. On TV, talking . . . 'bout that boy. I know him.'

'And that's the whole truth, so help me God,' Jack concluded.

Time was called at the bar. Dawn drained her second vodka and lemonade. She felt Jack's eyes upon her. She wondered what reaction he expected. How do you react to something so horribly absurd? She wanted to laugh, to cry, to scream, to reason with him, to hold him close, to run away and hide her son from this softly-spoken lunatic. She did none of these things. She went back to the beginning and tried to consider things logically.

After they left Jamie with her father, they had gone to the Four Feathers. It was a favourite haunt of off-duty coppers. Ringo, the landlord, opened up the function room in the back so that they could talk without fear of interruption. Dawn had listened without comment to Jack's story. During the more fantastical episodes, she expected him to look away, but it was when describing those incidents - the accident, his mother's 'murder', the creatures - that he held her eyes. Whatever the real story of his life, it was clear that this catalogue of insanity was the version he believed.

She looked around the function room. Her eyes moved from red felt wallpaper to the dull brasses, from framed lithographs of this quarter of the city a century ago to the humming jukebox.

Jack's phone rang. He cancelled the call. She decided her tack:

'What happened afterwards?'

'She was buried . . . I knew my dad wondered sometimes, but he was too smart to see the truth. That I did kill her.'

'You didn't kill your mother, Jack.'

'Well, let her die then. It was murder by omission.'

'And these things. They're still . . .'

'In here,' he tapped his temple. 'I tried to keep my promise. Gradually, I gained some kind of control over them. They hated logic, so I used logic against them. I found that, having seen inside my mind once, I could impose a structure upon it. I think we all do that anyway, on a subconscious level. But mine was a conscious effort. I constructed a place for them. A prison that they would find it hard to escape from. Every day since then, I've fortified that prison. I've trained my mind. And I've kept myself alone.'

'Your mother never said you had to live alone.'

'She told me to fight them. This is the only way I know how. They draw energy from intimacy, affection, hatred, love . . .Touching. Emotion is so close to imagination, Dawn. There's a symbiotic relationship between the two things. Imagination can shape emotion and emotion can fire imagination. Both weaken logic, and it's only logic that keeps them locked away. That's why I couldn't . . .'

'Then why did you even try? With me?'

'They'd become so weak. I could barely sense them. For more than twenty years, I ground them down; for all I knew they were dead. And then my father passed away. He was the only one who loved me without needing to know the whole truth. For the first time, I really was alone . . . But there was you. And I thought that, one day, there might be a chance that I could explain it all to you. That first day we met, you remember? I touched you. I saw you. So kind, so loving. So afraid. I was drawn to you, to your compassion. I wanted to be happy, just once. It was selfish. I can never forgive myself for the risk I took. The danger I put you and Jamie in. But I thought they might be gone.'

'But they weren't. You felt them again?'

'The first time we . . . I sensed them. The slightest flinch. I had to stop. To pull away from you. As the weeks passed, I began to convince myself that I had imagined it. Then, the night we tried again, the last night, they broke free and flooded back through my mind. It was all I could do to stop them reaching out. From hurting you.'

'You think they're evil.'

'Of course they are. They killed my mother. They tore her . . .'

'Your father didn't see that. And they saved your life. On the Death Bank.'

'They saved themselves. They were parasites protecting their host. If I died, they died.'

It was time to stop this.

'*They*, Jack? They are not real. What did the doctors say your mother died of . . . ?'

'Embolism.'

'And you were guilty? You saw it and you couldn't help her. You know this is all make-believe, don't you? You've skewed your memory. Changed your past. Your accident happened, but you've worked these things into a retelling of it, to give them an origin story. A genesis. Those things are mental projections of your guilt. Nothing more.'

'Spare me the pop psychology, Dawn. If I'd created these things to project my guilt onto, then why do I still feel guilty?'

'Because guilt is a fluid emotion, and the story you've constructed to contain it is like a leaking paper bag. Jack, your mother died naturally. It *wasn't* your fault.'

'We don't have time for you to be sceptical, Dawn. They're back. I brought them back by trying to get close to you. In the long run, it may have been a blessing. Albeit in the best fucking disguise ever seen. The touching shows me things from a person's past. With the dreaming, they paint the future. I had my first waking dream in years last Friday . . .' he breathed hard. 'Dawn, it showed me how Jamie is going to die.'

'Don't, Jack.'

'Please. I have to tell you.'

She listened as he revealed what he claimed to have kept hidden for the last few days. In his dreams, he had seen a man murder her son. He told her that he had discovered that Simon's body had been taken over by Peter Malahyde according to some arcane ritual. Oliver Godfrey and Stephen Lloyd had been murdered in order to complete a second ritual that would involve Jamie. Jack believed that Peter had tired of his son's form and wanted a new one.

'You have to believe it, Dawn.'

His phone rang.

'Answer it,' she said.

'Jack Trent . . . Yes, hello . . . Calm down. Where are you? Stay there . . . I'm coming.'

He stared down at the phone, as if he mistrusted what he had just heard.

'What is it? Jack?'

'That was Doug Winters. He's just seen Simon Malahyde.'

Thirty-eight

The *Lazarus Club* on Lexington Avenue was only three streets from the Four Feathers. It was a gaudy super-club, complete with neon lights, plastic Doric columns and a huge Medusa bust, sporting dramatically coiffured steel snakes. Doug Winters waited for them in the foyer. Joll, the six foot seven wall of hair that had let them into Doug's house on Berwick Street, was holding him up.

'Doug, what have you seen?' Jack asked.

'He's here. Simon. He wants to see you. He's . . . different somehow.'

'What has he said?'

'Bring Trent. That's all. Bring Trent.'

The boy shuddered. His housemate led Doug to a red leather sofa and whispered something to him. Then Joll held Doug to his chest and kissed the kid's head. Leaving his friend, Joll waved Jack and Dawn into a far corner.

'Look, I don't know what's goin' on,' Joll said, in a deep baritone. 'I managed to get Dougie out tonight because I thought it'd do him good, but maybe he's still too freaked. He says he saw Simon in the VIP bar upstairs. I run this club-night and we don't open that bar, but I've put two bouncers outside.'

Jack started up the stairs.

'Whoa, you're not going alone,' Dawn called after him.

'Please, Dawn, trust me this once.'

He did not wait for a response. A wall of sound hit him as he stepped onto the mezzanine level of the club. The VIP bar stretched the length of the upper floor. If someone watched from behind its tinted windows, then he watched unseen. Jack began pushing his way through the crowds. He felt ridiculous in his sober suit, a dull grey pike swimming against a shoal of exotic fish. The dance beat rose, heavy on the sweat-laced air. A lighting rig sunk from the ceiling and pulsed sheer white flashes in time to the beat.

He reached the stairs. Moving the barriers aside, he climbed up to the VIP lounge and flashed his ID at the two bouncers. They looked relieved to see him.

'Has he come out?' Jack asked.

'No. He's still in there,' the stockier, bearded bouncer said. 'Is this guy really the one who killed them little lads?'

'We oughta go in there and tear him to pieces,' the smaller bouncer shouted.

'Be my guest,' Jack said.

The two men looked towards the red leather cushioned door.

'Something's not right about this fucker. Am I right?'

'You're right,' Jack answered. 'Look, there's a lady downstairs, dressed in a navy business suit. I don't want her coming up here, could you keep her out the way?'

They nodded and descended to the mezzanine. Jack stood on the balcony before the lounge doors, summoning courage and wondering who or what had sent for him. The bass track pounded over the squeal and groan of a thousand conversations. Down there, bodies moved and ground against each other. In the lounge, a cool, clean quiet waited for him. Oliver Godfrey's dead face, staring out of the catacombs, snapped into his mind. *The Doctor will see you now . . .*

Anne stood inside the bricked-up room, feeling the weight of lost years and the acuteness of her betrayal. Simon had been here . . . She imagined her ten-year-old son hearing the voices that called to him from this place. His hand touching the warped panels. Pushing. And inside, in the gloom, two figures waiting for him. They hadn't taken him at once, of course. The picture the policewoman had found showed that

264

they had coaxed the child for a while. Perhaps, before the end, the little boy visited them many times. Brought his drawings and his toys. Here, in the dark, he had played with ghosts.

Her penance must now be for Simon, for not being a mother to him. But for the first time in years, she was finding penance hard. Every time she closed her eyes, she saw her son's (*the thing's*) crumpled skull. The horror of his revelation, and what it had driven her to, set a mist over her thoughts. Now, in the room that she had feared for so long, and which no longer held the same horror for her, she relived it again.

Monday. Only a week ago. She had heard . . .

. . . gravel beneath tyres. A car door slammed shut. The crisp tread up to the front door. Scraping shoes on the tiled floor of the hall. Low, sweet humming.

The lounge door opened. Simon, blood of her blood, flesh of her flesh, yet unknown to her, entered the room. She had been staring into the fire for hours, mesmerised by the flames.

'Why do we make faces in the fire,' he said, circling her, 'when we don't see the faces around us? Are you still grieving for Papa? How tedious.'

She was surprised by his words. He had never mentioned Peter before.

'You - you don't understand, Simon. Your father . . .'

'Don't I? Did he talk about me before he died? Pass on any messages or pearls of wisdom to the son he would never meet? Of course, you wouldn't know. You left him to his lonely end. Now, *I* know cruel, but even I doff my hat to you. That's fucking heartless. But don't grieve, Mother. He wasn't really alone. I was *always* with him.'

Anne looked up at her son and saw him - really *saw* him - for the first time. A young face with an inexplicable weight of age stamped upon it.

'What do you mean?' she asked.

'Just what I said. I was with him in the last hours. When his face was gone, when his heart burst. So much pain. So much blood. Darkness in the darkened room . . . And all that *screaming*. You still hear it, don't you? Poor Mother, your life hasn't been easy . . .' He passed behind her. 'And I'm sorry, but I'm afraid it's about to get much, much worse.'

Pain tore through her scalp. She gasped and reached back, scratching his strong fingers. He drew her head over the lip of the couch.

'The time has come, the Walrus said, to talk of many things: of shoes and ships and sealing wax of cabbages and kings . . .'

Strands of hair loosened at their roots.

'And how your husband never died, and whether souls have wings.'

The wooden back of the couch cut into her neck. A thread of saliva hung from Simon's mouth and wound down to touch her lips. She tried to bring her hands up to scratch him, but her spine was twisted, taut as a crossbow, and her arms had no strength. It was as she stared into his eyes that fear began to temper her pain. Something was changing in those cold blue pools.

His lips traced the contours of her cheeks and jaw. Her skin crawled under his caress. He kissed her, full and deep, his tongue searching the barrier of clenched teeth. Then his mouth moved to her ear and breathed soft, devastating words. The years rolled back and forth in her mind as the truth was revealed. She listened to Simon, while at the same time echoes from the past returned to haunt her. What had she overheard the nurses say?

'*Poor man. So lonely. Sometimes he even speaks to himself, as if there really is someone else in the room with him . . .*'

What had the priest told her?

'*You must listen. That thing you call your son contains only a bare trace of Simon. It is something else.*'

His revelation done, she saw the bitter irony of the last seventeen years. All that grief for a dead man who still walked.

All those days and nights, all that life, wasted. Yet her anger was nothing compared to her horror. Her child had been taken and she had let it happen.

'Now you know.'

He wound her hair tight around his fist and tore a clump of it from her scalp. She didn't make a sound.

'They're still here, you know. Peter and the boy,' the deep, sweet voice continued. 'We all live together quite harmoniously. They know who the master of the house is. Every now and then, however, they try to have their say. Especially the child. Wilful little tyke, he is. They're trying to stop me now . . .'

'Who are you? How did you . . . ?'

'Haven't you been listening? I couldn't have done anything without Peter. He was my way in, you are my way out.'

'What do you mean?'

'Let me show you.'

The thing thrust its hand into the fire. Flames licked between the fingers, but there was no crack of roasting skin, no cry of pain.

'I could douse myself in petrol and walk through the fire unscathed. There are only two ways out of this arrangement. One I do not care for. The other . . .'

Before she could react, he dragged her from the couch and threw her onto the floor. He sat astride her, splaying her arms wide and pinning them beneath his knees. The points of his hair combed her face.

'The other might prove rather fun.'

He stretched a hand behind his back. The pressure of his weight on her breasts was agony. Then came the touch of his fingers as they spidered along the inside of her leg. He rode the skirt up to her stomach. She tried to buck him forward, but his knees dug into her biceps. Those cold fingers began to tease beneath the band of her knickers. She felt his nails graze through her pubic hair. At the same moment, through his trousers, his penis rocked hard against her. With his free hand, he ground fingertips into the raw patch he had torn from her scalp.

'I'm gonna fuck you, Mummy. How do you think that'll make little Simon feel? He can see all this, you know.'

The thing smeared two arcs of her blood beneath its eyes.

'He watches through these. All Simon can do is watch while I rape his mother with his own . . .'

A kick of adrenalin rushed through her. The torn muscles in her arm rallied. She punched upwards. He pitched forward, his hand snapping from between her legs. She heard the crack of his head against the grate. Sparks from the fire flew into his hair, burned low and went out. He made no move to get up. He smiled, showing her a row of smart white teeth. So like Peter . . .

'That's the spirit. Why don't you finish it? Why don't you *live* for once?'

She grabbed the poker from beside his head and stood over him. His hair fanned out like a mane of dark blood. She hesitated.

Mad. Surely he was mad. It couldn't be true . . .

His face began to change. It was not a violent process, but one of calm fluidity. Accompanied by a strange susurration, features rustled out of the skull or crumbled away. The skin weathered, the hues hardened; an autumnal change worked across the landscape of the face. Hair receded and the pigmentation of his eyes darkened. The transformation complete, a new mouth gasped for air. Peter. Peter as he had been before the illness. Peter, wracked with pain that was not physical.

'Annie . . . Jesus, I'm so sorry . . .'

'Peter. Why?'

'The things he's done. The things he's made our boy do . . . I'll burn for this, Annie. I'll *burn*.'

'You let him . . . Your own son.' Inside she was screaming. Outside, she was surprised at how level her voice sounded. 'I deserved anything, but Simon . . .'

'I made the bargain. I didn't realise . . . Finish it, please, Annie.'

Peter's face contorted. His heavy brow shortened and smoothed out. The large nose contracted into a tiny snub. Colour suffused the greyness, and autumn turned to spring. Lying in the outsize clothes on the marble surround was her son as he had been at ten years old. The boy's face twisted. She could hear the grind of his teeth.

'It hurts so much,' he whispered. 'Please make it stop hurting.'

'Simon? I – I can't . . . . You're still in there . . .'

'He makes me do things. He says he won't ever let me go.'

The child-face crumpled. Between the tufts of flaxen hair, long dark strands began to grow. The features lengthened, the eyes darkened.

'Fucking kill me, you bitch. Fucking kill me. I'll do things to your child you wouldn't believe. Kill me now.'

The thing had returned to its usual guise. It lay very still, waiting for her move. Heat licked along her arms as she raised the poker.

'That's it. Do it,' it laughed. 'Do it for love.'

She did not hesitate. She rained down the poker, tearing the creature's head to pieces. Blood flecked her face; so warm and so wet. Her arms grew heavy, but she did not stop. She pummelled the yielding head until she heard the prang of metal upon stone. When she opened her eyes, she saw her son's skull crushed almost flat against the marble. Blood ran in rills over the lip of the surround and onto the carpet. Chips of bone, no larger than baby teeth, adhered to the grapnel of the poker.

'My, my.' The fat little priest from the village stood in the doorway.

Why had he been there? She could not remember. Something about having seen Simon driving erratically through the village and wanting to check he'd made it home all right.

He had helped her. He told her that he knew what Simon was. An abomination. She had been right to end that life. He cleaned the gore from the fireplace and sponged the blood from the carpet. They wrapped Simon in cut up bin bags and taped him tight. Then they carried him from the house and placed him in the boot of his car. As the priest started the Triumph, he had given her some final instructions.

'You'll have to report him missing. It'll look suspicious if a friend goes to the police first. When they come, your story is you heard nothing, saw nothing. Don't overdo the worried mother routine, but if they drag their heels kick up a fuss.'

'Where're you taking him?'

'The less you know about what happens now the better.'

'What do I do?'

'Go back to your daily routine. I'll help you as much as I can. Now I need to take care of the body.'

The tail lights drew away down the drive and passed between the trees like blinking red eyes.

Why had he helped her? Because he'd really known what Simon had been? Because he thought that such a thing deserved death? Perhaps, but something had struck her the day she had gone to see him at the *Old Priory*. There had been a kind of relief in his eyes. An impression of quiet victory.

Whatever his motives, the priest's help had robbed her of the punishment she yearned for. As she stood now in the bricked-up room, staring at the bed in which Peter had died (not died, *changed*) she longed for the retribution of others. Seventeen years of self-imposed punishment had drained her. She took out Trent's card and punched his number into the cordless phone. While she waited for the connection, Anne took off her headscarf. Her fingers went to the soft, wet infection on her scalp. She dug deep into the mush until the pain blinded her. Still it was not enough.

'*Jack Trent. Leave a message.*'

'Mr Trent, this is Anne Malahyde. I must speak to you. I don't have it in me to punish myself any more. You have to help me. You have to make them punish me . . . I killed him. I killed my son. I didn't see . . .'

She stopped. She had heard something. Door opening. Door closing. Footsteps below. Footsteps on the stairs.

'*Thank you. If you wish to rerecord your message.*'

Across the landing. The door creaked open. Dust swept into her eyes.

'Praise God, Mrs Malahyde,' the priest said. 'Your punishment has come.'

WEDNESDAY 30th OCTOBER 2002

Like one, that on a lonesome road
Doth walk in fear and dread,
And having once turned round walks on,
And turns no more his head;
Because he knows, a frightful fiend
Doth close behind him tread.
>   Samuel Taylor Coleridge,
>   *The Rime of the Ancient Mariner,* 1798

Thirty-nine

In the crucible below, the press of young bodies ground and melted against each other. How strange they looked, moving without the context of sound or the stale blend of sweat and perfume. Behind soundproofed windows, a man, and something that was not a man, watched.

'They fritter their youth away, hardly conscious that time is bearing down upon them. They will only recognise the value of what they have now when their eyes are dimmed and their flesh is wasted.'

'Quite the philosopher,' Jack muttered. 'Shall we cut to the chase?'

'Sarcasm, Mr Trent, is indicative of fear.'

'And bullshit is indicative of a bullshitter. Let's start with a couple of easy ones, shall we? What am I talking to? Are you even alive?'

Jack didn't turn to look at the figure beside him. As the thing wasn't really there, then conversing with its reflection in the tinted glass seemed just as appropriate as talking to it face-to-face. Jack guessed that the almost opalescent features in the glass were those of the grown Simon Malahyde.

'Let's say I'm between properties. I spent seven interesting years in my last place. Now I've got my eye on a new prospect. You might know it: pubescent, lovely green eyes. Just my sort of thing.'

'I won't let you take him,' Jack said. 'I know how you do it and I can stop you.'

'Well, well, Mr Trent, I believe you have paid a visit to the best little metaphysical library in town.'

'Cut the crap. Tell me what happened to Simon Malahyde.'

'Simon and his father are gone. The boy may be at peace, such an innocent. His father? Who can say? His pact with me *was* rather naughty, don't you think?'

'You're not Peter Malahyde?'

'Hasn't Asher Brody told you about me yet? He does have a somewhat irritating habit of being deliberately mysterious. No, I'm not Peter. And Simon, 'the vessel' that is, is wrapped in plastic and rotting at the bottom of a river.'

'How did he – the body – how did it die? Did you kill yourself?'

'You haven't read the *Transmigration of Souls* very closely, have you?'

'I ran out of time.'

'The sands wait for no man, eh? Especially not in the Yeager Library. I'm surprised you found your way out. But no, I'm afraid that, once the transition is made, the soul is bound to the body in such a way that suicide is impossible. There are only two ways to end the taken life. The first is natural, psychic decay. Depending on the body and how it is used, the spiritual cohesiveness of it will begin to fail after a certain time. It's the delayed reaction of the body rejecting an alien soul. Much like in organ transplantation, often the host rejects foreign tissue. But it is a slow rejection, usually taking decades. In the special case of Simon, the period was only seven years . . .'

'Why?'

'I'd've thought you might have guessed that. In the usual practice of the ritual, one living man imposes his soul over that of a child. With Simon, things were different. I could not impose my will exclusively. Weak as they were, I had to share the body.'

'Simon and his father . . .'

The face in the glass flashed a serene smile.

'A dark trinity of father, son and a less than holy ghost. It appealed to my sensibilities. A grand 'fuck you' to the Almighty.

276

This crowding, however, impacted on the longevity of the arrangement. Psychic decay kicked in earlier than usual. That particular route out of the body is rather . . . messy. I decided to expedite matters. Suicide isn't possible, but murder is. I could easily have paid someone to kill me, but I have always taken a rather twisted delight in poetic justice. I convinced someone who had blamed herself for seventeen years for the death of her husband to kill him again. It was rather funny, I thought.'

'You're telling me Anne Malahyde killed her own son?'

'With a little prodding.'

'So you *are* dead.'

'Dead, alive. Indelicate, absolutist terms. Since my soul left Simon's body, I have a certain physical presence, which is almost spent. By Thursday I shall be, in the common parlance, a ghost. I have tasted that level of existence once before. I do not plan to let it happen again. The boys are dead, their fat already harvested, the baptism dresses ready to be burned. All I need now is Jamie.'

'Then why haven't you taken him? He told me he's seen you . . .'

'Time is a factor, but I'm in no real hurry. I'll be spending many years inside the child, so I'd like to get a good feel for him first. And, I must admit, I do enjoy a little sadism along the way.'

'Why are you telling me all this?'

'I'm telling you, Mr Trent, because we've already met. Do you recall?'

'The work shed.'

'Bravo. I'll wager you've only just remembered that. People always seem reluctant to remember me when I meet them with my true face. I've adopted Simon's appearance just now, so that we can have this tête-à-tête without all the tedious screaming. Yes, that's the first time we met, but I have a vague memory of seeing you before that day. As if through a veil . . . What remarkable dreams you have . . .

'When we met in the work shed, I saw two things through

277

your eyes. The first was Jamie. He rather upset my plans. You see, I originally had young Oliver Godfrey's brother in mind to be my vessel. But there was something about young Mr Howard I found irresistible. The second thing I saw was some power within *you*. I like a challenge, Mr Trent. I see no purpose to this existence, this perpetual rejuvenation, without challenges. This is a battle of wills between us, but I want to play fair and lay my cards on the table. I know how far I will go to get what I want. How far, I wonder, will you venture? The music is playing. Will you, won't you, will you, won't you, will you join the dance?'

'Okay, you've jawed for a while. Now let *me* tell *you* something,' Jack said. 'You may have lived a long time, know a lot of things, but you won't take this boy. You can't frighten me.'

'Fancy yourself as something of a hero, Jack? Well, we shall see. You do know, however, that you're quite wrong.'

'About what?'

'I can frighten you. The Doctor knows where it hurts.'

Jack turned and looked at the figure beside him. In a moment, Simon Malahyde's face was gone, replaced by that blood-splattered horror that had stared at him from *the dreaming*. The skin tightened around the skull until the bone shone through. The eyes rolled back and sank into their sockets. Jack stared into those hollows. He shuddered to see what was written there: failure, despair, death, and an endless torment.

'No. It . . . won't be like that,' he shouted. 'I'll be there for him.'

The face smiled pityingly and melted away.

'Jesus Christ, Jack. What the hell's wrong with you?'

Wafts of skin settled across Jack's face. He brushed the dust from his eyelashes and saw Dawn standing in the doorway.

'Who were you talking to?'

'Dawn, he was here. You – you must have seen . . .'

'I saw no-one. You were talking to yourself.'

'He wants Jamie. He's going to take him. I can't stop it.'

'You're insane. Jesus, you *are*.'

278

'Dawn . . .'

'Don't you ever come near him. Don't ever come near my boy.'

'Please. Please wait.'

The door swung to. Jack ran after her. Once outside the air-conditioned saloon bar, the heat hit him. He reeled back and vomited down his front. Disorientated, half-blind, he groped for the handrail. Reaching the mezzanine level, he pushed aside the bouncers and their questions. Hands jostled him, mouths screamed obscenities in his ear:

'Bastard spilt my drink.'

Pain exploded along his spine as a fist smashed into the small of his back. He fell to his knees, choking as he tried to catch his breath.

'Leave him alone, he's fucked . . .'

It took a while to muster the strength to stand. He staggered to his feet. A welcome blast of cold air prickled his face as he shouldered through onto the outside landing. The foyer was empty.

They had left her car at the Four Feathers. She had a start on him, but if he ran all the way he might catch up with her. He raced out of the club and turned left down a side alley. Vaulting bin bags, he banked left again into a dimly lit mews. His footsteps reverberating off the cobbles sounded like a fusillade of gunfire. As he ran, he relived the horror of what he had seen in those gaping, dark eyes: The End. How the game would be played out; how the cards would fall. The truth of it - for he believed he *had* witnessed the truth - terrified him. For the first time, he felt his resolve waver. In the vision, he had seen himself running, like he had wanted to in the first dream. The reality was, Jack Trent was no hero. The time would come, and he would leave Jamie to face his fate alone in the clearing.

Jack emerged from the mews. The car park of the Four Feathers was across the street. He saw Dawn climb into her Range Rover. There was no time to think through what he was going to say. *Please God, just give me the words to make her believe* . . . He started forward. Stopped. Through plumes of steamed breath, he watched her. She was crying. She was crying for him. He took something from that sight. Something powerful.

He felt a hand on his shoulder.

'Leave this to me, Mr Trent. You need to rest.'

Jack turned. Behind him, he heard the growl of the engine. Headlights spilled down the mews and swept over the windows of the old stable buildings. The light flashed across the strong, grey face of the old man.

'Brody?'

'The confluence of old and new. I feel like a hoary Old Testament prophet handing the sword over to a new champion. You have only a short time now. Take this.'

Brody handed Jack an oblong package wrapped in brown paper.

'Rest first. A few hours at least. Then read.'

'I can't. I must . . .'

'Will she listen to you? Tell me where she has gone. I'll protect the boy tonight.'

With faith in his own power to save Jamie all but spent, Jack gave Dawn's address and that of her father's house. He also told Brody his own address.

'You've seen him, haven't you?' Brody said, buttoning his ragged coat.

'I saw the end.'

'Take heart. You saw the end as he would have it. Horror, Mr Trent, is in shadow. Throw light on the shadow and the horror falls away. This,' Brody indicated the package in Jack's hands, 'is a candle.'

Forty

Elvis' dashboard gyration wound down. Bob Peterson set the toy dancing again. For the thirtieth time that night, he flipped open the glove compartment and ran his finger along the cold body of the Walther semi-automatic. Jesus, this was fucked up. He should have just told Jack 'no'. But the guy had sounded scared, and Bob knew that Jack Trent was a man, like himself, not easily scared. This kid must be in real trouble. Be that as it may, tomorrow he'd call the whole thing off. Bob Peterson didn't put his cock on the block for nobody.

He scrunched down as the Range Rover pulled into the cul-de-sac. She was alone. Eyeing the Walther one last time, he made up his mind and heaved himself out of the car. Despite Jack's instruction on the issue, Bob felt that he had to tell this woman that her son was in danger. She had a right to know.

'Miss? I . . .'

She spun round and demanded, 'Who are you?'

Bob was struck at once by her strength. Occasionally, he met clients like her. Very occasionally. The sort who thanked you after you'd shown them the photos of their hubby porking the nanny. No hysterics, no tears, no threats. She just gathers up the kids, leaves home and takes the bastard for everything he's got. Not insensitive, not inhuman; just real strong. Bob admired those women.

'My name's Bob Peterson. Look, you know someone called Trent? Jack Trent?'

He told her the full story: about Jack asking him to follow her son, about the man's insistence that he carry a firearm.

He supposed that, having reflected on the sort of woman she was, he should not have expected a reaction. Still, her calm acceptance of it all made him feel as if he hadn't explained things very well.

'You know, Jack, he's no fool. He must believe . . .'

'I know what Mr Trent believes. What do you believe, Mr Peterson?'

'Me? I don't . . . You see, I'm clever in my own way. Wily, I suppose. But Jack, I've known him a long time. Well, not *known* him, I don't reckon nobody *knows* him. But he doesn't do things for no good reason. My opinion: your boy's in trouble. Believe it.'

She thanked him for his frankness and, before he could say another word, she stepped into the house and closed the door.

Still confused and worried, Bob began retracing his steps. It wasn't until he was within a few feet of his car that he saw the man leaning against the driver door, drumming sausage fingers on the roof. Pat Mescher's huge head turned from contemplating the interior.

Bollocks, Bob thought, as he looked past Mescher to see the Walther P99 sitting in the open glove compartment.

'Mr Bob Peterson. Well, well. What are y'doin' here?'

'Mescher. Free country, isn't it?'

'It certainly is, Roberto. But, and this may come as news to you, this ain't the Alamo. Now, you're goin' to tell me what your heart-to-heart with Miss Howard was all about, or there'll be all the Jailhouse Rock and corn-holing you could wish for.'

Grinning, like the fattest Halloween pumpkin Bob had ever seen, Mescher opened the passenger door.

Jack moved from empty street to empty house. He tried calling Bob Peterson for an update on the surveillance, but the bastard's phone was switched off. Sitting on his bed, he thumbed through the comic Jamie had been reading earlier. His knuckles started to throb. He went to the bathroom and peeled back the filthy bandage. On the way to the Four Feathers, Dawn had expressed concern that he had not properly tended the wound. He told her that he hadn't given it much thought. It wasn't bravado, in the last few days his physical wellbeing had not been foremost in his mind.

He ran scalding water over the cuts, grinding his teeth as thick strands of infection bled away. He reached over to the sparsely equipped medicine cabinet. The nearest thing to antiseptic was mouthwash. Hissing, he trickled *Mr Gumshine* over the cuts.

As he picked the old dressing from the sink, clean blood trickled from his fingers and stained it afresh. Something shifted in his mind. The image of the dirty bandage, spotted red, moved like a gear release in some forgotten mechanism. It began a chain reaction. Teeth of small cogs intersected with larger wheels until the whole memory of his escape from the Yeager Library was active.

' . . . I have to go. Please, I have to save the boy.'

'As I read the situation, Jack, you have things somewhat upside down. Much better for you to remain within these walls. Out of reach. Out of Time.'

The possibility of forcing his way out of the room was only just occurring to Jack, when the librarian slipped into the corridor and locked the door behind him. Jack sent the rickety wooden chair crashing to the floor. He hammered on the door until the sides of his hands were raw. After what may have been half an hour, he heard footsteps in the stone flagged corridor outside.

'Do you require a book, Mr Trent?' came the voice of the librarian.

'No. Jesus, please, just let me out.'

'If you do not require a book, please hush. This *is* a library.'

'A boy's going to be taken. His *soul's* going to be taken. Don't you care?'

There was no answer. Exhausted, Jack turned back to the

room. He was shocked to see how small the chamber looked. When he entered, the ceiling had been high, reaching up twenty feet or so and arched across with great ribs. Now the roof was a few feet above his head. Likewise, the room seemed much shorter and narrower, barely allowing enough space for him to pass between the wall and desk. And where was that small octagonal window? Now there was just bare brickwork making up the rear wall.

It's like a tomb, Jack thought. *Like a recess . . . like a catacomb.*

Ridiculous as it seemed, he went about the room, pushing and tapping at bricks, hoping that one would slide back and reveal a secret passage. Having tested all the flagstones and bricks within reach, he dragged the table around the walls and probed the roof, inch by inch. As he went, he could hear faint murmurs, as of reading aloud, from the neighbouring rooms. And once, high-pitched, crazed laughter. It was hopeless. He jumped down from the desk and kicked it into a corner. He slumped to the floor and started twisting handfuls of straw around his fists. If there was no way out for Mewes and Marlowe, then there was no way out for Jack Trent. Jamie's young life would be taken while he endured here through the centuries. And he would never see her again. Never be able to touch her or explain. All he would have now was the aged skin of paper between his fingers.

They stirred.

That grit, that kernel at the back of his brain. He closed his eyes and swept down their corridor, threw open the door of their prison and stood over the toy box. He could hear the thick sound of their bodies forming from the gestalt mass. As he listened to their motions, a new kind of despair settled over his thoughts. There really was no way out. He knew that he could plead with the librarian until words ran dry, but would never be set free. Not because the man was cruel, but because some laws truly are immutable.

Inside his mind, he saw himself taking the tiny key from his pocket. He fitted it into the padlock that harnessed the chains to the toy box. *Why not?* He thought. *Better this than eternity alone.* He tore off the chains and straps and threw open the lid.

This was where the memory stuttered. He remembered the rest in snatches:

The pain as they pierced his eye. The black pool of emerging shapes. The six, half-formed, growing from the puddle. Then the sight of them: slinking, clawing, padding across the floor and to the back wall of the chamber. Blood running from his nose and spotting the dressing across his hand. His excitement, as he crawled after them, suddenly unafraid. Afraid of nothing now. Their hands, their talons, their barbed legs tearing at the brickwork. Dust flying into his face, shards of stone scratching his skin. Bricks thrown aside, missing his head by inches. Hurried footsteps in the corridor. A key grinding in the lock. The librarian looking down at him.

'We don't encourage visitors, Mr Trent.'

'They're with me,' Jack smiled.

'Very well. You go blindly to your fate, Jack. Better you stayed here.'

The librarian closed the door. Cold, odourless air roared through a fissure in the wall. The pages of the *Transmigration* were torn from their binding and swept about the room in a tight cyclonic swirl. A wave of exhaustion passed over Jack. He couldn't keep his eyes open. He felt a hand reach around his throat and pull him over the lip of rubble. Then, the tip into nothingness. There was a rush all around him. Perhaps he opened his eyes, but if he did he saw only unending darkness. He slept.

When he woke, he found himself back in the grounds of Jericho. Before taking in his surroundings or the questions of PC Dawling, he had reached into his mind. They were there. Lodged safely in the toy box again.

Standing now in front of the smashed mirror, where it had all begun, he wondered about what Dawn had said in the Four Feathers:

'And they saved your life, Jack . . .'

Perhaps they had saved him in the Yeager Library. Or perhaps they had wanted to show that they were merciful where he was cruel. He still held the keys to their prison.

Wrapping his hand in fresh bandages, he went through into the lounge. He shifted a box of clothes from his favourite tattered easy chair, switched on a reading lamp and opened the package Brody had given him.

The manuscript was written in pencil on thin paper. Jack recognised the crabbed handwriting from the later Brody diaries he had found at the nursing home. In some places the paper was torn through where agitated corrections had been made.

Jack made short work of the introduction detailing the history of Crow Haven. He was not surprised by what he read. Ever since coming to that village in the vale, he had felt that something abided there. Some pervasive, unfocused force, of which Simon Malahyde might be only one facet.

He turned to the rest of the bundle. From the back of the house came the moan of the wind and the constant flutter of tarpaulin, like the flapping of huge bird wings.

The night noises faded as he read.

Forty-one

Brody's Story

Fittingly perhaps, it was on the eve of the Feast of Epiphany in 1976 that I came to Crow Haven. Those grey, indefinite moments before dawn found me standing on the hill that overlooks the little community. Light played through the trees around me, but if anything the village grew darker, as if it was gathering the last of the night into its tiny pocket. These first impressions inspired a childish bout of homesickness. I found myself longing for the broad plains and mist-laced mountains that I had left behind only forty hours before. And for the quick-waking town at the foot of the Andes that had been my home for the last ten years. So high and wide everything seemed in my memory; so low and mean this English village appeared to be.

I shook myself. I had no right to feel miserable. I had requested this transfer myself, thinking I was becoming too comfortable in my pretty Peruvian parish. Not having been to England, I had asked for an appointment here. If I was stuck in a backwater that was my own fault. In any case, this pessimism was no more than the effects of exhaustion. I had arrived in England the previous evening, hired a car and driven through the night. Jetlag had kept me alert into the small hours and now my long journey was beginning to tell. I must not let tiredness spoil my first impression. I took it in again.

The road before me rolled down and arced around the village until it rose again, at a shallower pitch, over another

287

rise. The cluster of houses, the obelisk war memorial, the school building, the church and a small farm sat in the basin. All of it hemmed by a forest, whose tall trees, I now realised, kept night cast over the village. Such strange trees. Even the branches of the youngest saplings were contorted, like arthritically twisted fingers.

I surveyed the full expanse of the forest. It seemed to me the apotheosis of those dark, enchanted woods from the pages of Grimm's Fairy Tales.

Despite my tiredness, I could not sleep. My bed at the *Old Priory* was too soft and my internal clock had not yet readjusted. I got up and decided to go through my predecessor's papers, in order to familiarise myself with the parish. I was surprised by the absence of old sermons, notes for upcoming festivals and personal reflections that one would expect a priest to keep. In fact, I discovered only one piece of writing in the late Father Tolly's hand. It was a brief note, stuffed between bills and receipts in an old tin box. Mystifyingly, it was addressed to me. To my knowledge there had been no talk of Tolly retiring before his stroke, and even if there had been, he could not have known that I would be his replacement. I could make no sense of it.

Holding the half-page up to the light, I read:

My dear Brody,
    Its evil abideth within and without; until the Darkness exhausts Itself and the Flood taketh away all Sorrow.
    My blessing goes with you.
    The unhappy Father Robert Tolly.

I had been in the village almost two months when I heard about the house being built in the forest. I knew all my parishioners by this time, if only by name. Most of the congregation came from neighbouring villages, where I would preach on a cyclical basis, my base remaining in Crow Haven. They gave me a friendly honeymoon period, plying me with enough homemade preserves to turn a WI committee green with envy. The few Crow Haven parishioners, however, were quite different. They took Communion, seemed willing to pitch in at functions or festivals, listened attentively enough to my sermons, but they kept themselves set apart from the rest of the flock. Cornered, they would pass the time of day, but their speech was always short and guarded. Even taking confession, I sensed reticence in the outpouring of their sins. After a few weeks in the job, I asked an outside parishioner what he thought of the village.

'Unlucky place,' he said. 'Bad things happen here, but *they* never say. Bad history. Outsiders come in sometimes, but as a rule they keep to themselves. And I'll tell you summat else: these Crow Haven folk, they've been here since it all began. Way back. Same families as when the witch was burned. They don't never leave.'

'Witch?'

''undreds of years ago, when it were all marsh. Some say she cursed 'em. Bad luck to the town that was raised.'

'Come on,' I smiled, 'all these people afraid . . .'

'Sins of the fathers shall be visited on the sons. You should know that, Father.'

To be honest, I laughed inwardly at what my friend, the outsider, had told me. Superstitions grow up all too easily in such places, I reflected. I determined that I should do something to break down this silly barrier between Crow Haven and the other communities. To achieve that, I would have to make a real effort to get to know my local flock.

I paid my first visit to a family called Rowbanks who lived on the farm at the outskirts of the village. All the family attended church, and I knew they were a large clan. There was the grandmother, old Ma Rowbanks, her sons Jim and Michael, Jim's wife, Valerie and their three boys, James, twelve, and the twins Luke and Josh, ten. When I called, only Ma Rowbanks, the grand matriarch, and her eldest son were home. They greeted me courteously enough, and I sat trying to engage the old woman in conversation while her son made tea.

'Nice to have such a large family, Mrs Rowbanks.'

She leaned back and peered into the kitchen.

'Yes, lovely. So, you been in the tropics I hear, Father.'

'South America. Peru, actually. As you can tell from my accent, though, I'm originally from Down Under.'

'That's nice . . .' she focused on me. 'Why'd y'come 'ere then?'

'Keep y'beak out, Ma,' Jim Rowbanks said, elbowing open the door and setting a tray with three slopping mugs on the coffee table. 'Sorry, Father, no fancy china, I'm afraid. And apologies for the stink, we're manuring the fields tomorrow.'

'Don't worry, Mr Rowbanks. When I was in Peru, I spent some time at a ministry near the islands where they harvest the guano. I hardly notice such smells nowadays.'

'What's guano?' Ma Rowbanks asked.

'Bat shit,' her son answered.

'Well, this kind was bird dung, actually,' I said, sipping my tea.

We sat in silence for a time. Jim, looking as if he had work to be getting on with, continued to glance out of the window and tap the side of his mug. Ma Rowbanks sipped and sighed and sipped and sighed. I ferreted around in my mind, trying to come up with a topic of conversation.

'Well, Mr Rowbanks . . .'

'Jim, Father.'

'Jim. I hear your wife is soon to add to your happy family. Twins, I believe?'

'That's right. Month or so 'til she pops . . .'

Silence again.

'Lot of trucks going through the village,' I said. 'They pass right by the *Priory*.'

'Someone's coming,' Jim said, looking into his drained mug. 'Some outsider. Started building a house in Redgrave.'

'Really? I would have thought that was protected land.'

Jim gave a short laugh and snorted: 'Protected?'

'Well, National Trust or something.'

'No-one should live in there,' Jim said. 'We don't go into the forest as a rule.'

290

'Do you think it's unlucky?' I asked.

He turned and gave me a sharp look.

'Railway used to go through Redgrave. They cut down the trees, ripped up the earth to make way for it, just like they choked the marshes all those years ago. They'll tell you the railway was shutdown because of cuts, but you live here awhile longer, Father, you'll see this place always has things its own way.'

I think Jim would have told me more, but I saw his eyes wander to his mother. I didn't catch the look she threw him, but his mouth clamped shut, as if she had pinched his lips together.

'I'd like another cuppa, Jim.'

Jim obeyed, collecting the mugs and ducking back into the kitchen.

'Now, Father, tell me about them bat islands.'

Time inched across the calendar. From my study window, I watched the winter retain a cold grasp on the village. It was rare to see anyone moving in the streets and Crow Haven appeared to me, with its grey skies and heavy falls, like a miniature scene in a snow globe. I saw few of my parishioners, except at services. Occasionally, I would run into a knot of them, standing by the bus stop or in the butchers. Their whispered conversations would halt and they would nod, smile and watch me pass, like a flock of secretive sheep. My only diversion was the walks I took in the woods. I ploughed through the snowdrifts of January and set my face against the knifing winds of February. Save for the few evergreens and firs, everything was sleeping or dead. Many stretches of the wood appeared so forlorn that I felt a superstitious dread of them. But even in those more menacing pockets, where light and shadow seemed to play against their natures, there was a dark beauty.

It was on one of these winter walks that I first encountered the Crowman.

I set out in the early afternoon. The day was cold, but I

was in the mood for a good long ramble. Jim Rowbanks had not exaggerated when he said no-one ever walked in the woods, for I had found no beaten paths through Redgrave. It would be easy to get lost in the thicket, but I had always prided myself on having an almost infallible inner compass. On this excursion, however, I must have got myself turned around somehow. I had been walking for over an hour, planning a sermon in my head, when I realised that I was on unfamiliar ground. Through the branches overhead, I could make out only a uniform grey sky, with no hint of sun to tell me which direction I should take. Standing stock still for a moment, I listened for the hammering, sawing and swearing of the builders at work on the new house. All was quiet.

After two more hours of stumbling around and finding myself passing familiar trees, I wondered if I should make it home at all that evening. The sky darkened in the east and snow began to fall, thick and deep. I had knelt down to scoop a handful to my lips when, through the trees, I saw a glade a little way off in the distance. It was set on higher ground and might give me an idea as to where on earth I was. As I tramped towards it, I felt a strange sensation. It was as if a force, pressing on my shoulders, wanted to keep me away from the rise.

I hacked through the bracken and entered the open space. I was mystified to see that there was not a flake of snow on the ground. The rest of the forest was already carpeted white. More disconcerting still, those trees bordering the clearing were very tall, and I could make out nothing of the lie of the land. I did not like to admit it, even to myself, but I was truly lost. Mumbling under my breath, I made a circuit of the glade, slapping my arms as I went to encourage the circulation. It really was bitterly cold.

I arrived back at the point where I had broken into the clearing, and had decided to try my luck again through the wood, when I was struck by the stillness of the place. Even in this season of hibernation, it was unnaturally quiet. No wakeful owls, no snuffling foxes. Just silence, heavy silence, lying steadily across the wood. I looked up. Night was falling fast, and it was as the shadows thickened at the forest edge that I noticed the shape of the trees. All around the perimeter, the oaks leaned back, arching their branches and trunks away from the clearing, as if they were repelled by it.

Nonsense. I was letting my imagination unnerve me. I started back towards the forest.

I had taken only a few steps when I saw him.

A tall, spindly figure standing between the trees. So still. So very still as he watched. It was the twilight playing tricks, nothing more. But, for a moment, I could have sworn that those branches nearest the figure's head were slowly drawing themselves away. I was about to address him, when the stranger spoke.

'You . . . you *see* me . . .' The voice steadied. 'We meet where it began.'

For several seconds, I could do no more than stare at him. At last I found my tongue.

'Hello? Could you help me? I'm afraid I've gotten myself lost.'

He came forward into the clearing.

'Where it began, so it begins.'

The first bright hint of the rising moon crept over the treetops and played through the fine wisps of his yellow hair. It looked for a moment as if he were haloed. The shadows fell away from his face and, in the mercurial light, I saw a skull inset with the darkest eyes.

293

Forty-two

Father Garret stared at his balled fists. Blood ached in pockets across his hands. He couldn't bear to look at his palms outstretched now. When he did, he saw the shaft of the spade, the haft of the axe, the grip of the scalpel. He had not flexed out his fingers since last night, so he did not yet know if he would see the rope.

'*And priests dare to babble of a God of peace,*' Garret quoted. '*Even whilst their hands are red with guiltless blood.*'

Once his hands had been clean. Once . . .

It had begun in the early days of October the previous year. Arriving home from evening worship, he had suffered his first blackout. During the fevered dream that followed, he heard his own voice telling him:

It's real now. No longer just a vague set of prognoses. I am dying.

Scotch on his lips brought him spluttering into consciousness. Through streaming eyes, he stared into the face of his saviour. It did not then occur to him to ask Simon Malahyde how he had gained entry to the house.

'How long do they say you have left?' the boy asked.

'A year . . . maybe less . . .'

Strong arms bore him to an easy chair. Piercing blue eyes held him.

'A final turn of the seasons. That's all you have?'

'Yes.'

'Perhaps not. Death is an illusion, Father. And like all illusions, if you strip away the façade of magic, if you look deep

294

into the workings of the thing, you can adapt the trick to your own purpose.'

'Heresy. Blasphemy,' Garret croaked.

'What of it?' the boy answered. 'Die if you want to, but in the end, as the God you love revels in your agony, what comfort will your principles be to you? You saw your father rot. Did God show him any scrap of mercy? Will he show any to you?'

'I love the Lord.'

'You love a lie. Patches of myths that have been stitched together, overlapping and forced to fit. The God you know is a wishful dream. Ask yourself, what manner of monster could hear the cries of his children and leave them to their misery? But don't be afraid, Christopher. For *I* am the resurrection and the life: he that believeth in me, though he were dead, yet shall he live . . .'

And then Simon Malahyde had breathed the barest hint of a dark secret. Something deep inside Christopher Garret rejoiced and cringed at the words, for there were conditions to meet and tasks he must undertake. When the full miraculous horror had been revealed, he felt a dirty hope rest within him.

'Do these things and you will keep your soul safe for judgement. He . . .' eyes that were not eyes looked up at the crucifix on the wall, ' . . . is dead. Let me show you what He only dreamed of.'

And so the die was cast. And so his hands now run with blood.

It took a whole year of scouring church registers to find two boys who matched the Doctor's very specific needs. They could not both be taken within a short space of each other, connections would be made. They must look like random abductions. Even now, when the end was so close, Garret found it hard to believe that nothing had gone wrong. Children. So trusting, so blind. Only in these last few days had he found any reason to be concerned. Those two detectives, especially the woman, had come so close.

Keep your head for a little longer, he told himself. Tonight it would be over. Tonight the promise would be kept and the secret would be given.

Pain tore at Jamie's eyes, as if fish hooks imbedded there were being reeled back in. At last, he was forced to look again at the thing standing by the back gate. It was the misshapen man from the photographs that he had found in his mother's car. It was the face from the bridge, from the TV, from the toilet stall, from his nightmares. The floppy hat was gone, its head, naked now, save for the few tufts of yellow hair. The features were indistinct. All except for the dark caverns that were its eyes.

Jamie stood at the window of his grandfather's back bedroom, desperate to move. That paralysing terror was working through him again, reducing him to mute catalepsy. Screams shivered in his throat but he could give no voice to them.

There's only one person who can make me go away, and he's not here . . .

It was beckoning him, but it couldn't move beyond the gate, and Jamie knew why. A few hours ago a tall, broad-shouldered old man had circled the house, crumbling something between his fingers and whispering as he went. Jamie had watched enough old Hammer films to guess that it had been a ritual of some kind. A spell perhaps, to keep evil at bay. An hour after the mysterious protector had left, the scarecrow-figure emerged from the shadows on the bridge. Rain swept in waves across the fields, yet the thing laid no footprints in the wet earth. It had reached the gate, and there it stayed.

Jamie was frozen, unable to scream for his mum and grandad, but at least the old man's magic was working.

She sat on the floor, the bath tub like a wall of ice at her back. The window was open a crack and slashes of rain licked across her bare feet.

'So, Dawny, what are you going to do?' Her father's voice through the door.

'Please, leave me alone.'

Silence then. But she knew he was still there.

'He was talking to himself, Dad. I've told you, he was having J followed.'

'All I'm going to say is this: when you first told me about him, you said he made you feel safe. You remember? Does he still make you feel safe?'

She heard him pad away down the corridor.

Jack had lied and lied. He had employed a man to follow her son. He believed outrageous, impossible things. That imaginary creatures were living inside him. That they had murdered his mother. That someone, some *thing*, had taken possession of Simon Malahyde and was now threatening her son. How did that make her feel . . . ?

She threw open the window. Rain billowed inside and drenched her nightclothes. Water ran down her body. She looked into the growing pool at her feet.

'He makes me feel safe,' she whispered.

Garret woke with a start. He had been dreaming of his father again. Picturing his own chubby boy hand clasped in those yellow fingers. Smelling the decay, the disease, almost believing that there was an odour to pain. And his father, managing a grimace-smile, thinking that it would comfort the boy.

The matter-of-fact nurse had, for once, not been in the dream. He wondered why. She was usually ever present, plumping the dying man's pillow, administering injections with ill-tempered impatience. How he had hated that nurse with her barking voice and her spade-like hands that rooted through his father's smart medical kit. He had longed to reach inside the bag when her back was turned, to draw out the bright, shiny scalpel and drive it home at the base of her skull.

But in this dream, the nurse had been replaced by the Doctor. The mysterious Doctor, who Brody had told him was living inside the young Malahyde boy. The Doctor who held the secret. And there were crows all around him, flapping about his body, clothing him. He was bending over Ethram

Garret, reflected in the dying man's glassy eyes.

'You did it, didn't you, Christopher?' the Doctor said. 'You took the pain away.'

And Garret saw his boy-self nodding.

The memory was in his hands. The left soothing the fevered scalp, pinching the nose. The right planted over trembling lips. Squeezing and pressing, squeezing and pressing, ignoring the tongue that fluttered against his palm, the eyes that fixed and rolled, fixed and rolled. Fear mounted as the seconds passed. Fear that the disease would not be cheated out of its long-fought victory. That the man would be forced to live, only so that he might suffer further agonies before death took him.

Ethram Garret plucked at his son's sleeve. His atrophied legs jerked beneath the covers. In the final moments, the capillaries of his eyes burst and shit poured out of him. Then his chest dropped and his cheeks sank.

'Yes. I took the pain away,' the boy said. 'But I don't have to be scared now, do I?'

'Oh, I think you do,' the Doctor said, covering Ethram's face with the soiled sheet. 'I think you have a great deal to fear.'

Then that deep, velvety laughter filled Father Garret's ears and he had woken. He prayed that the laughter he now heard was no more than a mental echo. But no, it was not a dream-figure that stood beside him, stroking his face.

'Bring me the fat,' the Doctor said. 'Then your work is finished.'

'You'll tell me?' Garret sobbed. 'Please. You promised . . .'

'I'm sorry, Christopher, but your father was right. You don't have the stomach to cheat judgement. It's time you went down into the cellar. They're all waiting for you. In the shadows. In the dark.'

Forty-three

Brody's Story

'My name is Dr Mendicant. I'm sorry if I startled you, Father.'

The man who strode through the clearing, his bony hand outstretched, was not the skeletal creature I had first imagined. Hunger, cold and twilight shadows had done their work to unsettle me, I supposed. He was, however, a strange-looking man, excessively lean and tall. If it wasn't a skull that had grinned through the darkness a moment before, then the head was only saved from being one by the tightly drawn, oddly opalescent skin that canvassed it. In their hollows, his eyes shone, black and doll-like. I took his hand and felt the slip of small bones beneath the skin.

'And you are the lost Father Asher Brody,' Mendicant said in a slow, warm voice.

'Yes, stupid of me. I didn't realise the woods were so extensive.'

'Tricks of Nature. You've not wandered as far as you think. If you would care to come back to my house, I'd be pleased to offer you some soup to warm you up.'

'I'd be happy to, thank you.'

'Good. Then let us see if we can find a way through the woods.'

As I followed my new friend out of the clearing, I noticed that his long black coat was very thin and he wore no gloves, yet he gave no indication that he felt the cold. I, on the other hand, shivered beneath my many layers. He passed lithely across the scrub and bracken, and had to wait at intervals for me to stumble after him. I supposed that it was my imagination again, but whereas steam billowed from my panting mouth, I did not see the faintest plume rise as he breathed.

'So, what are you a doctor of?' I asked between gasps.

'A little of this, a little of that. Theology, metaphysics, history . . . .'

'Aha. And what were you saying back there? About beginnings?'

'You must have heard the local legend,' he said over his shoulder. 'The isle witch. Elspeth was her name. A murderer of children. She took of their essence to rekindle her youth. That clearing was her home. That was where it all began.'

He told me the story that I have already related in my History. As he finished, we emerged from the woods onto a drive lined with barren elms. I had, of course, already guessed that Mendicant was the owner of the new house. This then was the approach that had been cleared before work began. And here was the gateway, an imposing structure of twisted metal, surmounted by a trio of imploring figures. Mendicant must have followed my gaze.

'They are the three wailing women,' he said. 'Those who stood by the Cross in the last moments. The Virgin Mary, her sister, and Mary Magdalene.'

'Where is the Saviour?' I asked.

'Where indeed?'

Throughout my life, I have often heard the spiteful edge in the voices of those who not only believe in nothing, but are viciously jealous of those with faith. In that simple question of Mendicant's, however, I did not discern ignorant ill-grace. Instead, I heard a kind of polite conceitedness that did not begrudge faith, but laughed at it as a childish fancy.

'I'm not sure I understand you,' I said.

'There was no offence meant, Father,' he said, opening the gate and beckoning me through. 'You have your beliefs, I have mine.'

'I respect that, but why build something to mock . . .'

'I do not mock. You are allowed to hold out the symbols of your faith.' He pointed to my crucifix. 'Am I not allowed to give expression to my doubt?'

'It seems odd, that's all,' I replied, privately acknowledging that he had a point.

'I've seen odder things,' he smiled.

We reached the house. Save a few rough edges, it was almost complete. I will not bore you with its description, as I'm sure you have seen it, or will in due course. Suffice to say, I was taken aback by its flawless, cold beauty. Mendicant did not take out a key, he simply pushed the door open and walked inside. A welcome waft of warm air greeted me as I followed my host up a spiral staircase.

'An unusual house,' I observed. 'Do you plan to name it?'

'I mistrust names. People make too much of them. Are too readily fooled by them.'

'You mean like 'Mendicant'?' I laughed. 'Perhaps you have family connections to the mendicant friars? Did you beg alms to get this place built?'

He stopped before a door to the right of the landing. For a moment I feared that I had insulted him. His dark eyes held mine until I felt compelled to lower my gaze.

'Mendicant is a fitting name for me,' he said at last. 'Does not everyone take from others on occasion? Do come in, Father.'

I knew this had to be the part of the house suspended on pillars, but I was surprised that only one room occupied the large space. Small windows punctuated the walls and, between them, rows of bookcases reached to the ceiling. There had to be hundreds of thousands of books, journals and pamphlets.

'Are you a man of letters, Brody?'

'I wouldn't go that far, but really, this is fascinating.'

I think Mendicant was pleased with my obvious appreciation for his collection. He walked along the stacks, pulling out a few items as he went.

'This is my library of Catholic writings and incunabula. Here is the Apostolic Letter condemning the slave trade by

Gregory the Sixteenth. Pius the Ninth's *Ineffabilis Deus*, on the Immaculate Conception, as you know. A Fifteenth Century copy of the Chinon Parchment, wherein Pope Clement the Fifth secretly absolved the Knights Templar from charges of witchcraft and heresy . . .'

He passed me each of these precious documents in turn. I handled them as a man might cup a rare pressed flower.

'One of the Cotelier editions of the Clementine Homilies . . . and here my Protestant collection. *The Book of Concord: The Lutheran Confessions*, a 1580 German print; an original of John Wycliffe's magnum opus, his *'Summa Theologiae'*, attacking, among other things, the temporal authority of the clergy. And here . . . my pride and joy. My *Daemonologies.'*

I placed the books and letters on a small occasional table. We stood now before the largest collection. Four separate bookcases full of arcane and modern texts.

'See here,' the Doctor said, 'the translations of the ancient cuneiform hieroglyphics of the Assyrian and Babylonian demonologies. King Assurbanipal's copies of a great magical work, from the clay tablets preserved by the priestly school of Erech in Chaldea. And here, the Iranian *Avesta,* with the temptation of Zoroaster by Anro Mainyus, *Daevanam Daeva,* the Demon of Demons. Then the *Daemonologie* of James the First, that was cited at the trial of our friend, Elspeth Stamp. And the *Malleus Maleficarum* . . .'

Opening this last book my eye scanned the first few lines of text:

Question I

WHETHER the Belief that there are such Beings as Witches is so Essential a part of the Catholic Faith that Obstinacy to maintain the Opposite Opinion manifestly savours of Heresy.

Not for the first time in my life, I felt ashamed of my Church's history. Doubtless, Mendicant saw the emotion in my face.

302

'Written by two Dominican inquisitors, Sprenger and Kramer,' he said, giving weight to each word. 'Prefaced by the papal bull of Pope Innocent the Eighth. Validated and championed by your Church. Responsible for the mass murder of innocent men, women and children.'

I said nothing. He took the volume from me and slipped it back into its alcove.

For the next few hours, we talked of theology and mystery. Throughout our discussions, the Doctor outwardly gave my views due respect. Yet, as we spoke of the early writings of Origen and Tertullian, there was the ever-present impression in my mind of a huge intellect reining in its scorn as it watched a smaller mind fumble about in its wake. Looking back, I can see how skilfully he steered the conversation towards the suggestion, made in certain apocryphal texts, that Adam, the first Man, sired children with the creature Lilith. The so-called Mother of Demons.

'The belief that Adam laid with a she-demon is based solely on a faulty reading of Genesis Chapter Five,' I said.

'Not *solely*. The Talmud tells us that, after Adam's expulsion from Eden, he separated from Eve and "became the father of ghouls and demons". And in Isaiah, Lilith is a recognised figure. Remember the passage? "And demons and monsters shall meet, and the hairy ones shall cry out to one another, There hath the lamia lain down, and found rest for herself". "Lamia" representing the original Lilith. Do not be too comfortable in your reading, Father,' he said. 'Demons may be all around us. Thousands to every man, as the Jews once believed. And perhaps the demon half-breeds of Adam still walk side-by-side with men, unheeded by them, because the demon-sons of Adam were also made in "his own image and likeness".'

'I don't believe that. I have my faith.'

'Always the last words of the ignorant when their arguments falter. I wonder, though, what you truly believe. What you would admit to yourself if you had the nerve.'

'It's late,' I said, taking my coat from the chair back.

'But you haven't had your soup.'

'I've lost my appetite.'

'Oh, dear. I've upset you again, haven't I?'

'Not at all.'

'Will you come again? So nice to have an enlightened clergyman to talk to.'

Did a sneer play across those thin, colourless lips?

'Perhaps. Maybe we shall see you at a service some time?'

'You know, Father, I think you will.'

I saw myself out.

Reaching the gate, I stood for a moment, contemplating the three mourners. I put my palm to my breast and felt the impression of the crucifix hanging around my neck. It gave little comfort. Below it, in the barrel of my chest, where I often felt my love of God swell, there was a dry emptiness. The light of faith had burned low and now I sensed it, flickering like a candle against an encroaching darkness.

Mendicant had managed to slither under my skin. For the next few weeks, I sat in my study, while work and unanswered letters piled up around me. I often rationalised my feelings. I was missing Peru; I was unaccustomed to the climate; I was having a mid-life crisis. And yet, during those contemplative nights by the fire, my thoughts always turned to him. As all my interests and passions waned, I longed to return to the nameless house in the woods, to devour those precious books and tease out the forbidden secrets locked inside the Doctor's mind. Often, I almost succumbed. Once or twice even venturing as far as the mouth of trees. Like a drug-starved addict, begging for the faintest whiff of marijuana smoke, I peered down the avenue, hoping to see that blasphemous gate. Even it seemed to speak some terrible truth to me. But in those moments, when the storm grew around it, the candle within burned brighter and lit my way home.

The February snows melted and Crow Haven was treated to an early, if phantom, spring. Even the desolate trees of Redgrave awoke and stretched out tentative blossoms. Every day, I expected to see migratory birds return to the woods, or those that stayed the course of the winter emerge from their hiding places. Where were the noisy parties of jays, the low-gliding cuckoo or the *si-wick* call of the woodcock? All I had seen were the jealous crows.

Nevertheless, as the season changed, so my mood recovered. I began to answer my correspondence again and re-doubled my efforts to become part of the community. Just as the early spring had given colour back to the village, so I felt a little contrast moving into my own grey life. The lure of the library and the spectre of Mendicant faded from my mind. The candle burned brighter.

Valerie Rowbanks presented her husband with twin boys on the 22nd March 1976. The evening after the birth, Jim Rowbanks came to see me. He asked if I would baptise the children as soon as possible. One of the babies was very weak and, although the doctors had assured him that there was no cause for concern, he did not want to risk the child dying without receiving the Sacrament. I told him he was worrying needlessly but, to set his mind at rest, I proposed the baptism should take place the following afternoon.

Jim seemed reluctant to leave. He circled my study, picking up oddments that I had collected from my travels, asking idle questions about each of them.

'Jim, sit down. Tell me what's on your mind,' I said.

He looked towards the door, ran his palms down his jacket and finally took a seat.

'Ma says that the secrets of Crow Haven must stay the secrets of Crow Haven,' he said. 'Even if he is God's voice on earth, he ain't God's ears. But I say you are, you hear confession, don't you? Father, if you are to bless my babies, you should know what sort of life they're coming to . . .'

He hesitated again. I offered him a tot of brandy but he shook his head.

'No, gotta keep a clear head . . .' He bent over in his seat, resting his elbows on his knees, as if the burden he was about to unload possessed a physical weight that sat heavy on his shoulders. He exhaled and said, 'It's like this: my babies won't *ever* leave this place. Some have tried, but if you're Crow Haven born, then here is where you'll live out your span, and in this earth is where you'll be buried. Maybe you've heard the old tale of my kinswoman, Abigail Rowbanks? She was due to marry a man named Stephen Lydgate; this was Eighteen Sixty-Five. They planned to up and leave Crow Haven, start a new life in Manchester. Everyone told them they couldn't go. They didn't listen. Some don't. Abigail was found drowned in a barrel of pig's blood the morning of the wedding. Lydgate, he was hanging from one of those big old oaks. Bowels torn out, as if by some animal . . .'

'If you truly believe this,' I said, 'why did Valerie give birth at home?'

'If a Crow Haven woman has her child outside the village, the baby will be born dead. It's always been the way.'

'I can't deny that I've felt something was wrong with this place,' I said, 'but why does this happen?'

'Because Crow Haven should never have been. It was raised up out of the marshes. Out of a bad place that was never meant to be home to anybody. Anybody except her.'

'You mean Elspeth Stamp?' I said. 'That was four hundred years ago.'

'Makes no matter. What they did to her was like setting off a nuclear bomb. The fallout is still in the earth, the trees, every fibre of this place. It reaches down the years and infects us all. It'll infect you too, if you stay long enough. It's Evil, Father. The Legion Evil from the gospels. Old evil. And it doesn't work alone. Often times it brings other things to the village.'

Other things. Bad things. Unholy things. A skull-like face between the trees.

'Now you know,' said Jim. 'Believe it or not, I've done what I thought I should. You can't do anything about it. Father Tolly tried. He could never accept the rottenness here. He thought his faith could stand up to it. Well, I pray he rests easy now.'

He got up and went to the door. His face was turned into the corridor, his hoary, dusty hands clenching at the jamb.

'We'll live with it 'til the marshes roll up again.'

'And so, Mark Jeremiah Joseph Rowbanks and Paul Ezra Ezekiel Rowbanks, I baptise you in the name of the Father, the Son and the Holy Spirit. Amen.'

All of Crow Haven had turned out for the service. Despite Jim Rowbanks' story, I still felt my heart lifted by the turning season and by the faces of those infants that the Lord God had freed from the burden of Original Sin. I sprinkled water on the brow of Mark and handed the boy back to his mother. This was the sickly child, and he did seem much paler and thinner than his brother.

I turned to the congregation.

'We all labour under dark shadows,' I said, 'and perhaps there is cause to believe that we, residents of Crow Haven, labour under one of the darkest . . .'

I caught old Ma Rowbanks throw a reproachful look at her son. Jim looked up, worry written across his weathered face, but I felt that candle blaze within. The clouds that Mendicant had spread there had weakened and now drew back further.

'But in the Lord we are strong. At the End of Days, when all other lights are extinguished and Man is left alone, facing the end of all things, His Light will be a beacon, shining yet in the darkest hour. And it shines here. No shadow, no Evil can triumph before our faith, for by its nature the shadow is weaker, coming after Him and perishing before Him. 'I am the Alpha and Omega', He has said, 'the beginning and the end, the first and the last'. We here must face our fears or they will . . .'

The baby choked.

Its eyes fixed and dilated. Its chest shuddered and sank. Little hands twisted into claws. Jim Rowbanks tore the limp child from his wife and laid it out on the Communion Table. Frozen, I watched the crowd press around, heard the confused babble of advice, the screams and cries. Only Ma Rowbanks stayed where she was. She sat in the first pew, staring directly at me. I imagined that I heard her thoughts:

This is what comes of facing our fear, Father. This is the price we pay.

Through the throng, I saw glimpses of the tiny dead thing. Jewels of water still adhered to its brow. Its eyes were rolled back, its lips turning blue. Valerie flipped the baby over and started rubbing its back.

'Father! Quickly, the rites.'

Jim was grief-stricken. Desperate. But the horror that I might be responsible for the child's death, robbed me of my senses. I had wanted to stamp out the hopelessness of this place. I had wanted these people to feel that they could face their demons in the strength of God. I had challenged the power that moved here and it had lashed out. I managed to walk to the table. To lay my hands on the unmoving child. To mumble a few broken prayers. The light within burned to its lowest ebb.

A breeze whistled down the aisle and into the chancel. I looked up. Over the heads of the confused, wailing congregation, I saw the church doors open. The wind picked up, threw the service sheets from the pews and splashed the water in the font. There was shuffling in the crowd, a parting of people. Through them I saw snatches of dark clothes and striking white skin.

Mendicant.

He moved, without hurrying, up the steps to the Communion Table. Gently, he took my hands from the dead child. A voice, that sometimes answers my prayers, told me to reclaim the tiny body. That whatever was being done, it was better that the child remain as it was. I could not obey. Black marble eyes held me. His fingers arched over the baby and dug rhythmically at its chest. His lips moved, but I could not hear the words.

The barest movement. A twitch of legs. Then the baby's eyes focused. His breathing came in gasps. He started to cry. He was bundled into thin arms and given to his mother.

'Yours, I believe.'

'Oh, God. Thank you. Thank you God,' Jim Rowbanks muttered.

'No need to thank God, Mr Rowbanks. You can thank me.'

'Who are you?' Jim asked. I noticed the farmer's expression as his eyes flitted across Mendicant's features. It was as if he saw something there which disturbed him.

'I'm a doctor. An old friend of Father Brody here,' the man smiled, showing worn, yellow teeth. 'My name is Mendicant.'

Forty-four

Brody's Story

BUNDLE 1 –
MENDICANT IN CROW HAVEN – 1976

The next few hours passed in a blur of shifting faces and locations. I dimly remember moving outside and watching Jim, Valerie and the baby disappear in an ambulance. Then old Ma Rowbanks herded us back to the farmhouse where a buffet tea was laid out. I chatted to Michael Rowbanks, all the while keeping an eye on the saviour Doctor as he moved among my parishioners.

There were no faltering conversations, no conspiratorial glances. They cooed over the new local celebrity, patting him on the back and calling him 'a good chap'. Some of the mothers even passed their children to him, as if he would give the infants a benediction. The Rowbanks children tried to get him to pose for a photograph with Ma Rowbanks, but he demurred politely. If truth be told, I was jealous as well as anxious. When I had arrived in the village, I had been greeted by a cold, indifferent congregation. Now those same people took this *thing* unquestioningly to their bosom. At last, he glided over to me. I cannot now recall the words he whispered, but I found myself following him to the door. We left the Rowbanks' as the call came through reporting that the baby was out of danger.

Before I knew it, I was in the library, taking the drink Mendicant proffered. The light from the fire danced through the cut glass of the brandy decanter, dappling his face with motley colour. His voice was quiet, soothing almost.

'You ask: Why do they not recognise him for what he is? They should. They are used to seeing the darker heart beating beneath the skin. But, like many people whose lot it is to suffer, they are fooled by small acts of kindness. Only you, Asher Brody, see me as I really am. I do not know how you look beyond this . . .'

His appearance altered in a moment. Instead of the skeletal figure beside me, there sat a young man. Handsome, with golden hair about his shoulders, beautiful as the Morning Star.

' . . . and see this,' he said, his face falling back to its shrunken dimensions. 'Some, like Jim Rowbanks, may catch the smallest glimpse, and I cannot fool the camera, but you *see*. You pierce the veil of my adopted flesh. I appear to you as I am, withering in the last stages of my current incarnation. But soon, like young Master Rowbanks, I shall be reborn . . .' he gave a hollow laugh. 'I am the Resurrection and the Life.'

'You are nothing,' I said.

'And yet you are drawn to me. You yearn for the truth that I know.'

'I yearn for nothing outside my faith.'

'If you truly believe that, then you should be able to stop what's coming. You have dreamed of such a match all your life, have you not? Your brother was the hero; your time never came. I offer you a chance that few men ever have: to become everything you ever dreamed.'

'How do you know me?' I asked.

'I see your dreams, Asher. I see your faith, wide and shallow. Have the strength to put it to the test. Prove me a father of lies, or accept the truth you have always known. That Man is truly alone in his suffering.'

'The Lord is with me.'

'Then end me, if you can. A new metempsychosis is coming. Let's see if you can stand against it.'

He leaned forward. Against his skin, the red light thickened and appeared to run. He opened his mouth wide. The library fell away and I was drawn into that darkness.

I found myself in the transept of the church, kneeling before the altar steps. Candles in sconces burned along the walls of the nave and, placed before the Communion Table, a vigil light flickered. It must have been night outside, for the stained windows were bleak and colourless. Was I really now inside my church or slumped and dreaming in Mendicant's curious library? Clenching the crucifix around my neck, I rose to my feet. As I did so, I heard the mewling cry of a child. Then I saw it. A bundle wriggling upon the Communion Table.

'In time of trouble, he shall hide me in his pavilion,' I murmured, mounting the steps and approaching the altar. 'In the secret of his tabernacle shall he hide me. He shall set me upon a rock . . .'

My feet echoed in the stone heart of the church. The candles flared, throwing my shadow across the tiny form. Its head was covered in the folds of the blanket. I reached out, my hand trembling.

'And now shall my head be lifted up above mine enemies . . .'

I plucked back the blanket. The candles guttered and died. By some unknown light, I saw it.

'Sweet Christ.'

Innocence desecrated, grace polluted, here, in the fortress of my faith. How can I describe what lay twisting before me? I cannot. I will not. I saw the wounds of lust upon Mark Jeremiah Joseph Rowbanks, and my soul balked. Yet I knew, instinctively, that as hideous as this physical defilement appeared to be, it was nothing more than an illusion. A cruel amusement conjured by Mendicant to unnerve me. What the Doctor really had planned, however – this metempsychosis – would *not* be mere illusion. Whatever evil was about to transpire, it would be very real.

While the baby cried, I screamed prayers and obscenities into the roof of the church. The echo of my voice resounded like laughter between the beams. Laughter that stayed with me as the scene faded, and I awoke in my bed at the Old Priory, my body twisted in sweat-soaked sheets.

★

For days, I hardly ate or slept. Functioning on some auxiliary level, I gave Mass, heard confessions, wrote my sermon, while all the time checking and re-checking my memory for some mention of 'metempsychosis'. I had many friends who studied arcane mythology, but none who believed it had any practical application. There was only one man who might believe me, and I did not want to burden his last days with worry.

At the end of a week of heavy research, all I could gather was that metempsychosis, or the transmigration of souls, was an ancient belief, spread across a startling number of civilisations. In different forms, it was present in many of the religions of Asia and the Ancient World, cropping up in early Judaic and Christian writings, and even in the rich beliefs of the tribes of North America and Australia. The central tenet in all these versions was that a soul may be disconnected from the body (temporarily in sleep or permanently in death) and that it might then be transferred between organisms.

I was lost. I knew only two things for certain. One, that Mendicant, whatever he was, believed that he could prolong his life. And second, that the Rowbanks family was central to his plan. On a rare excursion into the village, I heard that the good Doctor had become a regular visitor to the farm. That he had been virtually adopted by the family and had lavished gifts on the children. I made up my mind that I had to speak to Jim about my concerns. Surely, with all that he had told me, he would believe my story.

It was in the early hours of the morning, eight days after my last encounter with the Doctor, when I happened upon something. I had been ploughing through a dry tract on Orphic religions that I had picked up in Venice years ago, when an illustration of a woodcut caught my eye. It was a picture of a blank-faced child, encircled by runic designs and the legend: *TABULA RASA*. I had a vague memory of seeing something like it in one of Mendicant's books. Beneath the illustration was the following text:

313

Note should be made of a short-lived sect that existed on the southern coast of Thessaly. They were known as either the Keepers of the Soul Springs or the Metempsychosists. They worshipped Dionysus as the god of life, death and rebirth. During bacchanalian orgies, it is claimed they practised a rite of rejuvenation, during which child sacrifices were offered up and the souls of the old and worn were put into the empty vessels of the slaughtered young. Mention of this sect is made in the writings of Pliny, who noted that the rituals were attended by 'hosts of dark and rapier-beaked birds'. (See *Birds of Thessaly* n.23 or the *Stymphalian Birds* (article: *Behind The Labours of Hercules*)). This woodcut was found among the few remaining papers of Don Amone, the so-called 'People's Saint of Castile'. Amone was brutally murdered in 1590, his vast collection of incunabula destroyed or stolen.

I could wait for no further confirmation of my fears. I might spend another month searching through dusty archives and discover little more about the ritual than I had already ascertained. Meanwhile, Mendicant would have found his new vessel.

I knew that Jim Rowbanks would be up and about early. At four a.m. I put the tract in my pocket and started out for the farm. The morning was warm, but heavy rain clouds had rolled over the forest and spread across the village. A band of crows circled above the lower field of the Rowbanks farm, tormenting the horses that pawed and grunted at the ground.

I was halfway up the dirt track when I heard the farmhouse door snap open. Jim came striding down the path. I read in his face that I was too late.

'Tell me,' I said.

'The little ones. The twins. Dead.'

I held out my hand to steady him.

'How?'

'Doctor says it was probably an infection, passed by Mark to his brother. It wasn't an infection, Father. It was *him*.'

'He's been here?'

Grief twisted Jim's features.

'Last night. He kissed them both before he left . . . None of them can see,' he looked back at the house. 'I knew, Father. I *knew*, and did nothing to stop him. I saw, that day in the church . . . Something in his face. And the wind, did you hear it? I don't think it came from outside. It came from the mouths of the saints in the windows. From the Madonna. They were speaking to us, but we didn't hear.'

'Jim, take hold of yourself . . .'

'I told you, didn't I, Father? This place draws things to it.'

'Listen, has he been back?'

'They've called him already. Ma and the others. They're sitting around in the house like statues. None of them have cried. They won't, until he comes . . . .'

I saw the grief and violence brimming within him.

'Don't do anything rash,' I said. 'I have to contact an old friend. I will return.'

I left the broken man and went back to the *Old Priory*. I had wasted a week poring over thousands of pages, when a footnote and a phone call might have given me the knowledge to save those children. I did not hesitate now. I reached the house in double-quick time and went straight to the study. The connection, stretching halfway around the world, crackled and fizzed.

Samuel Willard had taught me the true, joyous love of God. 'Taught' is not the right word. Inspired. Even as I heard his age-cracked voice at the end of the line, I imagined him as the young priest who had nurtured my faith all those years ago. If I had been faced with such a predicament in days gone by, my first instinct would have been to contact him. Recently, however, he had been very ill. In his eightieth year he had contracted pneumonia. This, coupled with a collapsed lung, meant he was very frail. The doctors had advised that he should be admitted to hospital, but he would not leave the Seminary that had been his home for over half a century.

None dared to contradict the kindly but determined 'Grand Old Man of St Patrick's'. It was with grave concern, therefore, that I called my old friend.

'Asher, my boy,' he said. 'How are you? Have you settled into your new parish? Why you ever wanted to go to England I don't know. Grey country. Grey people.'

Hearing his voice again was too much. Despite his years and the poorness of the line, he heard my emotion.

'What is it, boy? We'll put it right, whatever it is.'

I can't remember exactly how I told him the story of my time in Crow Haven. I'm sure it was very confused. When I finished, he was silent for a time. Over the hum of the line, I thought I heard the pounding waves of Manly and the screech of the gulls.

'Did I ever tell you, Asher, that I am English?'

'No. I always thought . . .'

'I came over when I was twenty-two, after the Great War. I took a job at the convict prison in Fremantle before moving east. Before my twenty-fifth year, I had seen all the horrors that one lifetime could bear. The hell of the trenches and then the degradation of humanity that was the hillside prison. But in those darkest hours, He shone in my heart the brighter. You told me of the illustration in your book. The boy with *Tabula Rasa* printed over him? When you live through horror, that is what you must become. *Tabula Rasa*. An empty vessel for God to fill with strength. Knowledge will get you so far, but belief will give you the power to stand.'

'But what can I do? Love of God will not tell me what Mendicant wants.'

'It may surprise you to learn that, when I was a boy, I studied at a college not far from your parish. Jericho was its name. There was a rather extraordinary legend attached to the place. A great store of ancient knowledge that moved between worlds. One night, coming home from vespers, I passed an archway and thought I saw . . .'

My old friend proceeded to tell me the most impossible story.

316

'I must admit,' he continued, 'that, aside from that experience, I have no knowledge of ghosts and demons, but I do believe in them. And I believe in you. Go to Jericho. I will phone ahead and make the arrangements. Ask for Willard at the gate . . .'

He gave me some further instructions. I noted down things that weeks before I would have called superstitious nonsense.

'Remember, Asher, *tabula rasa*. Clear your mind of prejudices and limitations. Be as an empty vessel and allow God's love and His wrath to fill you.'

I said goodbye to Father Sam. I would never hear his voice again.

I set out for Jericho.

Forty-five

Brody's Story

BUNDLE 1 –
MENDICANT IN CROW HAVEN – 1976

I don't know why I translated the *Transmigration of Souls*. Perhaps, even then, I had some inkling that the Doctor's end would not be of my making. That I was, like John the Baptist, only the precursor; preparing the way.

As I drove away from Jericho, I looked at my watch and found that it had stopped at a quarter-to-midnight: the time that I had entered the archway and left the world. The translation had taken a good three hours or more. Yet, when I passed the cathedral, the solstice clock chimed twelve. Either that grand old timepiece was wrong, or time itself was out of joint. Perhaps those hours of work within the confines of the library had occupied only fifteen minutes in the real world. I had been absent from Crow Haven for a few hours at least and, although I had put Jim Rowbanks on his guard, I knew that Mendicant had a way of warping a man's perceptions.

I left the city lights behind. The twisting, shadow-thick country roads were so still and unmoving that my imagination betrayed my fears. Above the rattle of the engine, I thought I heard whispers telling me that I was too late and that everything I feared had come true. In the headlights, I glimpsed the dark shimmer of blood on bark and, occasionally, a gaunt face staring between the bracken. Rolling down the hillside into Crow Haven, I passed deserted streets, silent houses and windows with curtains tightly drawn.

I pulled up at the *Old Priory* and collected the war souvenir my brother Charlie had left me. I prayed I would not need it. Then I drove on to the farmstead. Like all the houses in the village, the Rowbanks' was in darkness. My headlights arched over old Ma Rowbanks who sat in the doorway, her body heavy against the jamb.

'Jim and Mike have gone to the house,' she called. '*He* took the boys.'

'I know,' I answered, getting out of the car. 'Jim told me. The babies . . .'

The old woman shook her head. She had spoken in an even voice, but her natural authority had abandoned her. She had lived all her years in this pinprick-tumour on the world and had faced down the Darkness within it. But, in her last days, a new evil had come to Crow Haven and she had thrown open her door and invited it in. She saw this now and the fight had gone out of her. Ma Rowbanks would be dead and buried within a fortnight.

'No, Father. Not the bairns. Jim's boys. James, Luke, Josh. He has taken them into the woods.'

'When did this happen?'

'They've been gone since this morning. First light.'

'No. That can't be. I saw Jim this morning. He told me about the twins . . .'

'The twins died two days ago, Father,' the old woman snapped. 'Jim's waited for you all this time. You've been gone two days.'

My blood turned to water. So time *had* run in the Yeager Library, just not as I had first thought.

Mendicant must have tricked the children into giving him their dead brothers' baptism dresses. Now, two of the boys would power the metempsychosis with their deaths. The third, probably James, the eldest, would become the tabula rasa. The empty vessel into which Mendicant would pour his spirit.

'We didn't see until it was too late, Father. We didn't *see*.'

I got back into the car, threw it into reverse and tore down the dirt track, making for the Conduit Road and the tunnelled approach to the Doctor's house. I left the car ticking over on a gravel siding and ran up the avenue.

The house slept, austere and beautiful in the darkness. I was ready to force an entrance, but found the frame already splintered and the door slack on its hinges. I crept into the hall and stood listening. There was a creak of boards from above. Someone was moving in Mendicant's library. Deftly as I could, I climbed the iron staircase, slipped across the landing and opened the library door. All the baize antique reading desks and the red leather chairs had been pushed into the corners. The fire was dead, the coals raked over. In the centre of the library lay the bodies of two children. Both just ten years old.

They were naked. Mutilated. Laid out, face-up. Their heads were turned, so that they stared into each other's dead eyes. As detailed in the *Transmigration*, cuts of flesh had been taken from their abdomens. There were dark contusions around their throats. I prayed that they had been strangled before the tearing had begun. The carpet was still wet to the touch. I put my hand over their hearts, felt the hardening musculature beneath the skin, and tried to think of an appropriate prayer. All the liturgies I knew seemed inadequate, both too grand and too pure. I reverted to the simple Prayer for the Dead.

'We found them like this. Together,' said Jim, coming in from the hallway. 'They were twins you know, Luke and Josh. Just like my other babies.'

His face looked almost as pallid as Mendicant's. The emotion contorting it, however, was of a kind that I doubted had ever knotted the Doctor's features. He came at me, tearing my hands from his children. I felt his blows, sharp and keen. The attack was a short one.

'You left us . . . you promised . . .'

'I've done my best,' I said, wiping blood from my mouth.

'But where've you been, Father? My boys'd still be alive if you'd let me . . .'

'I've been finding answers,' I said.

I had a good reason for my absence. What could I have done without the knowledge that the Yeager Library had

320

afforded me? How was I supposed to know that time would pass so quickly outside its walls? I was not to blame for this. Yet there was blame thrown at me by Jim. And there was blame in the dead eyes of those boys.

'Finding answers,' I repeated. 'And finding them too late. How did it happen?'

'He came to the house the morning you left us and cried his crocodile tears. He kept asking me where you were, making snide comments about us being abandoned in our hour of need. It was all I could do to stop myself from beating him to death there and then, in front of my family. He stayed late. Then, this morning, Val came screaming across the fields. "The babies' clothes are gone, the babies' clothes are gone . . ." Just kept repeating it. We searched all over, but couldn't find the dresses. I went to wake the boys. Their beds were cold. Michael said he'd seen them walking into Redgrave at first light. Couldn't say why he didn't stop them. Something was walking with them. No more than a shadow passing across the corn rows. That was when they snapped out of it. Michael and Val cottoned on straightaway, started believing what I'd been saying all along. That Mendicant wasn't right . . . But Ma, it took her some time . . . We found the boys this morning. Broke down the door and searched the place. There're strange things here, Father. Rooms full of statues and idols and pictures. Paintings of things you read of in the Bible. And some things even the Bible won't name. The boys were already . . .'

'And you've not found James?'

'We've searched the woods. Tried to get men from the village, but no-one'll come out.'

'Have you called the police?'

'Trouble in Crow Haven is handled by Crow Haven. Outsiders don't understand.'

Only a month or so ago, I would have told Jim he wasn't thinking straight. That his children had been abducted and murdered and the authorities must be contacted. But now I knew the truth of his words. Outsiders would not understand. I did not, at that moment, stop to consider that word. *Outsider.*

Crow Haven was now my home. It was aware of me.

'Have you been to the clearing?' I asked.

'Where do you mean?'

'The island. The place where your forebears burned the witch?'

'No-one has ever seen it. Or, if they have, they've never come back out of the woods to tell.'

'I've been there,' I said. 'Have no doubt, that's where he's taken your son.'

We carried the children outside. Lying them side-by-side in the forecourt, we covered their faces with our coats. The house stood like a great lowering insect, gazing down on the little corpses with its clusters of glass eyes. I said a few words. Then we tore two heavy cudgels from an oak and entered the forest.

I thought I would know my way back to the clearing. It had been only a month or so since Mendicant had found me there. In vain, however, I looked about for familiar knots and whorls in tree trunks, shapes and patterns in the bracken. It was not that everything looked the same. A few steps one way brought us to a glade filled with the coppiced trunks of young trees. Straying in another direction, we found ourselves among a grove of ancient sycamores, coming together overhead and blocking out the sky. In so varied a forest the short route that Mendicant and I had taken should have been obvious. But without the Doctor, I was lost.

'Stop for a moment,' I said. 'Let's get our bearings.'

Jim grimaced: 'Now you know why we don't walk in the woods. It likes to play games.'

We stood in an avenue between two elm groves. Overhead the clouds were so distended they almost grazed the treetops. I have walked in many forests in my life, from the *El Infierno Verde* rainforest of Peru to the eucalyptus basins of the Blue Mountains near Sydney. In all of these, the prospect of rain, the lifeblood of the forest, is welcomed by the sweet, cool scent of the trees. As if they reach out and invite the downpour. But in this wood there was only the smell of rot and decay. A rumble passed through the clouds and rain pattered on the mulch at our feet. Jim opened his mouth to say something, but a gesture from me stopped him. Above the smell of putrefying vegetation, I had caught a whiff of something else. Something that I had expected, but which still hit me like a punch to the gut. An acrid scent of burnt cloth, mingled with an aroma of cooking meat.

Jim Rowbanks had not read the *Transmigration of Souls*, but I saw a half-realisation in his eyes nonetheless. We did not speak, but hurried as noiselessly as we could between the trees.

I held out every prayer I knew before me. In those moments, before I saw the full horror of it, I was a child again, ready for adventure. The very darkness of the wood around me seemed to retreat, just as the darkness within fell back against the renewed glare of the candle. I was God's champion at last. Facing a truly elemental battle.

Forty-six

Brody's Story

BUNDLE 1 –
MENDICANT IN CROW HAVEN – 1976

We were too late.

Volleys of rain rattled through the tree to which the boy was tethered. From this distance, we could not see what Mendicant had made of him, but his head lay slumped against his chest and he was not moving. In a rough circle around the tree, the grass was dyed dark red. At the boy's feet, rags smouldered in the embers of a collapsing fire. The last of the smoke from the burnt baptism dresses rolled up and disappeared as it touched James Rowbanks' face.

'I confess, I had expected better from you, Father.'

Mendicant stood in the shadows. A skeletal creature, running his fingers through the boy's hair. He stepped forward, into the light.

His eyes had shrunk further into his skull. The skin was so taut around his head that his lips had drawn back over his gums. Blood smeared his mouth and stained his teeth. I felt hollow – *tabula rasa* – but I was filled only with rage. I grasped the cold metal in my pocket.

'I am strong in the Lord and the Power of His Might,' I whispered.

The rotting face smiled. He started across the clearing towards us. With every step he took, it was as if some invisible force flayed him alive. His nose was now no more than two thin slits. The rain slipped beneath the cracks in his scalp and ran inside his face. Only a strip or two of skin connected his cheek and jaw. Glistening in the gap sat a long tongue, visible from tip to root. The orbs of his eyes, robbed of lids, rolled in their sockets. Membrane and muscle, sinew and cartilage were torn back to the bone. The stink of decomposition bowled ahead of him. Putrefying juices dribbled from his mouth, and I could smell the work of spilled stomach acid as it burned through soft tissue.

I called out to Jim to stand his ground, but the man looked at me with an expression of dazed horror and lurched back into the forest.

'It's almost done,' Mendicant spat. 'All you can do now is kill me.'

I pulled the weapon. The Doctor stopped in his tracks. A look of satisfaction passed across the remnants of his features. He thought I meant the bullets for him; that I would speed his regeneration. I told myself that it was just an empty carcass now, ready for him to fill. Just *tabula rasa* . . .

I aimed Charlie's Webley MkVI.

'No, Father. God, no,' Jim called.

'The boy's dead, Jim,' I shouted, keeping Mendicant in my sights. 'If I don't, he'll have him. He'll keep James locked inside . . .'

Sweat lathered my hands. My finger slipped on the trigger. Was there another way? No time to think now. No time for anything except . . .

The Doctor was almost upon me when I emptied all six chambers. Fire whipped out of the barrel. With a sickening report, the top half of the boy's head exploded against the tree. The force of the impact bucked him free of his bonds. As if a desperate penitence had taken command of him, James fell to his knees. His torso remained upright while a dying nervous system galvanised his hands. They snatched and searched for a face that was no longer there. It was a cruel animation; a false life persisting inside a form that could not endure. Broken tombstones of teeth still adhered to the lower jaw, but everything above had been obliterated. Inside the angry red star that now adorned the tree, slivers of brain tissue flopped like earthworms along the bark. Finally, the body ceased twitching and collapsed to the ground.

Mendicant screamed.

Jim came to his senses. He ran, and dashed his branch against Mendicant's skull. There was a crack followed by the sound of splintering shockwaves. A valley had been punched into the Doctor's head, cleaving his temple into a spear of bone. As Jim tore the branch free, a needle of wood caught like a fish hook and ripped Mendicant's left eye from its socket.

The Doctor turned his head and laughed.

'I fucked your son before I ate him.'

The words were the spite of a frustrated child.

'I fucked him and I ate him.'

Jim's grasp on the branch tightened. I saw his knuckles wet and white.

'I fucked them all.'

Jim rained down blow after blow, until he could no longer lift the branch. Despite the massive trauma to his head, and the crippling blows to his body, Mendicant was still alive. His degeneration halted, he lay on the earth and whispered words beyond my comprehension. I thought I recognised a fragment of Aramaic, but I may have been mistaken. Whatever the origin of his utterances, they rang in my ear as both poetic and ancient.

The storm eased. The clouds rolled away and the night sky domed the clearing with cold, indifferent moonlight. I kept watch over the Doctor while Jim, gasping and sobbing, gathered up the remains of his son.

We lifted the Doctor between us and lashed him to the same tree that had held James Rowbanks. There was no murmur from him, only a thin, reedy breathing. When he was secured, I suggested that Jim find Michael and go back to the farmhouse. I would watch Mendicant until the end.

'You're sure he was dead, Father?'

'Yes. There was nothing else we could do,' I said, and

wondered at the lie.

Had I been sure? Wasn't it the case that I had been so desperate to stop Mendicant proving the impotence of my faith that I had deceived myself into thinking that I could not help the child? Every time I closed my eyes, I saw the sparks from the gun barrel and asked myself that question. I ask it still.

The hours passed in blessed silence. Not until dawn touched the treetops did Mendicant speak his last.

'The end of one life, the beginning of something new.'

He lifted his head and stared at the light cresting the forest.

'*Non omnis moriar*. So said Horace in his Odes. Do you know what that means?'

As I crossed the clearing, the sun reached out a tentative finger and shone upon the strange creature we had crucified.

'Come closer, Asher, I won't bite. It means *I shall not altogether die*. Others have attempted to stop the metempsychosis before. I was ungenerous in my earlier estimation. You *have* done rather better than I expected. But this is not the end. I will still dance on your grave. When darkness creeps from the corners of the room, I promise that you will see my face before you die.'

'What are you?' I whispered.

'I am all you fear. I am the manifestation of your creeping doubts. Because if I am tolerated, then all you believe is a lie and all you thought of as heresy is true. Did Adam lay with the Lilith, and am I her child? I was shaped from fear, Asher, and I show you yours. Do you feel it now, as your faith closes in about you?'

He looked beyond me, sweeping the clearing with his gaze.

'But do not look to me to find the proof of your doubts. There is great evil here. Even I do not quite understand it. What I do know, is that it is *aware*. And it is focused on this sad little village. Before I came here, I heard it calling to me

327

in my dreams. Telling me to compound the misery of these wretched people. It was the sacrifice of the witch that did it. Her will gave a once undisciplined force a kind of intelligent determination. Do you know what she said as she burned?'

I shook my head, like a dull child.

'"*Each generation shall be mine. All shall be bound to the town that will come; all shall perish according to the choosing of the Darkness I lay upon you, or until the Darkness sickens of Itself and can bear no more. Then shall the town fall back into the shifting wastes*". The Darkness endures and I shall, for the time being, endure with it.'

I heard its call before I saw it. A crow, like tattered black cloth, flew into the clearing.

'Goodbye Asher,' Mendicant said. 'We will meet again, by and by.'

They passed in a wave from the trees: hundreds of crows following that first scout. The birds reached the centre of the clearing and wheeled in a huge black column. The clamouring cyclone soared forty feet overhead, its shadow cast across Mendicant and myself, the sun rippling over its body. Then, from the conical top, one bird broke away and plummeted back towards the clearing. Bending low, I staggered to the shelter of the tree line.

Mendicant was soon cocooned in a shrieking mass, each bird fighting for its chance to pluck and gorge. I heard no murmur from him, but it would have been difficult to hear anything above the cackling of that host '*of dark and rapier-beaked birds . . .*'. As if they wanted to show off their work for a moment, the curtain spread apart and I glimpsed what they had made of him. His remaining eye had been plucked out, and now two deep hollows stared at me. His clothes hung from him in shreds. The fingers of his ribcage were visible, arching through the husk of his torso. Most of the remaining skin on his face had been snatched away and his throat had been exposed. As they vied for the slivers of his cheeks, Mendicant's head turned from side-to-side in a strange, almost rhythmic motion. *Left to right, left to right, left to right . . .*

When they were done, the birds cawed happily at each other and took flight. Like a storm cloud caught on the breeze, they passed over the treetops.

I cut down the dead thing they had left and buried it in a shallow grave.

There was still work to be done. Grief would have to wait. I collected Jim and Michael from the farm and we returned to the house. While they went from room to room, collecting up the belongings of the late owner, I sifted through his papers. I could find no identifying documentation. The date of birth given on a few official forms was the sixth of January 1910.

He had bought the Redgrave land through an agent from the present Earl of Walmshire. I found evidence of an extensive share portfolio, handled by a stockbroker in Berne. From even a cursory examination of his assets, I could see Mendicant had died a very wealthy man. Last among the papers was a copy of a letter, dated a week before, and addressed to a firm of London solicitors. It revealed the well-laid plans of the late Doctor:

My dear Sirs,
Due to my failing health, I have decided to make a Will, which I would be grateful if you would draw up in the proper fashion. It should be a simple document, as there is only one beneficiary. Being of sound mind, I leave all my property, real and personal, to Master James Rowbanks, in recognition of the friendship extended to me by his family. You will find all the relevant documentation relating to my affairs enclosed, as well as the details of my worthy beneficiary. The Will should not be challenged, as I have no living relatives, but I set here on record my reason for bequeathing my fortune to the boy.

The tragedy of the Rowbanks family has touched my heart. I, too, have led a tragic life and would have their grief eased a little. Of late, James has lost his four younger siblings. The babies, Mark and Paul, died in their sleep.

Within the same week, his brothers, Luke and Joshua, were killed in a terrible fire. I feel the pain of this family keenly. I hope this gift, given in friendship, may bring them happiness when their benefactor is dust, scattered to the winds.

E Mendicant.

He had laid the way carefully, ensuring that the fortune he had accrued would not be lost. And he had revealed his plans for the disposal of Luke and Josh.

Having collected all the books from the library, and the statues, idols, puzzle boxes and paintings from the rest of the house, Jim, Michael and I met in the courtyard. Luke and Josh still rested under our coats, shaded by the mountain of Mendicant's strange collection. Once I had finished telling the brothers of my discoveries, I outlined a plan of action.

'As I see it, there is only one thing we can do,' I said. 'We must follow the Doctor's last instructions. We must burn the bodies so that the true cause of death cannot be identified. If we don't, there will be questions that none of us could answer.'

'I won't burn my babies,' Jim said.

'We have to, Jim,' Michael sighed. 'We can't explain it any other way.'

'They're at peace now,' I said. 'Fire can't harm them. But we can't do it straight away. Suspicion might be roused by the death of the babies and the boys within so short a time of each other.'

'The same would've been true with Mendicant's plan,' Michael said.

'Why should he have cared?' Jim snorted. 'He might have even made it look like me or Val had murdered our own kids. He'd've used my boy to do that.'

'Very likely,' I said. 'But in this we have no choice. If we store the bodies for a month in a cool dry place, then we could arrange the fire to look like an accident.'

'You seem to have the stomach for such things, Father,' said

Jim. 'I do not.'

I heard the fermenting bitterness in Jim's voice. It would go on to poison his life. After that day, he would never speak to me again.

By some strange alchemy of thought, which I have witnessed often among Crow Havenites down the years, the secret was shared among the village without a word of it being spoken. The community pulled together in a silent conspiracy. Old Arabella Nugent, headmistress of the school, kept a fictitious register of attendance for Luke, Josh and James up until the night of the fire. The Rowbanks did not blame those who had stayed behind their doors that night. It was, after all, the centuries-old practice of the town never to defy the Darkness. But perhaps it was a sense of guilt that made Crow Haven so readily complicit in the lie regarding the deaths of the boys. When questioned by the police, several eyewitnesses came forward to testify that they had seen the children screaming from the windows of the Rowbanks barn. Unfortunately, the fire was too fierce for anyone to attempt a rescue. With so many witnesses, with no cause to suspect foul play, and with pressure from the local press to leave the grieving family be, the police investigation was brief and delicate. Death by misadventure was the verdict.

After six months without communication from his client, the Swiss stockbroker contacted the English police. They made a cursory investigation, but it appeared that Mr Mendicant (he was never referred to as 'Doctor' in his papers) had vanished, along with all his belongings. He was filed as a Missing Person and soon forgotten. I have often wondered whether Jim Rowbanks, as James' next of kin, ever received Mendicant's fortune. I guess that, if he had, he must have given it away, for year on year the Rowbanks farmhouse fell into a sad ruin.

Jim is now the last of the Rowbanks left. Valerie killed herself five years after these events, wrapping stripped wire around her body and switching on the mains. In the early

Eighties, Michael, sickened by memories, defied superstition and left the village for a new life in America. He made it to the States, the farthest any Crow Havenite has ventured in centuries. When the maid at the *Golden Plaza Motel* on Orlando's International Drive could not get into Mr Rowbanks' room, she called security. Michael was naked, sitting on the floor, his back against the door. There was a half-written letter to his brother between his legs and a complimentary hotel biro thrust through his left eye. Suicide, of course.

And so the first chapter of Mendicant's life in Crow Haven is finished. The next chapter begins with the arrival of Peter and Anne Malahyde in 1984, eight years after the Doctor's death. Yet there is no definite demarcation between these periods, for Mendicant continued to exist on some level, as he told me he would.

I stopped walking in the woods after his death but often, on my way to and from the church, I would catch, out of the corner of my eye, the hint of a face watching me from the trees. And I was not the only one. The children of the village began to see him. In their nightmares, and sometimes at their windows in the dead of night. Come Halloween, they drew pictures of him and a song sprang up around him:

> *He walks in the woods and he talks to the crows,*
> *A bent old man, with a hole for a nose,*
> *And holes for eyes: black as sin,*
> *A man tore one out and a bird poked one in,*
> *And he waits for a child, pure and good*
> *That he can whisper to and take to his home in the wood.*
> *Be very afraid of the trees and the grasses*
> *When they move on their own,*
> *The Crowman passes.*

Forty-seven

Dawn decided to forgo the lift and trudge up the six flights to CID. It gave her time to think things over. She wondered whether it was possible that both Jamie and Jack were suffering from a kind of infectious hysteria. She had read about such cases at university: shared delusions and paranoia, mass hallucination. Maybe they had met while she had been abroad. That was possible. Just before she left, Jamie had been very keen to see Jack. What if they had got together and her son had been drawn into Jack's madness?

As she added layers to the theory, the awkward pieces that did not fit - the fact Jamie had recognised the old man from the photographs; the question why Jack would fixate on the Malahyde case - were swept aside. By the time she reached Jarski's door, she was feeling a little better. She knocked and entered.

Jarski was leaning back in his chair, his fingers pressed into a spire. A familiar smell, the herald stink of Pat Mescher, crept into her nostrils: a mix of dried sweat and something like Roquefort cheese. Mescher was trying to look grave, but couldn't disguise the grin spreading over his ample face.

'Well then,' Jarski sighed, 'it seems the shit has well and truly hit the fan.'

Jamie woke with a start. Questions immediately started buzzing in his head. What had happened last night? How had he fallen asleep? Was the *thing* still waiting outside? He scrambled out of bed and tore back the curtains. The figure was gone. He scanned the rest of the garden and the farmland beyond. Nothing.

The morning sun sat beneath a brow of black cloud. All across the fields, and in the garden, a pale mist crawled low to the ground and slunk, cat-like, through the picket fence. It was shaping up to be a shitty sort of day. Jamie reached for his watch on the bedside table. Nine-thirty a.m. His mum must have thought he needed a day off school. He knew, however, that she had gone to work. He had overheard her last night say that she would report in, explain 'the situation' and request a few days' leave: 'So we can get J some help.'

Fair enough. With her gone, he might be able to give his grandad the slip and find Jack. He pulled on a T-shirt and jeans and scraped his hair into a parting. Before he left the bedroom, he took another quick look out at the back gate. There was no-one there.

At the head of the stairs, he stopped and listened. There was the rattle of the washing machine on rinse. The late chime of the half-hour from the clock in the hall. The hiss and spit of frying bacon. But the burr of Johnny Yolendy, the football pundit who his grandad listened to religiously every morning, could not be heard. As the spin of the washing machine wound down, Jamie called over the banister:

'Grandad? You down there?'

He descended, gripping the weft of the carpet with his toes.

'Yo, anyone about?'

The smell of burnt bacon. The pop of the toaster. Grey smoke threading out from the kitchen.

'Grandad . . . ?'

The post lay scattered on the mat. The cat was crying to be let in. The kitchen door stood open a crack. Jamie padded down the hall, feeling his guts knot tighter with every step.

'Grandad, are you all . . . ?'

A hand rested on the linoleum, like a huge upturned spider.

Dawn listened to Pat Mescher's bullshit story. It seemed that he had decided to check up on 'his old pal' after Jack's no-show at work yesterday. Mescher then gave a long-winded account of how personnel had given him Dawn's father's address. His intention had been to head on over and see if he and Dawn could figure out between them what was up with Jack. Finding Bob Peterson's car parked outside the house, he had questioned the private detective and got the full story.

'Now, I didn't want this getting all over the papers,' Mescher said, 'that's why I brought it to Roger.'

'Bullshit,' Dawn spat. 'You're a self-serving, arrogant prick and . . .'

'Cut it,' Jarski exploded. 'Right, let's get straight what we're looking at here. Professional misconduct - dereliction of duty - inciting a member of the public to commit a serious offence - vagrancy — and . . . and pissing me off!' After each indictment, Jarski brought his fist down hard on his desk. 'How much did you know about this, Dawn?'

'She knew the whole story,' said Mescher. 'She was outside the house last night. I saw her talking to that crackpot Elvis wannabe.'

'That was the first I knew about it,' Dawn snapped. 'I was coming to speak to you this morning, Sir. Jack . . . He did have my son followed by this Peterson guy.'

'Why?'

'Because he's fucking nuts,' Mescher said. 'You wanna know how he caught that freakshow Greylampton? Because it takes a schizo to catch a schizo.'

'He had Jamie followed because he thought my son was in danger,' Dawn said.

'From who?'

'The same man who's been killing these kids.'

'What? Malahyde?'

Dawn hesitated. 'It's complicated.'

'Well, you better *un*-complicate it,' Jarski muttered. 'Give it to me nice and easy. No big words.'

'Jack spoke to me in confidence, Sir.'

'Confidence? No such thing in police work.'

'You're asking me to betray a trust.'

'I'm asking you to save your career, Sergeant. I don't want to put you on suspension. I don't even know if I have the grounds, but there are ways and means, believe me. You tell me now what Jack Trent said to you or . . .'

'Don't threaten me. I don't care what you . . .'

'I've got Jack for inciting use of an unlawful firearm. If you don't tell me what you know, I'm going to make life very, *very* unpleasant for him. If you *do* tell me, we'll get him some help, but you've gotta be up front with me.'

'Okay! Fuck!' Dawn breathed deeply. 'Jack believes . . . he thinks Simon Malahyde . . . Christ! He thinks Simon was possessed. He thinks the spirit of whatever possessed Simon committed these murders. He thinks this spirit wants to take my son.'

Guilt flooded her mind. All the logical arguments she had summoned to defend her view were washed away in that moment. A small voice railed against the tide: *I had to do it. For his sake . . .*

For your own - the tide answered - *to protect your safe little world. To protect the world you feel you must control. Order, order, order. Ever since Richard left. Order in parenting, work, love. Control, control, control.*

Pat Mescher was laughing. A full, thick, guttural laugh. Jarski cut him short.

'Get out.'

Dawn looked up. Jarski had swung round in his seat and was staring at the Lowry print on his wall. Dawn and Mescher threw bitter, questioning looks at each other.

'I mean you, Mescher. Out.'

Mescher crossed the room and leaned over the desk. His moist bottom lip trembled as he stared at the back of Jarski's head.

'But, Sir . . . I thought, seeing as Trent's . . . incapable of . . .'

'Let me tell you something, *Pat*,' Jarski spat the name as he faced the DI. 'If I had to choose who to head up a major investigation, a fully lobotomised Jack Trent or *you*, I'd choose Trent every time. Now, fuck off.'

Dawn watched the two fleshy slabs that were Mescher's hands tense and discolour. Jarski returned his gaze with steady indifference. As he went to the door, Mescher seemed to collapse into himself, like an accordion. Then he rallied and turned to her.

'Next time you see that freaky fuck, ask him how he enjoyed the pussy-for-hire. He didn't want me to tell you,' Mescher said, glaring at Jarski, 'but I was tipped off about just how off the rails Jacky boy is. His whore told me. How does that make you feel? To know he's been picking up pussy behind your back? Guess you couldn't give him what he wanted.'

'Out now!' Jarski roared.

Mescher slammed the door behind him.

'You okay?' Jarski muttered.

'Fine.'

'You don't look fine.'

'I'm not,' Dawn said. 'What's next?'

'Next,' Jarski sighed. 'Next, we bring him in.'

Forty-eight

Jack woke to find the last page of Brody's story still clasped in his hand. He stretched, and felt the muscles in his back and shoulders knotted from the few hours of sleeping upright. He blinked and took in the room.

'Jesus, what time is it?' he groaned.

'It's a quarter to ten.'

Jack started. He wondered how he had overlooked the man sitting opposite. Perhaps it was the exhaustion that still lay heavily upon him, making his senses dull. Or maybe it was because he had become so familiar with Brody from reading his story, that it would have been strange, in a sense, had the old priest not been there.

'I thought you were watching Jamie.'

'The boy's as safe as he can be at the moment,' Brody said. 'But for the sake of his future well-being, the time has come for us to talk.'

Jack held up the manuscript bundle. 'Do you really believe all this?'

'Are you playing devil's advocate, Mr Trent?' Brody snapped. 'We don't have time for you to start setting the world back to its proper order.'

'Okay, let's say it all happened exactly as you describe. I find it hard to believe that no-one ever let slip about the deaths of the children.'

'Secrets of Crow Haven are secrets of Crow Haven. I can't explain the nature of the place any better than that.'

'But you're talking about a community-wide conspiracy. There're always weak links . . .'

'I'm talking about a way of *life*, Mr Trent. I'm talking about something that is so ingrained in these people that to behave in any other way, given those circumstances, would have been as impossible for them as it would be to change their genetic makeup.'

'Well, let's talk about genetics,' Jack countered. 'This whole thing about them never being able to leave the village. How can a people survive that long in isolation?'

'You misread the situation. Outsiders do come in occasionally. To flavour the gene pool, if you like. Some talk of dreams that drew them to Crow Haven. Other unlucky souls stumble across the place and find they cannot leave. Those outsiders are soon made complicit in the ways of the village. There *are* cases, however, showing that centuries of related genes rubbing against each other is not a healthy thing. I have seen children born that . . . that had no chance of living. And sometimes you will also notice a lesser deformity; something in the arrangement of a face that will strike you as wrong, but which you cannot describe . . .'

Jack kneaded the corners of his eyes.

'All right, let's say I buy the Village of the Damned scenario. What about Mendicant? What was he?'

'What *is* he. That's the proper question. And the answer: I've no more idea now than I had twenty-five years ago. After his death, I read a great deal of ancient writing on the story of Lilith, the she-demon who Mendicant claimed had sired demonic children with Adam. Certain things did strike me in those old legends. In the Sumerian myths, Lilith lived in the desert beyond the Euphrates. She would go to the river and steal unbaptised babies and murder them, possibly drinking their lifeblood. In the epic of Gilgamesh, it was written that Lilith, maid of desolation, built her house in the trunk of the huluppu tree, between the dragon at its root and the bird in its branches. And in all these stories, she was identified as a succubus: a night-creature who confused the minds of men with dreams. The taking of children. The affinity with trees. The ability to manipulate dreams and inspire obsessions . . . It made me wonder whether Lilith had passed her powers down to her half-breed children.'

'But if Mendicant was a demon, why perform the ritual?' Jack asked. 'Aren't demons immortal?'

'If he was as he claimed, then he was tainted with humanity. He was Adam's son, too, remember. Perhaps he had a long life, like the patriarch Methuselah, but was not content with the years given to him.'

'What I don't understand,' said Jack, 'is how he resurrected himself inside Simon Malahyde. I thought that, after ten days outside a body, the spirit could not possess again. He was left roaming those woods for eight whole years. Just a ghost . . .'

'But you've read the *Transmigration*?'

'There was a problem. I ran out of time.'

'Then how did you get out?'

'I found a way. It's not important.'

'This makes a little more sense, then. I had not anticipated you leaving Yeager so soon. As I wrote,' Brody indicated the bundle on the floor, 'time runs differently there. How far did you get with the transcript?'

'I reached the end of the ritual.'

'You didn't read my later translation?'

'Later translation? I thought you could only visit the Library once . . .'

'Only one visit is gratis,' Brody muttered. 'It's time I told you the rest of the story. How Peter Malahyde died; how his son, Simon, was taken; how Mendicant came back.'

He took a brown paper bundle from his bag, similar to the one he had given Jack the previous evening.

'Read quickly. And while you do, I'll amend the later portions of my story to include the addendum to the *Transmigration*. Then we'll talk some more.'

'Can't you just tell me all this?' Jack asked.

'I don't trust myself,' Brody said. 'You see, I believe I overlooked something in my experiences with Mendicant. Some vital clue that I should have realised, and which might have saved Simon. I've written all I can remember, but if I simply tell you the story, I fear I may omit that one detail.'

'Fine,' Jack said. 'But coffee makes me extra attentive, Father. You'll find the percolator in the kitchen.'

BUNDLE 2 -
AFTER MENDICANT - 1976 - 1985

A few weeks after the murders, I received a final letter from Sam Willard. It reminisced, joked and flattered, and wished me long and happy years. There was a postscript, added seemingly as an afterthought, but which struck me as the real thrust of the letter:

> 'Recently I have been bothered by bad dreams, and look forward now to a long, untroubled sleep. In these dreams, I have seen something of the man, Mendicant, of whom you have spoken. His end is not of your making, Asher. A voice spoke to me in the dream. It told me that you are to make the way clear for another. You will have to pay a great price if you attempt to end the life of this thing before the hour appointed. This other shall seek you out, appeal directly for your assistance, though his first entreaty shall not be made face to face. You shall know him by this entreaty and also by his eyes. Eyes that meet across a white and crooked bridge.

'That's how you knew me, you old bastard.' Jack touched the scar that bridged his nose.

'What did you say?' Brody called from the kitchen.

'I said, how's the coffee coming?' Jack smiled, returning to the manuscript.

★

I often thought of leaving Crow Haven, but its sorrow held me there. Guilt also, and the sense that the Darkness had not been spent by the murders. So the years passed and I found the old weariness, which had pressed on me after my first meeting with Mendicant, dog me once more. Day by day, I parcelled up my interests and passions and stowed them away in the cellar of the house. It felt as if I was putting my soul into a kind of storage from which it might never emerge. For a year or more, letters still arrived from my friends, but they remained unopened. What good was it for *me* to read them? The Asher Brody they were addressed to had died with James Rowbanks in the clearing.

James Rowbanks. I tried not to think of him, but he haunted my dreams. Most nights, I would see him staggering from the forest, crossing the Conduit Road and tapping at my study window. Sometimes he pleaded, more often he stood in silence. Always he was faceless. He would cry, telling me that he *was* alive. Begging me not to fire the gun. I closed my eyes against him and blocked my ears. I knew, of course, with every rational instinct that he was never there. Yet still, when morning came, there would always be the handprints at the window.

I remained lonely, with only prayer and my strange little flock for company. I grew as sullen and reserved as any of them. So much so that the congregation from outside soon dwindled. They saw me as one of 'the Crow Haven folk', I suppose. Tainted now by the bad luck of the place. By the late summer of 1984, when Peter and Anne Malahyde arrived in the village, no-one from outside came to Crow Haven to worship.

I was coming out of the church one morning in early September, when I saw the trucks trundle by and turn into the avenue of trees. It was as if the past was replaying itself and I had been thrown back to that time when men and mortar had arrived to build the Doctor's house. A bright pain bloomed in my heart. Somehow he has come back, I thought; somehow he has found a child.

That was impossible, of course. I had read the *Transmigration of Souls* and knew that Mendicant was spent. If he still walked in the woods, then he was as frail as gossamer, unable to perform the rite. No more than a whisper in the wind. For all those inward reassurances, however, that parade of trucks worried me. If not the Doctor, then some outsider was coming to Crow Haven.

A few simple inquiries of a local land agent gave me the name of the newcomer. I sent Peter Malahyde a note of introduction suggesting that, once he had settled in, I might pay him a visit. A few weeks later, I received a phone call from Peter, and we arranged that I should call upon him and his wife the following afternoon.

I was on tenterhooks all the next day. I felt duty bound to put the Malahydes on their guard, but was at a loss to know how to do so. Perhaps Peter Malahyde was a spiritual soul, open to the impossible story that I might tell him. But what if he was pragmatic and unimaginative? If I laid out my story in plain terms, then he might think me mad. He could turn me out of the house or, worse still, inform the Bishop or the police. Then there would be questions about the deaths of the Rowbanks children. The best course was to ease myself into Peter's confidence and introduce him slowly to my story.

By this time, as I have instructed, you will have spoken to Geraldine Pryce and already know of my first meeting with the Malahydes. I had planned to segue gently into the proposal of blessing the house, but the shock of Peter talking about entering Mendicant's library forced it from my lips. I could see that Peter and Anne thought me only somewhat eccentric, but the suspicion was evident on Geraldine's face. I have got to know that lady well over the years, and have found her to be a person of extraordinary perception. The second shock was when I discovered that Anne Malahyde was pregnant. If Mendicant did still exist, there were many barriers to him achieving another possession. Still, the thought of a child growing up in this house filled me with horror.

As I said my goodbyes, I made Peter promise that he would not open the library until I had performed the blessing.

Having researched the protocol for the blessing of homes, I arrived back at the house the following afternoon. The day was fast expiring, and I felt that summer might be dying with it. Long before dusk, wisps of autumnal cloud had skulked in from the north.

I was somewhat early for the appointment. Caught up in my thoughts as I approached the house, I did not notice that the front door was ajar. A raised voice echoed from upstairs.

'It matters to me.' Peter, sounding angry, but also dejected. Then the flat, muffled tones of his wife.

'Don't lie' – Peter again – 'I hate lying, I told you. It's not the pregnancy, you're still beautiful. I'm too fucking old, that's it. Fucking worn out.'

A door slammed and I heard feet passing across the landing. Embarrassed, I stepped away from the front door and tried to make it appear that I was just arriving. Peter collided with me as he barged out of the house. His high colour drained as he looked me up and down, as if he couldn't remember who I was.

'Hello, Father,' he said, his brow clearing. 'Did we have an appointment?'

'The blessing,' I said. 'I've underestimated my schedule. Now's the only time I can fit you in.'

'I see,' Peter glanced over the upper windows of his new home. 'You better come in then.'

We passed through the house. I made the blessing in each room, and at the entrances and exits, my mind always on the Doctor's old sanctum upstairs. The last room on the lower level was the conservatory that spanned the space between the L-shaped wings of the house. Jim and Michael Rowbanks had described this place to me after they had cleared it of the Doctor's possessions, but I had not seen it myself. It was an impressive ruin, overrun with weeds and trailing plants. As I prayed, I caught sight of a balcony set into the back wall of the sealed second storey. On my visits to Mendicant's library, I had noted that door, wondering where it led. On both occasions, however, the subject of our conversation had driven such idle questions from my mind.

I felt cold now, as I saw it standing wide open.

'A little confession,' Peter said.

He led the way out of the conservatory, into the hall and up the iron staircase. As feared, the lock of the library door had been pried apart.

'I told you to stay out,' I said.

We were standing shoulder-to-shoulder on the landing. Peter shivered.

'I know,' he whispered, then seemed to rally himself. 'Come on, Father, why so grave? We've stampeded through the rest of the place. What's the trouble with . . .'

'Have you been inside?'

'Yes.'

'Did you see anything?'

'Not then, no,' he was thoughtful again. 'Later . . . a dream. I was in the room. There were books. Hundreds of books. And a fire: burning pages and wooden statues. And children with dead faces . . . There was a man . . . It was just a dream.'

'What did he say to you?'

'Nothing . . . It was nonsense.'

I did not want to push him. I crumbled a wafer of Host and read from Paul's letter to the Colossians. I kissed my crucifix and laid it on the upper panel of the old library door.

'We beseech the Lord to enter this home, to bless it with His presence, to draw out any Evil that lies against its walls and in its secret heart. We pray for Peter and Anne and their unborn child, to be strong in the Lord and in the Power of His Might.'

'So, what is it about this place?' Peter asked in a half-laughing voice. 'You been here before? Did the last owner sacrifice nubile young virgins or something?'

'Can I take a look inside?' I asked.

Peter nodded. The library was almost exactly as I remembered it, save for the thick carpet of dust and the empty

345

shelves. The leather chairs, the simple, elegant fireplace, even the phantom smell of musty books was familiar.

'Make a great study.'

'Why did you come to Crow Haven, Peter?'

'It's a beautiful house,' he said. 'And the countryside. Who wouldn't want to live here? Good clean air, perfect place to bring up a child . . .'

'Why did you come to Crow Haven, Peter?'

I went to the balcony. A bittersweet scent of rotting flowers rose up from the conservatory on a wave of warm air. A stone imp peeked at me from between gnarled vine-fingers.

'To take Annie away. From people . . . People her own age.'

'Don't you trust your wife?' I said, turning to him.

'If I were her, beautiful, young . . . Why should I trust her?'

I think he was surprised at what he had admitted. I was puzzled myself as to why I had questioned him about so intimate a matter – thereby risking his anger – when my plan had been to ingratiate myself by degrees. For a moment, I had felt a connection with him. A connection which I controlled and with which I could bend his thoughts to answer my questions. Mendicant must have felt something like it during our conversations: the thrill of dominance over a weaker mind. Had some echo of the Doctor's power been left in this sealed room? The thought that I might enjoy using so invasive a talent frightened me.

'Sorry,' Peter said, 'what were you saying?'

'Doesn't matter.'

'Shall we get some fresh air? I'll show you the work shed I've had built.'

Peter led me down a new path that had been cut through the forest. He chattered about this idea for the house or that project for the grounds. I knew what he was feeling. It was the same brew of nausea and confusion that had followed my own interviews with Mendicant. In time, his memory of our conversation would return. What would he make of it, I wondered?

The path ended at the door of a sizeable cabin. Aside from the corrugated roof and metal chimney, the dark wood walls of the shed fitted neatly with its surroundings. A positive chameleon, in fact, compared to the glass house.

'Had it thrown together a week or two ago,' Peter said, ushering me inside. 'Thought I'd try my hand at a little wood-work.'

'You've lost your interest in local history already?' I asked.

'Look at these beauties,' he said, taking down tools from their racks.

'You've not asked me about the man who built your house. I thought you might. You were very keen to hear about him the other day.'

'Cost a pretty penny. Never believed a simple hammer could cost so much. Thought I'd start small, a dollhouse for the baby or something.'

'I thought you wanted a boy.'

'No,' he snapped. 'Annie, she wants a girl. Boys are hassle.'

'Peter. What did the man in your dream say to you? Did he ask for something?'

Peter began replacing the tools with exaggerated care. Through the window at the far end of the cabin, I could see flares of purple light stream over the forest. The last show of defiance from the aged summer. A moment later, the light failed.

'Listen, Peter, I had hoped to introduce you gently to what happened here. I see now that he is moving faster than I ever anticipated. You know of whom I speak. The man in your dream. It's imperative you tell me what he said to you.'

'Why?' Peter replied, *sotto voce*.

'I know how this must seem, but you must believe . . .'

'I do.'

It was difficult now to make out anything, save for the rough shape of Peter's back against the gleam of the tool rack.

There was not a breath of wind outside. The only sound was the creak of the cabin.

'What did he say to you? You must tell me.'

'All good things to he who waits.'

The voice was not Peter Malahyde's.

The sickle moon rolled over a ragged collar of trees. It threw yellow light onto the cabin floor. Something hot teased at my heart, then clenched and wrung it. There was a silhouette cast on the bare boards: a tall, thin man, his head moving left-to-right with metronomic steadiness. I looked up and expected to see those sightless eyes boring into me. The wasted face was not there, and when I glanced down, the shadow was gone.

My left arm was numb. A tingling sensation passed an inch or two above the skin. Beads of sweat dripped from my face and watered the floor.

'Peter . . . I feel . . .'

'Ssshhh. Quiet now.'

My vision swam. I had to catch hold of the worktable to steady myself. Peter was facing me, but he did not seem to notice my discomfort. He was brushing the side of his face with long, languid strokes. I was about to plead for help, when I saw him pluck a pleat of skin from his cheek.

'Will you look at that.'

In one smooth motion, he pulled the pleat into a long strip and tore it free from his neck. As the pain gripped my heart again, I recalled that final vision of the Doctor's face between the curtain of crows. I saw a tongue of skin, caught in a beak and torn from Mendicant's throat.

Falling to the floor, I stared up at the underside of the tin roof. There was a fresh access of pain and I knew no more.

Forty-nine

Brody's Story

BUNDLE 2 –
AFTER MENDICANT – 1976 – 1985

'How long have I been here?'

'You were brought in the night before last. You slept through yesterday, which was good.'

The young doctor noted observations on his clipboard.

'Who brought me in?'

'Ambulance. Mr . . .' he checked the paperwork. 'Malahyde came with you. Said you collapsed at his house. Now, Father, you've had a mild heart attack, a warning. There may be some damage to the heart muscles, but fairly minimal . . .'

'When can I leave?'

'Whenever you choose,' the doctor sighed. 'But let me tell you, if you leave this hospital in less than five days, you're risking a second, perhaps fatal attack.'

I pulled the sheets back and tried to sit up. My arm collapsed under me and I sent the water jug crashing to the floor. Exclamations of surprise and grumbles of complaint came from my immediate neighbours. The doctor settled me back into bed.

'You're too weak to go anywhere,' he said, checking my hands for cuts. 'No damage done. Listen, Mr Brody, I know you feel you have duties to attend to, but the world's not going to fall into vice and sin just because you're laid up for a week. Even Jesus took a rest in the Garden of Gethsemane before the Big Day, didn't he?'

★

As it turned out, I was much weaker than even the young doctor had guessed. By the end of the week, I was just about able to reach the toilet with the support of two sticks. I was told that my frugal diet, lack of recent regular exercise and irregular, though copious, consumption of scotch, had contributed to my poor recovery. There may also be psychological factors, one particularly sterile-smelling doctor told me: had I been under any stress of late?

The Bishop visited twice, picking his way down the ward, his hand to his mouth, as if the microbes from a few ragged coughs might carry a pestilence of biblical proportions. He gave me strict instructions that I was not to discharge myself until the doctors saw fit. Then he told me that a temporary replacement had been found to take up the reins in Crow Haven. Father Christopher Garret would stay for as long as was necessary.

These injunctions washed over me. I had remembered the shadow on the cabin floor and the strange spectacle of Peter Malahyde peeling skin from his face. As soon as I had the strength to lift the receiver, I requested the telephone. The operator told me that Malahyde's number was ex-directory. Lies about a sick relative would not budge her.

I lay still all night while, inside my head, I twisted and turned. Logical thought was made all but impossible by an undefined fear that locked the gears of my brain. What had Mendicant done to Peter Malahyde? What was being whispered to him in his dreams? I should have told Peter everything at our first meeting. I hadn't, of course, because I was *of* Crow Haven. I had become indoctrinated with that firm conviction that outsiders would not appreciate the reality of the evil that abided there. I should have realised, however, from my own swift introduction to Mendicant, that the Darkness does not always creep slowly into one's consciousness. Sometimes, almost as soon as an outsider enters the village, he feels the hand of it on his shoulder. Hears the whisper of its agents - of whom Mendicant was only the latest - until after a short, intense inculcation one was ready to believe impossible things. Peter

Malahyde was already of Crow Haven. My reluctance to expose the heart of the place to him had delivered him to Mendicant, weak and undefended.

In the bleakness of these thoughts, an idea came to me. It was the middle of the night, but I managed to convince the nurse that the call was urgent. She wheeled in the telephone and left me. I allowed it to ring for some time.

'Hello? Old Priory,' said a weary voice.

'Father Garret? This is Asher Brody . . .'

'Father Brody? Are you all right? Is anything wrong?'

'Listen, I'm rather anxious to contact Mr Malahyde on a private matter.'

'The man who went with you to the hospital? You want to speak to him tonight?'

'Perhaps you could pay a visit tomorrow? Tell him we must talk. It's a confessional matter. Ask him if he'll be good enough to visit me.'

'Certainly, if it will set your mind at rest. I'll see him tomorrow morning.' Garret sounded uncertain. 'Well, good-night.'

Sleep was difficult. I seemed to be highly tuned into the motions and workings of the hospital: the whirring machinery, the whispers of the nurses, the calls and croaks of my fellow invalids. I was irritable all the next morning, ignoring the chatter of the old lady in the next bed and passing back, without comment, the endless snapshots of grimy-faced grandchildren. At a little after one, I called Garret again.

'Have you seen Peter yet?' I asked, as soon as I heard the click of the line.

'Father Brody? Erm. Well, yes. I've just got back, actually.'

'How did he *seem*.'

'Seem? He was fine. Said you shouldn't worry about that chat you were having. He's cleared his conscience. He also said not to worry about the vase.'

'Vase?'

'The vase you knocked over in the kitchen. When you had your attack. A joke, I suppose . . . Are you there, Father?'

'He told you I had my attack in the kitchen?'

'Yes.'

'Did he look all right to you?'

'What is this all about, Father? I think you're worrying yourself needlessly. Perhaps your recollection of your last meeting with Mr Malahyde is a little skew-whiff.'

'Maybe you're right.'

'He does have a nasty case of eczema or some such,' Garret said, in a throwaway tone. 'Quite noticeable. Told me not to mention it, said it might upset you. Can't think what he meant by that . . .'

After nine days' bed rest, I was allowed to leave hospital. Father Garret drove me back to Crow Haven.

He seemed a conscientious fellow, about forty or so years of age. A very practical sort of Christian: quiet, hardworking, devoted. I got the impression that he viewed God as some all-powerful librarian, keeping the sins of Man neatly indexed, apportioning fines for overdue acts of devotion and for any dog-eared souls returned to Him. There wasn't much spirituality to Garret, but a good deal of humble service. On the ride home, I asked him about his past. Like myself, he had been trained in a seminary from an early age and, after a few novice posts, he had taken a parish somewhere in North Wales. I read between the tight lines he drew that his congregation had not warmed to his stilted and distant ministry. He had come here at the request of the Bishop and would stay as long as he was needed.

(As it turned out, Garret remained in Crow Haven long after my final, foolhardy involvement with the Malahyde family. After my convalescence, the Bishop insisted that I was not strong enough to see to all parish duties myself. It was nonsense, of course. There was not enough work for two men. I wondered later whether Garret had reported a few of my eccentricities to the Bishop, and, between them, they had decided that it would be best for him to remain by my side.

It is very strange, for Garret is the only person I know

who seems immune to the Darkness. I have seen many people come to Crow Haven down the years. In some cases, like Peter Malahyde and myself, the atmosphere of the place catches hold at once. In others, such as Geraldine Pryce for instance, there is a slow osmosis. Geraldine has never seen anything in the village that defies all rational explanation, yet she now knows, by instinct, what Crow Haven is. Christopher Garret, however, has never succumbed to the evil that walks at his elbow. Perhaps his lack of spiritual imagination has saved him).

As we pulled up at the *Old Priory*, I told him I might take a stroll and maybe pop in on the Malahydes.

'You should be resting,' Garret said, helping me out of the car. 'In any case, Mr Malahyde is not at home.'

'Where is he?'

'Abroad. Three-week holiday. I saw him in the village yesterday. His skin complaint is getting much worse. His doctor thought it might be stress related. Though what kind of stress a wealthy man like that can be under, I don't know. Anyway, they've gone to the Caribbean or some such.'

His *doctor* had recommended it. A strange coincidence that the Malahydes should leave the day I returned from hospital.

A month passed before I saw Peter again. My convalescence was now well and truly over and I was once more active about the village.

As I left the *Old Priory*, en route to the post office, Peter and Anne passed by in their car. Neither waved. I wasted no time in following them. I was breathing hard when I came out of the elm-tunnel and approached the house. I hammered on the door, waited a few seconds, and hammered again. Anne Malahyde, still beautiful, but tired and almost bent double under the weight of her unborn child, opened the door.

'Is Peter here?'

'He doesn't want to see anybody.'

'I'm afraid it's urgent.'

I pushed by her and went directly to the old library. Perhaps it was a trick of the light: the paintwork of the door seemed ever more cracked and peeling, as if years, rather than weeks, had passed since I had last seen it. I knocked and entered.

Peter Malahyde sat in Mendicant's red leather chair, his frame thin and crumpled. His face shone, though the only light in the room came from the cold autumn sun that yawned through the little windows.

'Come in, Asher,' he said. 'And close the door. I can't bear the light.'

Fifty

Brody's Story

BUNDLE 2 -
AFTER MENDICANT - 1976 - 1985

'What's happened to you, Peter?'

'Change . . . change inside a dream.'

As he spoke, grains of dead skin fell from the corners of his mouth. I could not know then how far the transformation would go, but already there were signs pointing to the final phases of this living decomposition. His lips were cracked and close-knit sores punctuated his skin. The arrangement of lesions on his face was no coincidence. I knew at once what I was seeing: a slow re-enactment of the tearing apart of Dr Mendicant on the person of Peter Malahyde. In this case, however, the ripping beaks were invisible and worked with a cruel leisureliness.

'You've seen him, haven't you?' I asked. 'The man who used to own this house.'

'He came to me in my dreams,' Peter whispered. 'Spoke to my fears. Promised me . . .'

He held a raw hand up to the light.

'Like Job, he said, you must first be put to the test.'

A breeze pushed against the library door, opening it a crack. A spear of light cut in from the landing.

'He made a dream seem possible.'

'And dreams are all he can give you, Peter,' I said, leaning toward him.

'No. He hands out nightmares, too. He has been with me every day since the dream. No-one else can see him. He

355

whispers to me in the night. He watches me from the shadows.'

'Listen,' I urged, 'you must tell me what you wished for.'

'I wished . . . I wished to put time in a bottle,' Peter laughed. 'To stopper time in a bottle. To make it run backwards. I wished for youth.'

'He can't give you those things. His only interest is to find a child. He has no use for a man.'

'Oh, I have my use. I am his conduit. He speaks plainly to me now, though it's fair to say he never actually lied. Just left a detail out here and there. I *will* be young. Young and unable to touch her . . . Unable to know her . . . How did he make me agree to it, Asher?'

'Tell me everything.'

'Can you help me? Can you take it back?'

'I can try. If you tell me.'

'No. No, I won't. It wasn't real . . .'

'You're being torn apart, Peter. Inch by inch, you're being stripped away. That's real. It's how I saw him die.'

'And how Peter must die,' he said. 'He has chosen the path; he must share the fate.'

'Is it *you* speaking?' I said, breathless, suddenly aware of all the physical weaknesses that my illness had inflicted on me. 'You - you have deceived him. He thought it was a dream. He thought . . . He didn't know what he was agreeing to.'

'Poor Asher. Time has not been kind, has it? You speak of dreams? It is *in* dreams that we are at our most honest. He has pledged his word and he will be rewarded.'

Peter whimpered and started scratching at his already raw skin. I snatched his hands away before he tore his face to the bone. The boils that hemmed his thinning hair broke out and wept. At that moment, I felt something slip out of the room. Perhaps it was Elijah Mendicant. Perhaps it was God.

There is little point in picking over the details of those last two months. With each passing day, Peter grew less intelligible and, physically at least, more like the corpse of Dr Mendicant that I had cut down and buried in the clearing. After our conversation in the library, Peter became very withdrawn. I could coax no more from him regarding the bargain he had made. I guessed that, in those weeks during my convalescence and Peter's absence from Crow Haven, there had been a period of transition. A time during which the Doctor's hold over him had grown stronger until it could not be prised away. Now Mendicant didn't even bother to prejudice Peter's mind against me.

In those first few weeks, when Peter was still well enough to move about, I took him to a number of holy places. We prayed, within the sight of blessed relics, that his affliction might be lifted. I scoured all the books on sympathetic illness and possession I could find, and we tried several rites of exorcism. None was effective. I wondered whether it was because the decay had not been forced upon Peter. This supernatural infection endured because a part of him still wanted the reward Mendicant had promised. There was only one way to break the effectiveness of that enticement. Anne Malahyde had to make what reassurances she could to her husband. If she could persuade him that his feelings of inadequacy were imaginary, then that part of him that yearned for renewed youth might die. But here was the problem: as the illness progressed, and Peter became increasingly unsightly, his young wife would not go near him. Worse still, by the time he was bedridden, she had insisted on him being cared for in the unused part of the house: Mendicant's old library.

I sat with him through the long nights. Often he would scream for Anne until the nurse quietened him with a cocktail of drugs. In the early weeks, while he could still speak, Geraldine Pryce paid a visit. She was very brave. I had hoped she might, in time, help me convince Anne to see Peter. As it turned out the 'disease' worked through him much quicker than any of us thought possible.

It was in the early hours of 6th January 1985, the anniversary of my arrival in Crow Haven, that Peter gave up the ghost. Leading up to that day, I had little chance to converse with him. His condition had deteriorated to such an extent that there was always a nurse or the live-in doctor on hand. Conversation was now nigh on impossible anyway. Peter's vocal cords were peppered with cankers.

I was dozing in the bedside chair when I felt a cool, flesh-less hand in mine.

'Ash–her, way–ka . . .'

'Peter? Jesus, how . . .'

Since the windows had been bricked over, at Peter's deter-mined insistence, he had not been able to sit up unaided. Now he was perched on the edge of the bed, his hand twitching spasmodically in mine. The nurse, who had been half-asleep, bolted awake as she heard Peter's voice.

'What's happening? What . . . . Oh, my . . .'

'Get Dr Stoker,' I told her. 'Go.'

She hesitated, looking from me to the wasted figure. Peter turned his torso towards her. To my horror, his head began to rock from side-to-side. Something in that see-saw motion must have decided her. She ran from the room.

Peter turned back to face me. His jaw strained. The mouth hole in his bandage mask opened wide. It was Peter who spoke, his tones as they had been before the rot took hold.

'This is the end, Brody. The end of one life, the beginning of another . . .'

'Peter, you must tell me what you promised him.'

I felt my thumb, which was pressing lightly against Peter's palm, push through the papery skin. The fingers cracked and splintered. I cried out, but Peter paid no heed.

'I've tried to take back whatever promise I made,' he said. 'He told me I could put an end to it: if I truly did not want what he offered. But he *will* take the boy.'

Pinprick bloodstains broke out on the bandages. Little tributaries ran into each other so that, within moments, the mask was etched with a grid of shaky red lines.

'What boy? Peter, you must tell me . . .'

'Be vigilant, Asher. The time is some years away. You must wait. You must watch.'

Blood seeped from beneath the layers of dressing. The mouth opened wider and the screaming started. He clawed at the bandage, exposing raw musculature, veins and cartilage. What I could see of his face resembled one of those anatomical drawings of a partially flayed human head.

I sat, riveted, repulsed, but unable to flee or to help the dying man. It was then that I heard the scratching upon the sills outside. Hoarse cawing filled the room. It was as if the crows had broken through the bricks and were tearing at the bandages, for now the remaining dressing was ripped from Peter's face, but not by his own hand. A great, lateral tear exposed both eyes, rolled white in their sockets.

I just about managed to find my voice:

'Peter, please tell me, what did you promise?'

'A trinity. A dark trinity. My boy . . .'

He fell back onto the bed, clutching at his throat. The screams died. His head stopped twisting. His hand twitched once more and then lay still on the counterpane.

Simon was born on 1st February 1985, less than a month after his father's death. In the early days, I tried to keep up a friendly acquaintance with Anne Malahyde. Her own consuming guilt and grief, however, forbade any lasting relationship. A few weeks after the funeral, she asked me to stop coming to the house. That was the last I saw of her for many years.

To begin with I also saw very little of Simon. A nanny would sometimes take him for a walk and, as soon as I saw the pram pass my study window, I would rush out and inquire after the child. (The nannies, by the way, never stayed for long. Often they would leave in the middle of the night without giving notice). He was a bonny baby and he grew into a happy child. I was filled with hope by his carefree ordinariness. Ordinary I say, and yet surely extraordinary. How did he manage to develop into so normal a little boy inside that house? I thought of him as a resilient bud, flourishing in a desolate wasteland.

As time went on, we got to know each other pretty well.

I made it my business to walk him, each day, between home and school. No-one in the village ever commented on my behaviour. No doubt they trusted that I had good reason to act as I did. Father Garret, who stayed on despite my reassurances to the Bishop that I was quite well, was generally too busy with the minutiae of office to notice my comings and goings. Simon never asked why I took a special interest in him, and I did not tell him that I had known his father. I grew to like the boy very much. Indeed, I might say I loved him.

Some months after his tenth birthday, they came for him.

Fifty-one

'Okay, I think I get the picture.' Jack laid the bundle on the floor.

'There is one final chapter of the story,' Brody said. 'The soul-rape of Simon Malahyde.'

'Look, I understand why you think what happened back then is important, but first I have to get what's happening *now* straight in my head.'

'All right,' Brody sighed. 'Let's talk recent history.'

Jack told Brody the story of the past few days, from his first dream to his encounter with Mendicant in the private saloon of the Lazarus Club. He was frank about *the dreaming*, without explaining its genesis or telling Brody about the creatures inside his mind. The priest listened and seemed remarkably uninterested in the details or antecedents of Jack's powers. Instead, he concentrated on Mendicant's reference to them.

'The Doctor is playing your fears against you,' Brody said. 'I guess you're not entirely comfortable with your abilities and have kept them hidden. He has seen that fear within you. He is an emotional sadist. He loves to see a soul in anguish. Look at how he threw doubts on my faith; how he played on Peter's fears of inadequacy. He wants to undermine you . . .'

'So he's partial to mind games. Is that the extent of what he can do?'

'That's enough. Fear can be a seductive thing you know. Look at this.'

Brody took a faded newspaper clipping from his pocket and passed it to Jack. It was from an English paper printed in Germany and dated April 1999.

'After the catastrophe of my attempt to save Simon Malahyde,

I tried to keep an eye on the boy. I had local papers sent to me from the areas in which he schooled. There are many clippings such as these that I destroyed before I left St Augustine's.'

BOARDING SCHOOL TRAGEDY

The pupils of Wistinghausen Boarding School are today mourning the loss of Albert Speno, 14. The unfortunate child was found last Thursday, locked in a tiny broom cupboard in a disused part of the school. He had suffered a fatal stroke, brought on, doctors have suggested, by a pathological claustrophobia. The child's fear of confined places was well known in the school and Albert was on medication to regulate panic attacks. Albert's body was found by schoolmate Simon Malahyde. The police do not suspect foul play but are at a loss to explain why . . .

The rest of the article had been torn away.

'It's proof of nothing, of course,' Brody said. 'Just another person who encountered Mendicant and fully realised something he dreaded.'

'You allowed this to happen,' Jack said. 'Albert Speno. Oliver Godfrey, Stephen Lloyd. They didn't have to die. Why didn't you finish it that day you abducted Simon?'

'You're right,' Brody said. 'I am responsible. When it mattered, I wasn't strong enough. But what will you do? If Mendicant is successful this time? If he takes Jamie and speaks with the boy's voice? Will you have the strength to finish him?'

They were both silent for a moment.

'Okay,' Jack stirred. 'In the Lazarus Club, he said he had only two days left to complete the rite. That means we've got roughly twenty-four hours. Short of shooting Jamie through the head, Jesus Christ knows what we can do.'

Jack regretted that last sentence as soon as he said it. Brody, however, did not react.

'He is not as strong as he would like us to believe, Jack,' the priest said. 'He fears God and he fears us. If he was really

362

so confident of his powers, why did he try to get me out of the picture during his whisperings to Peter Malahyde? And why did he try to kill me before I could tell you my story? But what has been worrying me is this: if Mendicant did incite Anne Malahyde to kill him a week ago, then he cannot be operating alone . . .'

'Why not?' Jack asked. 'Wasn't he alone in the Rowbanks and Malahyde cases?'

'Yes, but in the first he was flesh and blood when the rite was performed. He could murder the Rowbanks children, drink their fat, burn the baptism dresses himself. In the case of Simon Malahyde, the ritual only needed to be slightly adapted. His spirit was still suffused with the power given to him by the fat of the Rowbanks children. Remember, that ritual wasn't completed. All he needed was Peter to show the path into Simon. You remember what Peter said? That he was a conduit? In this case, however, Mendicant proposes to possess a child while in his spiritual form, and without the advantages he had with Simon. He does not have the physical substance to arrange the murder of the Godfrey and Lloyd boys and to burn the baptism dresses. Someone must be helping him. Someone he has seduced, perhaps with promises similar to those he made to Peter Malahyde. All that matters is that we now know he has the means to take Jamie as his new body. And this body will last him maybe fifty years. If we don't stop him this time, I will be long dead at the hour of his next metempsychosis and you will be as old and frail as myself.'

They were quiet again for a moment. Then Jack asked:

'Why haven't you asked me about my dreams?'

'It is not for me to question who God chooses as his champion,' Brody said. 'You are His sword, Jack. It is His business how He wields you.'

There was a knock at the front door. Jack twitched back the curtain and motioned Brody to the back of the room. They had been so absorbed in their talk that neither had heard the car pull up outside.

'It's the police,' Jack whispered.

He showed Brody through to the kitchen and opened the back door.

'Out this way,' he said. 'Keep to the backs of the houses.'

Brody retrieved his few belongings from the corridor. From his bag, he took a slim bundle, wrapped in the same brown paper as the other parts of the manuscript.

'That's the last of it. I've included the addendum to the *Transmigration of Souls*; the part you didn't have time to read at the Yeager Library,' he said. 'The days are almost up, Jack. Time is running out.'

Jack watched the old priest scramble across the uneven ground and disappear behind the house that backed onto his own. The house with the patio doors in which he had first seen the creeping corpse of Jamie Howard. The knocking from the front door became more insistent. Jack stuffed the package into his pocket and made his way from the kitchen to the hall. He eased back the latch. There were two uniformed officers outside.

'DCI Jarski wants to see you, Sir.'

'I'm sure he does. Look, I've been ill. Can you tell him . . . ?'

'He wants to see you *now*.'

'I can't. Not today. I'll call him and . . .'

There was the slightest of glances between the two officers. Before Jack could stop them, they had spun him around and the large forearm of PC Dawling was pushing into the back of his neck, pressing his face against the wall.

'Jack Trent, we are arresting you on suspicion of inciting another to carry an unlawful firearm and inciting the use of that firearm. You do not . . .'

Jack tried to struggle free. A blow to his ribs knocked him sideways, forcing all the air out of his lungs and bringing tears to his eyes. Between them, the two constables hauled him upright. His feet clattered on the floorboards. As the officers dragged him from the house, Jack's vision began to clear. Through the last of his tears he saw '1' flashing on the digital display of his answering machine.

Fifty-two

'Dawn, he's in danger. Please, you must believe me. Call him. Make sure he's . . .'

Dawling and the others forced Jack into the interview room. Dawn hesitated, wanting to follow but mindful of Jarski's instruction: *If you see him when he's brought in, don't talk to him. I don't want you making him excitable. We've gotta keep a lid on this.*

She went straight to Jack's office. Here she could step outside the chaos for a moment. Here she almost believed him . . . She snatched up the phone.

'Dad? It's me. Is J all right?'

'He's fine, love. We're just setting up the Risk board.'

'He's not mentioned last night or . . .'

'No. Nothing about that. Speaking of which, maybe I got a bit overexcited. I'm sure you're right about everything. Must be a logical explanation for all this . . . You still there, love?'

'Yes . . . Yes, listen, I'll be home late tonight. Is that okay?'

'Late as you like, darlin'. Me and the boy're gonna have some fun.'

She hung up and stared at the phone for a long time.

Quickly, Jesus Christ, quickly.

Jack took the package that Brody had given him from his pocket and placed it on his knees beneath the desk. He shot a glance at PC Dawling. The constable was standing at the door of the interview room, looking out into the corridor. Any moment now another uniform would arrive and Jack would be searched.

His hands shook. If they found Brody's story on him, he was in deep shit. Scratch that: even *deeper* shit. He drew as much saliva into his mouth as he could and spat into his palms. He smeared his hands over the vast collection of chewing gum that had accumulated under the desk. Thank Christ the station's contract cleaners were less than thorough. When the remoistened gum began to catch at his fingers, he pressed Brody's slim bundle against the tacky mess. As he did so, Jarski entered the room.

After almost thirty years on the force, DCI Jarski could count on one hand the number of times he'd been surprised. He looked now at the change in Jack Trent and realised that, from here on in, he would need to start counting on two hands. This transformation was not the slow-burn weariness under which he had seen many a good officer crack. Jack's disintegration had taken place in a matter of days. His shoulders were bowed and his skin was looser somehow. His fingers, drumming on the table, were grey with dust, his knuckles scabbed and yellow. He looked beaten down. Finished.

Jarski ushered the duty doctor into the room and closed the door.

'Now then, Jack,' Jarski said, taking his seat, 'how're you feelin'?'

'I've had a couple of rough days, Roger. How 'bout you?'

'Ditto. You gonna tell me where you've been?'

'Well, to start with I had this call from an old white rabbit. He sent me down this rabbit hole to Wonderland and I nearly didn't find my way back again. Next up, the rabbit sends me to see Old Mother Hubbard. She doesn't live in a shoe, but she does have lots of children,' Jack put his hand against his mouth, as if about to communicate a delicate secret. 'Some of them are a bit weird.'

'Aha. I see. And what's this I hear about you asking Bob Peterson to follow Dawn's son with a loaded weapon?'

'You need a gun to hurt the bad guy. The old white rabbit told me that.'

'Do you believe Simon Malahyde was possessed?' Jarski asked in a weary voice.

Jack, his manner switching to solemn contemplation, laid his hand flat on the desk and traced the callused ridges of his knuckles.

'What makes you think Sergeant Howard's son is in danger?' Jarski persisted.

One of the scabs crumbled under Jack's probing finger and began to weep.

'Why did you have the boy followed?'

'How can I answer these questions?' Jack whispered. 'None of you understand. Everything you know is a scar, thin and ready to crumble, if only you probe it a little.'

Jarski cast a look at the doctor, who nodded and slipped out of the room. A runnel of yellow fluid from Jack's knuckles mingled with his blood.

'I'm going to leave you now, Jack,' Jarski said. 'I'll send someone in to stay with you.'

'Dawn?'

'No, Dawn's busy. Maybe she'll come and see you later.'

'I don't want to stay here. Not on my own. I see things when I'm on my own . . . I caught Greylampton. The bank manager. He killed little girls, didn't he? He smelled of old paper. I saw how he cut them up. I saw it in here,' Jack tapped his forehead.

'But you stopped him, Jack. You probably saved . . .'

'He's coming for the boy,' Jack laughed, smearing blood between his palms. 'Not Greylampton. He hanged himself, didn't he? No, Malahyde, or the spirit that was in Malahyde. He's coming for the boy and he'll take him to the dark place. To the forest. To the clearing. And then, abracadabra, the magic will be done. I like magic. Bunnies in top hats and women sawn in half and dead things made alive again . . .'

Jarski closed the door behind him. Outside, he could still hear Jack jabbering away. The duty doctor pressed through a crowd of officers.

'I've got a friend coming over to evaluate him,' the doctor said.

'Evaluate him? What's to evaluate? He's doo-fucking-lally, isn't he?'

'Well . . . yes. But I'm not a psychiatrist. In the meantime, I'll give him a physical examination, sedate him if necessary.'

'Christ in heaven, spare me,' Jarski said, marching away down the corridor.

Father Garret had brought with him all the various tools that he'd purchased from the army surplus store over the past four months. The bolt cutters with which he had forced the roller door at the Steers Mill paper factory; the axe used to remove Stephen Lloyd's head; the shovel that had beaten in Oliver Godfrey's skull; the sheets of tarpaulin in which he had wrapped both bodies. Also on the trailer behind the car was the large army supplies container in which he had transported Oliver and Stephen to the Old Priory.

Now, he must remain focused. This was his revenge. If he was to die, if he was to be damned, then he would take one last parting shot at the creature that had promised him eternity and now laughed at his fate. He would *not* go to the cellar just yet . . .

The estate was deserted. What a stroke of luck that Jack Trent lived in such a place. No prying eyes, no fat mouths to tell what they saw. With a final look around, Garret got out of the car and approached Trent's door. He knocked. Waited. Knocked again.

He got to his knees and examined the lock for a good while. Then he took out his tools. Unscrewing the mechanism, revolving the barrel and drawing back the bolt was child's play, but he took his time, careful not to leave any telltale scratches on the brass plate. With the slow, methodical care of a surgeon, he laid out the innards of the lock, memorising its fitting. Then he pushed the door open.

He stepped inside and began to search out the best hiding

place for his prize. Not too obvious, that was the key. The flashing red digit on the answering machine caught his attention. Beforehand, he had decided to touch nothing unless absolutely necessary, but something told him to punch the play button.

'Mr Trent, this is Anne Malahyde. I must speak to you. I don't have it in me to punish myself any more . . .'

Garret pressed 'delete'.

Brody stared into the darkened windows. Something was wrong, he could feel it. Throughout the day, he had paced to and fro between the public telephone box and Tom Howard's house. He would wait another quarter of an hour - 'til eight-thirty - Dawn Howard might be home by then. If not, then he would have to chance it. He would have to go to the house.

There was not a breath of wind. The moon, tinted a smokey shade of red, glowered across the fields. It cast a strip of light against the body of a water tower and dyed a scarecrow's rags maroon. Nothing stirred in the fields. Nothing stirred in the house. Thoughts crept unbidden into Brody's mind. Was he sure of Jack Trent? It was only instinct and that vague prophecy in Sam Willard's letter that had told him Jack was the one. Well, what of that? What else did he have to guide him? Yet shouldn't he be wary of a man who had hinted that he possessed such strange abilities? No. It was too late for second thoughts.

Something caught his attention. A movement in one of the upper windows of the house. Black moving against black. The flash of a lustrous eye, the tap of a beak against glass. Brody pulled open the gate and hurried to the back door. Shading his eyes, he put his face to the kitchen window. Four rounds of bread sat upon a plate, a knife with a curl of butter perched on the upper slice. A pan steamed on the cooker top. Evaporated foam had made a tidemark around the sink, just above where the washing up sat in cold, oily water. Drawers had been pulled out and cupboards opened, as if someone had been preparing a meal. The door was unlocked. Brody eased it open.

The pan groaned. Otherwise the house was quiet. Brody turned off the gas. Blue shadows fell away and dusky moonlight lit the room. *S'like the galley of the Marie Celeste*, he thought.

Scuffmarks had scored the linoleum, two parallel furrows that stretched into the hallway. The door was open; the corridor, empty. The grandfather clock at the foot of the stairs tolled the hour, catching at Brody's heart with its discordant chime. Footprints marked the carpet. Wet, muddy footprints.

Had he already taken the boy? No, not here. A modern house, with all its suburban banality, would hardly appeal to the Doctor's sensibilities. Jamie would be taken to the clearing, Brody was sure of it.

'Jamie? Can you hear me? Are you here?'

He reached for the living room door. It opened a crack and he smelled the faint miasma of decay.

A shadow fell over him and grew against the wall. He saw the pendulum sway of the head. The pan in the kitchen gave a sudden prang. The clock stopped ticking. For a moment, everything remained cold and still.

Fifty-three

After his physical examination in the presence of PC Dawling, Jack had been taken back to Interview Room Six. The duty doctor had asked him a few questions; all rather obvious attempts to tease at the edges of whatever mania lay behind his delusions. It was easy to play up to the doctor's preconceptions. Hadn't this guy seen *One Flew Over the Cuckoo's Nest*, for Christ's sake? It had also been easy to divert the doc's attention by spilling hot coffee in his lap. While the physician danced around the room, swatting steam from his scalded groin, Jack peeled Brody's manuscript from under the desk and stuffed it in his shirt.

The doctor suggested that Jack's paranoia would not be improved by being locked in the cells downstairs. After some persuasion, Jarski had agreed that Jack could be lodged in his office until the psychiatrist arrived. Again, it was simplicity itself to fool the doctor into believing that he had taken the sedatives: hand to mouth, pills dropped into sleeve, drink of water. Jack looked back with gratitude on all those childhood hours spent boring his father with sleight of hand tricks.

He stretched out on Jarski's couch, eyes shut and a sliver of drool hanging from the corner of his mouth. He heard the doctor and the DCI leave the room, locking the door behind them. He waited a few moments, ears straining. Then he sat up and tore open Brody's final testament.

When I think of Simon, I remember snatches of afternoons. Bright summer, windswept autumn, winter, thick with snow. I picture our walks, from mouth of trees to village school, from village school to mouth of trees. The boy, always cheerful, full of questions and energy. He had an infectious thirst for life. A good thing in any child, you may think. I often wondered, however, whether he had inherited such lustiness from his father, and to what ends it might drive him in later life. I need not have concerned myself on that score. For this child, there would be no later life.

It was in the spring of Simon's tenth year when Geraldine Pryce came to see me. I would not say we had become friends since Peter's death, but a sort of familiarity had grown between us. I think it was based on that shared experience of witnessing Peter's illness. Neither of us ever discussed it, yet somehow she had divined something of the truth behind the tragedy. Indeed, through that experience she began to understand the nature of the village. Ten years after Peter's death, she had become yet another piece on the strange chessboard that was Crow Haven.

'He is . . . different lately,' she said. 'Withdrawn. Have you noticed?'

We sat in my study at the *Old Priory*. The sound of children playing near the Rowbankses' farm sallied across the fields and through the window. Soon Jim Rowbanks would stagger onto his porch. He would curse and holler until the children tired of teasing him. All children haunted him, as they haunted me.

'He's started asking about his father,' Geraldine continued. 'Have you been talking to him about Peter?'

'Never.'

'Then how does he know?'

'I've no idea.'

'Asher . . .' she gave a sudden, violent shudder.

'What is it?' I asked, her quiet terror catching hold of me.

'Simon . . . He's been inside *the room*.'

Ever since my first talk with Mendicant in that library, I have had a kind of Pavlovian response to the mere mention of the place. As Geraldine spoke of it, sweat trickled down my back and my throat dried up. I did not want to think of Simon inside that terrible room. I refused to imagine him there, his tiny form dwarfed by the shadows of those huge, empty bookcases. Alone . . . No, not alone . . .

I had been waiting for this for ten years. Had always known that the day would come. But now, I didn't want to hear. It would be all right, I told myself. She couldn't be sure.

'He told me . . . Jesus *Christ* . . . He says he's *seen* Peter. Spoken to him. Inside the bricked-up room . . .'

Not again. Please, God, not again. I had to ask the question, but already knew the answer.

'Was Peter alone?'

She shook her head. 'No.'

It was a cool afternoon. A mist curled about the trees. Snowdrops speckled the grass and frogspawn furred the forest pools. Simon walked beside me, a solemn little figure with his head bowed, his feet scuffing the ground. I put my arm around his shoulder, but he didn't look up. I would not let this happen. I'd die before I let this happen.

'Don't worry, son,' I said. 'It's going to be all right.'

I was angry. Scared. And I didn't believe my words.

We cleared the avenue of trees and I looked upon the Doctor's house for the first time in a decade. The years had taken their toll. Peeling paint and weatherworn brickwork seemed to have softened its rigid geometry. It remained, however, an imposing structure.

Simon opened the door with his latchkey and we ascended to the old library. The door was ever more warped and buckled in its frame. I took my time over the blessing, sprinkling holy water, crumbling wafer.

'Will this hurt my dad?' Simon asked.

'No, it will release him.'

'What about the other poor man?'

'Tell me again how you met your father,' I said.

'I told you . . .'

'I want to get it clear in my head.' I didn't need to know. I was playing for time, wishing the future away.

'I was playing here, on the landing. Mother was asleep. I thought it was the wind at first. The wind in the trees can sound like crying sometimes. Even like voices. But trees don't speak. Not really. Not words. I heard words. They said: *Open the door, Simon. Please let us out. We're so lonely in here by ourselves. Be a good boy and open the door.* It was voices, inside here.'

Simon laid his hands flat on the door and rested his ear against the panels.

'Weren't you frightened?' I asked.

'They sounded so sad. Like lost children. I wasn't frightened. I looked through the keyhole. I didn't see anything at first, it was so dark. But then, faraway, I saw a bed, all covered in webs. There was a man by the bed, waving at me. He was real tall and thin and he was laughing. He looked weird, but he seemed very happy. Then I saw this other man. He wasn't so happy. His waving was sad, like he didn't want to wave at all. *Hello, Simon* - the thin man said that - *we've been waiting so long to see you.* I said: *Who are you?* I just whispered it, but he heard. *Well, this is your father, Simon. He wants to meet you very much. And I'm Daddy's friend. But I don't have a name, isn't that sad? Will you give me a name, Simon?* I thought a bit. *What about Funnyface?* I said, because he *did* have a funny face. Horrible funny, not ha-ha funny. But it wasn't a scary face. He laughed loads when I told him his name: *Funnyface it is!* he said. *Clever boy. Oh, I can see we're all going to be good, good friends. Now, your daddy wants so much to meet you. Why don't you open the door?* I told him it was locked. *Oh, no, not to you, Simon. Say Open Sesame! Go on, give it a go!* And I did. And it opened. And I went inside. Then I can't . . . I can't remember . . . I think we played . . . I drew them a picture, I think.'

'And you've seen them again?' I asked.

The boy hesitated. His eyelids flickered, as if he had just remembered something. He backed away from the door.

'Simon, what is it?'

'Later. His face *was* scary later. They want to do something to me. They want to . . .'

'Listen to me, Simon. You must never go into this room again. No matter what you hear, no matter what you dream. Never. Are you listening to me? Do you understand? Your father is dead. He was a bad man and he died. The Devil lives with him in this room and you will burn in Hell if you go in here again. I . . .'

The child looked at me as if I had struck him. I told him to get out of my sight. He ran headlong down the stairs and out of the house. Every day, I question the wisdom of using those harsh words. I had wanted to frighten him, but I wonder whether Simon spent sleepless nights during the following weeks, desperate for my help but remembering that rebuke. Is this just another instance where I failed those who sought my comfort and counsel?

I crossed the landing and knocked on the door of the master bedroom. A moment later it was opened by Anne Malahyde.

'What are you doing here?' she snapped, glancing over my shoulder to the sealed door across the hall. 'I told you to stay away.'

She was still beautiful but only vestiges of her youth remained. Her eyes were very old. As gaunt and frail as she looked, however, her alteration from the fey young woman she had been had given her a certainty of purpose.

'Simon is in danger,' I said. 'If he stays here, something terrible will happen to him. He must leave this house immediately. Both of you *must* leave.'

She seemed terrified by the suggestion: 'I will not leave. I can't leave.'

'You must. Don't you care for your son?'

'He's well provided for.'

'That's not the same thing. You know what I'm talking

about, don't you? Why else is that room sealed up? You know something is alive inside there.'

'Are you mad?' she laughed. 'I keep it as it was when Peter died, as a shrine to his memory. I won't leave.'

'Then send Simon away. To boarding school or something. Even if you don't believe me, please humour me. Send him away before it's too late. I was with your husband when he died, remember. I know things you don't.'

'Leave now,' she said, closing the bedroom door, 'and I'll think about what you've said.'

Anne Malahyde did as she promised, but by the time the child was sent away to boarding school, he was Simon no longer. We continued our walks to and from school, but since my outburst the boy would no longer confide in me. I asked him repeatedly if he had heard the voices or seen the figures again. He shook his head and stared at the ground.

It was in the early days of June that Geraldine Pryce visited me again. She said nothing. She simply laid a school portrait on my desk and left the room. Puzzled, I called after her until I heard the front door snap shut. I looked down at the picture.

The faces of Simon's schoolmates, smiling, grimacing, frozen, stared out of the photograph. There was a spectrum of emotion there, from elation to subdued misery. In that gamut, humanity was displayed in many forms. In the face of Simon Malahyde, however, there was no humanity. There was nothing but distortion.

Too late. Too late for James and Josh, for Luke and Michael, for Jim and Valerie. Too late for Ma Rowbanks and for Peter Malahyde. Too late for little Simon, and much, much too late for Asher Brody.

They had taken him.

I stood before the cornerstone of the Yeager Library and heard the bell reverberate inside that prison of minds. The door opened. The librarian, as before, seemed to have anticipated my arrival.

376

'Good evening, Father.'

'I need . . . I must . . .'

'You wish to see the *Transmigration of Souls* again?'

'Or any addendum to it. Something that details any special circumstances in which the metempsychosis ritual might be performed. Please, a child's life . . .'

'There is an addendum to the text,' said the librarian. His voice was like a balm to my frayed nerves. 'It was penned by the author on his deathbed. Due to the delirium the writer suffered in his final hours, however, the veracity of the document is questionable.'

'May I see it?'

'Only one visit to the library is gratis, I'm afraid. If you wish to enter again, Father, you must pay for the privilege.'

'Pay? With what?'

'With a little of what you hold most dear.'

'I don't understand.'

'Your faith, Father. You must bequeath some of it to Yeager. You see, we are not just a depository of knowledge, but of experience. I find your faith fascinating, Mr Brody, full of passion and contradiction. I should like to examine it at my leisure. Are you agreeable?'

'But how can belief be dissected?' I argued. 'It's not like tissue; it's an indivisible whole.'

'There are ways,' the librarian smiled. 'Are you willing?'

To save Simon? To give him back his soul? For that, God might forgive the bartering of my spirit. I agreed. The librarian led me to the same chamber in which I had translated the *Transmigration* all those years before. There were a few pages of parchment on the desk, together with the lamp, notepad, quill and hourglass. The librarian set the sands running and I began to transcribe the text.

377

I am a coward. I would not have admitted that when I first put pen to paper and recorded the original of this work. I fooled myself into believing that greatness of intellect is, in some measure, superior to largeness of heart. I see now that my learning was meagre enough, but my soul was poorer still. Since I wrote of my experiences, I have led a half-life, fearful of shadows, timid of my fellow man. Loneliness has broken me. I scribble these, my last words, in a tiny garret, watching the passing of people in the street below. I am frightened by them, for all the world seems to me to be populated by angels and devils.

This addendum should have appeared in that part of the *Transmigration* in which I tell of the few variations of the rite and its limitations. I omitted it from the original text because it seemed manifestly hideous, even in the company of so many other hideous things. I set it down now, as twilight draws in.

On my fourth night in the chateau between the mountains, my changed host came to my prison chamber.

'Time for our latest lesson in the Art of Rebirth,' the man-child said. 'And time you heard a few of the modifications that may be made to the rite. It is not always performed as you witnessed. You may believe that a spirit must take possession of the vessel almost as soon as it is released from its own body. Not so. A spirit may survive ten days or so outside a body, and still take possession of a child. If he has not performed the functions of the rite before he died, however, he will not have the physical substance to perform them after death. It is essential, therefore, that some servant murder the children, feed his master their fat and burn the baptism dresses.'

'Yet after ten days the spirit is utterly spent?' I asked, taking down my notes.

'Not quite,' the child said. 'There is one other way for a spirit to work the rite. Let us imagine a ritual goes badly. The spirit is released from his own body, but cannot take up residence in a new form. If the spirit has consumed the fat of the children, then the power to possess remains with him. The problem is that, as a spirit, he will not have the substance to procure the baptism dresses to show his way into a new child.'

'So he is trapped. He is a ghost.'

'And will remain so unless he is very fortunate. It is possible, you see, for a parent to sell a child's soul. The pact must be made while the father or mother is alive, but possession can only take place with the guidance of a *dead* parent. The child, as with the normal rite, must also be on the cusp of puberty. Then, unlike the usual metempsychosis, where the spirit of the child is utterly subjugated and the possessing soul has free reign, the ghost must share occupancy of the body with both the child and parent. A trinity of souls.'

'No father or mother would do such a thing,' I said, horrified.

'It has been known. Though hardly an ideal arrangement, it saves one from being a mere shade. But there are disadvantages. The older, possessing ghost will be the master, but the other spirits may war against him. And there is the question of longevity. The life of the vessel taken in this way is severely reduced. Three spirits warring inside will take its toll.'

'And what will happen when that body wears out?'

'Well, then the dominant spirit is free to resume normal metempsychosis. He has a body to use, so he can prepare the sacrificial children, take of their fat, burn the dresses, etcetera. The only problem he may come across is the one I have already outlined. The resistance of the parent and child souls. They may interfere with the necessary preparations. It is remarkable how many fathers, having willingly sold their sons, discover a conscience after the deed is done. For this reason, it has been known for spirits to seek the assistance of a human helpmeet who will take care of the messy business of the ritual . . . Why are you not writing?'

'It cannot be true,' I said. 'Good God, it cannot be true.

Fathers selling their sons . . . what promise could be made to induce such betrayal?'

'We all have our price, my poor friend,' he laughed. 'And children are bought and sold the world over for less than the promise of renewed life, for no more than the feel of brass in a clutching hand. Man does not prize innocence as highly as you think.'

He went to the door and rapped three times. I heard the bolt draw back.

'Do you still look on me as such a monster now?' he asked. 'I have murdered children who are strangers to me. Yet your own father might have promised your life away, had he but known what I could grant him.'

All the horrors I heard during the remaining weeks did not affect me so much as that interview. What kind of world is this, where we must have life at whatever cost? And where the perversity of that demon, who now spoke with child lips and looked upon me with child eyes, was naught compared to the twisted nature of Man?

I thought I would die in that chamber, teased on my deathbed by only the narrowest touch of sunlight on my face. But my little host was true to his word. When I had completed my account of the ritual and its permutations, I was released. The surly coachman guided me out of the chateau, gave me a bindle of bread and cheese and showed me the road.

At the great door of the castle, I looked back, searching every window, hoping that I might see the beautiful face of the changeling. Perverse as it may sound, I had fallen in love with him, and it broke my heart to leave without a final look at that strange incubus. All the windows were empty. I set my face against the wind and started the descent.

Many years have passed. I have squandered the fortune left to me by my father on diversions: drink, dice, women, boys. Anything to take my mind from those memories. I sleep now in these filthy rooms, playing deaf to the threats of my creditors. My solace is that I have not long left. The corruption works as speedily on gentlemen as it does upon whores.

I seldom dream, but if I do I see only his face. The face he stole from that angelic child, I mean. He will have aged now, of course, yet will always be young, unto the ending of the world. Will he visit my grave, I wonder? When the worms are set to their labours, will he wonder what became of the soul of his poor scribbler? The pen falters in my hand . . . the ink spills across the page . . . darkness spills across my heart . . .

I was hardly aware of leaving Yeager. I have a vague memory of the librarian speaking to me, though what he said, I cannot tell you. Arriving home, I pulled down the books I needed from the shelves, lit the lamp on my desk and poured a very large scotch. A few hours of reading and drinking, and I was ready. I would attempt one of the exorcism rituals that I had tried with Peter Malahyde ten years before. Pray God that this time it was successful. I set out for the forest.

The day was warm. The trees crackled and the breeze bowed through the long grass. Overhead, the clatter of crows followed me through the branches. I paid them no heed. Finding a sheltered spot, I stayed hunkered down in the undergrowth all afternoon. From my vantage point, I could see the tree-tunnelled drive and the gate leading to the house. As I waited, the same questions echoed in my mind: *Am I strong enough? What can I do to save him? What have I lost to the Yeager Library?*

My heart burned. My nerves wound themselves ever tighter. I ploughed the earth with my hands, plied it with my fingers. Waited.

Footsteps on gravel. I plucked the rope from my pocket and wound it around my fists. I glimpsed a face moving between the trees. A satchel slung over a shoulder. Feet skipping down the avenue. Simon came into view.

I stifled my cry.

It was the body of a child: slight, narrow-shouldered, short legs, small hands. But settled upon that torso was the shrunken, wasted head of Elijah Mendicant. The crows cawed. The thing stopped, looked about itself. I burst through the under-growth.

Mendicant (I will not call him Simon, as Simon was now lost to me) woke and struggled for breath. I had dragged him to the clearing and tethered him to the same tree on which he had been crucified almost twenty years before. I had bound the little hands so tight that the rope cut into them. Once or twice, I thought I would give way to grief and horror, but my heart was hardened, as the rite demanded it should be. I could not bring myself to gag him, however, it would mean touching that tiny, rotting face.

I stood outside the circle of crumbled wafer ringing the tree.

'Father? What are you doing?'

It was Simon's voice. I would not listen to it. I stepped forward, made the Sign of the Cross and dashed Holy Water over him.

'Lord have mercy. God the Father in heaven. God, the Son, Redeemer of the World. God the Holy Spirit. Holy Trinity. One God . . .'

My head was bowed, but I heard the familiar ripple of laughter.

'Pray to a new Trinity, Asher.'

'Holy Mary, pray for us . . .'

My voice remained steady while my soul trembled. I recited the Litany of the Saints, the Lord's Prayer, the fifty-third psalm.

' . . . snatch from ruination and the clutches of the noonday devil this human being made in your image and likeness. Strike terror, Lord, into the Beast now laying waste to your vineyard . . .'

The afternoon wore on. During the latter stages of the exorcism, though the sun was at its zenith, the shade that it granted to the clearing made everything seem quite dark. When at last I looked up, I could not make out the face before me. Summoning whatever courage I could, I stepped into the circle and laid my stole upon the taut cheek. Shadows fell away and I saw a sardonic smile beaming up at me.

'I'm still here, Father. I wonder why. Perhaps something burns less bright within you.'

'I cast you out, unclean spirit, in the name of our Lord Jesus Christ. Begone and stay far away from this creature of God . . .'

'I see a tiny flame in a vast cavern. You see it now, don't you, Asher?'

'It is He who commands you. He who once stilled the wind and the sea and the storm . . .'

'Imagine a hand reaching from the darkness. Reaching for the candle . . .'

' . . . author of pain and sorrow . . .'

'Two fingers reaching . . .'

'Begone then, in the name of the Father and the Son . . .'

My hand was shaking so badly I could not make the final Sign of the Cross.

' . . . snuffing out your candle.'

I stumbled back, kicking a path through the white circle as I went.

'The light is gone, Father, and now it is my turn for a little fun.'

The knots around Mendicant's wrists and ankles tugged themselves loose. He ran his hand across the bark of the tree.

'Was this where I died? It seems a lifetime ago.'

He moved out of the circle. I knew that running was pointless. I must make my stand here. I must gather up the waning vestiges of my faith and truly believe the words of the rite. Now, however, for the first time since I had been a child, I felt alone. The candle, whipped by a cold wind, flickered one last time, hissed, burned to a point, and was extinguished. A sigh passed out of the clearing and through the forest. I mumbled my final entreaty, knowing it was wasted breath:

'Lord God, heed my prayer. Please let my cry be heard by you . . . *Please,* Sweet Jesus.'

The changed child strode towards me. His face tightened. His pupils grew large and the whites of his eyes vanished. Like hollows, I thought. At a distance of ten feet, Mendicant stopped. His mouth fell open and a long, agonised cry tore its way out of his throat. It was Simon, screaming as if in great torment. It rang around the clearing, answered by the call of the crows that had gathered in the trees. Then those dark eyes cleared and fixed upon me. The boy's spirit had been trammelled.

'Do you have the courage to do more than speak pretty verse and canticles, Father?' Mendicant asked. 'Simon is alive inside. There is only one way to free him. You'll find the answer in that bag behind you.'

I had thrown the school satchel aside when I dragged the unconscious boy into the clearing. Now I unclasped the bag and felt inside. Something sharp met my fingers. I drew out a long, thin piece of flint.

'I knew you would come to do what you could. You will find that blade better than any mumbo jumbo,' said Mendicant, pulling back his head and exposing his throat. 'I will never let the boy go. He is bound to me now. The only thing you can do is kill him, as you killed James Rowbanks. Can you do it?'

The shaft of the flint dug deep into my palm. I grasped a fistful of hair, brought the blade to the beating artery. Child eyes looked up at me. They were not hollows.

'Can you? The heat of his blood on your hands. Can you bear killing *another* child?'

The tip nicked. Blood trickled down the flint and touched my fingers. One final effort. The simplest movement: to slash or to press home. To release, to free, to murder . . . In my mind's eye, I saw James Rowbanks' head explode against the tree. I snatched the blade away and Mendicant laughed.

'I was going to kill you,' he said, 'but to leave you with the agony of this memory is much better. You deserve pain, however, somewhat more visceral . . .'

384

Mendicant raised a balled hand, mirroring my own grasp on the flint. I tried to release it, but my fingers gripped tighter. The child winked and brought the fist down hard into his open palm. I could not resist. I drove the blade into my own hand. Roaring through the pain, I saw Mendicant roll his fist, as if he were working a pestle in a mortar. Small bones moved aside to accommodate the weapon as I ground the flint into my hand.

'No reason to whimper, Asher. I am making you in His image.'

He then brought his fist level with his head and mimed little stabbing motions around his temple. I tore the flint free, flecking my face with blood. I could do nothing except mimic him. The tiny cuts ran fast. My eyes stung in the hot flow.

'Perhaps if I make you suffer as He suffered, I will bring you back to Him . . .' He held his fist at waist height, a foot or so from his body.

'Dear God, no,' I cried. 'Please . . .'

'But it's the only way you'll learn,' the voice deepened. 'Goodbye, Asher.'

The child's hand thrust against its side. I saw the blade – the spearhead – puncture beneath my ribs. Then the flint was withdrawn, red and glinting in the sunlight. Mendicant collapsed to the ground, exhausted. Here was a final chance to finish it. I staggered towards him. My lung rasped as I tried to breathe. I felt the sac drain and flutter against bone. Falling to my knees, I rolled onto my back. My vision darkened and all I could hear was thin, child-like laughter.

Fifty-four

Dawn stood in the photocopier alcove at the end of the corridor. Two officers were collating files in a room nearby. She could not risk being seen and it being reported to Jarski. With each minute that ticked by she felt her chance slipping away. Finally, yawning and bleary-eyed, the officers slouched down the corridor.

'Christ, what time is it?'

'Just after ten. Fancy last orders at the Feathers?'

'Mm-no. I think I'll go home and spend some quality time with a Pot Noodle and a stack of pornography.'

Dawn waited until they stepped into the lifts. Then she hurried to Jarski's office. The glow of the desk lamp fractured through the frosted glass. She tapped. No reply. The doctor must have popped out for coffee or a fag. It would mean awkward questions later, but if she went downstairs she might be able to persuade the duty officer that Jarski needed a file and had sent her to . . .

The lock clicked. The door opened. Jack peered through the crack and ushered her in.

'Idiot forgot to take the spare key from his desk,' he whispered.

She had rehearsed so many questions. All she could do now was stare at him. He smelled institutionally clean, his own warm scent lost beneath the odour of cheap soap. His hand was swathed in fresh bandages, but the cloth was already stained with blood. The wound was tied in her mind with Crow Haven and Malahyde and all the madness since that first morning. She felt his fingers brush her hand.

'He told you. Mescher. He told you about the girl.'

He knows.

'And you wonder how, if I touched her, anything I told you can be true . . . That first day, the day you came back, all day so near you. I had to touch. To feel human. But I didn't *touch* her. Not as I touched you.'

'I'm not sure I can believe that,' she said. 'And if I can't, how can I believe any of it?'

'Perhaps you don't have to believe completely. Just entertain the slimmest possibility.'

'I won't validate your fantasy, Jack. If I do, you might always be lost.'

'You found me. For a time. That's the best I could ever have hoped for. Our little time of being together. I *am* lost.'

His voice stayed calm, but he was trembling.

'*Are* you mad?' she asked.

'Perhaps. But not in the way they think.'

'Then why the act?'

'Because I stand more chance of escaping a hospital than from the cells downstairs. The end is coming. I have to be there to meet it.'

'I could . . .'

She hesitated. Here was where the choice would be made. The sane, real world she had known, defined on her own concrete terms for thirty years, or his version of reality.

'No,' he said. 'You have to go to Jamie. Please, Dawn, just go.'

'Goodbye, Jack,' she said, turning away from him.

'Dawn? I want to say thank you. In case . . . well, just in case we don't see each other again.'

She closed the door behind her.

The hallway of Tom Howard's house was like a deep freeze. Brody shivered, and it was not just from the cold. He looked up at the figure that watched him from the landing.

Mendicant was exactly as Brody remembered. The hollow eyes, the sunken, undulating skull with its straw-like hair and tattered skin. Crows fluttered onto his shoulders. Beaks plucked at his face.

'Where's the boy?' Brody asked.

'Is that all you have to say to me after all these years?' the Doctor asked, the melodic tones of his voice in counterpoint with the cawing of the birds. 'After I had the good grace to leave you unmolested in your quaint Home for Rotting Flesh and Mind? You know, I was very tempted to pay you a visit. I had a special end in mind for you: something in the line of how St Peter was martyred. Yes indeed, I would have enjoyed seeing you strung up in the clearing, your body lashed to an inverted cross.'

'But Simon and Peter proved more difficult to manage than you thought, didn't they?' Brody countered.

'That is in the past. The wheel has turned and here we are again. You, older, frailer, but still admirably intractable.'

'This time I am not alone.'

'Jack Trent?'

Mendicant drew his lips over his stunted teeth. With that strange fluidity of movement, he came to the head of the stairs.

'What do you imagine he can do?'

'God has brought him to face you.'

'*I* have brought him' – the Doctor's long fingers arched around the banister – 'I have laid the trail and he has followed, blind as a mole sniffing worms. I have led my unwitting disciple into the mountain where I shall be transfigured.'

Mendicant descended.

'Transfigured?' Brody echoed. 'Is this some new obsession? You see yourself as Saviour now? This is just the same filthy ritual you have performed countless times.'

'Not quite. Tonight I shall unlock divine powers. I shall not simply be reborn, but reconfigured. Re-spiritualised. A new light shall shine from me.'

The door behind Brody opened. Out of the corner of his eye, the priest glimpsed the figure of an old man sprawled across the sitting room floor. The boy emerged from the gloom, stepping over his dead grandfather. He was holding something aloft. Before Brody could speak, he felt a bright pain splinter across his skull. He fell to his knees, clutching his head. His vision blurred, tunnelled and dimmed. He saw his fingers, huge and red, and the boy staring down between them.

'Sleep well, old friend . . .'

Mendicant. Twin hollows. Unending blackness before his eyes.

'Dream of signs and wonders.'

All ideas had run dry. She drove in blissful thoughtlessness. The tinted moon accompanied her homeward. Hooded by the clouds and rimmed by the flat fields, it stared across the earth like a great red eye.

She pulled into her father's street and tucked the car into the driveway.

Not a blade of light shone between the curtains. Something was wrong. She got out of the car, fumbled for her latchkey, thrust it into the lock and pushed open the door.

At first it seemed as if there was nothing beyond the doorway. A breeze chased about her legs, whipped into the void and whistled out again, its tone anxious. Before her eyes began to adjust, Dawn thought of Jack: of that tear between worlds; of the creatures that had slithered from it and made a tiny principality in his mind. Then the darkness appeared less complete. She saw the hallway and the stairs. Then the old man, his face laced with blood.

'The boy's gone.'

There were no questions in her mind now. She stumbled into the house and clattered up the stairs. Wrenching open doors, pulling aside beds and furniture, she screamed for her son. The lights would not work and, at first, she did not notice the scratches on the sills, the shit dripping from the mirrors, the torn curtains and the feathers. She tried to rush past the old man, but he held her fast.

'Please, Miss Howard. I don't think you should look downstairs.'

'Where is he? Tell me NOW.'

'Taken.'

'Where?'

'Only one place. We must find Jack Trent.'

She managed to twist loose. She went to the kitchen, the study, the cubby-hole under the stairs, the sitting room . . .

'Dad? Wake up. Please, Dad, wake up.'

She kicked the lifeless body.

'He's been dead some hours. I'm sorry.'

'How?' Falling to her knees, she cradled her father's head in her lap. 'How?'

'Miss Howard, we must reach Jack Trent. Your son's life depends upon . . .'

She was not listening. She just rocked back and forth, holding her father.

Silhouettes passed and re-passed across the glass. They whispered, but Jack caught the odd phrase here and there.

' . . . Dr King's been delayed by a spate of severe psychotic episodes . . .' - the duty doctor - ' . . . says they're all acting up tonight . . . Halloween tomorrow, silly season for some . . .'

'Bloody fruitloops,' Jarski muttered.

The DCI pressed his nose against the glass. Jack froze. The Picasso face drew away.

' . . . Greylampton case . . . best officer in the department . . .'

' . . . Dr King will be here soon . . .'

' . . . always weird though . . .'

Jack started. Jarski's words had not segued into muffled incomprehensibility. They just stopped, as if his voice was a recording cut short. Jack eased himself off the leather couch. He tiptoed to the door, inched it open, peered through. The corridor was deserted. Jarski and the doctor had vanished.

As Jack stepped out of the office, the lamp on Jarski's desk exploded. Grains of glass showered papers, files and the DCI's collection of stress balls. The lights in the corridor flickered and went out. From the end of the long hallway, illuminated lift buttons blinked at Jack. They looked very far away.

He started down the hall, checking the doors of the offices as he went. Each was locked. Everything, above and below, seemed unnaturally quiet. The sudden absence of background noise unnerved him. No rumble of traffic, no hum of conversation, not even the gasp and gurgle of a guttering toilet. And it was becoming very cold. He could see his breath now, and the glass in the doors he passed dripped with condensation. Where the hell was everyone? Jarski? The cretin doctor? The four hundred or more souls that routinely occupied this cavernous station?

A door slammed to. Jack turned. He could make out the shape of a man standing outside Jarski's door. Its head was swaying rhythmically . . .

Jack ran. Reaching the bank of lifts, he jammed his finger on the call button.

Come on, come on, come on . . .

The doors trembled and opened. Jack sidestepped into the carriage and punched the ground floor button.

Jesus Christ, come on.

The doors jarred halfway, grumbled and started to meet again. Karen Carpenter, singing the opening line of 'Rainy Days and Mondays', looped through the speakers. Between the closing gap, Jack caught his last glimpse of the figure. Was it smiling?

The lift jolted and bore him down.

The wind came in waves through the rolled down passenger window and sent a dull ache through Brody's ears. The needle dropped to forty as he drove Dawn's Range Rover out of the countryside and into the city hinterland. They sped past a gang of kids carving a pumpkin on the pavement; impatient commuters and taxi drivers outside the railway station; the cathedral, robbed of its textures by the night, towering and cyclopean in the darkness. Brody noticed these things in passing, but his mind was on the road and on the woman beside him.

She had hardly spoken since he had prised her away from the dead man. The most he could get from her was that Jack was at the station. Somehow they would have to make contact with him. It was happening again. The time of Mendicant's labour was almost up. Soon he would emerge, bloodied, triumphant. Reborn.

Brody pulled the car into the station car park. Automatically, he slipped into neutral and pulled up the handbrake. He could make no sense of what he was seeing. The police station looked like a massive, featureless earthwork. No lights, no-one coming or going. Nothing seemed to move inside it.

'Stay here.'

The crunch of his feet on the tarmac was thrown around the concrete precinct, amplifying the sound unnaturally in the stillness. He approached the station. The automatic doors were stuck halfway open, flinching as they tried to meet. There was no-one behind the reception desk. No-one waiting on the rows of plastic seats. A sudden breeze caught an empty crisp packet and span it in balletic swoops around the foyer. Brody looked back at the car. Reflected in the windscreen, superimposed over Dawn's face, he saw a flicker of white. He turned towards the station. Someone was staggering from the lifts, reaching as if for some invisible support.

'Mendicant,' Jack said, as Brody caught him. 'He's here.'

'Why?'

Jack shook his head. High above, lights began to pierce the windows. A murmur of voices reached them. The station was reawakening.

'Dawn,' said Jack, looking beyond Brody. 'She's with you?'

His eyes were bright. Dazzling.

Almost mad, Brody thought. *Something working behind them.*

'It's time, Jack. He's taken the boy. You must face him now. You must go to the clearing.'

Fifty-five

'I've organised a body of uniform to search the station,' said Pat Mescher, 'but I don't think Trent'd stick around.'

Jarski kneaded his temples and looked from Mescher to the doctor. They were all sat in the office that Jack Trent had disappeared from not ten minutes before. Jarski knew that Pat's concerned offer of assistance was yet another cynical attempt to worm his way into the case, but he didn't have the energy for an argument.

'How'd ya think he got out?' Mescher asked. 'Is the freak Houdini now?'

'Christ knows. We were stood outside talking. The lights flickered for a second and the doc reckoned we should check on Jack. We opened the door, he was gone.'

'Strangest thing,' the doctor observed, tapping his digital wristwatch. 'See this? Stopped at five to eleven. Might have been affected by the power surge, I suppose. But, when we came into the office, I saw the clock there was at five minutes *past* eleven.'

'Maybe they came for him,' Mescher grunted.

'Who?'

'His brothers from beyond the stars. Stopped watches? Lost time? Classic alien abduction stuff.'

The telephone on Jarski's desk rang.

'That's it!' Mescher laughed. 'He phoned home.'

'Please don't let this be the press . . .' Jarski groaned. 'Hello? Yes, this is Jarski. What? Please, I can't hear you, can you repeat . . . ? Holy *fucking* shit.'

Jarski felt his stomach tighten and his balls shrink against his body. As the anonymous caller made his statement, a dim, impossible truth started to slot into place.

Jack whispered. The only response he got was an occasional flicker of her eyelids. As he drove, Brody explained what had happened in a few words. She was in shock. Her father dead, her son taken, the world she had known pulled from under her. And all of it, my fault, Jack thought. He looked at the road ahead. The red moon was high now, bleeding through the clouds. As they turned east, he could make out the jagged tree-line of Redgrave in the distance.

'Did you finish my story?' Brody asked.

'I did.'

'And?'

'And nothing. No eureka moment. That detail you thought I might come across; if you don't know what it is, I sure as hell don't.'

'I know there's something there, Jack. Something we're missing.'

'Well, if you haven't figured it out after three failed attempts to stop this lunatic, what chance have I got?'

Brody did not react, but in the brief silence that followed a knot of regret tightened in Jack's stomach.

'I was wondering about your injuries,' Jack said. 'The ones Simon . . . Mendicant, inflicted.'

'Mere scratches when I came to,' Brody replied. 'You must never believe what he shows you.'

Jack sat back and stretched his arm around Dawn, making sure their skin did not meet. He tried to concentrate on Brody's story. Had there been anything that might help him? Some clue that . . .

A human helpmeet who will take care of the messy business of the ritual . . .

'Mendicant's accomplice . . .' Jack whispered. 'You said someone might be helping him. Someone who killed Oliver and Stephen, someone who extracted their fat. Someone . . .'

'Garret . . . Father Garret . . .'

Dawn's voice was very weak. Spittle hung from her mouth and she shivered. Jack held her close. Her eyes remained fixed and staring.

'Dawn? Can you hear me? Listen, you . . .'

'In the cellar . . . Something in the cellar.'

As she spoke, they crested the hill. Below, in its basin cradle, Crow Haven waited. They wound down into the village and passed darkened house after darkened house, until they reached the *Old Priory*. Having covered Dawn in a blanket he had found in the boot, Jack followed Brody up the rise to the rectory.

'Just like the night the Rowbanks children died,' Brody observed, looking over the village. 'Curtains tightly drawn, doors firmly bolted. They know, you see. They have an atavistic sense of when the darkness draws in . . . Do you sense it? The *feel* of the night. As if it's the same moment, playing over again . . .'

Brody's hand went to his breast.

'Are you all right?' Jack asked.

'Not at all,' Brody sighed. 'I see his face all around me. James Rowbanks. I seem to feel the gun in my hand again. Was I sure . . . ? I can't think about it. Look, you should go.'

'You're taking a risk going into that house alone . . .'

'I'm not alone.'

'Didn't your faith abandon you? Wasn't that the librarian's price?'

'For a time, perhaps. But true faith can't be taken; only undermined if one allows it to be.'

'And the protections you set for Jamie? How much of your faith was in them?'

'Well, let's be pragmatic if nothing else,' Brody countered. 'If Garret has been the Doctor's puppet, he may know something. Go.'

Jack was reluctant to leave the priest.

'Stopping him, that's all that matters, Jack.'

'And saving Jamie.'

'If possible,' Brody said. 'But if . . .'

The man hesitated, and Jack saw the effort written in his face as the old priest tried to give expression to his thoughts. There was a tangible sense that Brody was disgusted with what he was about to say.

'If you're too late, he will speak to you with the boy's voice,' Brody said. 'Try to convince you he is still Jamie. But remember, this will not be a metempsychosis like Simon's. In the normal working of the ritual, the child's soul is eclipsed. There will be nothing left of him.'

Jack looked down, unable to disguise his distaste.

'Remember, Jack: God is with you.'

Jack put out his hand. A few spots of rain pattered onto his palm.

'God's a fair weather friend, Father,' he said, 'and the forecast don't look too bright.'

'Well, goodbye. Good luck.'

Before Jack could stop him, Brody had grasped his hand.

They were loose in a moment, firing through Jack's arm, dragging him into the priest's thoughts and memories. There were a thousand doubts and horrors that plagued the old man, yet the creatures drew out only one image. Jack saw Brody, semi-conscious on the ground in the clearing, blood pouring from the wounds Mendicant had inflicted. He did indeed look like an aged Christ, brought down from the Cross before his time. Beside Brody lay the child. He was not moving but thin, age-cracked laughter came from his lips.

Jack looked around himself. He stood in the dim, peripheral edges of Brody's mind. The scene from the 'final chapter' played out before him, as if he were in a darkened theatre, watching actors on stage. Making up the rest of the audience were the creatures that had murdered his mother. *They* stood beside him, chattering, braying and screaming. They were looking at Jack, but pointing towards Brody's memory. They seemed to be trying to tell him something. One of them came forward. Jack backed away, but the creature's arm stretched out to meet him. A cold hand was laid upon Jack's chest.

Suddenly, he understood.

'*Yes, that's how it will end,*' he said. '*We'll do it together.*'

And they smiled.

Jack pulled his hand from Brody's. His vision returned. The priest looked very grey.

'I saw,' Brody whispered. 'What are they?'

'You have the Doctor,' Jack said. 'And I have my own demons.'

He turned away and headed for the Range Rover.

Brody walked towards the house. A moment later, he heard the roar of the engine. At the door, he looked back and saw headlights spill down the mouth of trees. *Who is this man?* he thought. *And what kind of dark angels are those that haunt him? How did they bear him into me? How did he see . . . ? Too late to wonder now . . .* Yet, a persistent thought nagged him. Had he sent one form of evil to meet another?

There were no lights in the windows of the *Old Priory*. Perhaps Dawn, her mind addled by the tragedy and inexplicability of what she had seen that night, had been wrong. Perhaps Garret was tucked up in bed, dreaming innocent dreams.

Shadows sat beneath the portico, and Brody did not see that the door was standing open until he was within a few feet of it. Autumn leaves had been blown into the house, laying a brown, chattering carpet across the floor. On the wall were the familiar portraits of the old priests of Crow Haven. His own photograph nearest, then the monochrome face of Father Tolly . . . Robert Tolly, who had died alone in this house.

Its evil abideth within and without; until the Darkness exhausts Itself . . .

The leaves rustled at Brody's feet. He went to the study and tried the lights. Nothing. The electricity must have tripped out. The fuse box was in the cellar. He pulled back the curtains and looked out onto the road and forest. Something cracked beneath his foot. He bent down and picked up a broken

397

crucifix. His eyes snapped to the wall. There was a ghostly impression where he had hung the cross years before.

He went to the cellar door and ducked into the stairway. He tried the cord and tapped the bulb. Nothing. A shadow passed over the wet stone flags at the bottom of the stairs. Brody descended.

At first the cellar appeared to be empty. Brody's eyes wandered over the changes that had been made. The coal chute had been ripped out and the ground-level hatch boarded up. The floor had been cleared of debris. A flame burned behind the grate of the old furnace and slashed bars of light across the walls.

'Have you ever thought, Asher, what a terrible thing it must be to have great faith and a weak nature?'

Garret stepped out from the alcove on the far side of the cellar.

'Of course you haven't. You are a Samson among men. But I know. I know, without question, that Hell waits for me. I have known it since the day I smothered my father. I prayed for forgiveness . . . But I have faith. Faith that Hell is waiting . . .'

'What did he promise you?' Brody asked.

'He came to me when the cancer was young. My doctor had given me a timetable for damnation. Mendicant promised me a way to keep my soul from judgement.'

'Christopher, why didn't you tell me? I could have . . .'

'We lived together for ten years and never knew each other. You want to absolve my sins now? You are too arrogant, Asher. There are works beyond even you.'

'He's false. Whatever he's promised . . .'

'Deceived. Yes, I know.'

'Then help us. Tell me how and why he fixed on the child.'

Garret took a thin blade from his pocket and waved it before his eyes.

'Stay back. I could be taken at any moment, you see,' he laughed. 'Too close and you might be pulled down with me.

Down into the depths. It is because '*I wept not, and so to stone within I grew . . .*' My father comes to the cellar; they all come here, Asher. Little Oliver is waking just now, he crawls across the stones. He pleads . . . I wrapped his body in fine linen and laid him in the sepulchre hewn from rock.'

'You left him naked at a lay-by. His brains were beaten in . . .' Brody suppressed his revulsion. 'Tell me how Mendicant selected the boy.'

Garret held up the scalpel, delighting in how the light played across the blade.

'He wasn't the intended vessel,' he said, shaking his head. 'No, no, no. We had another child selected first. Oliver's brother, his twin. But then the Doctor saw Jack Trent. In the cabin. In the woods. Saw inside his mind . . . saw the child there . . .'

'But why *that* child? If Mendicant changed his mind, if he altered his plans at so late a stage, there must have been a good reason. Why does he want Jamie?'

Garret knitted his brow. He looked at Brody and said in a plaintive voice:

'Who is Jamie, Father?' Then turned to his right and fixed his gaze on some imagined figure. 'Who is Jamie, father?'

Why did *they* return so easily to the toy box? Jack hadn't even needed to recite the mathematical formula. Why hadn't they tried to flood out of him and murder the old priest? A tantalising sliver of memory teased him. *They* had tried to communicate something. Some pact had been made; promises given on either side . . . He could not remember.

Jack continued to focus on the unmoving face in the rear-view mirror, hardly aware of the blur of passing elms and the trembling arc of the accelerator needle. His heart burned in his chest as he watched her. After her outburst, Dawn had lapsed back into an almost comatose state. He tried calling her name, asking her mundane questions about her age, her favourite flowers, but she remained insensible.

He had brought them to this. During their meeting in the

Lazarus Club, Mendicant said that he had first seen his new vessel by looking into Jack's mind. His fucked up brain had betrayed Jamie.

Dawn's scream cut through his thoughts. At the last moment, he saw a black figure swaying against the gate. He tried to wrench the steering wheel left, but it locked. He slammed on the brakes. The back of the car swung around, tyres screeching, and smashed into the gate. A branch, thick as a caber, punched through the windscreen. Wet bark tore through Jack's earlobe. From behind he heard the sound of crumpling fibreglass. For a moment he thought the gate, with its flutes of barbed metal, might topple, crushing the car's roof. It gave an ominous groan, but remained upright. The car came to a steaming standstill.

Jesus Christ, be all right . . .

The branch had sloped down and punched through Dawn's seat. He tried to lean round, but the seatbelt pinioned him. He could not see her from this angle. He tore the buckle from its fitting, kicked his way out and threw open the back door.

The tears rolled hot against the cuts to his face. She lay crumpled beneath the branch, her breathing steady. As gently as he could, he pulled her from the car and carried her some distance along the road. Laying her on the dank grass, he checked her for injuries. Her ankle was purple and swelling, but she was otherwise unharmed. He held her close. A few, shuddering sobs rose from him.

'No-one will cry for her,' she whispered.

Dawn stared at the gate. Sorrow wrote itself across her features. Jack had forgotten the cause of the accident. The black figure . . .

Anne Malahyde. Strung from the cross-section of the gate. Her arms tied behind her back, her feet pointing downwards, her body twisted with the rope as if she were a pirouetting ballerina.

'Someone should cry for her.'

'Dawn, can you hear me? Can you . . . ?'

'I believe,' she said. Her hand rested against his face. 'Save him.'

And then, impossible as it was, they heard the toll of the cathedral's great solstice clock. The sweet, heavy tones they had heard on their summer walks, reaching them from a distance of over twenty miles. As the last chime faded, the screams rang out.

Midnight had come to the forest. And with it, the tenth day.

THURSDAY 31st OCTOBER 2002

This is what I believe: That I am I. That my soul
is a dark forest. That my known self will never
be more than a little clearing in the forest . . .

DH Lawrence
Studies in Classic American Literature, 1923

He was transfigured before them

Matthew 17:2

Fifty-six

Jack ran along the path. His soul was not split, as it had been in *the dreaming*. The forest, born out of the ancient marshlands, really did press about him. Thorns scratched his skin and roots caught at his feet. He followed the acrid scent of fire and the screams which called to him from the clearing.

Primitive instincts railed against the strength he had drawn from Dawn's belief in him. He wanted to go back, to escape, to be far away from what would happen. What must happen. Mendicant would have his new vessel. What could he do to stop it? He did not even possess Brody's depleted faith. He had nothing . . . Except that wasn't quite true. Before Dawn and Jamie he had had nothing. He might have faced the Doctor willingly then, welcoming the end of his lonely existence. But now she believed him. Wasn't there a chance that they could build a real relationship based upon that belief?

No.

He must bury such temptations and hopes. It had been that kind of thinking that had brought them to this. If he had not chanced happiness, if he had not touched her, then his years of training would have bolstered his mind. He might have withstood the Doctor's probing. If for nothing else, then for the sake of his own sanity, he could not allow Jamie to be taken.

He reached the border of trees. The mist cordoned the clearing, banking in a wall around its margins. A deep croak sounded from above. The crows had not abandoned the forest as they had in *the dreaming*. They stood sentinel in the branches, their eyes blinking against the mist.

Jack switched on the torch he had taken from the glove compartment of the Range Rover. As he stepped into the clearing, the screams stopped dead. He rattled the torch against his palm, but the beam continued to flutter. He glanced up, hoping for a break in the clouds that had blotted out the blood-red moon. There was a frisson in that dark blanket, a simmering of elements, like the prelude to a summer storm. Streaks of purple light bloomed against the belly of the cloud, but there was no clap of thunder.

The smell of burning charcoal strengthened. His torch died. It did not matter.

In the low light of the coals, he saw them.

'Mendicant didn't tell you who he had chosen as his new vessel,' Brody said.

'Of course he did.'

Garret raised the scalpel to his mouth and let the flat side play against his tongue.

'But Jamie Howard . . .'

'I told you, I don't know who that is.'

'You must. If Mendicant told you . . .'

'You don't see at all, do you?' Garret laughed. 'Clever Asher Brody, with all his book learning, and still you stumble around in the dark.'

'Then tell me, Christopher: what am I missing?'

'Everything. The Doctor spoke to me moments after he had seen it. He was so excited. Plans had changed.'

'*What* did he see?'

'Power. A kind that he had never known before. A dark power, chained but rising.'

'Oh, God . . .'

The truth fell like a brick into Brody's consciousness.

'A child,' Garret whispered. 'Inside a man's skin.'

Brody pushed past the craven priest, sending the scalpel chinking over the cobbles. Garret screamed after him:

'Don't leave me down here alone. They're coming again.

From the walls, from the earth. They want me to go with them now. Please, Asher, I'm sorry. I don't want to die.'

Brody reached the top of the stairs and slammed the door. He fitted the padlock and he shouted through the panels, 'Remember your Chaucer, Christopher. Each man's death is written in the stars. Embrace yours.'

'Good evening, Jack. Your timing is impeccable.'

Jack had stitched together an image of Mendicant's face from the descriptions in Brody's diaries. That inconstant patch-work of features had been frightening enough, but the reality was worse still. He could only bear to run his eye over tiny portions of it at a time.

Jamie knelt at the Doctor's side, a bundle of clothing cradled in his lap. Mendicant's desiccated fingers brushed the boy's hair.

'Let him go.'

'Dear me, Jack. Still not sunk in, I see? You know, I've been acquainted with many seers down the years, but few so obtuse. From your first dream to this realisation, you have failed to read the signs. Of course, the boy may go.'

Jamie started forward, like a pulling dog released from its lead. The bundle fell beside the fire. He ran and buried his head in Jack's coat.

'The crows ate the wafer. . .' he whispered. 'Grandad . . .'

'Brave lad,' said Mendicant. 'I had to do terrible things to make him scream.'

'I don't understand,' Jack said.

'No. You haven't understood at all. Poor Jack. Well, it is the night for enlightenment. Tell me, that *first* remarkable dream you had, what did you see?'

'I saw you. I saw Jamie . . .'

'No. Think harder. Be more precise. What did you *see* . . . ?'

A pulse of light crackled through the clouds and lit up the Doctor's cavernous eyes.

'A *boy*, Mr Trent. You saw a *boy*. Just that. Though you see glimpses of the future through those dreams of yours, they

407

operate in the same manner as any normal dream. They are interpretive. Pray, tell me, when you dream how do you see *yourself?*'

The realisation shivered in Jack's brain. Or *was* it realisation? Didn't he know all this? Hadn't he seen it before? Mendicant was speaking:

'You see the boy you were when your mother died. If you hadn't woken yourself so dramatically from that first dream, it would have been your own face coming at you from out of the shadows.'

'No . . . that's impossible,' Jack murmured. 'The rite can only be performed on a child.'

'You really must read more carefully, Jack. *The Transmigration of Souls* states that only a child *spirit* may be subsumed by the possessor. A child on the cusp of adulthood. The self-image in your dreams is very telling. You see yourself just as your spirit is shaped. You *are* still a child. A being trapped in time. Your spirit has not aged a day since the night your mother died. Why?'

Jack drew Jamie closer. He could feel the hammering of the boy's heart against his own. Truths, hard won, slotted into place.

'Because I can't touch.'

'You come to it at last. What marks the difference between a boy and a man? Not years: there is no arbitrary point at which we can say: this is a child and this is an adult. It is how he begins to experience the world, not through his eyes or ears, but through the different ways that he begins to touch. It is tactile experience which bridges the gap. For some reason I cannot fathom, you have never touched as a man.'

'Then why this charade? If you wanted me, why take Jamie?'

'Details, Mr Trent. Again you have failed to read the signs. What does the *Transmigration* tell us about special cases of metempsychosis? Cases in which the possessor wants to tap the potential powers of a vessel? Like those of a witch, for example.'

Jack plucked the text from his memory: the last few words of the original document.

'The powers must be accessed.'

'*Fully realised*, Mr Trent. Fully realised at the point of possession. On that day we met in the cabin, I saw the potential within you. And I saw that you had spent years grinding down that potential. I knew that if I wanted to take advantage of your gifts, I would need to draw them out. But how? The solution was very prominent in your conscious mind. You are a would-be hero. You harbour great guilt for the death of your mother. You live out fantasies in your head in which you save her. In which you save everybody. Also present in your conscious mind are two special people: Miss Howard and her son. If I could make you believe that the boy was in danger, you might access your abilities. Reinvigorate them. Then I could take you with all the fringe benefits thrown in. The priest was a nuisance, of course, but in the end he played his part rather well, convincing you of the danger. Pushing you to the fore.'

'So you took my face out of *the dreaming* and transplanted Jamie's.'

'It wasn't difficult. I just laid a suggestion here and there in your subconscious. Heroes never dream of their own demise, Jack.'

'But why the wait? Why not push me into accessing the dreams sooner?'

'Subtlety, my boy. Though appearances are against me, I am a very subtle man. Time was on my side. I had a week to play with you, to force you into accepting your gifts. And now you are ready. Tonight, through our metempsychosis, the cloak you have wrapped about yourself will be thrown off. You shall be radiant. You shall be transfigured. Yes, there is a similarity, is there not? Remember what the good book tells us: that Jesus revealed his identity to the disciples and, six days later, he took them into the mountain and was transfigured. Six days ago, in that little cabin, I revealed myself to you. The road to the mountain has been long, has it not? You know,

409

Jack, I've performed this rite countless times; have occupied countless vessels. But tonight *we* shall achieve something very special. You are the thing I have craved for centuries: a new challenge, the next step in my evolution. I shall not just be immortal, but truly set apart from humanity. It is your gift to me, and I thank you for it.'

'You've no idea what you're doing.'

'I admit, I only glimpsed your abilities when I laid the suggestion of Jamie's fate in your dreams. You've buried so much so deep. But I have a few gifts of my own. I will draw out your secrets.'

'How? What are you?'

'Fear. Living fear. To Peter Malahyde I was the spectre of advancing age and decrepitude. To Christopher Garret, I was his coming judgement. To Asher Brody I was the confirmation of those doubts he harboured about his faith; a demon who fired his intellect. I am all of my guises and none of them. But to you, Jack, I am redemption. A monster to be vanquished. A final labour to be completed before, like Hercules, you can be forgiven by the family you allowed to die. But I am not so black and white. Strip away all my faces and I am the primal urge in everyman. I am the will to survive, at all costs, which lives even in you. Can you condemn something so primal? Something so pure . . .?'

Jack levelled his eyes with Mendicant.

'Let me tell you what you are,' he said. 'You're not some grand corrupter. You'd like to be an affront to God, but I doubt you register on his radar. You're a petty sadist. I once knew someone like you. Greylampton was his name. He was a pathetic, bland little man, desperate to be seen as important. He killed children because it was the only way he knew that he existed. I found him and I ended him. I will end you.'

'Feel better for that?' Mendicant smiled. 'Now, listen. If I can't have you, then I *will* take the boy. You won't be able to stop me. Brody tried and failed, and at least he had some belief inside him. All you have is your misery. But if you allow

410

me in, you have my word I will not harm the boy or his mother.'

'Don't, Jack. He's a fucking liar!' Jamie screamed.

'You won't hurt them?' Jack whispered.

'What a spirited child. In other circumstances . . . But yes, you have my word.'

'Jack, no.'

The voice came from the forest. Dawn, her face ashen but determined, was making her way towards them. She grimaced as she put weight on her torn ankle.

'Dawn, stay there,' Jack shouted, holding his hand out towards her. 'Trust me, please.'

She stopped twenty or so feet away from the fire. She met Mendicant's gaze and it was with pride that Jack saw there was no fear in her eyes. There was anger, there was concern, but she was not afraid.

'Dawn, I want you to take Jamie. Find Brody and leave the village. Tell him I tried.'

'No, Jack, I won't leave you with him,' Jamie said, choking on the words.

'You'll do as I tell you,' Jack shouted, pushing the boy towards his mother.

Jamie stumbled backwards, wiping tears from his face.

Jack's voice faltered and broke: 'Go . . . Both of you . . .'

'Jack . . .'

He shook his head and turned away from her.

A low rumble rolled through the sky. The fire sizzled and Jack felt the rain touch his face. There was a break in the cloud and the red moon bathed Mendicant's marble-white skin. For a moment, the Doctor said nothing. He was looking over Jack's shoulder, watching Jamie and Dawn . . .

They were leaving. Reluctantly, he knew that. But Jack was glad that they would soon be gone. He had been lonely all his life. Lonely and afraid. Wasn't it fitting that he should end it that way?

Fifty-seven

'Throw the baptism dresses into the fire.'

Motes billowed from Mendicant's exposed throat and glistened, like the rain in the firelight. The smile was gone and the Doctor's face was impassive. Even so, Jack could sense a malign satisfaction, sapping the last of his resistance. He snatched up the bundle that Jamie had guarded and unwound the tiny garments.

'Did you murder these babies, too?' Jack mumbled.

'Natural causes, I assure you,' Mendicant said. 'Perhaps you'll soon be able to turn that righteous anger against God; ask *him* why he took them. Now, throw the clothes into the fire.'

'And if I don't? You're fading by the minute. What if I just left you here, as Brody did, hoping against hope that another Peter Malahyde will come along?'

'So predictable, Jack. Look behind you.'

And there they were. The wind billowed their jackets, rain streamed down their faces. Dawn and Jamie, clutching at each other, mouths slightly agape, stood not ten feet from the fire.

'We could see the gate; we could see the road . . .' said Dawn, her voice tremulous. 'Jack, what's happening?'

'Just a game, Miss Howard,' Mendicant answered. 'One that Jack here insisted we play. I brought you back to take your part. Now, tell me . . . what do you fear?'

The Doctor stretched out his hands to Dawn. She flinched, but held her ground.

'What haunts you in the small hours? What secret dread

412

will you admit only to the dark?'

'Dawn, don't listen to him,' Jack bellowed.

'Let me draw it out of you,' Mendicant said. 'Let me make it real.'

'Dawn, go NOW.'

'I . . . I can't. Jack, I can't *move.*'

As she spoke, Jack found that his own body had become immobile. He strained every muscle until veins roped his neck. It was no good. He watched the Doctor pass through the flames of the dying fire, approach Dawn and put his thin arm around her shoulder. Beside her, Jamie was also unmoving, but whereas Jack and Dawn strove against the force binding them, Jamie was silent and expressionless. Dawn's face contorted as she tried to turn her head away from the rotting lips.

'Don't touch her,' screamed Jack. 'Don't you lay a fucking finger on her.'

'Look at your son,' Mendicant whispered, ignoring Jack's commands. 'What are your fears for him?'

Dawn screwed her eyes tight shut.

'Come now, tell the Doctor, he'll make it all better.'

'I'm . . . afraid . . .'

She hissed the words through clenched teeth, as if the confession were being wrung out of her.

'Yes, go on.'

' . . . he'll . . . one day . . . be . . . abandoned. He'll . . . one day . . . be . . . alone. Frightened. Lost. Unloved.'

'I know a place where your fears can be realised,' Mendicant said. 'Where Jamie can wander blind forever. A place where he will never see another human face again. And I can make him believe that it was *you* who sent him there. That his mother has abandoned him. Look at your son. Do you want that?'

A milky-blue gauze crept from the corners of Jamie's eyes. The whites marbled and Dawn cried out as the pupils filmed over with thick cataracts. These, in turn, smoothed out into layers of skin, meeting and fusing the eyelids together. This process then moved on to the boy's ears, nose and mouth.

413

Soon all physical traits were gone. Jamie's head writhed, smooth and egg-like, with only hints of features shifting below the surface. Suddenly able to move, the boy held his hands before his face. Beneath the canvas of skin, his mouth split into a silent scream.

'Please, no,' Dawn cried, as her son staggered forward, snatching at the air. 'Give him back his face.'

'Well, that's up to our friend Jack,' Mendicant said. 'I wonder, does he love Jamie enough to save him?'

'It's an illusion, Dawn. It's not real.' *Was he sure of that?*

Jamie tore at the sheathing, but to no avail. Tremors seized his Adam's apple. He caught at his throat and fell to his knees.

'He can't breathe,' Dawn cried. 'Please, he's choking.'

'What say you, Jack? Will you save the boy?'

'It's not real,' Jack repeated.

'Very well. Now, my child . . .'

His panic forgotten, Jamie's hands fell to his sides. His crease-less head twisted towards Mendicant.

' . . . you will show me what *you* fear.'

For a moment, nothing happened. Jamie remained kneeling, while Mendicant intoned soundless words. The boy was so still he resembled a shop dummy with the features sanded away. A pulse throbbed beneath the skin and the likeness was lost. Jack watched the bulge press against the fleshy lid that covered the kid's mouth. At first, he thought it was Jamie's tongue trying to poke through. And then two black pincers split the skin. The tear rounded out into a tiny, surprised 'O'. The new mouth grew wide, and the thing that had made it scuttled down the chin, mandibles snatching and feelers tasting the air. In its wake, a repellent host poured forth: centipedes and scorpions, millipedes and spiders, bowing locusts and clicking beetles. With them came the crack of hatching cocoons and the slow, wet passage of larval sacs. Jamie did not move, did not even seem conscious of the grotesque life that he evacuated.

'No!' Dawn screamed. 'Please, Jack!'

'Not real. Not real.'

Jamie's throat pulsated with the stream of insects moving up from his stomach. The single route of escape was becoming blocked. His mouth stretched wider, but the flood was dammed with convulsing bodies. New avenues had to be opened up. The nostrils broke first. Earthworms wriggled free and roaches skittered out, making their way into the boy's hair. The ears were breached and then the eyes. Strange inverted legs and the alien head of a mantis rose up into a vacant eye socket.

Jack's will broke.

'Stop it! Please, stop it. I promise, I'll do whatever you want.'

'Very well.'

The insects melted away. Jamie's eye rolled back into position. His features pushed through the mask of skin. Disorientated, the boy screamed and ran fingers across his face. He buckled over, sobbing and shivering. Dawn, now able to move, held her son close.

'But they stay until it is finished,' Mendicant smiled. 'Now, burn the clothes and allow me in.'

Jack breathed deeply. He threw the garments into the flames. Beads of red ember touched the edges of the cloth and the dresses caught. Smoke crept from the heart of the fire. It furled around Mendicant and rolled inside those sightless eyes before sending out tendrils towards Jack. When the vapour was within a few feet of him, it rose and touched his face.

It felt as if a hundred icy fingers were probing his body, testing invisible weaknesses. In some areas, like his scalp and chest, he felt a strong barrier. In others, like the base of his spine, he sensed frailty. The smoke touched his eyes, teased and violated . . . And now it searched inside him. Through the gauze, Jack saw the Doctor move towards him. They stood for a moment, face to face. A charnel stink filled Jack's nostrils. Then the Doctor fell to his knees. Jack felt claw-like fingers open his shirt and stroke his chest. Nails dug into his skin. Pain seared through him. Blinding, tearing pain.

Jack clutched Mendicant's head to his breast. Rain poured into the indentation in the Doctor's skull and ran down his back. It made the flesh more pliable, and Jack's fingers sank into the scalp. Mendicant had faded to little more than a shadow, but his teeth were still tearing and ripping.

The Doctor made quick work of his meal. Jack could feel the black tongue lick across his breastbone. He could hear the thrum of his heart in his ears. Exposed to the night air, it felt so cold inside him.

Over the groan of the wind, someone was crying.

She was still there. Dawn had not abandoned him.

And then, in a moment of exquisite realisation, disconnected memories knitted together. He laughed out loud.

He had the answer.

His hands passed through Mendicant and covered his gaping chest. He fell to his knees, the sound of his lungs in his ears. For a moment, it all seemed too unreal to credit. The pain was distant and he sensed it only empathetically, as if it belonged to someone else. With this new detachment, he watched the fire collapse into itself and die.

It was the fire, wasn't it? That dull red flame before his eyes? So like the blood-moon that had watched their progress to Crow Haven. It was coming closer . . . Mendicant . . . Plunging into his eyes, delving deeper and deeper. Finding the path laid out for him.

She said nothing. She had no words, nor did she need them. All she had to do was cradle his head. In her peripheral vision, she could see his trembling torso and the wet edges of the wound torn out of his chest. The blood beneath her knees was cooling.

His eyes did not seem sad, but a few tears rolled over the white scar that bridged his nose. She felt his hand, cold and shaking, against her cheek, and she held it there, warming it.

'I want . . . to see him . . .' he whispered.

She turned his face towards the forest. Jamie stood between

the trees, his head buried in his hands. Her own voice sounded distant in her ears. She heard herself calling to her son, telling him to let Jack see his face. Jamie pulled his hands away.

'Go now . . .' Jack groaned. 'He is fi . . . finding his way . . . inside.'

'No.' She passed her hand over Jack's lips.

'Please, for me . . . Live, for me . . .' he sighed. 'Be happy, for me.'

'I can't . . . I can't leave you here. Alone.'

'Always alone . . . Please, Dawn . . . Something is coming . . .'

His pale blue eyes pleaded with her. At their corners, she saw a fleck of darkness. It began to streak out in veins, swallowing the whites. Without hurrying, she laid him down on the wet grass. Rain dripped from her hair as she leant over him. She tasted his blood as their lips touched. The final, warm breath left him and passed into her.

When she reached Jamie, she took hold of his hand and pulled him behind her.

'We can't leave him . . .'

'He's dead.'

A scream erupted from the glade. Dawn felt herself give way. Jamie fell against her and they both collapsed to the ground. The birds exploded from the trees, their calls lost against the resounding power of the cry. It was not of pain, but of anger. Of a primal, desperate rage.

It was Jack. Still alive. Fighting against something back in the clearing. And at that moment, as if mimicking the scream, the sky roared.

Asher Brody was standing at the door of the *Old Priory* when the scream tore out of the forest. Looking over Redgrave, he saw a flare of red light shoot above the trees. He knew that it came from the clearing.

Just as he managed to regain himself, the clouds, hanging low over that scarlet firework, were rent open. A deluge, the like of which Brody had seen only during the season of El

Niño, roared from the rift. The foaming edge of the clouds looked like the lip of some huge crevasse, down which a booming torrent of water cascaded. The rain that swept across the village, though not comparable to the wall of water that pummelled the clearing, was strengthening. Within a few minutes, the drains that serviced the Conduit Road had flooded.

Brody ran back to the rectory. He went to the study and turned out all the drawers. While he searched, he felt his heart rattle in time with the drumming on the window. At last, he found the keys in an old biscuit tin and tore back out of the house. Ignoring the sting of rain against his face, he managed to unlock Garret's car and threw himself into the driver's seat. He turned the key and flipped the wipers. They did little good. He ground the gear stick into first and roared down the drive. The engine gargled and the tyres span as the car hit the running stream that had once been the Conduit Road. With minimal control of the vehicle, Brody headed towards the mouth of trees.

'Its evil abideth within and without;' he quoted, 'until the Darkness exhausts Itself and the Flood taketh away all Sorrow . . . Godspeed, Jack.'

Jack opened his eyes. He felt gingerly across his chest. The wound was sealed. Mendicant was inside. There was not much time.

Save for the beat of blood in his ears, he could hear nothing. He guessed that the searing crack from the heavens moments before had ruptured his eardrums. He was standing, though he did not remember getting to his feet. Rising to a level of about three feet all around him was a wall of running water. The source of it, a great cascade falling from the sky, sent up a spray that reached the tops of the tallest trees. The water did not touch him, however. Somehow, it was held back, either by Mendicant or himself.

The rush pressed against the trees and undermined their foundations. Those that bordered the clearing stood resolute,

418

but beyond they were falling like dominoes, ancient earth flying from upturned roots. He prayed that Dawn and Jamie had reached the village and were safe.

But now he must concentrate.

Find him, Jack, he told himself.

He shut his eyes on the world: the weeping moon, the harried sky, the dying forest. He prepared to welcome his visitor.

Fifty-eight

He stood in a long stone corridor. There were archways and passages leading off in all directions. Blue light shone on the bare walls and floor, but he could not see its source. For the first time in centuries he was afraid.

He had seen it in the eyes of so many but, for countless lifetimes, he had only observed the mechanistic effects of fear. The tears, the trembling, the pleading and the screaming. If asked, he could not honestly have described the shape and texture of terror from memory. But now his flesh began to creep and fear slithered inside him again. The sensation acted like Proust's madeleine, bringing back memories he had thought long buried. Memories redolent of pain and horror.

It had started in a corridor much like this. A sweet-sour smell pervaded the place; the stink of horse piss on straw. The windows had been so high that all he had been able to see was a hint of troubled sky. He could not now remember how old he had been. Ten years? Certainly no more than that. And his name had not been Mendicant or Elijah. His name . . . Nathaniel. Of course, Nathaniel. But somebody had called him Natty. An affectionate nickname.

He had been very cold, waiting in this corridor, and his little fingers had turned almost blue. Someone had wrapped them in her skirts. Someone beautiful. Someone warm. His mother.

She cried when the men came out of the room, their terms negotiated, a price bartered and agreed. Catching one of them by the arm, she had pleaded. What had she said? He could not remember. The man, dressed in a threadbare shirt, slack trousers and worn shoes, tried to comfort her. The other, a face as hard as granite, sneered at the display and barked:

'I will keep him well enough. Would you rather he shared your fate and starve in the street? Just remember my condition. You are never to see him again.'

The poor man nodded, knelt and shook hands with his son. Then he turned, masked his tears, and dragged his wife away. She had screamed, as if her soul were tearing itself apart. Then the man, whose face was a mass of pockmarks and sores, said to him:

'Tell me, boy, what dost thou know of God?'

'That He is good. That He loves all little children.'

Nathaniel felt an iron grip on his arm.

'Well, my learned friend, we shall test your theory. In here.'

And then the man had opened the Room of Fear.

There was more he could dwell on if he chose. The branding, the scorching, the fracturing and resetting of his bones. The lectures on the purity of pain. The twisted philosophy of his master, who believed that one might hold counsel with God through the ecstasy of a child's torment. It was memory drowning in tears and blood. Neither in prayer, that was swiftly abandoned, nor in his fear, which endured for years, did he hear God's voice.

But he heard other things. Secrets whispered when his master thought he slept. Tales of ancient mysticism, lost knowledge and heathen rites. And of a path to eternal youth. Eternal perfection. He listened down the dark years, while his own youth wasted away and his body was contorted until he dreaded the sight of a mirror.

When the old man died, and Nathaniel had ground the tormentor's face beneath his foot, he stayed on in the Room of Fear, reading all he could. He might have left, of course. Hidden his face beneath sackcloth and gone to seek his mother. But could he bear her horror as she looked at him? No, let the poor woman retain the unspoilt child of her dreams, rather than return to her a crippled devastation to haunt her nightmares. His family would not know him, but Nathaniel determined that he would be allowed to live again. The world owed him much for his suffering, and now its debt must be paid.

Having learned to read by surreptitiously observing his master, he sought out the clue that might restore him among the dead man's papers. A veritable library of uncatalogued myth, superstition and heresy awaited him. It took two long years to piece together the rite, but there it eventually was, laid out before him. His path back home. To his youth, to his fairness. He gazed across what he must do and his soul balked at the ugliness of it. And yet, by degrees, he overcame his squeamishness. With each possession, his remaining shreds of pity dwindled. He was changed. But he could not now escape his old lessons. Fear, he had known. Fear he became. Forgetting his mother, forgetting his name, he adopted his old master's moniker: Mendicant.

And now, was *this* that long forgotten corridor? Did one of these doors lead to the Room of Fear? Was his master waiting for him? He felt very small. Just as he had found it difficult to remember his past, he was now confused as to who he was and what he had done since those days spent poring over his master's papers. Why was he here? Was this Hell? And if it was, what had he done to bring damnation upon himself?

He shuddered and sobbed. It occurred to him that his voice was higher than it had been. He had changed again, but from what? A shadow passed over him and he covered his head with his hands. His master had come. The pain must soon begin.

'Are you afraid, Nathaniel?'

'Yes . . . He hurts me. I'm just a little boy . . . I don't want to go back into the room . . .'

'There is a room you must enter, but it's not the one you're thinking of. There are no rooms like that here. Will you come with me?'

The man's voice was soft. Nathaniel put his crooked hand

into the stranger's. He looked up and seemed to recognise the man, though he could not remember from where.

'What's your name?' Nathaniel asked.

The man smiled. 'My name's Jack.'

The water reached the level of the drive, flushed the gravel away and made the tyres skitter on the track. In the deep gullies on either side, a bisected river was felling young trees and tearing through the subsoil. The car skidded to a halt. Brody jumped out and ran to the wrecked Range Rover. There was no-one inside.

Just as he caught sight of Anne Malahyde hanging from the gate, the frame gave a violent shudder. Anne pivoted forward. There was a groan of rust-furred bolts. Then the foundations gave way. Brody raced back to Garret's car. With a chorus of splintering glass, the gate crashed into the Range Rover, trapping Anne's body beneath.

They waded waist-deep in floodwater, Jamie helping to shoulder the weight off Dawn's torn ankle. The destruction of Redgrave continued to roar on all sides. Creepers and roots caught at their feet, tripping them into the filthy water. Occasionally their hands met the silky touch of dead things floating by. As they tried to traverse a small trench, the uprooted remains of a tree swept over the rise above them. Dawn saw the thorny arm rip through Jamie's shirtsleeve. He stifled his yell. She urged him on; even if the gash was deep, they could not stop now. They must reach higher ground.

They scrambled up a dirt bank. A sturdy oak was resisting the barrage. With some difficulty, they managed to use the trunk to lever themselves over the ridge. This level, though unstable, was at least free of running water. They hobbled through the undergrowth until they came to an opening in the trees. And there stood Simon Malahyde's work shed, the rain drilling on the tin roof.

Jack first saw him here, she thought. *Only a week ago.*

But now Jack was surely dead. And Mendicant was safe

inside his new body.

They left the cabin to its certain destruction. Up the incline, not even noticing their pain and grief now. Listening only to the ravaging of nature by Nature. They came out of the forest and stood before the house.

A lifetime ago, she had thought it incongruous. This cold, magnificent structure, so obviously a design of man, set in the tortured heart of Redgrave. Now she wondered. There was a detached pitilessness in the spirits of both house and forest. Neither cared for living things. As they stepped onto the driveway, the windows exploded outwards. Razor-sharp shards fell just short of where they stood. In the dusky moonlight, the ground glinted, as if spotted with tiny red pools.

It's bleeding, Dawn thought. *The house is bleeding.* She was glad.

It was hard to believe that the misshapen child walking at his side was Elijah Mendicant. And now that Jack had glimpsed the torment he had suffered all those centuries ago, he pitied him. Still hidden, however, because at present Mendicant was too weak to remember it, were lifetimes of fear that he had inflicted on others. Soon enough the Doctor would regain himself, and this last vestige of purity, here represented by his child-self, would be gone. Jack could waste no time on sympathy. He must take the child quickly through the avenues of his mind. He must bring them both to the room.

He had first glimpsed the answer during his connection with Brody, when he had witnessed the last scene of the priest's story. It had not been until he had despaired, however, that a possible solution hit him. With his chest gaping open, his blood watering the ground, he had laughed and given thanks to Father Asher Brody. The crazy old bastard had been right. The answer *had* been buried in those dread memoirs of his:

The way Mendicant had collapsed after forcing Brody to inflict the stigmata injuries upon himself – The fact that the Doctor stayed away for three weeks after his first attempt to drive Brody's faith from him – The mystery of why Mendicant had not taken the time to prejudice Peter's mind against Brody during the 'supernatural infection' – The relative lack of resistance Mendicant had shown when Brody and Jim Rowbanks set about destroying him. These and other instances pointed to the fact that, after he expended a great deal of psychic energy, Mendicant was very weak. Already tonight, the Doctor had used his powers during his trick at the station and in his manipulation of Dawn and Jamie. If Mendicant was left disorientated by these acts, then Jack might be able to corner the creature on his own terms.

Of one thing Jack was certain: he was well versed in the manipulation of his own mind. If he found Mendicant temporarily suggestible, he would be able to effect his plan. So far that plan was working. He did not know, however, how much longer Mendicant would remain pliable to his will. Soon the Doctor might regain himself and tear down the rooms and corridors that imprisoned him. Then would he really honour his promise to leave Dawn and Jamie unmolested? Fate had twisted and broken his nature, just as his old master had broken his body. Jack could have no confidence in any promise the creature had made.

'It's getting darker,' Nathaniel said, drawing closer to Jack. 'And the passage grows thin and low. There is a fell air to this place.'

It was darker in this, the farthest corner of Jack's mind. The air was dank, like that of an abandoned lighthouse. Jack felt inside his pocket and brought out a single key. As he slipped it into the lock, a high chittering sound came from behind the door.

'I don't want to go in there.'

Jack looked at Nathaniel. He saw the child behind the deformity.

'We must,' he smiled, 'and we must not be afraid.'

He threw open the door. The air was fresh. Jack's mother always opened the windows first thing. There was the bed with the homely patchwork eiderdown, his unfinished homework strewn across it. The neat row of the Junior Encyclopedia that he had hardly ever touched. The old hornbeam tree outside, tapping the window with a familiar *tick-tick-tick*. It was night in the fantasy world outside, but the nightlight was on and there were his precious comic books.

'Where are we?' Nathaniel asked.

'My room,' Jack said. 'My bedroom when I was a boy.'

And there was the toy box, harnessed with straps and chains and a sturdy padlock. The lid rattled. A clawed hand reached through the gap and tore at the bonds. Jack took another key from his pocket and knelt before the box.

'Please,' Nathaniel cried, catching his sleeve. 'Don't let them out.'

'I must. Go sit on the bed.'

His fingers shook and he found it difficult to slide the key into the lock. Finally, it clicked home. This was surely madness . . . He remembered Dawn's words:

They saved your life. On the Death Bank.

It was over quickly: the snap release of the lock, his hands tearing off the straps and chains, throwing back the lid . . .

They were running. Dawn registered the pain in her ankle, but stayed focused on the dim figure of Asher Brody. The drive was falling away beneath their feet, and there was now a river, maybe six feet deep, tumbling and gouging out its path on both sides of the causeway.

They reached the gate. It was lying against her car, at a forty degree angle. The body of it pivoted on the narrow drive. On either side, two feet of the gate's span was suspended over the broken channels of the river. The frame was too heavy to lift. They would have to climb. She sent Jamie first, stepping on the base to steady it, while he clambered up the irregular ladder of latticework. Brody, positioned beneath the gate, grasped the sharp metal tracery. Despite the loss of blood from his arm, Jamie managed to scamper over the frame and onto the roof of the wrecked Range Rover.

'Fast now!' Brody shouted. 'The ground's giving way!'

426

She put her foot on the first artificial rung. Her heart skipped. The base of the gate ratcheted further into the earth. The three mourning figures squealed against the roof of the car. She looked ahead and saw that, if the gate subsided another foot, it would slip off the Range Rover, crushing Brody beneath.

'I can't risk it!' she called, 'It'll fall.'

'Do it,' Brody bellowed. 'Just fucking do it!'

She grasped the rung above, then the next. Halfway across, her ankle lodged in a whorl of metal. She looked down and it was only then that she noticed the figure crumpled into a foetal ball beneath the gate. Anne Malahyde, eyes glazed, stared up at her. The rope hung loose about the dead woman's neck. Again, Dawn felt a stab of sorrow. Her head swam.

'Come on!' Brody roared.

Dawn grunted against the pain, gripped the tender skin and tore her foot free. The effort sapped the last of her energy and she fell sideways. She heard Jamie's frightened cry and the gruff exhortations of Brody that she should '*Get the hell up.*' Beneath her, inching closer as the gate rolled, the foaming swirl of water.

She pulled herself back to the middle of the gate. It see-sawed with her and the frame juddered downwards again. She ignored the sudden give, dragging herself up and over the final few feet of sharp metal. Her legs were raw and bleeding when she reached Jamie. Together, they scrambled to the ground.

As Brody released the frame and ducked from under it, the gate slid off the car roof. It hit the ground and that section of the driveway crumbled on impact. A terrible composite sound – the cracking of many bones and the liquid splatter of flesh – echoed down the avenue as Anne Malahyde's body was crushed beneath a tonne of iron. Water gushed into the new channel. The river was complete.

The great black body of Mendicant's gate sunk below the churning waters. The rope around Anne Malahyde's neck pulled taut. Her body, now an almost featureless pulp, was dragged over the tongue of the causeway and consumed by the swell.

The river started eating away at the rest of the drive. Its erosion was swift and the waters were still rising. As Brody hollered and waved them to Garret's car, Dawn's Range Rover pitched forward. A huge spray sprang up and moments later the rest of the car toppled into the water.

There was no room to turn round, so Brody threw the car into reverse. The engine gave an asthmatic gasp and puttered out. Cursing, he tried again, gunning the accelerator. The car grunted, whirred and died. The river had now reached to within a foot of the front tyres.

'We'll have to run,' Dawn shouted.

Brody nodded and they jumped out. Within seconds, they heard the rumble of Garret's car joining the Range Rover.

The going was tough, their feet forever slipping on the wet ground. At one point the earth was torn out from under Brody. The old man reeled for a moment before Jamie caught his arm and pulled him back. They were within two hundred feet of the opening when they heard the pounding rush behind them.

'*Run*,' Brody wheezed. 'Landslide.'

Dawn could feel the spray sting her legs. She pictured it gaining momentum, dirty white horses cresting at their backs, ready to grind them into the bed of the forest.

A curtain of rain thundered at the end of the row of wych elms. It darkened suddenly. They saw the rough shape of a car. The smoke from its exhaust swelled down the avenue to meet them. They shot through the mouth of trees, groped, found the doors already open, and piled in. The car rocked against the onslaught. The windows broke. Before they had time to brush the glass from their faces, the car jerked forward. Dawn was vaguely aware that they were speeding through the village. There were other vehicles joining the exodus, but the angry protest of horns was almost drowned by the storm.

She checked Jamie over. The gash was deep, but not life threatening.

'Geraldine,' Brody gasped, 'good God. It must be fate.'

'Or good timing,' said the woman driving the car. 'I saw you drive in there twenty minutes ago. Thought you were cutting it fine.'

Dawn was surprised at how the wind had picked up. Sheltered by the older trees and deafened by the water, they had neither felt nor heard the gale. But it was strong, howling from rooftop to rooftop, throwing tiles to the ground in its wake. A power line had smashed through the roof of the post office. The wires sparked and struggled like harpooned eels. Garbage from toppled dustbins twisted in little cyclones. All around, there was the sound of breaking slate and glass.

Her mind focused on Jack as she stared out of the window. There was a man lying on the Green. He was pinioned beneath uprooted fencing, a spear of wood piercing his side. The water had risen to his chest. He clutched at the ankles of friends and neighbours. They kicked him away and clambered over him to reach their cars. He was abandoned.

'Stop the car!' Dawn screamed.

'No,' Geraldine said. 'You can't help him. It's the last gasp of this place and it will have its pound of flesh. Am I right, Father?'

Brody said nothing. The car sped on, snaking between obstacles until it reached the outskirts of the village. They hit the rise leading out of Crow Haven and left the water behind. Brody turned back. A faint whisper passed his lips. It sounded to Dawn like *Crows*.

A runnel of black fluid slipped over the lip of the box and pooled on the floor. Almost at once, sets of eyes, teeth, nails, clots of hair and a tiny, gasping mouth took form. *They* were coming.

Jack shot a glance at the bed. Nathaniel sat there, twisted and malformed, yet a child still, and desperately frightened.

'They won't hurt you,' Jack said, 'I won't let them.'

There was a shift on the surface of the pool. Four rudely formed arms, each ending in crabbed, three fingered hands, broke through. Between them they held up a dripping ball of dark matter, about the size of a large pumpkin. For a moment the ball remained spherical. Then it folded inwards. A head was shaped while the fold twisted into a torso, not much thicker than an umbilical cord. The thing remained limbless while its face defined: a pouting mouth and a single, blinking eye.

Jack was shocked as this semblance of a mutated foetus began to speak. *They* had never spoken before.

'*If we do this, you will keep your promise?*'

'Yes. I wouldn't be able to stop you, would I?' Jack said.

'*You know that we cannot return. The rift is long closed to us. We must abide here. We must find a new home. The externals of this world cannot support us.*'

'I know.'

The eye bored into Jack. The rich, slurping voice made him shudder.

'*You have never understood our intent. Our only desire was to please our host. We showed you wonderful things; gave you powerful gifts, and to you they were a curse. We have tried to understand your morality, Jack. Have you ever tried to understand ours? It was* you *who called to us through the rift. It was* you *who failed to shape the gifts we proffered. And we have tried to keep you safe, not only in our own interests, but because you saved* us *as we stumbled from the void. Your mother . . .*'

'Don't speak of her,' Jack murmured.

'*We cannot understand . . . It was our gift; she was hurting you. But we will not speak of it. Your enemy draws closer. We have felt him near us before, when he re-shaped* the dreaming. *He sensed our power then, but did not know our nature. You hid us well. But he grows now from the weakened form of that child. If you are to give us our freedom, it must be done soon. We will not be able to resist him, should he overthrow your mind and draw us back. We would not care to serve him.*'

'You are free,' Jack said. He stepped away from the door. 'End it.'

The creature nodded. Its features melted away. With a

430

slippery gracefulness, the limbs sank back into the body, which in turn formed itself into a ball. Supporting fingers flexed and gripped and the columnar arms bore the orb down into the black pool. Before the surface settled, the mouth reformed.

'*You thought you were alone, Jack Trent. We were always with you.*'

They crept towards the door. The replica of the door that his mother had retreated to as *they* tore the life out of her: *Jack, you must fight them . . . Keep them from the world*. He was sending them back to the world now. In these final moments, he was breaking his promise.

They slipped beneath the door.

'No. You can't let them out. Don't you know what they'll do?'

It was Nathaniel, but his voice had grown deeper. A grey tinge streaked through his skin. Jack watched the last thread of darkness slither away. Then he went to the changing child. Nathaniel cringed against the bedpost. His hands pawed at his face. Jack pulled the twisted fingers away.

'It's going to be all right,' he said. 'It'll be over soon.'

Nathaniel shuddered against him.

'Someone's coming,' he said. 'Someone cruel . . . He whispers to me. He wants me to let him in. He says I'm just a memory. He does bad things. He is like my master and yet . . . Oh, God . . . I know that he is me. He is what I will become, because I *am* a memory . . .'

'You are as you should have been,' Jack whispered. 'You must not let him in. Stay with me. We'll be together. In the darkness.'

While he spoke, Jack could feel *them* racing down the twilit corridors of his mind. They tore through stone and blasted open doors that segmented his thoughts and memories. He found the sudden disorder unsettling. He tried to remember his father's name and found that it was lost in the debris. Finally, *they* reached the weakest and, paradoxically, the strongest point of his mind construct. This was the place where discipline broke down and a quiet chaos of emotion ruled. It was

431

a corridor but, unlike the others, there was not that air of cold bureaucracy about it. The light was softer here; a sweeter, freer air.

The corridor came to a dead end. The wall was papered over with a photographic enlargement. It was a replica of the souvenir he had of their summer picnic. A time when he had felt freedom . . . love . . . She had moved just as the shutter closed, so the image was blurry, motion trails flying from her hair.

They tore through it and he felt his bedrock crumble. Who was she? The woman in the photograph . . .

As they shattered his mind, so he felt the needle pierce his eye. He could see a spidering flare of pain coat his brain, but it seemed so far off as to be inconsequential. *They* were fulfilling their promise. Slipping over his body.

Consuming him.

'It's cold,' Nathaniel said.

It *was* colder. And it was growing darker. The corners of the room were gathering shadows. Jack could hear the tap of the hornbeam at the window. Beyond, the garden had been smothered by the night. Soon the door was only an outline. Then a smear of colour. Then it was gone. As the rest of the room was covered in the rolling darkness, Jack held the crippled child tight.

'He wants to come in,' Nathaniel said. 'He's crying. He says you want to kill me.'

'Don't listen. Keep him out just a little longer.'

The boy's head slumped against his chest. Jack felt the last of his body being filmed over. Soon...

'I'm afraid of the dark,' Nathaniel whispered. 'My master used to tell me that if the Devil caught you in the darkest darkness, then your soul was lost. I can only see the bed now... Jack, have I done bad things?'

'No. Not anymore.'

Half the bed was gone. They sat on an island in a growing void. But it was peaceful here, and Jack was grateful to the nothingness that awaited them. The darkness crept steady fingers across the patchwork. It touched Jack's legs. He had the dimmest sensation of his body being torn apart. Then, from below, they heard a whispered sound.

The opening bars of *Mister Sandman*...

'What is it?' Nathaniel asked, his voice unafraid.

'It's my Dad,' Jack said, smiling. 'Playing music downstairs. But I think he's happy...'

The nothingness rolled over them, like night over lonely tundra. But they were not lonely. They held onto each other. It drew a steady veil over their faces, until only their eyes remained, shining yct against the darkness.

'Her name was Dawn.'

And then they were gone.

Epilogue

In the valley, the rush of boiling river was abating. The moon had lost its fire and glinted on the silt-filmed surface of the water. A few of the taller houses and the church spire stood out as islands, but little else of the drowned village was visible. Of the forest, there were only intermittent patches of older trees, bowed over like the buttress ribs of a demolished cathedral.

The emergency services were arriving on the scene. Brody stayed with Dawn and Jamie while their wounds were tended. Then he walked up the rise to join his flock. On the hill above the village, bewildered Crow Havenites huddled together. A few were occupied in searching for family members among the crowd, but there were bodies enough floating on the surface below to account for the missing. Most just stood, surveying the devastation of their homes. Brody knew that an unspoken hope passed between them. A hope so fragile that they dared not give expression to it, for fear that it might crumble under brutish words. Was it possible? Were they free? He came amongst them and they did not seem surprised to see him.

'The crows,' he said.

The birds circled in an unbroken black thread. Beneath them was a raised area of land, a barrow perhaps, bordered by a strangely uniform circle of trees. They were timeworn, monolithic oaks, arranged as if they were a convocation of mystic standing stones. It was the place where the forebears of these people burned Elspeth Stamp almost four centuries ago. And the place where Jack Trent had ventured to meet

Elijah Mendicant. Brody's heart beat, slow and heavy. Had Mendicant's last cruelty sickened the Darkness? Were these the shifting wastes that the witch had prophesied?

A clear night sky, dusted with stars, domed the ruined village. Only over the clearing did a troubled arc of cloud persist. The hollow at its centre was no longer the source of a thundering downpour, but its kinetic mass crackled with streaks of light. It was too isolated to be a thundercloud, and after the flashes, there was no rending crack. It seemed to be waiting.

A string of piercing shrieks broke out. The eyes of the people on the ridge turned to the crows, but to Brody, the cries had not sounded like the caws of a bird. It had seemed like a clarion call of victory. At the sound, one of the crows broke away from the rest. Brody could see it struggling to turn its body into a downward swoop, but however it twisted, it was tugged inexorably upwards. Then, as one, its fellows joined it. They rose up in a wave, like a swarm of locusts. Spinning wildly as they ascended, the first bird was soon swallowed between the teeth of the cloud. Moments later, the entire flock was devoured.

There was a low rumble. The lights shivered on the skin of the cloud and died. Then it simply dissolved, and only the stars and moon looked over the remains of Crow Haven.

'Dawn? Where the fuck are you? Do you know what's happened? I tried calling you last night. Did you have any idea that Jack . . . ?'

'My father died last night. Heart attack. We were at the hospital.'

'Oh, fuck.'

She heard Jarski draw a deep, exasperated breath.

'Look, I'm sorry. How's the boy? You've got a boy, haven't you?'

'Yes. He's shaken up . . . He was here alone when . . .'

'Christ. Okay, you need some time. Okay. Shit. Have you seen the news?'

'Yes.'

'Fucking vultures. I still can't figure out how he got out of the station . . . Did . . . err, did you have any inkling, about what he was *really* like?'

'Look, Sir. Jack and I . . . I always thought he was odd. Not that this sort of thing ever crossed my mind. But, yes. With hindsight I suppose it makes sense. About as much sense as these things ever make. I think he *was* disturbed. Maybe Mescher was right. Maybe Jack only caught Arthur Greylampton because they were birds of a feather. It's possible he saw his opportunity with the Malahyde disappearance.'

'Yes. Makes sense. I still can't believe it,' Jarski groaned. 'Okay, he was a freak, but this? Anyway, I hate to ask, Dawn, but when might you be back?'

'I need a few days. I'll be back next week.'

'Great. Fine,' said Jarski, with evident relief. 'The fucking press are going ape shit . . .'

Dawn replaced the receiver. Please, God, let that be her final betrayal.

She stared down at the empty space of carpet. An hour ago, an ambulance had come and taken her father away. Jamie was sleeping upstairs. The house ached with silence. She was alone with her thoughts. For the first time in years, she cried freely.

It had taken Brody all day to write up the five pages of foolscap. So simple a tale, yet he could not adequately describe the sacrifice that had been made.

He was still dissatisfied when he found himself before a familiar door. He rang the bell pull and waited. From across the Cardinal Quad came shouts and laughter from those fellows of the old university, trapped in time as surely as the brothers of the venerable library. Yet another exception to God's laws. Brody had seen so many that he wondered whether anything was truly forbidden.

'Father Brody. How strange. I was not expecting you.'

The librarian was dressed in his usual black robes, but his hood was pulled back. Brody remembered the chaotic arrangement of bones in the face, the soft musicality of the voice, and the forceful sense of knowing that emanated from the man.

'You have not returned to consult my books for a third time, I trust? If that is the case, I'm afraid I would insist upon you staying . . .'

'No. I have here something you may wish to add to your collection. If your archivist could attach it to the *Transmigration of Souls,* I think it might be of use, should anyone need to consult that document in the future.'

Brody held out the pages of yellow paper.

'Your contribution is most welcome, Father. It is a testament, too, is it not? An attempt to immortalise a great deed?'

Brody nodded. The librarian folded the papers and placed them beneath his robes.

'A very interesting individual. Tortured, of course, as all interesting people are. I was glad to have met him . . . And the other?'

'I cannot say. I pray he is gone.'

'Your prayers matter little. Things are as they are.'

Brody said nothing. He turned his back on the library.

'It may be of some comfort to you to know that he was successful,' the librarian called. 'And he was not alone when the end came.'

'Our top story: the remains of missing ten-year-old, Stephen Lloyd, were found late last night at the home of Inspector Jack Trent, the man heading the investigation into the deaths of Stephen and eleven-year-old Oliver Godfrey. We pass over now to our correspondent at the scene . . .'

The picture switched to a journalist standing in front of a police cordon. In the background, there stood a uniformed officer guarding the door of Jack's house.

'Yes, Clive, I'm here at the home of the missing Inspector Jack Trent. Now, the police aren't giving away much information relating to this startling new development. We heard from the DCI in charge earlier, Roger Jarski, who told us that, acting on information received from an anonymous caller, Mr Trent's home was searched last night. Several items of clothing belonging to the missing children were discovered here, as well as a number of ghoulish trophies. Now, we know that the partial remains of Stephen Lloyd, who was reported missing a few days ago, were discovered in playing fields near Renton. It is possible that the torso of Stephen has been found inside the house behind me. This remarkable twist of events has left the local area in complete shock. People are asking how the police did not know that so seriously a disturbed mind was working amongst them. I have spoken to Dr Kent Fincher, an expert in cases of post-traumatic shock. He had this to say . . .'

'Garret's work,' Brody said.

Dawn refilled his glass and gave herself a top-up. She joined him on the sofa.

'He knew that Jack was Mendicant's intended vessel,' Brody continued, 'and when Mendicant refused to share the secret he had promised, Garret took his revenge. Mendicant would have his new life, but it would be spent behind bars.'

'And this is how Jack will be remembered?' Dawn said, swilling back her whisky. 'He saved my child. He suffered to save us, and this is his ending.'

'No. It doesn't end like this for him. There are no real endings, are there?'

A black and white photograph of Jack appeared on the screen. They were both quiet for a moment while the reporter leapt from one unfounded conclusion to the next.

'How is Jamie?'

'I don't know. He woke earlier. I didn't . . . I couldn't talk to him.'

'You must, for your sake and for his.'

The report ended.

'In related news, the village of Crow Haven, south of the B136, was the sight of a freak storm last night. Over to a rather wet Jan Phipps.'

The reporter was on the ridge overlooking Crow Haven.

The water had dropped several feet, but was still lapping at the upper windows of some of the houses.

'In the early hours of this morning the small community of Crow Haven was the scene of some of the worst localised flooding on record. So far, meteorologists are confounded as to how a storm of the proportions needed to devastate this area could have been missed on satellite surveys. As you can see, all the homes in this little vale have been largely destroyed. Most of the residents of this close community did manage to escape unscathed. Unfortunately some did not survive. Among those missing, believed drowned, there are local farmer, James Rowbanks, Post Mistress, Estelle Gilchrist, parish priest, Father Christopher Garret and Mrs Anne Malahyde. Mrs Malahyde was the mother of Simon Malahyde, a young man who disappeared a week ago. Simon was the prime suspect in the murders of Stephen Lloyd and Oliver Godfrey. That line of inquiry, however, was pursued by Jack Trent, and so must now be regarded as a blind. The whereabouts of Simon Malahyde are still unknown . . .

'I have here with me Mr Sandhurst from the local council. Mr Sandhurst, what can be done for this devastated community?'

Mr Sandhurst, a ruddy-faced councillor in his late fifties, exuded sympathy.

'Well, we have arranged temporary accommodation for all residents. I'm afraid, as you have pointed out, it is unlikely that the current buildings will be allowed to remain standing. Health and safety, you know. We will be helping the people of Crow Haven in their arrangements with their insurers. But I am not optimistic that, from a financial point of view, rebuilding will commence here any time soon.'

'And what of Redgrave Forest?'

'Well, as you see, the area is completely destroyed. We . . .'

Dawn switched off the set. Brody looked into the shifting prism of the cut glass before finishing his drink.

'Well, I'd best be off,' he said.

'Where will you go?'

'I . . . humph,' he heaved himself off the sofa. 'I shall go abroad. There's a village at the foot of the Andes I've been dreaming about. I was happy there once.'

She went with him to the corridor and opened the front door while he hauled on his coat. He fished in his pocket and brought out a string of rosary beads and a small crucifix.

'Say goodbye to the boy for me,' he said. 'And give him these; just as a keepsake. I don't think I shall need them anymore.'

He closed her hand over the gift and held her gaze.

'Mourn him,' he said. 'He should be mourned.'

Before she could respond, he had closed the door behind him.

It was very late, but Jamie had not eaten all day. She went to the kitchen, took eggs from the fridge and cracked them into a bowl. They'd had omelettes with ham and cheese that night in the flat. When he had first met Jamie.

There was her father's mug on the side, stained through with rings of tea. What had he seen in his last moments? What had Jack seen? And if, as she now believed, there were such things as ghosts, was Jack out there somewhere? Perhaps one day she would see him again. His face on steamed glass. In a mirror. Or in her dreams. That playground of the mind, in which terrible, wonderful things happen all the time.